P9-DCL-815

DISCARDED

WOULDN'T

— IT BE —

DEADLY

WOULDN'T
— IT BE —
DEADLY

D. E. IRELAND

MINOTAUR BOOKS

A THOMAS DUNNE BOOK
NEW YORK

MYS
Ireland

This is a work of fiction. All of the characters, organizations, and events portrayed in this novel are either products of the authors' imaginations or are used fictitiously.

A THOMAS DUNNE BOOK FOR MINOTAUR BOOKS.
An imprint of St. Martin's Publishing Group.

WOULDN'T IT BE DEADLY. Copyright © 2014 by D. E. Ireland. All rights reserved. Printed in the United States of America. For information, address St. Martin's Press, 175 Fifth Avenue, New York, N.Y. 10010.

www.thomasdunnebooks.com
www.minotaurbooks.com

Designed by Molly Rose Murphy

The Library of Congress Cataloging-in-Publication Data is available upon request.

ISBN 978-1-250-04935-3 (hardcover)
ISBN 978-1-4668-5035-4 (e-book)

Minotaur books may be purchased for educational, business, or promotional use. For information on bulk purchases, please contact Macmillan Corporate and Premium Sales Department at 1-800-221-7945, extension 5442, or write specialmarkets@macmillan.com.

First Edition: September 2014

10 9 8 7 6 5 4 3 2 1

SEP 29 2014
Gift

Dedicated with many thanks to George Bernard Shaw and his immortal characters Eliza Doolittle and Henry Higgins. Shaw's celebrated play *Pygmalion* inspired this mystery series; an added thanks to the Irish playwright for inspiring our pen name. We hope Mr. Shaw would have approved of our reimagining. If not, we take comfort in Shaw's own statement: "A life spent making mistakes is not only more honorable, but more useful than a life spent doing nothing."

ACKNOWLEDGMENTS

We would like to thank the Talbot Fortune Agency, for their lightning-quick offer of representation and for landing a publisher in such a short time; editor Toni Plummer Kirkpatrick, for believing our book was a winner; and our long-suffering spouses, Barry and Randy, and our brilliant daughters, Amanda and Emma, for their love and support. But our deepest thanks must be extended to Wayne State University, where the two of us first met. To this day, we've never used anything we learned from that Theory of Anthropology class, but it was well worthwhile. At the end of the semester, we left the class as lifelong friends—and future writing partners.

HENRY HIGGINS:

"There's only one way of escaping trouble; and that's killing things."

— George Bernard Shaw, *Pygmalion*, Act 5

WOULDN'T

— IT BE —

DEADLY

ONE

LONDON, 1913

The shadowy hallway seemed as black as the heart of Jack the Ripper.

Eliza Doolittle paused at the top of the stairs. Why were the lights turned off on the second floor? Since there were no windows along the corridor, the housekeeping staff normally kept four electric lights burning. But all she could see before her was darkness.

Although she had no idea where it was located, Eliza fumbled for the light switch. She cursed these newfangled devices. How was a soul to know what to do when the electricity went out? When she'd needed illumination when she'd lived in her old digs on Drury Lane, she'd reached for a gas lamp—assuming she had a penny for the meter. Now every building in London was awash in the dim glow of electric lights. Maybe the storm caused the lights to go out. Today's weather was especially foul as thunderous rains and wild winds swept over the city.

If she felt her way, she'd reach the room where she gave phonetics lessons. Her fingers brushed the flocked velvet wallpaper as she inched along the corridor. With her other hand, she grasped a heavy cloth sack weighted down with the tuning forks she used for her lessons.

What a silly goose she was. For years, Eliza wandered through alleyways darker than this, with murderous dodgers lurking in them. That's what civilized living did to people—made them fear every sound. Put a Whitechapel girl among the gentry and she became as jumpy as a Brighton maiden aunt. After all, she wasn't walking along the corridors of a Bethnal Green council house. This was fashionable—and sedate—Belgrave Square.

The distant ring of a telephone downstairs reminded her that she was far from alone in the building. Not only did a prestigious company of solicitors rent offices on the first floor, her employer Maestro Emil Nepommuck lived and gave lessons in the apartment directly across from her classroom. In fact, she could probably hear him moving about his rooms as he prepared for the arrival of his own students.

Eliza stopped and listened. Not a sound. There wasn't even the usual smell of Nepommuck's Turkish cigarettes, which often permeated the whole second floor. Only the relentless pounding of rain on the roof broke the eerie silence.

Raised in the slums of Lisson Grove and London's East End, Eliza was uneasy with too much quiet and stillness. A year ago at this hour, she would have been selling violets under the skylights at Covent Garden Market as dozens of costermongers hawked their wares around her. Now that she'd learned to speak like a lady, she had a more genteel occupation teaching others to speak the King's English. But she missed the cacophony and lively crowds of market day. And at this moment she would have given five quid to hear just one greengrocer sing out, "Who'll buy me fresh strawberries? Strawberries ripe from Kent! Sixpence a pound!"

She even harbored a regret or two that she was no longer living with Professor Higgins and Colonel Pickering at 27A Wimpole Street. For certain there was never a quiet moment in that house with Henry Higgins holding court from breakfast to bedtime. However, if she were still living there, Higgins would never cease to remind her how grateful she should be to him for turning a Cockney guttersnipe into a proper lady. No, she had made the right decision to become Maestro Nepommuck's teaching assistant.

She strained again to hear any sound from Nepommuck's apartment. The Hungarian was not fond of mornings so perhaps he was still asleep. It was unlikely he had ventured outside. Eliza couldn't imagine Nepommuck stepping outdoors on such a wet and miserable day.

As she crept down the hall, a floorboard creaked beneath the carpeting. Eliza froze. Had she caused that sound? Blimey, if she swooned after hearing her own footsteps, she'd best head back to the stairs before she made a complete fool of herself and yelled for help.

Another creak, louder this time, but she hadn't moved an inch. The sound came from farther down the hallway near Nepommuck's apartment. Eliza held her breath.

Was someone slowly walking toward her? If so, why didn't they speak? Unless they didn't realize she was here. After all, if she couldn't see a foot in front of her face, neither could anyone else. Eliza opened her mouth to call out, but hesitated. A childhood spent living on the London streets had taught her to trust her instincts. Just now they told her to keep quiet.

When thunder crashed overhead, she jumped. Hand over her racing heart, she heard the floorboards creak yet again.

Eliza refused to stand still like a frightened bird. How many steps had she taken since she left the stairwell? If she turned and fled, she might fall headlong down the steps in the dark. And she didn't fancy breaking her neck because a noisy hallway gave her the vapors.

The carpeted floorboards squeaked two more times, the sounds closer. No doubt about it, someone was in the hallway with her. Her eyes had adjusted to the dark, and Eliza thought she saw a shape move in the shadows.

Instinct be damned. She had to do something. "Who's there?" Her voice sounded especially loud in the unnerving silence.

Nothing.

"I hear you, mate." She put as much bluster as possible in her voice. "No use pretending you're not there. If you're lost, speak up. And if you're lurking here in hopes of cutting a purse, it'll be slim pickings."

Again, only silence. Eliza heard a furtive footstep, and another. Suddenly a rush of pounding feet headed right toward her. She spun around and ran for the stairs, the bag of tuning forks banging against her hip.

"Leave me alone!"

Behind her came the sound of a grunt as whoever chased her drew near.

"Get away from me, you blooming—" Without warning, she lost her footing and fell hard to the floor. The bag of tuning forks slammed against the opposite wall. Eliza tried to get to her feet, but something hard pressed against her spine.

Her face flattened against the carpet, Eliza shouted, "Get off!"

A shaft of light broke through the darkness. She heard Maestro Nepommuck call out, "Who's there? What is happening out here?"

The weight against her back released and a slight breeze ruffled her hair. Sprawled on the floor, Eliza turned her head and spied a figure darting into the shadowy stairwell.

"Miss Doolittle, is that you?"

"Yes, Maestro."

She heard him mutter in Hungarian. A moment later, the lights flashed on. Her shiny new tuning forks lay scattered across the carpet.

Nepommuck crouched beside her. "Are you hurt?"

Shaking her head, she sat up. A tuning fork slipped off her back. "I'm fine. I just tripped."

"Whyever did you turn off the lights?" He helped Eliza to her feet.

"The lights were already off when I came upstairs." She readjusted her hat, which still dripped from the rain. "Did one of your pupils switch them off when they left?"

"I do not have pupils until after ten. You know I do not like to rise early."

Eliza now saw that the Hungarian wore a gold brocade dressing gown and embroidered black-and-gold slippers. He had obviously not been awake long. What really caught her attention was the black netting covering his hair. And when he moved his head, she spied two strips of tape holding down his luxurious mustache. She tried not to stare.

Clearing his throat, he seemed to realize he was dressed inappropriately. "If you are not hurt, I shall return to my apartment. I trust you can pick up your tuning forks." Nepommuck sniffed. "Although I do not agree with the practice of using such devices. We are teaching people to speak correctly, Miss Doolittle, not tune violins."

"Professor Higgins sometimes used them during his lessons with me." Eliza knelt to collect the scattered forks. "A person may have a speech problem because they do not hear properly. A tuning fork helps to uncover that. And they also are good for—"

"Enough. I do not wish to hear about the Professor or his silly tricks." He tugged at his dressing gown's belt. "If you are done tripping about in the dark, I would like to get dressed before our pupils arrive."

"One moment, Maestro. Did you see anyone in the hallway when you turned on the lights?"

"I saw only you and your tuning forks lying on the floor. A most unladylike sight, too."

"Someone was in the hallway with me. It was too dark to see, but I heard the floor creak."

He gave her a patronizing smile. "Floors often creak, Miss Doolittle. Old buildings make all sorts of odd noises." A roll of thunder accompanied his last words. "Add thunder to the dark, and you would not be the first young woman to take fright."

"It takes more than a thunderstorm to make me run for the stairs," Eliza said. "I'd bet a week's wages there was someone hiding by your door." She nodded toward his apartment. "He chased me when he realized I was here. That's why I fell."

A strange expression briefly crossed the Maestro's face before he shook his head. "Nonsense, Miss Doolittle. The storm and the dark hallway caused these fancies. Besides, why would someone stand outside my doorway only to run away when I appear?"

"I don't know, but it's not likely they had a pleasant purpose in mind. I think—"

He held up his hand to cut her words short. "I think you are imagining things. You may have hit your head when you fell. Perhaps you are . . . how do you say in English? . . . hallucinating."

With a muttered curse, Eliza bent down to pick up her tuning forks. "Please don't let me keep you from getting dressed, Maestro. I am sure it must take you some time to become presentable."

"Impertinent girl." He kicked a stray tuning fork with his foot.

She bent to retrieve it, but stopped when she saw the metal button that lay beside it. "Is this yours?" Eliza held up the button. Brass or even gold, she thought, and carved with an intricate design of a lion surrounded by stars.

Nepommuck stared at her in disdain. "Do you think I stand outside my door ripping buttons off my clothing?"

Eliza examined the item closely. Did it belong to the person who'd fled in the dark?

When the clock inside his apartment chimed the hour, Nepommuck gave a great sigh. "Please stop wasting time picking up trash, Miss Doolittle. Our students will be here soon." He stalked back to his apartment. "And don't turn off the lights again."

"But I never touched them!"

He slammed the door behind him.

Eliza glanced up and down the empty corridor. "Someone switched them off on purpose," she mused aloud. "Someone who wanted to hide in the dark."

And since the stranger had lurked in the hallway between Nepommuck's apartment and her classroom, he must have wanted to harm the Hungarian.

Or her.

Henry Higgins was in a murderous mood. After a long scholarly tour of Spain, he was impatient to once more listen to the fractured English of his own countrymen. For the past eight weeks, he'd heard nothing but Basque consonants and lisping Catalonians. Enlightening as the Spaniards had been, all he wanted now was to listen to the glottal stop of a dockworker from Newcastle-upon-Tyne. And he itched to correct a tradesman from Birmingham when he stressed the wrong syllable. He had half a mind to grab a hansom cab and head for the East End just to enjoy the riotous street cries of a Cockney newsboy.

He stormed over to the bell rope and gave it a yank. Then again, the last thing to raise his spirits would be the sound of a Cockney voice. It would remind him of Eliza Doolittle. In a mere six months, he had taught that ungrateful little cabbage leaf how to speak like the Duchess of Manchester. Yet after all he'd done for her, there'd been no word from the girl since her father's wedding two months ago. Even more irritating was the fact that Eliza was still the houseguest of his own mother on the Chelsea Embankment.

"Blast," he muttered as he pulled the bell rope again.

Not that he expected anyone to answer his summons. The household didn't run properly with Eliza gone. The parlor maids seemed indolent, and even Mrs. Pearce acted inattentive. Worst of all, he still hadn't found his damned slippers.

After several fruitless minutes of waiting, Higgins walked into the empty foyer. "Mrs. Pearce, I need you!"

His bellow echoed off the walls. Colonel Pickering, who opened the front door at that exact moment, jumped in surprise.

"Higgins, my good man. You gave me quite a fright." The Colonel shook out his umbrella, spraying drops on the polished floor. "I hope nothing has gone awry with your latest pupil." He gestured toward the laboratory.

"What's gone awry is that two pupils have canceled on me this morning. I've never had anyone cancel before. Now I have two cancellations in one day, and on my first day back from an extended leave. The boorish audacity." Higgins glanced toward the kitchen again. "Mrs. Pearce!"

"If you shout any louder, you'll burst a blood vessel."

"What in heaven's name is that woman doing? I haven't caught a glimpse of her since she brought my tea at eleven o'clock. The household has fallen into complete anarchy. We may as well be living in Italy."

Pickering checked the watch on his chain. "I hardly think you've been neglected. It's only half past eleven."

"Exactly. I've not yet had the morning paper brought to me. I am accustomed to having the paper and my slippers in my possession by ten o'clock. Eliza always made certain——" He stopped himself.

Pickering clapped him on the shoulder. "I miss her, too. What say we pay a visit to your mother later today? We've been away for weeks. Perfectly proper for a chap to call on his mother, wouldn't you say? And it's an ideal opportunity to see how our Miss Doolittle is faring."

"She is not *my* Miss Doolittle, and I am not playing the pathetic suitor. I'll leave that to the sorry likes of Freddy Eynsford Hill." Higgins frowned at the older woman coming down the hall. "The phantom housekeeper approaches. My dear Mrs. Pearce, it would be refreshing if you made an appearance once in a while."

Mrs. Pearce wore her usual long-suffering look. "Sir, if you want me to keep the household accounts, see that the bed linens are changed, and arrange the delivery of a beef joint for dinner, then you will have to let me out of your sight now and again." She took Pickering's hat, coat, and umbrella. "I didn't realize you'd returned from your appointment, Colonel. I'll bring some hot tea. The weather is foul. Seems as if April means to drown us all."

"What about me?" Higgins crossed his arms.

She glanced up at him. "What about you, Mr. Higgins?"

"I want more tea, I want to know why my pupils have canceled, I want my morning paper, and I want my bloody slippers!"

Mrs. Pearce nodded toward the newspaper folded neatly on a table by the stairs. "It was damp from the rain, so I had one of the girls iron it for you. I'm sure it's dry enough now." She grunted as she readjusted Pickering's wet coat and hat heaped in her arms. "Now if you gentlemen will go into the drawing room, I'll have tea sent right in. As for your pupils, a Mr. Giraldi sent round a boy not five minutes ago. He cannot come for his lesson this afternoon."

"What the devil is going on?" Higgins ran a hand through his hair.

"And I hope I do not have to hear another word about your slippers. We've turned the house upside down a dozen times looking for them. You'd best purchase a new pair." Mrs. Pearce paused. "Or ask Miss Doolittle what has become of them."

"If you think I am going to beg a single thing from that insolent female—"

But Mrs. Pearce had already disappeared beyond the kitchen's swinging door.

"I say, do you mind if I have a quick look at the paper?" Pickering asked. "Major Redstone will be arriving any day. He's an old friend from Bombay, and I'd like to check the ship manifests. Since the *Titanic* went down last year, I find myself worrying over every ocean voyage."

Higgins handed the newspaper to him before they retreated to what would have been a drawing room in any other Wimpole Street home. Here it served as a phonetics laboratory. Although the leather chairs, piano, and writing table were common sights in any proper drawing room, the filing cabinets, lamp chimneys, laryngoscope, and tuning forks were not. Pickering settled in the easy chair by the fireplace while Higgins began to pace about the room.

Three pupils canceling in one day was unheard of. He felt like the victim of some perverse practical joke. Without a student to terrorize, half the fun had just gone out of the day. If it weren't raining buckets, he'd grab his notebook and head outdoors. It was always great sport listening to his countrymen murder their native tongue.

Now he faced a long idle day inside. While Colonel Pickering was good company, they had just spent the better part of two months together touring Spain. Higgins suspected they had run out of conversation somewhere in Granada. Plus Higgins was in a combative mood and he didn't want to take it out on a fellow as congenial as the Colonel.

Indeed, he found it most fortuitous to have met Pickering last summer near Covent Garden's vegetable market. Higgins had been so impressed by the scholarly tome *Spoken Sanskrit* that he was determined to meet its author, Colonel Pickering, even if it meant traveling halfway across the world to India. Fortunately he was saved the tedium of a long ocean trip when the Colonel arrived in England for the sole purpose of meeting Henry Higgins, the author of *Higgins's Universal Alphabet*. That both of them happened to be standing outside Inigo Jones's St. Paul's Church that rainy evening was nothing short of remarkable. A certain young Cockney flower girl was also there that night, but Higgins wasn't certain if he would term that encounter remarkable or ominous.

As two confirmed bachelor scholars, it seemed only fitting they continue their research together at Higgins's home at 27A Wimpole Street. Soon after, Eliza Doolittle joined the household as their prize student, and the past year had been spent turning her from a caterwauling street urchin into something resembling a lady. If nothing else, Wimpole Street was never dull once that upstart had moved in.

Higgins plucked a tuning fork, threw it down, wiped nonexistent dust from the phonograph, and ran his hand over the life-size model of a human head. After straightening the Piranesi drawings on the wall, Higgins ate a chocolate cream from the dessert bowl on the piano. Just the sight of the candy reminded him of Eliza, who gobbled up his chocolates like a greedy child. Maybe Pickering was right. Maybe they should pay a call on his mother. And if the "Cockney duchess" happened to be in attendance, he would treat her with the profound indifference she deserved.

"Jolly good." Pickering nodded with obvious satisfaction. "Major Redstone arrived in Southampton yesterday. I wouldn't be surprised to receive a call from him later today as soon as he settles in at his club. Quite looking forward to seeing him again."

"Is this the chap who's an expert on Sanskrit poetry?"

Pickering nodded. "Redstone's not yet forty, but he's one of the best in his field. In fact, he's coming to London to present a paper next month at the Asiatic and Sanskrit Revival Society."

"Sounds like a fellow who enjoys a decent conversation. Have him stay with us. We've more than enough room here, especially since that ungrateful flower peddler left."

"Ripping good idea. I'll ask him as soon as he contacts me." Pickering gave the paper a shake, then turned the page. "Oh, my word."

Higgins glanced his way. "Did the suffragettes burn down another cricket pavilion?"

"Henry, I think I may know why you are losing pupils. Our Hungarian colleague has taken to advertising in the paper during your absence."

"Nepommuck? That peacock has been riding my coattails ever since I corrected his abysmal English. I find it absurd I would lose pupils due to an advertisement in the *Daily Mail*."

"It appears he has an assistant now." Pickering cleared his throat and began to read. "'Learn the King's English from the flower girl who successfully passed for a duchess at the Embassy Ball two months ago. Taught by the renowned Emil Nepommuck himself, Miss Doolittle will have you speaking like the gentry in less than eight weeks. Visit Maestro Nepommuck today at Belgrave Square and arrange a lesson with his star pupil.' I say, the man has more brass than the horn section at the symphony."

"The bloody liar!" Higgins grabbed the paper. "Let me see that."

"Try not to get too upset with Eliza. I'm sure there's a good explanation."

"That treacherous harridan!" He kicked the nearest table, sending a box of wax cylinders crashing to the floor. "How dare they collaborate."

"No need to tear down the laboratory, old man."

Higgins flung open the door. "Mrs. Pearce! Bring my coat and hat, I'm going out."

"What are you going to do?" Pickering looked pale.

"I am going to see our Miss Doolittle, as you suggested. And when I do, I intend to strangle her with my own hands. And that thieving Hungarian, for good measure!"

TWO

Every time Eliza lit a coal fire, she thought of her dead canary. Poor little Petey. Eliza sent a brief prayer his way as she added another lump of coal to the grate. While she blamed the blustery spring day for feeling so cold, this morning's strange encounter in the dark hallway had added to the chill. She smiled as the flames leaped higher. It had been almost a year since she left her shabby room in Angel Court, but Eliza still marveled whenever she sat before the loverly warmth of her own coal fireplace.

A pity she didn't have this coal the winter before last. She'd bought a little canary from a street seller in Brick Lane. The purchase of the bird and cage set Eliza back a week's wages, but the cost was well worth it. What a treat to return home to her lonely room and be greeted by the lilting song of her own bird. That is, until the harsh cold of winter set in. Without a coal grate or enough wood for the fireplace, Eliza could barely keep herself from freezing. Petey was dead by Boxing Day.

"How did that sound, Miss Doolittle?"

Feeling guilty that she hadn't heard a word of the vocal exercises, Eliza turned her attention back to her pupil. In two months, she'd taken on ten students. It wasn't difficult work, nor as unpleasant as selling flowers in a chilly downpour. But listening to people misspeak their native tongue reminded her of how recently she had been among them.

"Much better, Mrs. Finch, but you must avoid slurring your 'r's. Especially when your voice dips into a lower register." Eliza picked up a tuning fork and struck it. "Try to pitch your voice to this. The conscious effort to do so will cause you to slow your speech and better enunciate the 'r' sound."

After a deep breath, the woman began reciting the day's diction lesson in a higher key.

Mary Finch had newly come to London with her husband, Cornelius, who owned several woolen factories in Leeds. Prosperous and young, the pair decided to use their growing wealth to climb the social ladder. However, they quickly learned that wealth without the right accent and diction proved meaningless in the circles they aspired to. The sooner they learned to speak like the upper crust, the faster their ascent. Or so they hoped.

Eliza found Mrs. Finch an agreeable young woman, although with her sleek head of blond hair and propensity to wear bright colors, "Goldfinch" would have been a more apt name. And while Mary was a diligent student, she seemed more interested in fashion than in vowels.

This morning, it took twenty minutes to distract Mary from asking endless questions about Eliza's outfit. Where had she purchased her satin, faille, and leather boots? Was the color of her shadow lace blouse the celebrated peony hue all the fashion magazines were writing about this season? Did she find it troublesome to keep wrinkles from spoiling the silhouette of her gray linen skirt? She even asked to examine Eliza's kid gloves.

One more question and she'd hand the woman Colonel Pickering's card. After all, he had bought every stitch of clothing she possessed. Thinking of the dear Colonel sent a wave of sadness through her. Eliza missed the sweet man, and wondered if he'd returned from his research trip to Spain and Portugal. Henry Higgins had gone with him, at least according to his mother, with whom she was staying. And that insufferable man was the last person she wished to see again. Particularly since she was now working with the Professor's main competitor. She felt a bit guilty about that. Still, a girl had to make an honest living. And she had warned Higgins that she might become a phonetics teacher.

A loud banging erupted downstairs.

Mrs. Finch looked up in obvious alarm. Someone seemed to be battering down the door. Eliza frowned. This was turning into a day of oddities. What next?

The banging ceased.

"Nothing to worry about, I'm sure." Eliza shot a reassuring smile at her student. She tapped the tuning fork. "Shall we try again?"

Mrs. Finch cleared her throat and launched into her recitation. Eliza nodded with satisfaction when she finished. "Much better. You see, it only takes a bit of concentration to—"

"Eliza! Where are you, you ungrateful baggage?"

"Oh, no!" Eliza dropped the tuning fork in shock and ran behind the corner chair.

"Miss Doolittle?" Mrs. Finch looked wide-eyed with fear. "Whatever is the matter?"

Before she could answer—or suggest a good hiding place—Henry Higgins barged into the room. With his beet-red face and eyebrows twitching, he appeared ready to hurl a deadly thunderbolt or two at her.

"Go away." Eliza clutched the chair for support. "I am engaged with a pupil."

"A pupil?" Higgins pointed his dripping umbrella at Mrs. Finch, who sat with her mouth agape. "Do you mean this benighted fool has come to *you* for assistance in how to speak proper English?"

Eliza's fear vanished at that familiar mocking voice. "Who better to go to?"

He shook his umbrella again at Mrs. Finch. "You there. Say something."

Mary Finch looked over at Eliza for support. "I . . . I don't know what everyone is shouting about, but I have an appointment with my jeweler and really must run."

Higgins turned back to Eliza with a smirk. "She is lately come from Leeds in Yorkshire. Dreadful slurring of the 'r's. But she was raised in Sedbergh, hence the west Cumbrian inflections. In fact, I would guess the northern part of the village."

"However did you know that?" Mrs. Finch sounded impressed despite her obvious fear.

"He's showing off," Eliza said. "It's a favorite parlor game of his. I don't know why he simply doesn't buy a dog and train it to do tricks for his amusement."

"I did have a monkey quite recently who was very good at fetching slippers and mimicking her betters. She was more amusing than a dozen trained dogs." He glared at her. "But far less loyal."

"Monkey, was I? More like your best pupil. A pupil so talented the mere idea she decided to give lessons threatens you."

"Don't flatter yourself. I don't care if you teach the entire East End to hold on to their aitches. What I do resent is you giving that hairy Hungarian access to my hard-won methods!"

"Maestro has no interest in your methods."

"By Jupiter, Eliza. You're calling that buffoon 'Maestro'?"

"It's what you called him that night I won your bet at the Embassy Ball," she shot back. "And he hasn't asked me a single question about your phonetics techniques. Why should he? From what I can see, the Maestro charges twice your fee and has three times the number of pupils. Maybe you should be asking me about *his* methods."

"You imp of the devil! I should have instructed Mrs. Pearce to drown you in the bathtub the day you came begging at my doorstep. Judas Iscariot had more loyalty!"

"The gentlemen downstairs are beginning to complain about the noise," Pickering said as he entered the room.

"Hang them all," Higgins said. "And they're not gentlemen. They're solicitors."

Eliza hurried over to embrace the Colonel. "You are the only gentleman here. How lovely to see you again."

"And you too, Eliza." Pickering beamed at her with approval. "I've been thinking about you for weeks now, hoping you were well. And here you are, looking so pretty and proper. By the way, I bought the loveliest lace shawl for you in Seville."

"Please sit down, Colonel." She gestured to her student. "Colonel Pickering, this is Mrs. Finch. Mrs. Finch, I would like you to meet the esteemed Colonel Pickering, a renowned expert in Indian dialects."

"What about my introduction?" Higgins said with a growl.

"That's Henry Higgins." Eliza didn't even glance in his direction.

"Very pleased to meet you both," Mary Finch murmured as she hurried to pull on her gloves.

Eliza sat opposite Pickering at the lesson table. "Tell me all about Spain. How many Basque dialects did you record? What was the food like? And what about the weather? Did it rain much?"

"Bloody hell!" Higgins's curse elicited a gasp from Mrs. Finch. "Who gives a damn about the rain in Spain?"

"I do," Eliza said. "What would you rather talk about? Your wounded pride, your insufferable vanity?"

"Why don't we talk about your treachery? And the unethical tactics of that lying unskilled ape Nepommuck!"

"Why am I being called a liar and unskilled?" Emil Nepommuck stood in the open doorway to Eliza's classroom.

Since his phonetics laboratory and living quarters were directly across the hall, she was amazed he hadn't appeared when Higgins arrived. Indeed, if the Professor wanted proof of the Maestro's success, he need only peek into his rival's apartment, with its ornate furnishings and Persian carpets. She doubted the Duke of Edinburgh lived as lavishly as Nepommuck.

Higgins was unfazed. "Eavesdropping is a perilous occupation, dear boy. You may want to stop doing it if you don't want to hear insulting things about yourself."

"Eavesdropping? I could hear all this noise from the roof." He smoothed down his mustache. "And, Miss Doolittle, haven't we had enough excitement for one day? I thought you were a lady."

"No, you didn't, you deceitful oaf." Higgins banged his umbrella on the floor. "You knew she was a Cockney flower girl when you hired her. Or did you think I'd never read that blasted piece of fiction in the newspaper? I should pummel you over the head for those lies you had printed!"

Nepommuck flushed. "I have no time for this bullying nonsense. And I would rather you not come here to frighten Miss Doolittle and Mrs. Finch."

Mary Finch scurried to his side. "Thank you, Maestro. I feel so much better now that you are here."

He patted the woman's hand. "Look how you have upset the gentle Mrs. Finch. You ought to be ashamed of yourself, Professor."

"Oh, I don't give a tinker's dam about Mrs. Finch," Higgins said. "Why doesn't she leave if I make her so nervous?"

"Henry, really," Pickering said.

"It's true, I must be going." But instead of leaving, Mrs. Finch pressed closer to Nepommuck, who bent down to kiss her hand.

"No, my dear. I am sure Miss Doolittle wishes to finish your lesson."

"I certainly do," Eliza said. "As soon as we get rid of Professor Higgins. Unless he's not done threatening everyone in the room."

"The only person I mean to threaten is you." Higgins walked over to Nepommuck, clearly pleased that he towered over the younger man by at least six inches. Mrs. Finch took a step back. "Or need I remind you that I taught you literally everything you know?"

"I hardly think you taught me thirty-two languages, Professor. You taught me a little phonetics, yes, but the ear and the linguistic skills? Ah, they are of my own making."

"Nonsense. You made a career for yourself by posing as my apprentice. Every country you set foot in, you trumpet my name before you. Being my student has been your entrée to all the drawing rooms in Europe. Now you have the brass to steal away Eliza, the recent beneficiary of my latest phonetics methods."

"Steal? Miss Doolittle came to *me* after I made her acquaintance at the Embassy Ball. She asked for a job as my assistant, and I hired her."

"That's true," Eliza said. "I did."

"And why should I not hire such a clever girl, a girl so clever she fooled even the great Hairy Faced Maestro, as I am known on the Continent."

"She fooled you only because I taught her!"

"Congratulations, Professor." He clicked his heels together. "I salute you. But she has chosen to work with Emil Nepommuck, not Professor Higgins. And why should I not let the world know that my assistant is the celebrated flower girl who passed as a duchess? It is a genius advertisement for my business. Thank you for allowing our paths to cross."

"Do you expect me to believe that you have no intention of stealing my techniques and passing them off as your own?" Higgins's expression grew even more suspicious.

"Miss Doolittle, have I ever asked about this man's methods?"

"Never."

Nepommuck looked immensely satisfied with himself. "Ah, then. You see? Quarrel settled. I do not wish to even hear of your latest techniques, when I, Nepommuck, have developed excellent ones of my own."

Eliza noticed that a blood vessel pulsed in Higgins's temple, a sure sign his temper was growing worse. The Professor pointed his umbrella at her this time.

"So what does Miss Doolittle use to teach? What is recorded on those wax cylinders I spy scattered about the room, the phonograph records, the notebooks in her crooked handwriting? Are they your techniques?"

"Of course not. They are her techniques."

"She has no techniques except for the ones I gave her! Those are the only ones she knows."

"Stop." Eliza banged on the table. "I have every right to use what I learned and pass it on to those who want to improve themselves. I do have to make a living, after all. Unless you expect me to trot back to Covent Garden with a basket of violets dangling from my arm."

"Hang that. Pickering told you dozens of times he'd set you up in a flower shop."

"I will, Eliza," the Colonel said.

Eliza reached across the table and squeezed Pickering's hand. "Thank you, Colonel, but I've only been teaching for a few weeks. And while I find it satisfying work, I don't know what I shall do in the future. You've both controlled so much of my life this past year, I need time to breathe on my own for a while."

"Just so, Eliza. You are an intelligent young lady and need no further instruction from us." He rewarded her with a gentle smile.

For the hundredth time, she wished she had been born Colonel Pickering's daughter.

Higgins turned his attention back to the Hungarian. "At least have the decency to admit you've stolen my students. I lost three just this morning."

"If they become aware of a better teacher, why should they not come to me?" Nepommuck straightened one of the dubious decorations he loved to pin on his suit coat. "You cannot blame me for that."

"We're back to the root of the matter," Higgins said. "They want to be taught by the man who trained the flower girl to speak like a duchess. And that is me, not you. However, you boast in the advertisement that Eliza is *your* handiwork, you miserable mound of pomaded hair!"

Eliza agreed with Higgins. "I asked him to change the advertisement. He promised to do so."

Nepommuck now appeared uncomfortable. "I spoke to the paper on this matter. Blame them if they have been delinquent on moving forward."

"Lying mountebank," Higgins said. "You are nothing more than a linguistic charlatan, a predatory fraud who blackmails his clients."

"How dare you accuse me of blackmail," Nepommuck sputtered.

"But you yourself boasted to me at the Embassy Ball of how you made your clients pay, and not merely for phonetics lessons. So don't take me for one of these idiots who come to you with their awful grammar and sad secrets." Higgins nodded at Eliza. "And now you're exploiting gullible young women for gain as well."

"I am not gullible," Eliza said.

"Then you're stupid, which is worse. As for you, Nepommuck, I am off to see my solicitor. Your fraudulent claim affects my business, and I intend to bring a case against you."

"I see no reason to involve lawyers." Nepommuck nervously stroked his mustache. "Let us settle this like gentlemen."

"We are one gentleman short, I'm afraid."

He grabbed Higgins's arm. "But you will ruin my reputation!"

"Take your hands off me. I'd like nothing more than to throttle you right here and now. It's a wonder some desperate student of yours hasn't already plunged a dagger in your back. I'm tempted to do so myself."

"Get away from the Maestro, you dreadful man!" Mrs. Finch flung her arms around Nepommuck. "I won't allow you to harm him."

Higgins threw both of them a look of disgust. "Pick, it's time to be on our way. This is turning into a scene out of a penny dreadful."

"I agree." Pickering walked over to Eliza and gave her a quick hug. "But I expect to see you soon, my dear."

"You will," she whispered to him.

Higgins tipped his hat at Eliza. "You only have time enough for two or three more lessons before I bring an end to this sorry enterprise and the hairy-faced dog who runs it. Enjoy what's left of your brief career as a phonetics teacher."

"Scoundrel," Nepommuck muttered as Higgins and Pickering walked past.

Once they were gone, Eliza breathed easier. But like a summer storm, the Professor's visit left fallen debris behind. A trembling Mrs. Finch clutched at Nepommuck even tighter.

"I told you Professor Higgins would be angry," Eliza said. "The advertisement is a fraud."

"So you take his side, Miss Doolittle." Nepommuck glared at her. "After all I have done for you."

"Done for me?" Blast the man. In fact, blast all men, save Colonel Pickering. "What have you done for me except lie to all of London about how you magically turned a Cockney flower girl into a lady? I'm the one who has brought in over a dozen new students. You should be grateful to me."

"How can you speak to the Maestro like that?" Mary Finch looked stricken. "He deserves an apology, Miss Doolittle."

Nepommuck gave a dramatic sigh. "She cannot help herself, my dear. Do not let her lovely vowels fool you. Miss Doolittle is only lately come from the gutter."

"One more word, mate, and I'll kick your blooming arse!" Eliza clapped a hand over her mouth, dismayed at how easily her speech had reverted to the East End.

"Ah, just as I thought." Nepommuck looked smug. "Come, Mrs. Finch. I will finish your lesson across the hall. It appears Miss Doolittle has forgotten how to speak the English language properly herself."

The pair swept out of the room as if they were King George and Queen Mary.

Eliza grabbed a nearby inkwell and reached back to throw it at the door Nepommuck slammed behind him. After a moment, she lowered her arm. She would not lose control again. She was no longer an ignorant flower girl. And she'd see both Higgins and Nepommuck hang before she allowed herself to slip back into her old life. Except at this moment, she wanted nothing more than to sit in her cozy old "piggery" in Angel Court.

"I am a person of discernment and discretion, Maestro Nepommuck," she said aloud. "And I am an independent woman, Professor Higgins. No matter what either of you think, I deserve your regard and courtesy."

Then she felt her blood rise at the contempt with which both men often treated her. "I'm a bleeding lady, I am!"

Frustrated, she flung the inkwell to the floor. "Ah-ah-oh-ow-ow-oh-ow!"

THREE

"It's a blooming castle," Eliza said in wonder as she stepped out of the taxi.

The brick facade of Hepburn House did indeed gleam in the noontime sun like a golden palace. Eliza squinted up at its many turrets, windows of leaded glass, and trellis vines of ivy curling about the elegant stonework. The mansion stretched on either side, disappearing into a green profusion of beech trees and rhododendrons that concealed where the walls ended. Nepommuck told her that the widowed marchioness was a wealthy woman, but she didn't expect anything like this. Cor, how the rich do live.

Even though the day was unseasonably warm, she shivered at the prospect of mingling with the toffs all afternoon. She'd barely slept last night, sick with worry about attending such a fancy occasion as the Annual Foundling Hospital Garden Party of the Dowager Marchioness of Gresham. The Embassy Ball had been daunting, too, but she'd had Higgins and the Colonel with her. Now she would be entering the gilded lion's den alone.

She did ask Nepommuck if she could allow her suitor, Freddy Eynsford Hill, to escort her, but he refused. This didn't surprise her. Nepommuck had barely said a civil word to her since Professor Higgins barged in on her lesson twelve days ago. Even if Freddy couldn't come, she had an official invitation as well as an obligation to her students to be here. Not that she expected to enjoy a minute of it.

With a last nervous tug on her dress, Eliza marched to the entrance. The oak-paneled door swung open before she even raised her hand to knock. A tall young butler stood before her, as intimidating and handsome as the house itself.

She stared in amazement. The fellow was the spitting image of her favorite film actor, Bransley Ames. Blessed with the same wavy black hair, long-lashed dark eyes, and wide mouth, the butler also had a cleft chin like the actor. He might even be better looking than the real Ames. She should know, having spent far too much of her wages at the Shaftesbury Picture Palace.

The butler raised a curious eyebrow at her, which made him look as dashing as a pirate. It didn't seem fair that the rich got to live in palaces and have lovely young fellows waiting on them besides.

"May I help you, miss?"

"I'm Maestro Nepommuck's assistant, Miss Eliza Doolittle." Without waiting for a reply, she sailed past him, head held high. She may have been born in Lisson Grove, but she was going to act as if she belonged here. When she heard the door shut behind her, she let out a sigh of relief. She'd fooled the butler. That was a good start.

"Right, mate," she said aloud, forgetting she wasn't alone.

"I beg your pardon, Miss Doolittle?"

She took on her airiest tone. "Oh, I didn't say anything."

To hide her embarrassment, Eliza walked into the first room on her right. Had the temperature been colder, she would have thought she'd entered an ice palace. Everything was wintry white and silver.

Her admiring gaze took in the silver brocade sofas, crystal vases of white spring flowers, and sweeping silk curtains of palest ivory. Silver candelabra gleamed on the mantel of a white marble fireplace, while each piece of porcelain bric-a-brac on the silver tables and shelves was snow white. The plush white carpeting sank beneath her French heels. Eliza gasped at the sight of a grand piano, also painted white, that sat in one corner. Who knew pianos could be any color but black?

A sudden shriek made her jump, and she whirled around. Several feet away stood an enormous white birdcage designed to look like Buckingham Palace. From behind its polished bars, a large white bird with a yellow crest stared at Eliza. Cocking his head, he let out another piercing shriek.

"Am I the first guest here?" she asked the butler, who stood watching her from the doorway.

"No, miss. The other guests are in the gardens." He cleared his throat. "This is the drawing room."

Eliza felt herself blush. "Of course," she murmured.

The butler led her down a long hallway resplendent with gilt-framed portraits, carved wooden settees, and vases taller than she was. The tiled side corridor seemed to go on forever, but eventually she heard voices and saw glass doors that looked out on an expanse of green rolling lawn. She and the butler stepped out onto the terrace.

"Miss Eliza Doolittle," he announced.

Not a single soul bothered to look her way. "Thank you," she said.

"If you require anything at all, Miss Doolittle, you may ask for me." He gave a slight bow. "I am Harrison, Her Ladyship's butler."

His courtesy and good looks prompted an unexpected confession from her. "To be honest, Harrison, I'm a bit nervous about mingling with all these gents and ladies. I do thank you for being so kind."

"Don't let the toffs worry you, miss." He leaned toward her, his voice low. "The only thing separating us and them is a lucky ancestor or two."

Eliza had to restrain herself from planting a kiss on his handsome cheek. But after he was gone, her uneasiness returned. What would the Marchioness's fancy friends think of her? It was a marvel she had passed herself off as a duchess at the Embassy Ball. Perhaps she'd done it only to prove Higgins wrong—or to make him proud. Blast the infuriating man. But she would dearly love to see his irritating face just now.

Remember the ball, she told herself. You were a duchess that night, better mannered and twice as regal as any aristocrat waltzing about the ballroom. She had no reason to take fright at a little garden party packed with swells. Especially since out of the three hundred or so guests, twenty were pupils ready for their big test in the only classroom that mattered. If they could pass as one of those born to privilege, then Nepommuck could collect his final—and most lavish—fee.

She wasn't even a student to be tested, merely an assistant teacher here to shepherd her own pupils. Eliza looked out over the white tents, tables draped in linen, and beautifully attired guests enjoying pastry and tea on the lawn. A few guests played croquet, the ladies' elegant spring hats bobbing with every swing of the mallet. She was pleased to see that her own outfit would stand muster. Eliza had chosen the sage green gown with infinite care, along with a straw skimmer hat banded with grosgrain ribbon and topped by a darling tiered bow.

As she walked down the terrace steps, she nodded to one of her students. Mr. Corbett was a jolly older gentleman from Belfast eager to trade his Irish brogue for an Oxford cadence. He seemed deep in conversation with several people gathered around him, one of whom she recognized as a famous opera singer she'd seen during her Covent Garden days. Well done, she thought, and passed Mr. Corbett with a proud smile.

During the next hour, Eliza circled the elegant manicured gardens and observed most of her pupils. As the day grew warmer, she darted into a tent for some quick refreshment. The sight of tiered silver trays filled with pastries and cold sandwiches cheered her. Maids and footmen dressed in starched uniforms moved soundlessly among the tents and the tables. She noticed that they refilled every flute of champagne without being asked.

So far, the afternoon had gone better than expected. Each of her students had performed brilliantly. Mrs. Hazel Tinsdale might require one more lesson. Not that anything was wrong with her speech, but the matron from Newcastle had to learn to drink more tea and less champagne at a garden party. One more glass of the bubbly, and she'd be carried off the grounds in a drunken stupor.

Eliza spent the next twenty minutes enjoying the Charlotte Russe. She hoped no one noticed that she'd eaten three slices. Dabbing at her mouth with a linen napkin, she was grateful for the white canopy overhead. It felt as warm as midsummer even though it was only the eleventh of May. She fought the impulse to take off her hat and fan herself with it.

Only one student remained for her to observe: Mary Finch. Unfortunately Mary had yet to interact with any of the guests. Instead the young woman wandered aimlessly about the grounds, smiling only when Nepommuck came into view. But the Maestro kept company with the other bluebloods and took no notice of her.

Not that she was easy to miss. Mary had chosen not to wear her usual yellows or golds. Today she was dressed in pink tulle, positively girlish, with a pink feather aigrette bobbing above her blond head for good measure. Small wonder that Mr. Finch followed close behind his wife, a look of alarm on his face. Eliza was ready to take her leave, and Mary Finch stood in the way of her departure. She must insist that Mary converse with a baronet or two.

Before she could speak with Mary, however, Eliza caught sight of the Dowager Marchioness of Gresham. Dressed completely in white, the Marchioness—also known as Lady Gresham—commanded attention not only for her sleek-fitting lace gown, but for her air of majesty. She was as intimidating as a queen—and probably just as wealthy. The first time they met at Nepommuck's apartment, Eliza had to restrain herself from dropping a curtsey. She thought the Marchioness a most striking woman, even though Eliza guessed her age to be close to sixty. Her piercing gray eyes, which made Eliza nervous, were enhanced by perfectly coiffed snow-white hair. And it was doubtful there was an aristocrat anywhere in Europe with a profile half as regal.

Standing near a marble fountain, Lady Gresham raised a gloved hand. With the smallest of gestures, she summoned Eliza to join the guests gathered about her. By the time Eliza reached them, Nepommuck had joined the group. He looked his usual smug self, dapper in a well-brushed suit, polished shoes, and white gloves. His whiskers and mustache were groomed to perfection. Although he ignored Eliza's presence, Lady Gresham welcomed her with a gracious smile.

"Ah, Miss Doolittle, I told Emil that you both should be so proud of your pupils," she said. "Not one of my friends has guessed at their base origins."

So much for graciousness, Eliza thought.

Lady Gresham gestured to the woman beside her. "I do not believe you have made the acquaintance of Miss Rosalind Page, soon to make her debut in the West End."

The statuesque actress gave a little nod, which made her amethyst earrings glitter with the movement. With her vivid coloring and slender figure swathed in lilac silk and chiffon, Miss Page looked ready to make a grand entrance onstage.

Eliza bit back an excited grin. The celebrated Canadian actress had been Nepommuck's pupil for the past month, but Eliza always seemed to be elsewhere when she came for her lessons. Miss Page was reputed to be a theatrical sensation in North America, and the London papers were filled with stories of the young woman's talent and beauty. Now that Eliza finally set eyes on her, it appeared that the rumors of her beauty had not been exaggerated.

"Miss Doolittle," Miss Page said in a melodic voice. "How lovely to meet you."

What a pity that Miss Page and the handsome butler weren't a couple. Oh, the pretty babies those two could make. Miss Page's complexion was as perfect as porcelain, while her almond-shaped violet eyes boasted lashes longer than Eliza thought possible. If Lady Gresham reminded one of a haughty queen, Miss Page was the epitome of a Celtic fairy princess. Eliza admired the actress's mass of curly auburn hair piled fashionably beneath a broad hat festooned with lavender silk roses.

Up close, she also noted a touch of rouge on the actress's lips and cheeks that only heightened the dazzling effect. Eliza wondered if she dared dip into the rouge pots herself, although she could never hope for results anywhere near as gratifying.

"I apologize for staring, Miss Page," she said. "You're just so beautiful."

Rosalind Page laughed. "And you are much too kind."

Lady Gresham cleared her throat. Those gray eyes had grown hard. Flattering another woman was obviously not appreciated. "You already know Mr. Cornelius Finch."

Eliza murmured a greeting to the businessman, who was busy watching his wife make her way toward them.

"And this is Mr. Dmitri Kollas, one of Emil's oldest pupils." Lady Gresham pointed her white lace fan at a stocky man in a well-tailored suit.

"I believe we met at the Embassy Ball," Eliza said.

The burly fellow only grunted a response. She had a dim memory of him being a Greek diplomat, or at least posing as one, according to Higgins.

Lady Gresham next gestured to a young man with wavy chestnut hair and a mischievous expression. "This dear boy is James Nottingham."

"Very pleased to meet you, Miss Doolittle." Nottingham bowed over her hand, and gave her a quick wink when he straightened.

Although he was an attractive fellow, Eliza thought there was something a bit foxlike about him. Perhaps it was his long, thin nose that gave her that impression, or his shrewd and lively gaze. Whatever it was, Mr. Nottingham seemed like a man who could lead one on a merry chase if he wished.

"And of course you know Mrs. Finch, since you give her instruction," Lady Gresham said in a much cooler tone as Mary joined them.

"What a lovely party, Your Ladyship," Mary said, out of breath from rushing. "Even the weather has cooperated to make this an exquisite day. My dear husband and I are most grateful for the invitation."

But she didn't spare a glance for either Lady Gresham or her unhappy husband, Cornelius. Mary's attention was fixed on Nepommuck.

Mary took a step forward. "May I have a private word with you, Maestro? In the rose garden, perhaps?"

"That's enough, Mary," Cornelius Finch muttered.

Nepommuck looked uncomfortable. "Miss Doolittle is your instructor. If there is anything you must discuss, do so with her."

"But it is you I must speak with, Maestro," Mary said. "I have news that simply cannot wait."

"News? I cannot imagine what news you have that warrants interrupting Her Ladyship's party." A flustered Nepommuck turned to Lady Gresham. "Please excuse Mrs. Finch. It appears that she requires instruction not only in phonetics, but in etiquette as well."

Lady Gresham shrugged, her face a mask of icy indifference.

Mary's eyes grew wide. "Emil, we need to go somewhere private and speak. I insist."

Cornelius grabbed her arm. "Obviously my wife has been out in the sun too long. The heat is making her babble nonsense. If you will excuse us." With that, he pulled her away and the couple disappeared behind a privet hedge.

"What a pity," Miss Page said with an exaggerated sigh. "The second act will take place offstage, and it looks to be an interesting one."

"Let us hope Mr. Finch can get his wife under control." Nepommuck turned to the Marchioness. "Your Ladyship, both of us have more important things to attend to this afternoon. And we have spent enough time with these tiresome pupils of mine."

Eliza snorted. Who asked him to spend any time with us? The blowhard.

"Of course." Lady Gresham took his arm and they turned to go.

Nepommuck glanced back at her. "Miss Doolittle, why don't you tell the other students the amusing tale of the flower girl turned duchess. It will give them hope that anything is possible." With that, the pair sauntered off.

"Blooming bastard," Eliza muttered under her breath.

"Pig!" Dmitri Kollas's flushed face reddened further.

"Pay him no mind," Miss Page said. "The Maestro is so busy climbing the social ladder, he forgets good manners are a requisite."

"How much farther can he climb?" Eliza asked. "He's a Hungarian blueblood."

"Is he?" Miss Page raised a skeptical eyebrow. "Or does he merely pretend to be? People can pretend to be whatever they like. Mrs. Finch pretends to be a devoted wife. You pretended to be a duchess. 'All the world's a stage, and all its people merely players.' At least I get paid for it." She gave a charming laugh. "Now I am positively ravenous and must have something to eat. No pretense there. Mr. Kollas, would you care to join me?"

Struck dumb by that lovely face, Kollas followed Rosalind Page to the nearest white tent.

James Nottingham laughed. "Beauty and the beast."

"She is a beauty," Eliza said with an admiring sigh. "I don't think there's a woman in England who can compare with her."

He shook his head. "Not really my type. She's too tall and all that curly red hair puts me off. Plus I find those purple eyes a bit spooky." Nottingham cast an appreciative glance at Eliza. "I much prefer young ladies with straight brown hair, sparkling brown eyes, and charming little upturned noses." Nottingham gently touched the tip of Eliza's nose.

She took a step back.

"Please don't run away, Miss Doolittle. I've not heard the tale of the flower girl turned duchess. Would you enlighten me?"

"Miss Page is right. Everyone pretends. Right now you are pretending not to have heard a story that has been the centerpiece of Nepommuck's newspaper advertisement for weeks."

He smiled. "Forgive me for the white lie, but I wanted to keep you engaged in conversation. And the story seems a pretty one."

"Don't know what's so pretty about it. A year ago I was a poor Cockney flower girl, fit for little more than selling posies outside Covent Garden. Then I had the good fortune to study under the same man as the Maestro once did: Professor Henry Higgins of Wimpole Street. And while I'd never admit it to him, the Professor is quite the skilled phonetician and philologist."

"A philo-what?"

"A student of languages."

Nottingham waved away a lazy bumblebee. "And now you're Nepommuck's most famous assistant."

"Hardly famous, Mr. Nottingham. I have fewer than a dozen pupils."

"Why am I not one of them? If I had known I could improve my vowels with a temptress such as you, I would have banged down the door to your classroom."

Eliza was amused by his frank admiration. "Given your boldness, I wonder you simply didn't demand me as your teacher."

"I'll tell you this, I'd much rather you teach me than Nepommuck. He boasts so much, there's hardly any time for a real lesson."

"Surely he must be helping you."

"To a point, not that I need much instruction. A little polishing to hide my Liverpool accent so I can get a position as a London clerk. But he's insufferable. You'd think I was a gorilla who didn't know how to talk at all. I've learned more about how to speak properly by spending my Sunday mornings strolling about Kensington Gardens. Listening to the swells talk to each other—and talk down to everyone else—is far more instructive than being humiliated by our Maestro."

"He humiliates you?" she asked, curious.

"Absolutely. And I'm hardly the only one. One day the Maestro will get stuffed, mark my words. From what I've heard, he treats all his male students like servants, while he's far too friendly with his lady pupils. Case in point, the lovesick Mrs. Finch."

"Spreading rumors can be dangerous, Mr. Nottingham."

"Rumors? Before you became his assistant, my lessons preceded Mrs. Finch's. If you think I'm bold with the ladies, you've not watched Nepommuck. He couldn't get rid of me fast enough at the end of the hour, not with the lovely Mary Finch fluttering on the other side of the door. That is, until her husband caught on, so Nepommuck handed her over to you."

Eliza was about to question him about the Finches when she saw a familiar face. "Excuse me, Mr. Nottingham. But I've just caught sight of an old friend."

She hurried off, surprised to see Colonel Pickering at the party. The Colonel seemed as surprised to see her, and as pleased. After giving her a warm embrace, he presented his companion, a tall, distinguished gentleman with a high forehead and reddish brown hair slicked back.

"May I introduce Major Aubrey Redstone," Pickering said. "The Major is a friend from my days in India. He only recently arrived from Bombay. Major Redstone, this is the incomparable Miss Eliza Doolittle."

"A pleasure to meet you," she said, admiring his smart military bearing and neat appearance. "Welcome back to England."

"The pleasure is all mine, Miss Doolittle." He bowed over her hand and straightened with a warm smile. Eliza noticed that Redstone had remarkably pale blue eyes, made even paler by his tanned face. It seemed a friendly face, she decided, and took an instant liking to him.

Redstone glanced around the garden. "I don't know if I'm pleased to be back. I've spent too much time on the subcontinent. This all seems quite foreign."

Eliza looked at the rich people supping on cakes and champagne under white tents. "To me, too."

They laughed. She tucked her hand around Pickering's arm and the three of them strolled about the rolling lawn. "Tell me how you snagged an invitation to Lady Gresham's charity garden party," she said to Pickering.

"Her late husband, the Marquess, was my father's closest friend. I knew the family quite well. Such a pity when he died six years ago. He gave the best shooting parties in west England." Pickering nodded toward Hepburn House. "If these walls could talk, my dear, the *Tatler* could run stories for weeks."

"I insist on hearing a tale or two myself one evening, Colonel."

"I'd much rather tell you about Major Redstone. He's a renowned scholar of Sanskrit poetry and was kind enough to leave Bombay and journey all the way here to assist me with a transcription project. At least he will once he delivers a paper to the Asiatic Society tomorrow."

"I promise to devote the rest of my visit to helping you with that palm-leaf manuscript," Redstone said. "Luckily we have two years before presenting the paper at the Sanskrit Revival Society." He turned to Eliza. "The Colonel said you're working for Hungarian royalty."

"So he claims, but who knows for certain?"

"The Major has been in the army and in India too long," Pickering said. "Doesn't much care for the company of the upper classes, do you, Reddy?"

"Only if they are true aristocrats: civilized, charitable, well mannered." He paused. "And scholarly."

"A gentleman soldier perhaps?" Eliza asked with a smile.

"The best of all possible choices," he said, eyes twinkling.

"I'm afraid that if Maestro Nepommuck is as royal as he claims, he will only reinforce your low opinion of the upper crust." She nodded toward the couple by the topiaries. "There he is with our hostess."

"I say, Verena is looking exceedingly well," Pickering said. "She always was a handsome woman, but she looks even better now than when she was sixty."

Eliza stopped in surprise. "How old is the Marchioness?"

"Oh, I should not have mentioned her age. A gentleman should never discuss a lady's age. Quite unforgivable of me."

Perhaps that explained why Lady Gresham had been so kind and solicitous to the Maestro. Even a marchioness could be flattered by a younger man's attentions. And in return, she had introduced Nepommuck to the most important people in London. Every week he was invited to yet another dinner party or reception to hobnob with the country house set or those who had the ear of 10 Downing Street. No wonder he was such an obnoxious snob.

When she led Pickering and Redstone over to the couple, Eliza took a closer look at her hostess. A large white hat shaded the top half of Lady Gresham's face, but Eliza noticed fine lines around the woman's eyes. At most she looked sixty, and an impressive sixty at that. And her high cheekbones, so sharply defined, seemed as if they could cut glass. So could her penetrating gray eyes. Eliza suspected she was not a woman you wanted to cross . . . or disappoint.

Pickering and Lady Gresham greeted each other with a warmth

that surprised Eliza. Nepommuck looked at the Colonel with new respect. No doubt he would add Pickering to his list of people to exploit. Since Redstone was temporarily forgotten, Eliza spoke up.

"Major Aubrey Redstone is the Colonel's friend and a noted scholar of Sanskrit poetry."

"I am honored to meet a colleague of Colonel Pickering." Lady Gresham extended her hand. "And a scholar, too. My late husband would have been most impressed, as am I."

Nepommuck sniffed. "What is Sanskrit but another language? I speak thirty-two languages. As for poetry, nonsense fit only for spinsters. It doesn't interest me."

"You've never read Sanskrit poetry then, Mr. Nepommuck," Redstone said. "It is infused with both intellectual complexity and lyrical beauty."

"I have not read it, and have no intention of doing so."

"Now, Emil," Lady Gresham warned, "Sanskrit is an ancient and difficult language to translate, as the Colonel can tell you. I cannot believe you do not appreciate poetry. Would you have me think you do not care for Shakespeare or Tennyson?"

Nepommuck seemed to shrink under her steely gaze. "Shakespeare is different. Who does not love Shakespeare?"

"Indeed, who does not? You are instructing Miss Page, or should I say Ophelia."

"Excuse me, but I thought her name was Rosalind," Eliza said.

Nepommuck gazed at her with greater contempt than usual. "You are such a stupid girl."

"That is most uncalled for," Pickering said, his voice uncharacteristically angry.

"You owe Miss Doolittle an apology." Redstone glared at Nepommuck.

"Emil?" Lady Gresham had that steely look once more.

The Hungarian cleared his throat. "Please accept my apology, Miss Doolittle," he said with obvious reluctance.

Eliza nodded, hurt both by his insult and by the fact that she didn't understand why he had called her stupid.

Nepommuck cleared his throat. "It is two o'clock."

"Oh my. It is almost time." Lady Gresham picked up her skirt with one hand. "Please excuse us, Colonel, Miss Doolittle. And I hope to see you again, Major."

Nepommuck shot all of them a surly glance before hurrying after her. "You can see now why I doubt whether the Maestro is of royal blood," Eliza said.

Pickering shook his head. "My dear, there are boors in every social class."

"That man seems especially boorish," Redstone said. "The Colonel and I may have to find you another employer."

"I can't complain about my salary, but I don't fancy being insulted."

"Of course not. Verena ought to show that cad the door." Pickering remained upset, which touched Eliza. Neither of them mentioned the fact that Higgins regularly hurled sly insults at her. Then again, he treated everyone with the same arrogant impatience. "Let me ask a servant to bring us a nice pot of Earl Grey, and perhaps a bit of pastry, too. I believe someone mentioned Charlotte Russe. I know you love sweets, Eliza."

That was true enough. Drat Henry Higgins. She'd developed quite the sweet tooth ever since he'd plied her with those scrumptious chocolates last year as bribes for good behavior.

"Maybe a tiny slice of the cake," she replied. No need to mention it would be her fourth today.

"Excellent. Then we can relax and spend time catching up."

"I would love that. We didn't have much opportunity the last time we met."

They exchanged rueful glances, remembering the scene twelve days ago when Higgins and Nepommuck argued in her classroom. Pickering set off for the nearest white tent. After he left, Eliza looked over at Redstone. He was the Colonel's friend, a scholar, and he seemed kind. He would be honest, or so she hoped.

"What did I say that was so stupid?"

"Ophelia is a character in the Shakespearean play *Hamlet*," Redstone said. "Miss Page will make her debut on the London stage in that role."

Eliza nodded. For a terrible moment, she fought back tears. There was so much she didn't know—couldn't hope to know—not without years of study. Higgins could teach her not to drop her aitches, Mrs. Higgins could instruct her in manners, and Pickering could buy her all the right clothes. But God help her, she was stupid, a stupid girl who used to sleep in her street clothes at night because she had nothing else to wear. How dare she presume to think she could ever find a life outside the desperate poverty she was born into?

"I am stupid. The stupid daughter of a dustman who pretends to be a lady."

Redstone shook his head. "I see a lady before me, Miss Doolittle. A lady more gracious and refined than any peer listed in Debrett's. You are a lovely, intelligent young woman. And the Colonel believes you've accomplished more in six months than most people do in a lifetime."

"But I didn't know who Ophelia was. I've never even heard of her. In fact, I've never read a word of Shakespeare."

"It's just a play," Redstone said. "And plays can be read. Books, too. No one is born knowing who Ophelia is."

When he led her to a nearby table and pulled out a wrought iron chair, she sat down with a sigh. "That's kind of you to say, Major, but you're a great scholar."

He sat across from her, looking amused. "I certainly was not born knowing how to translate Sanskrit poetry, Miss Doolittle. It took many years and no small amount of effort. Everything in life has to be learned. And it's not simply what comes from books. We learn how to walk and talk when we are babes, how to act in polite society, and how to love from those who care for us." His pale eyes seemed to darken. "We even learn how to hate. That is perhaps the most difficult lesson of all."

Eliza was about to ask if someone had taught him that lesson, but Pickering returned with a footman. The man set down a silver tea tray filled with scones, cucumber sandwiches, and tarts with strawberries. A maidservant brought a tray of teacups and a teapot.

The Colonel perched on a chair. "I fear there is no more Charlotte Russe, my dear."

Eliza felt guilty about that. After tea was poured, she, Redstone, and Pickering enjoyed good food and conversation until Lady Gresham's voice rang out over the garden.

"May I have everyone's attention?" Lady Gresham stood on the terrace, with Nepommuck a few feet behind her. The guests at the farthest reaches of the gardens strolled within earshot of the terrace. "Ladies and gentlemen, I want to welcome you to my Annual Foundling Hospital Garden Party. Your donations will help the cause immensely. Countless children are abandoned on the streets of London each week. Please contribute to this worthy charity. And thank you for joining us today."

Eliza had a few crowns in her pocketbook. She made a note to drop them in the donation basket before she left.

Lady Gresham continued. "Some of you are pupils of the distinguished language expert, Emil Nepommuck, also known affectionately as the Maestro."

Even from where she was sitting, Eliza could see that Lady Gresham's cheeks had grown quite pink. Lord, she was blushing like a young girl. Nepommuck now stood beside her. He looked even more pompous than usual.

"The Maestro and I have personal news to share. It appears that I am about to add another title to my name, albeit a Hungarian one." Lady Gresham reached for Nepommuck's hand. "I am both pleased and proud to announce that just this morning, I accepted Emil's proposal of marriage."

Gasps from several hundred people greeted her words. Pickering choked on his tea. A crash of china sounded from one of the tables, and Eliza noted even the servants seemed stunned. The butler Harrison stood a few feet behind the couple, and she almost laughed at the look of shock on his face.

A smattering of applause finally erupted, overpowered by dozens of people talking among themselves. After a long pause, guests began to approach the couple on the terrace.

Eliza turned back to Pickering and Redstone. "I knew the Marchioness was taken in by the Hungarian, but not to this extent."

"Taken in? *Taken in?*" Pickering wiped the tea he'd spilled over his cravat. "Why, she has completely lost her senses! What is she thinking, to marry some foreign mountebank, and at her age. Nepommuck is no more than thirty-two. That fortune hunter should be horsewhipped for taking such cruel advantage of a seventy-year-old woman."

This time, Eliza choked. "Lady Gresham is seventy?"

"Seventy-one this November. And yes, I know it is not gentle-manly to speak of a lady's age, but this . . . this is too much!"

"Calm down, old chap," Redstone said. "You'll make yourself ill."

"He's right," Eliza began. "After all, if Lady——" She caught sight of Mary Finch running through the crowd.

Eliza stood up for a better look. Pushing guests aside, Mary raced from the other end of the garden. With her feathered aigrette askew, the sobbing young woman shouted, "I won't believe it! It cannot be true. Emil! Emil! Tell them it's not true."

Her husband ran after her.

Guests jumped out of the way as Mary barreled past. At one point, she knocked over a maid carrying a tray of tarts, which flew into the air. Cornelius grabbed her just before Mary reached the terrace steps, but the hysterical woman had now caught everyone's attention. Nepommuck stared down at her with a look of pure hatred . . . and fear.

Mary struggled in her husband's arms, but he refused to let her go. "You don't understand. He promised to marry me. You did, Emil. Tell her that you love me. Tell her. You can't marry that old woman!"

"Good heavens." Pickering gulped down the rest of his tea.

Lady Gresham said in a loud voice, "Harrison!"

The handsome butler appeared behind the Marchioness, who whispered something in his ear. He nodded.

Meanwhile Cornelius still held Mary tight, his face beet red. "Mary, stop this. You are making a fool of yourself. Of us both!"

"But I love him. And he loves me. We made promises to each other. Emil!"

Without warning, Mary suddenly went limp. Cornelius strug-gled to keep her from falling to the ground. When Harrison reached the couple, he picked up the young woman as if she weighed no more than one of the pink feathers bobbing above her head. She revived briefly as the butler carried her past. Eliza could have sworn she heard her sob, "The baby."

Cornelius muttered a terrible oath, his face a mask of fury and grief. After they'd left the grounds, the crowd began to buzz. James Nottingham stood by the fountain, a champagne glass in his hand. He raised it in Eliza's direction and mouthed, "I told you."

She turned to Redstone. "This can hardly be what you expected, Major. After all your years away from England, I can't imagine what you must think of us."

He smiled. "What I'm thinking is that English garden parties are far more interesting than I remember."

FOUR

If that's my son, send him away," Mrs. Higgins said. The doorbell chimed again. "Tell him I've gone to call on Cousin Bertie. Better yet, say Bertie and I left on a trip to the Hebrides. We won't be back for a fortnight."

"Yes, ma'am." The parlor maid dropped a curtsey and hurried off.

Mrs. Higgins settled back in her favorite chair by the window. Below, the Thames sparkled in the morning sunlight. Due to the mild weather, the drawing room windows were open and she smiled with pleasure at both the sight and fragrance of the potted hyacinth on her balcony. Reaching for her teacup, she took an appreciative sip. It was an exquisite Ceylon brew purchased on the recommendation of Colonel Pickering. She found him such an agreeable chap, always brimming with useful information about the most recent imports from the subcontinent and Asia. On his next visit, he promised to bring her a new tea blend from India.

Unfortunately Henry often accompanied the Colonel, and she did not need to see her dear boy more than once a month. Henry had already paid her a call over two weeks ago, filled with deafening rage over that Hungarian phonetician. And with no small amount of animosity reserved for Miss Doolittle. Ever since Henry and the Colonel met Eliza, her household had been filled with more drama than Drury Lane Theatre.

Mrs. Higgins almost spilled her tea when her son charged into the room.

"Mother, I don't understand why I must ring that bell half a dozen times before anyone answers the door." Henry thrust a large bouquet of flowers at her. "You ought to give me a key."

"Heaven forbid, and take off your hat. This is a drawing room, not the platform at Paddington Station."

He flung his hat and coat onto a nearby ottoman.

The parlor maid entered, looking chagrined. "Sorry, ma'am, but Mr. Henry insisted on coming up."

"If you thought that story about visiting Cousin Bertie would fool me, then you must think me as dotty as he is." He raised an amused eyebrow. "The next time you wish to lie about going on holiday, do not choose a place as lugubrious as the Hebrides."

"Daisy, I commend you for doing your best to rein in my son. But since he has already breached the walls, please take these flowers he manhandled. And bring more tea." She accepted his kiss on her cheek. "Well, Henry, two visits in two weeks. I don't know whether to be flattered or afraid. And bearing lilacs, too. I'm certain Mr. Eynsford Hill will not be pleased that you brought a spring bouquet for Eliza."

"The flowers aren't for that ungrateful ninny. I brought them for you." He sat back on the chintz-covered divan with a smug grin.

"For me? Whatever for, dear?"

"For helping turn that little traitor into something resembling a lady. And for being so charitable as to offer her a roof over her head after she ran away from Wimpole Street."

"I don't see it as a charitable impulse. I quite enjoy her company. Eliza is a charming girl. As I am sure you have had occasion to learn."

"Hah," he snorted.

"Eliza has wanted to pay room and board since she began working for Mr. Nepommuck. A proposition I would not hear of, I might add. The girl has pride. Although you seem to have done your utmost to break it."

"Is that what she's been saying? That impudent siren of Covent Garden."

"Henry, really. It is entirely too early in the day for such purple prose. I've a dressmaker appointment at eleven. Do you have some other purpose beyond delivering lilacs?"

"I've just come from Sibley & Moffett."

"Our solicitors?"

He nodded. "I am bringing charges of fraud and professional sabotage against Emil Nepommuck. They will be serving papers later today."

"I had hoped you would change your mind since we last spoke." Mrs. Higgins was not pleased. "This will play out in the papers, not just in the courts. Nepommuck will not take these charges lightly. Some of his clients move in circles close to 10 Downing Street. And numerous friends reported to me that the Dowager Marchioness of Gresham announced her engagement to him Sunday at her charity garden party."

"Pickering passed on the ridiculous news." His smile grew even more devilish. "Rarely have I been happier to hear some lunatic couple decided to wed. Ah, to be there when that worm learns he has lost Lady Gresham's fortune along with his students, and what is left of his reputation."

"Henry, try to be reasonable for once in your exasperating life. Is it really worth all this trouble and expense just to strike back at him for stealing Eliza away?"

"He did not steal that urchin away. She went to him, cap in hand, begging for a job. And with my teaching methods in her purse."

She put up a hand. "I refuse to sit through this litany again. My hearing has only now recovered from the hours of shouting you subjected me to on your last visit."

"You don't think I am going to let that hairy hog publicly take credit for my work, do you? Eliza Doolittle is my creation. No one else's."

"Eliza is her own creation, Henry. You simply provided the tools and the opportunity. A year ago she was fighting to survive in the East End. Now she's instructing businessmen and mill owners' wives on how to speak proper English. In less than a year! Give her credit for talent and intelligence. It wasn't only your vocal exercises."

"Damnation. Why does everyone take that girl's side against me?"

Mrs. Higgins sighed. "No tantrums, dear. You are much too old for that to be attractive."

"Well, I am not going to let those bald-faced lies continue in the paper." Henry paused. "I've responded in kind."

"Should I plan a six-month tour of the Continent so I can avoid the uproar?"

"No, you must stay here. I am sure that a court deposition will be taken from everyone who witnessed how Pickering and I turned that Covent Garden turnip into a lady." He grinned. "What a lark it will be exposing that pompous Hungarian. Let's see how many students he has after Sibley, Moffett, and I are done with him."

"Let's see how many of your students remain after this circus ends."

"Of course, poor little Eliza will be out of a job," Henry continued as if he hadn't heard a word she spoke. He gestured toward the drawing room door. "If she's at home, maybe we should have her join us. I warned her I'd engineer the demise of her Maestro. But it's only fair she know that she'll have to give testimony. Under oath, so if she doesn't tell the truth, I shall hang that Cockney cabbage from Tower Bridge by her—"

"Eliza isn't here," Mrs. Higgins broke in. "She had a nine o'clock lesson this morning, so she left here an hour ago. Afterwards, she plans to meet Mr. Eynsford Hill and his sister at Belgrave Square for a tour of the gardens and tea. If you wish to speak with her, you'll have to go to her classroom later today when her afternoon pupils arrive."

"She won't be giving lessons much longer." Henry stretched back on the divan. "I have seen to that. In fact, I doubt that any of Nepommuck or Eliza's pupils will be wanting lessons today."

"Why not?"

"Haven't you read this morning's *Daily Mail*?"

"Not yet." She pointed to the writing desk. "Daisy put it there with my letters."

Higgins retrieved the newspaper and unfolded it with a flourish. "Has Eliza read it?"

"She is courteous enough to wait until I have looked it over first."

He seemed even more satisfied with himself. "Then it will come as a complete surprise when she arrives in Belgrave Square."

"A nasty surprise, judging from your buoyant mood."

"Of course it's nasty. Is there any other sort of surprise one should spring on an enemy? I've been busy since I learned what that poser was claiming in the papers. So rather than bash his hairy head in—which I admit I briefly considered—I struck back in the newspapers." He handed the *Daily Mail* to his mother.

She started to read, then looked up. "Dear lord, Henry. What have you done?"

———

When would she learn that it was a mistake to send Freddy off to hire a cab? Eliza cringed as an omnibus almost ran him over. She waved in his direction, hoping to convince him to stop trying, or at least get out of the street.

Freddy's sister, Clara, let out a sigh. "Poor Freddy. I'm afraid he never acquired the trick of flagging down a cab."

Actually, Eliza suspected he'd have trouble stopping a rag seller pushing his cart.

"A pity we can't afford our own driver and car," Clara continued. "But that just isn't possible in our current situation."

"I'm sure that will change soon." She squeezed Clara's arm in a gesture of sympathy.

Eliza understood that Clara considered the family's financial condition as one step away from bleak poverty. But the girl was blissfully unaware how well-off the Eynsford Hills were compared with most Londoners. Thanks to a modest inheritance, the family lived a genteel—albeit frugal—life. Try hanging your food in a sack from the ceiling every night to keep the rats from eating it, Eliza wanted to tell her. But Clara was young and unsophisticated. And she regarded Eliza as the epitome of a modern young woman, the latest society fashion in brash elegance.

Freddy and his mother were just as unworldly. Even after learning that Eliza had been a Cockney flower girl, they treated her transformation as an amusing lark. Had any of them ever caught a glimpse of the East End's narrow dark streets? She didn't know whether to be amazed or angry.

Eliza bit back a scream as Freddy tripped mere inches away from a motorcar heading for Grosvenor Crescent. Hang the niceties. The fellow was going to get himself killed.

"Freddy, get your arse over here!" she shouted.

"Oh Eliza, I do love how you know all the new small talk," Clara said in delight. "Yes, Freddy, move your arse!"

Two dowagers marched past, glaring at them in obvious disapproval.

Eliza breathed a sigh of relief when Freddy reached the curb. He looked dashing as always, with his blue eyes, thick mane of blond hair, and skin as clear and rosy as a country milkmaid's. That such a refined and handsome young man should adore her was another miraculous event in a year that had been crammed with them.

"Darling, I couldn't get the attention of even a single taxi," he said with a sunny smile. "And I nearly got knocked down by an omnibus. It was rather exciting, though."

Eliza adjusted his collar. "Don't worry, Freddy. As I told you before, we can easily walk to Belgrave Place from here. It's only a few blocks, and the day is glorious."

Spring had made a stunning entrance the day of Lady Gresham's garden party. The weather had been almost tropical ever since. They stood along the edge of Belgrave Square Gardens, and the heady fragrance of its flowers was enough to make her swoon.

"But won't you be late for your lessons?" he asked.

"My next pupil doesn't arrive until one. It's not quite noon."

Big Ben began tolling the midday hour at that moment. "See, we have more than enough time for a leisurely stroll." Eliza linked arms with both Clara and Freddy.

"I do want to get there in plenty of time so you can introduce me to the Maestro," Clara said. "He must be very busy. I wouldn't like to interrupt his lessons."

"It's Thursday. He only has one lesson today at three o'clock."

"I hope he doesn't think me too forward. I've been longing to meet him ever since you became his assistant. Do I curtsey? He's the first person of royal blood I've ever met."

"Lord, no. Just shake his hand and say, 'How d'ya do.'"

"You're so funny, Eliza. What should I call him? Baron? Prince? What do they call him back in Hungary?"

Eliza suspected they called him "Emil" but didn't want to disillusion Clara. "I've no idea what the Hungarians call him. 'Maestro' will do for any Brits who make his acquaintance."

"Will he flirt with me? I've heard he's quite the ladies' man."

"Of course. He flirts with every female, and you're prettier than most."

"Has he dared to flirt with you, Eliza?" Freddy asked, clearly outraged.

"He does now and then, usually when he's bored. But since Professor Higgins called, he's barely said a word to me." Eliza smiled up at Freddy. "Don't be jealous, silly. I told you. He and Lady Gresham announced their engagement at the garden party last Sunday."

"Maybe he shan't pay much heed to me at all." Clara deflated like a pricked balloon. She dodged a pram pushed by a determined black-garbed nanny with a stern face. "I'm not a pupil, after all. Or a marchioness."

"That won't stop him."

Eliza knew that Nepommuck would lavish Clara with flattery and attention. Why not? She was a pretty young woman who thought the Maestro was as royal as the Hungarian king himself—assuming Hungary had a king. But once Clara left his sight, he'd forget he ever met her. Nepommuck preferred the company of older women: well connected, discreet, and wealthy.

"If he dares flirt with you, Clara, I shall have to get in his face," Freddy said.

"If you are going to fly into a temper every time a man flirts with me, I don't know how I shall find a husband," Clara said. "After all, why shouldn't I marry royalty? Lady Gresham is marrying the Maestro. And I heard she was the daughter of a Bristol engineer before she wed her late husband the Marquess. As for the Maestro, he must have aristocratic brothers or cousins. Do any of them ever visit him in London, Eliza?"

"You are not going to marry a Hungarian, Clara, no matter how royal his blood," Freddy said. "When the time comes, you will marry a British chap. Not a foreign bounder."

In defiance, Clara walked ahead of them, her heels clicking on the pavement. Eliza wished Freddy would be gentler with his sister. Until five weeks ago, Clara's energies had been directed at a prominent banker's eldest son. The pair even discussed an engagement until the banker learned the Eynsford Hills' only assets were good looks and a tiny trust fund.

"Freddy, I am merely introducing Clara to Nepommuck," Eliza said in a half whisper. "She's been low after that business with the banker's son. If this cheers her up a bit, we should let her be. A few flattering words from an overdressed Hungarian might do the trick."

Freddy stopped, gazing at her with naked adoration. "You are the most wonderful creature, Eliza. They ought to write songs about you in the West End. There simply isn't a woman more beautiful or kindhearted than you, my sweet darling."

Flowery nonsense, but Eliza loved every word. "What would I do without you, Freddy?"

In another second, they might have scandalized the traffic rounding Belgrave Square Gardens with an ardent kiss. A rude voice stopped them. "'Ey there, Miss Doolittle, 'old yer tracks. We got to be talking afore I soak that bloke in the river!"

A barrel-chested older man made his way toward them. Eliza recognized Dmitri Kollas, one of Nepommuck's pupils. Higgins suspected the Greek diplomat was actually from Clerkenwell. Although Kollas pretended not to speak English, she'd heard him arguing loudly with Nepommuck several times. What little she heard through the walls revealed that Kollas spoke like a Cockney native.

"Mr. Kollas, what's wrong?"

His face turned purple. "That bastard Nepo you work for. I been there twice this mornin' banging on 'is door, but 'e ain't got the knockers to open. Yellow as pus, 'e is. And after all 'is bloody nattering at me these months, about 'ow I be lower than a snake's belly. Well, I be putting a call to me mates in Clerkenwell what will pay 'im back for all 'is insults!"

"Perhaps the Maestro simply isn't at home," she said.

"Nah, I 'eard him moving around in there," Kollas said in disgust. "'E even told me to clear off through the bloody door. The bloke's a right dodger what ain't got the bullocks to admit 'e's bleeding worse than us fools what pay 'im."

"But why are you so angry? You've been his pupil for months."

"Played me, 'e did. Or maybe 'e thinks I can't read? Thinks maybe there ain't no one in the bleeding town that don't know 'ow to put words together! Well, Nepo best jimmy up some of my 'ard-earned sterling. I ain't been forking over so's I can get knocked down for being Cockney and not bloody Greek!"

"Do you understand this fellow?" Freddy whispered.

Eliza ignored him. "What is there to read?"

He held aloft a newspaper and struck the folded page. "You the only schooled filly not reading the dailies? Look on this, and tell me all us dusters ain't got cause to set his place afire."

Kollas thrust the paper into Eliza's hands before stalking off. She scanned the front page. Clara and Freddy gathered around her. "What was he saying, Eliza?" Clara asked. "I couldn't understand a word."

"Dmitri Kollas is one of the Maestro's students. Apparently he went to his lodgings twice this morning, but Nepommuck refused to open the door. For some reason the Maestro doesn't want to see him." Eliza stopped. "Oh, crikey."

"What is it?" Freddy peered over her shoulder.

"This article says Emil Nepommuck committed several crimes in his native Hungary, including rape, assault, arson, and fraud." She read for a moment. "And he served time in a Budapest prison."

Clara let out a cry. "It can't be true! Where is the paper getting such lies?"

But Eliza had no time to answer. She stepped out to the curb, her hand raised. A hansom cab immediately steered in her direction. "How did you do that?" Freddy asked in amazement.

"We must get to Nepommuck's lodgings before he runs off. A mob of people will be arriving at Belgrave Square any minute. And they'll all be wanting the truth." Eliza stared down at the newspaper article before getting into the cab. "I don't much care about the truth, but he owes me two weeks' salary."

When the cab reached their stop, Eliza jumped to the pavement before the horse halted.

"Eliza, wait for us!" Freddy and Clara called after her.

She ran into the building, then took the stairs two at a time. Breathless, she stopped at the top. The hallway was totally dark.

Freddy and Clara bumped into her, almost knocking her down. "What's going on?" Clara asked. "Why is it so dark?"

"Someone turned off the lights," Eliza said in a grim voice. "Again."

"We ought to find someone to turn the lights back on," Freddy suggested.

"No, I'll turn them on. The switch is halfway down the hall on the left." After the last incident, Eliza had made certain to locate it. "Enough of these games."

"Who's playing games?" Freddy asked as he and Clara followed close behind Eliza in the dark.

"Someone is trying to scare me. It worked once, but not this time." Eliza brushed her hand along the wall to the switch. With one click, brightness washed over them.

"There, that wasn't so hard." She turned to speak to Freddy but his sister let out a horrendous scream. He gasped beside her.

Eliza spun around to see what they were staring at in such horror.

Nepommuck lay facedown outside his apartment door, head turned to the side. Eliza could see that his eyes were motionless and wide open. She fell back against the wall.

With a strangled cry, Clara pointed at the dagger plunged into his back. Freddy grabbed his sister, who buried her face against his chest. "Eliza, we must get out of here. Now!"

But Eliza saw something else besides the dagger. Trembling, she forced herself to walk closer to the dead man. Blood streamed from his wound, staining his brocaded dressing gown and the carpet beneath him. She bent closer to the lifeless body. It was more gruesome than she feared. Plunged into his open mouth was one of Eliza's shiny new tuning forks.

FIVE

Any day spent in Scotland Yard was a fearsome day indeed. Eliza could barely control her mounting fear. After examining the Maestro's body and the hallway, the police brought her to the Yard for questioning. Shaken from the sight of the murdered Nepommuck, she expected the police to ask a few questions and then send her home. Instead they left her alone for hours in a small windowless room as cold as the North Sea. Eliza had nothing to do but worry and stare at the peeling paint on the walls.

She huddled on a tilted bench that threatened to collapse at any moment. But Eliza refused to move to the two chairs pushed up against a scarred wooden table. No doubt those chairs were reserved for the detectives who would eventually come to interrogate her. Although heaven knew what they expected her to tell them that she hadn't already said back at Belgrave Place.

The police had no right to keep her waiting for hours, alone and forgotten. She'd done nothing wrong. Unfortunately growing up in the East End had taught her that the law didn't give a fig about rights for a person such as her. And if they took it into their heads that she had killed the Maestro, she'd never see the gloomy skies of London again.

But she wasn't only worried about herself. Where had they taken Freddy and Clara? Poor Clara had been hysterical when they'd brought them all to the Yard. Freddy's genteel sister would never stand up to rough treatment by the police. Eliza wasn't even certain she could.

If only one of her tuning forks hadn't been found on Nepommuck's dead body. It was like an arrow pointed right at her. She hoped the police realized that no murderer would leave such an obvious clue. The tuning fork had probably been left to direct suspicion away from the real murderer, although why that bastard chose to involve her, she'd bloody well like to know.

She had no motive. Granted, Nepommuck had been a snobbish, irritating fellow, but he'd given her a good job with a salary to match. The police should see instantly that she had no reason to want him dead.

No, she blamed that explosive article in the newspaper. Someone who read that realized the Maestro was not who he said he was. Certainly that Kollas fellow was enraged about being lied to, given his harsh words earlier that day. And how many other students would also feel cheated or betrayed? But she didn't understand why that would lead to his murder.

Eliza rose to her feet and paced the small area between the table and the wall. Did she know the murderer? Was it someone she saw every day? Perhaps a jealous husband. She recalled the spectacle that Mary Finch made of herself at the garden party on Sunday. Had Mary driven her husband not only to distraction, but to murder?

And what about poor Lady Gresham? At the garden party, she

seemed as thrilled as a girl of twenty to be announcing her engagement to the Maestro. Tears welled in Eliza's eyes. How sad that the older woman's recent joy would now be turning to bitterness and grief. As for herself, Eliza found it hard to believe that she'd never again hear the Hungarian mock her English or watch him comb that ridiculous mustache. She may not have liked him, but over the past two months she'd grown accustomed to his smug little face.

The door banged open.

Eliza wiped the tears from her cheeks before turning around. Two men in rumpled suits entered the room. She could see that a bobby stood guard outside the door, helmet in hand. He threw her a stern look before shutting the door once again, leaving her alone with the two men. Terror clenched her gut. What were these gents up to? she wondered. Nothing good, that was for certain.

"Well, what 'ave we got 'ere, Grint?" the taller one asked. His beady gaze lingered on her bosom.

"Lemme see." His red-haired colleague consulted a notebook. "Seems this is Miss Doolittle, a teacher. Only that classroom in Belgrave Square don't look like any I ever seen before, Hollaway. Ain't no desks nor chalkboard. Found a bunch of those same metal things what was sticking up in the dead body. Dunno what they are. Fancy kind of weapon, most like."

"They're tuning forks." Eliza swallowed hard. "I use them as a teaching tool."

"Don't the tart sound fancy, Hollaway."

"I'm not a tart!" Eliza felt her anger rise, but she fought to keep it in check. "And you have no right to keep me locked up here."

"We got every right seeing as how something what belonged to you was found sticking out of the murder victim." He moved closer to her, and she took an involuntary step back. "So let's not be talking about your rights, because you don't got any."

Hollaway laughed. "Ain't that the truth."

"Now sit down and keep quiet." Grint pointed at the bench.

Eliza sat down with an audible sigh. She'd suspected as much. Despite her fancy clothes and proper elocution, they'd realized right off she wasn't a real lady. The swells and toffs ruled the world just as her father always said, and people like her mattered less than week-old bread.

Well, if worse came to worst, she wasn't going down without a fight. Eliza nudged her parasol lying beneath the bench with her foot. If either of these two laid a hand on her, she'd try to get in at least one good blow.

The red-haired detective seemed pleased to have cowed her. Beneath his mass of freckles, a chilling grin creased his face. "Now, I am Detective Colm Grint, and me and my partner, Detective William Hollaway, have been sent to question you. A course the way we see it, it seems pretty obvious what happened at that little love nest of yours on Belgravia Place."

"Love nest? That's ridiculous."

Hollaway sat across the table from her. "Don't seem ridiculous to me. You're a young unmarried woman living across the hall from a Hungarian gent who had a fancy title and too much money. Pretty cozy setup, if you ask me. Especially as the landlady said he was paying the rent on your rooms."

"Of course he paid the rent. I was working as his teaching assistant. And I didn't live in the rooms, I only gave lessons there." Eliza stared back at him. "Ask anyone in the building. They will tell you that I left every day promptly at four o'clock."

"A lot can happen between a man and a woman, even before four o'clock." Grint sat next to his partner, stretching out his legs beneath the table.

Eliza licked her dry, chapped lips. She thought she might indeed be capable of murder for a tall glass of water. "Maestro Nepommuck was my employer. Nothing more."

"Oh, he was employing you to do something all right."

If she weren't so exhausted and afraid, she might have found this whole conversation amusing. "I did not kill Maestro Nepommuck. I had no reason to want him dead. He paid me a good salary."

Both men looked over at each other as soon as she said that.

Grint smacked his notepad. "Funny you say that, Doolittle. That Eynsford Hill fellow told us you hadn't been paid in weeks."

Eliza sighed. Trust poor Freddy to remember something like that, when he usually forgot what blooming day it was. "Do you really think I'd kill someone for thirty quid?"

"People end up in the morgue for a lot less," Grint said.

Hollaway snapped his fingers. "You know, I'm thinking it weren't no love nest. I'm betting this dolly argued with her boss over the money."

"I did not! And we didn't argue at all. I gave my lessons, and he gave his. We barely saw each other. I don't know who stole one of my tuning forks, but I swear I'm innocent."

"Sure, sure. Every bloke in prison says that. Go ahead and tell the Detective Inspector that, too, when he comes. He ain't gonna believe you, neither." Hollaway grinned.

"Then I demand to see the Detective Inspector. Let me tell my story to him."

Grint whistled. "The tart is making demands now. Ain't she a brash piece of work."

"I tell you, I'm a respectable lady who earns a respectable living."

"Guess it's more respectable than what you were doing last year when you were selling yourself in Covent Garden."

"I sold flowers, and nothing else!"

Grint looked down at his notepad. "It seems you left your so-called respectable work in Covent Garden, only to take up living with two gents on Wimpole Street."

Hollaway cocked an eyebrow at her. "Nice work, Doolittle. Most tarts only land one gent at a time, but you took on two every night."

Eliza felt defeated. They were going to twist the truth so it came out ugly no matter how she protested. "Professor Higgins and Colonel Pickering were giving me elocution lessons."

"If we had more time, I might give you a lesson or two myself," Hollaway said with a leer.

"Be careful, Will. Looks like Miss Doolittle does more with gents than roll in the sheets. Now and again, she decides to stab 'em in the back." Grint got to his feet.

When he walked behind her, Eliza froze. Would he beat her? She'd tried so hard to act the part of an upper-middle-class lady, proper in speech and manner, decked out in a beribboned straw hat and an expensive silk peplum jacket. They'd seen through her despite it all.

"Have you sent for Colonel Pickering and Professor Higgins? Do they even know I'm here? As soon as I was brought in, I asked the sergeant at the desk to call them. And that was hours ago."

Grint leaned close to her ear. "And why should either of them care what happens to you, after you left 'em for the Hungarian?"

"You don't know what you're talking about," she said. "I want to see the Detective Inspector. I want someone to send for my friends. And I want to know what happened to Freddy and Clara."

"You want a lot of things, it seems," Grint said in a threatening voice. "Well, here's what I want to do." He struck Eliza viciously on the side of her head. Her straw hat went sailing to the floor, ribbons flying.

Pain and outrage washed over her in equal measure. "How dare you strike me! You have no right!"

"We have every right to do what we want." Grint grabbed her arm and twisted her around to face him. "So you'd best do as you're told, or you'll find yerself like them suffragettes—behind bars. An' a bit worse for wear, if you take my meaning." He gave her a shake for emphasis.

Her control was just about gone. "So where's this bloody Detective Inspector then? You can't shut me up 'ere like a rat in a trap. It ain't bloody right."

"Oh, I knew it, didn't I, Grint? She don't sound half the lady she looks." Hollaway laughed.

"You got that right, mate." Grint shoved her to the ground.

Eliza ducked before her head made contact with the table. Before he could lay his hands on her again, she grabbed her parasol and rolled under the bench.

"Hey now, what are you doing?" Hollaway said as she knocked the bench aside.

She scrambled to her feet, brandishing her parasol like a sword. "Don't either of you put your filthy hands on me again, you load of dog bollocks!"

Grint slowly moved toward her. "'Ere now, dolly, put that down. It'll go worse for you if you don't."

"Get away or I'll poke yer bleedin' eye out, I will!"

Hollaway feinted to the left and made to grab her parasol. Eliza whacked him in the chest. Grint was too fast, however. Before she could land another blow, he snatched it from her and cracked it over his knees. When he threw the broken parasol aside, Eliza couldn't help shrieking.

"Ah-ah-oh-ow-ow-oh-ow! You ruined it. It has a pearl handle, too. I'll have the law on you!"

"We are the law, you stupid whore." Grint reached for her.

"What the devil! Get away from that woman, Detective, or you'll be landing in a cell on your arse." A man dressed in a sharply tailored three-piece suit stood in the open doorway. "What in blazes is going on here?"

Grint backed off and Hollaway stood at attention. "She was giving us lip, sir."

"So you thought you'd break her parasol and scare her silly? Where do you think you are? At a bar brawl in Spitalfields? I should have your badge."

"Yes, sir," Grint muttered, his face nearly as red as his hair.

Eliza stood stock-still in awe. It couldn't be. But she'd know that shock of unruly dark hair on any East End street. And a familiar sharp blue eye fixed on her while the other squinted. She breathed hard.

"Jack, is that you?"

"Detective Inspector Shaw to you, miss," Hollaway said, but Jack waved him aside.

He took a step closer, his mouth falling open in recognition. "Lizzie? The police report said the lady that found the body was a schoolteacher called Elizabeth Doolittle. I didn't know it was my little Lizzie. But blimey, it is you!" Whooping with laughter, he lifted her off the ground in a bear hug.

"Jackie, I never thought to see you here," Eliza said when he finally set her down. "I'd heard you'd joined the coppers, but never suspected you were a detective inspector." She gave him a quick kiss on the cheek. "Lord, but your mum must be proud."

"Don't you look grand, and so grown up in your fancy dress. Last time I saw you, you were a skinny ten-year-old complaining about the free bread and milk at the Ragged School Mission Hall."

"The milk was sour and the bread always stale," she said with a shudder.

"So it was. But what the devil are you doing in Scotland Yard? There must be some mistake."

"No mistake, sir," Grint said. "She stabbed that Hungarian gentleman in Belgrave Square."

"I did not! Tell him, Jack. Why, I don't even like stabbing a pincushion." Eliza smiled up at him. "You can't imagine how happy I am to see you."

"Little Lizzie, all grown up. And dressed like a Mayfair deb, too. We've both certainly come up in the world, haven't we?"

"It wasn't easy," she said in a near whisper.

"Aye, not easy by half."

Grint cleared his throat, but Jack threw him a cold glance that made the fellow stare down at the floor once more. He was determined to get the last word, though.

"She's a murder suspect, sir, all the same."

"Miss Doolittle is no murderer, Detective Grint." Jack gave her a wink. "She's my cousin."

He'd gone too far this time. Henry Higgins stood at the railing along the Victoria Embankment staring at the Thames, now barely visible in the twilight. Guilt wasn't familiar to him, but as much as he hated to admit it, he was feeling a few guilty pangs now.

Don't know why I should, Higgins thought. If ever a scoundrel deserved a comeuppance, it was that blasted Hungarian. And seeing as how he had lied about so much else in his background, Higgins was amazed Nepommuck had been honest about being Hungarian. Since the lying bloke was fluent in thirty-two languages, he could have passed himself off as a native of any number of countries. It certainly would have made sense for Nepommuck—or Bela Kardos, as he was really called—to have taken on another nationality along with that fabricated royal lineage.

Higgins could only guess that the mountebank genuinely missed his homeland. The tiresome fellow loved to prattle about the glory of the Carpathian Mountains and the beauty of the Danube. He had even extolled the wonders of Hungarian cuisine, which as far as Higgins knew consisted largely of goulash.

Nepommuck wouldn't be suffering homesickness any longer. Higgins was shocked at how quickly word of the murder had traveled from the police to the evening editions of the penny dailies. For the past hour, newsboys had been crying out, "Disgraced Hungarian royal found murdered at Belgrave Square!" from every London corner. Of course, Higgins had felt compelled to buy a copy. And he was dismayed to read that a Miss Doolittle had found the dead body. Higgins knew that Eliza wouldn't forgive him for this, not with her damnable moral code.

In fact, he could hear her now: "Look what you've done, you arrogant bully. Just look what you've done!"

"Hey, guv'nor, can you spare a few coppers for an old soldier what lost a leg in the Transvaal?" a hoarse voice said.

A man dressed in a ragged army jacket held out his cap with one hand. A crutch supported his thin body. Even in the growing dusk, Higgins could see that the fellow did indeed have only one leg.

"And you don't want to be thinking about jumping into the river, guv. From the looks of you, I'm a damn sight worse off, and I ain't thinkin' of throwing meself in the drink."

Those South Welsh tones sounded familiar. "Corporal Ted Trent, is that you?"

The fellow squinted at Higgins in the fading light. "Professor Higgins? Didn't see it was you. Thought you was just some toff what was getting ready to end it all."

"So you thought it would be the perfect time to ask for a few coins?"

"Well, if a body is fixing to end it all, they got no more need for pound and pence, now do they?"

Higgins gave a short laugh. "Just so, Teddy. But I didn't plan on jumping into the Thames. I only needed to clear my head, think a few things through." He paused. "It's been an interesting day."

"They're all interesting if you ask me, as long as you're still breathing."

"I believe you're right, Corporal." This veteran of the last Boer War made him feel even guiltier about Nepommuck.

"Now that I sees that it's you, guv, how about if we talk for a while like the other times, and you can write down how a Swansea bloke like me sounds."

"For a fee, of course." Despite his glum mood, Higgins couldn't help smiling.

The fellow shrugged. "Seeing as how you're a well-heeled gent what lives in fancy digs, and I'm spending me nights shivering beneath Blackfriars Bridge—"

Higgins fished out his wallet. "Enough, Corporal. Here's a fiver. And I won't require a demonstration of southern Welsh dialect in return." He handed the old soldier the money. "Only don't make me feel any guiltier than I already do."

After the down-on-his-luck corporal shuffled off, Higgins turned his attention back to the river. He should go back to Wimpole Street. He'd been gone since morning, and no doubt Pickering, Eliza, and his mother waited to confront him about the newspaper article. And defend his actions he would. Despite how it ended, Nepommuck deserved to be exposed. Higgins had every right to set the record straight. How was he to guess that the Hungarian hid more secrets than Professor Moriarty?

When the private detective he hired two weeks ago presented him with pages of damning documents and photos from Hungary, Higgins was thrilled. He'd found the perfect weapon with which to take down an enemy who had blithely taken credit for Higgins's own accomplishments. And he had shown all of London—including Eliza—that Nepommuck was nothing but a deceitful bounder.

But Higgins hadn't factored murder into the situation. Scandal he had been prepared for, not a dagger in the back.

He sighed as he turned up the collar of his jacket. His mother would have at him even worse than Eliza for stirring up this hornet's nest. Higgins leaned over the railing and stared into the dark rushing waters below. Probably best that he couldn't see his reflection. He suspected that it might show a guilt-stricken man. Or worse.

———

"So what are we going to do about this dead man, Lizzie?"

"I don't know, Jack," Eliza said. "I was hoping the police had a few ideas."

Her cousin chuckled and drew out a chair for her. He waited for her to sit, like any real gentleman would. Then he turned the other chair around and straddled it to face her.

The door opened once more and Eliza let out a cry of delight. A constable entered with a steel tray holding two mugs, a pot of steaming tea, and a few biscuits. Jack took the role of Mother and poured, adding several lumps of sugar to both cups before handing one to her.

Grint and Hollaway stood near the wall, watching them with narrowed eyes.

Eliza took a long sip of the tea. She was so thirsty, she had to restrain herself from downing the entire hot brew in one gulp. "All I know is I don't like that one of my tuning forks was found in the Maestro's mouth. It makes me look suspicious, but also blooming stupid. As if I would kill a person, then leave something that obvious to point right at me. You and I learned better than that before we turned three."

Jack offered her one of the biscuits. "That we did."

She dipped a stale biscuit into her mug and devoured it. "I think I know how the killer got it, too. Last month I came into work with a bag of new tuning forks to use with my lessons. But when I reached the second floor, all the lights had been turned off. I realized I wasn't alone. Someone stood quiet as death farther down the hallway, right outside the Maestro's apartment. When I called out, whoever it was knocked me over like a feather trying to escape."

Grint gave a derisive snort.

Jack shot him a warning look before turning back to Eliza. "The killer most likely pinched the tuning fork from your sack."

"Sir, excuse me, but we have no proof that anyone was hiding in the hallway," Hollaway said. "Except for her word."

Grint cleared his throat. "Right. Miss Doolittle had access to the victim and ample opportunity to murder him. She also had a motive."

Eliza choked on the biscuit. "Motive? What motive? If you're going to bring up that nonsense about me killing the Maestro over my salary then I——"

"You're not a suspect, Lizzie," Jack broke in. "So calm down and enjoy your tea."

"Sir, just because the young woman is a relative is no reason to believe she's innocent," Grint said.

Jack nodded. "That's true. However, Nepommuck was last seen alive and well at eleven this morning by the housekeeping staff at Belgrave Square. Both Mr. Eynsford Hill and his sister insist Miss Doolittle was having tea at that time in Belgrave Square Gardens."

Hollaway took a step forward. "It looked to us that Mr. Eynsford Hill was a bit taken with your cousin, so the gent might be willing to say anything to get his sweetheart released."

Eliza didn't bother to protest. She knew that even if she were guilty, Freddy most likely would do just that.

"Exactly. Which is why my men and I spent the entire day tracking down every person who was having tea at the garden café this morning. At last count, we have at least eighteen people who swore they remember my charming cousin and her companions taking tea there from half past ten to eleven forty." Jack glanced at his notebook. "We also have several witnesses—one of them a policeman at Grosvenor Crescent—who remember the three of them strolling past at noon. Miss Doolittle and the Eynsford Hills discovered the body at ten minutes past noon. So where was the opportunity for Miss Doolittle to murder the victim? Unless you believe the Eynsford Hills are accomplices."

Both Hollaway and Grint looked sheepish at that suggestion. "The two of them don't seem like murderers," Grint said reluctantly.

"Neither does Miss Doolittle," said Jack. "And all three of them have witnesses which prove their innocence. From this point on, I will not hear a single word accusing them of anything criminal. Is that clear?"

Both detectives nodded.

Her cousin continued. "My main concern right now is the murder weapon."

"The dagger," Eliza said with a shiver.

"It's not technically a dagger. If it was, we'd have an easier time tracing where it came from. No, the weapon was an ordinary carving knife. A common brand made by Sheffield. You could find it in half the kitchens of London. Regent Street shops sell dozens of them every day. I'm afraid it isn't much of a clue."

"That's too bad," she said. "But did you release Freddy and Clara?"

Jack sipped his tea. "Hours ago. They weren't much help except for clearing you. The girl was totally hysterical. And truth to tell, the boy wasn't much better. I gave up trying to get a coherent story from either of them. And I am sorry that you've been kept here so long. But since some of my colleagues were convinced a young lady schoolteacher had done the deed, I decided to take matters into my own hands. I went out there myself like the footpad I used to be and started doing my job."

Eliza reached over and squeezed his hand. "Thank you. If I was still selling flowers, I'd send you a basket heaped with them." Her eyes widened. "Maybe I should send flowers, but to your wife. After all, you must be married by now."

He grinned. "Nearly. Miss Sybil Chase accepted my proposal of marriage just last week."

"How lovely. You must tell me all about her."

Grint cleared his throat, and Jack's expression turned serious. "We should probably leave that to another time," he said.

Eliza sighed. "For a moment, I forgot about the murder. And that I was a suspect."

"Not any longer. And you were never a likely suspect anyway."

She crammed another stale biscuit down. "I do know that some of his pupils were none too happy with the Maestro, and others were a bit too taken with him. But Professor Higgins has known Nepommuck far longer than I have. You should speak to him."

Jack exchanged glances with the two detectives. "We would very much like to question the Professor, but we've been unable to track him down. The last anyone has seen of him was this morning when he paid a call on his mother." He paused. "To gloat."

"About what? The article in the *Daily Mail* exposing Nepommuck?"

"You mean the article that the Professor is responsible for getting published."

Her appetite vanished. "What do you mean?"

"We spoke to the editor this afternoon. It seems the paper was given exhaustive and accurate information about the true background of Emil Nepommuck, also known as Bela Kardos, ex-convict. All supplied by Professor Henry Higgins of Wimpole Street."

"Blimey!" Eliza almost dropped her teacup.

"Did you know there was bad blood between the two men?" Jack asked.

Eliza hesitated. Even if Jack was her cousin, she hadn't seen him in a decade and he'd obviously risen far and fast. He'd been kind enough to rescue her, but he was a Scotland Yard inspector. And her ear still stung from the blow delivered by a Yard detective. How much could she really trust any of them?

"They didn't like each other," she said finally, "but there were plenty others that didn't like Nepommuck, either."

"So where has he been all day? His colleague Colonel Pickering said Higgins had no appointments on his schedule."

"You've spoken to the Colonel? Does he know I'm here?"

"Indeed yes. He and a Major Redstone have been waiting for the better part of the day trying to secure your release."

Eliza pushed herself away from the table. She wanted nothing more at that moment but to lay eyes on the Colonel's kind face. "Please. May I see him now?"

"Better than that. He and the Major can take you home." Jack turned to Hollaway. "Send the gentlemen in."

As soon as Pickering appeared, Eliza raced into his arms.

"My dear girl, we've been worried sick," Pickering murmured. "We had no idea what happened until young Freddy came to Wimpole Street half out of his mind with concern over you. Aubrey and I have done everything but petition the King to get you released."

Eliza blinked back tears as she looked up at him. "Thank you for that, Colonel." She turned to Major Redstone, who stood off to the side. "You too, Major."

"Are you all right, Miss Doolittle?" Redstone asked.

"I am now that both of you are here. Along with my cousin Jack, the Detective Inspector." She smiled. "We haven't seen each other in years."

"What?" Redstone threw Jack a puzzled look.

"It's true. The Inspector is my cousin. Both of us were raised hearing the bells of Bow Church."

Jack grinned. "She means we're East Enders—Cockney to the bone—although I'm proud we learned to disguise our old accents pretty well."

"How remarkable to meet your cousin in such circumstances," Pickering said. Redstone nodded in agreement.

"Lizzie has had a long, exhausting day," Jack said with a fond glance. "Best if she goes home, has a hot meal, and gets some rest."

"You're coming right to Wimpole Street with us, Eliza," Pickering said. "Mrs. Pearce will turn the larder inside out making you the best dinner you've ever had."

She gave Pickering another quick hug. "I'd like that. And you must come, too, Jack. We've had no time to catch up. I've no idea how you became a detective inspector, although I'm plenty glad you did. And I want to hear all about Sybil."

Pickering smiled. "Please join us, Inspector. Professor Higgins should be home very soon, if he's not already there. I know you have a few questions for him."

"A few." Jack looked at Eliza. "Yes, I believe I will join you."

He pointed at something beneath the table. "Here now. How did your hat get there?"

Eliza glanced over at Grint, who kept his gaze riveted to the floor. "Detective Grint dislodged it."

Jack bent down to retrieve her hat, sending a dangerous look Grint's way. After brushing a few specks of dust off her hat, he placed it back on her head. When he did so, his eyes widened. "There's a bruise on your neck and ear, Lizzie. How did this happen?"

Eliza looked over at Grint once more.

"This is unspeakable," Pickering said.

"Indeed it is," Redstone chimed in. "Whoever did that should be flogged!"

Jack whipped off his suit jacket and flung it over the table. "If everyone would please leave the room. Everyone, that is, except for Detective Grint."

Hollaway raced out of the room, followed by Eliza, Pickering, and Redstone. The door slammed shut. In the next instant, she heard something heavy being knocked to the floor. They all stood stock-still, listening to cries, grunts, curses, and repeated knocks and bangs from within the interrogation room.

At last, the door swung open and Jack emerged. He didn't have a scratch on him, but his knuckles were raw and bleeding. From behind him, soft groans could be heard.

"Sorry for the delay," he said, and shrugged into his jacket.

Eliza went over to her cousin and straightened his lapels. "Just like Saturday night at the Blind Beggar in Whitechapel."

"Aye." He kissed her forehead. "Now let's get you back to Wimpole Street."

Pickering clapped him on the shoulder. "Well done, Inspector. Henry will be as pleased as I am that you taught the brute a lesson."

"It's possible the Professor may not be as pleased to see me as you imagine," Jack said under his breath.

In that moment, Eliza knew she had never been the prime suspect in Nepommuck's murder. Henry Higgins was.

SIX

Although Mrs. Pearce had been given little time to cook supper for four, Eliza and her dining companions were duly impressed. The table was set with the best bone china, courtesy of a long-ago gift by Mrs. Higgins, and everything from the nut and celery salad to the boiled capons with cauliflower sauce was prepared to perfection.

So delicious was the meal that for most of it, there had been little conversation, everyone ravenous at the end of such a long, exhausting day. But as the maids brought out the blancmange and Madeira, Eliza thought it was time to put in a good word for the still absent Henry Higgins.

"It's a shame the Professor isn't here." Eliza reached for her dessert spoon. "Blancmange is his favorite. He's as lighthearted as a boy whenever Mrs. Pearce serves it."

"Don't worry." Mrs. Pearce stood near the dining room entrance, where she had overseen the serving of the various courses. "I've put aside an entire bowl for him."

Her cousin Jack cocked his head in the housekeeper's direction. "Does Professor Higgins often miss dinner without notifying his staff?"

"I should say not," Mrs. Pearce said in an affronted tone. "Mr. Higgins insists on punctuality for both his meals and his lessons."

With that, Mrs. Pearce gestured for the two serving maids to leave the dining room. She gave a last look of approval at the table before following suit.

Jack took a spoonful of pudding before speaking. "It seems as if the Professor's behavior tonight is uncharacteristic."

"Not at all, Inspector," Pickering said. "Henry takes to wandering the streets for hours on end for research purposes. He always has an ear out—quite literally—for an interesting dialect or a new turn of phrase. And where Henry is concerned, the study of phonetics trumps everything." He lifted up his own spoon. "Even blancmange."

"The Colonel is right, Jack. The Professor loves to eavesdrop on people. Despite what Mrs. Pearce said, we've known him to miss three meals in one day because he was so caught up listening to a south Putney bus driver." Eliza smiled. "Or a Cockney flower seller."

"Is that how you made his acquaintance, Lizzie?" Jack asked. "Last I heard from my sister, you were selling violets to the toffs."

"Better than selling fruit like I did when I was ten. Flowers smell nicer."

"How did you end up living with these three fine gentlemen at Wimpole Street?"

Redstone looked up from his dessert. "I have only recently arrived in London, Inspector. I regret to say that I had not made the charming young woman's acquaintance until Sunday last, when the Colonel introduced us at Lady Gresham's garden party."

Jack seemed puzzled. "I thought both you and the Colonel lived here with the Professor."

"That is true." Redstone sipped his Madeira. "But only this past fortnight. I've spent the last fifteen years in India."

"The Major and I are colleagues, Detective," Pickering said. "We've spent the better part of two years in Bombay working on Sanskrit translations and trying to revive the language, at least in the academic world. Our research was interrupted, however, when I came to London last year to meet Professor Higgins."

"I expected he would be gone six months at most," Redstone added, "but when he wrote that he was extending his stay indefinitely, I decided to journey to England myself. The Colonel and I have a paper to prepare for an upcoming conference. We'll need to work together closely until then."

Pickering nodded. "And when Henry learned a fellow language scholar was arriving in London, he insisted the Major stay with us."

Jack took out his notebook and scribbled something down. Eliza could sense the growing anxiety in the dining room.

"I don't know what you're writing," she said. "Major Redstone has nothing to do with the murder. He hadn't even met Nepommuck until I introduced them at the garden party."

"I see." Jack wrote a moment more before looking up. "What did you think of the Hungarian gentleman, Major?"

"I thought he was no gentleman," Redstone said.

"Why did you think that?"

"He insulted our Eliza at the party," Pickering said. "It would not take you more than ten minutes in his company to know him for an opportunist and a liar."

"Jack, no one in this room had any reason to kill the Maestro," Eliza said. "But plenty of others did."

Her cousin ignored her. "Major Redstone, while I'm not a language expert like you and the Colonel, it doesn't sound like you were London bred."

"You are correct, sir. My family is from Northumberland. I was born near Corbridge, just east of Hexham."

"From what I've learned so far, several of Nepommuck's students wish to remain anonymous," Jack said. "Perhaps you once had need of Nepommuck's services as a teacher and are reluctant to admit it. You do seem roughly the same age as him. Maybe at some point in the past, you wanted to get rid of your northern speech as much as I wanted to erase my Cockney vowels."

The Major smiled. "If my speech retains the echo of my Northumberland upbringing, I can only say I never found it to be an impediment. Certainly it proved no obstacle to my studies at Sandhurst or Oxford."

Eliza was growing irritated. "Really, Jack, you're acting as if a Northumberland brogue is as dreadful as our East Ender accent. And I consider myself lucky it was the Professor and Colonel Pickering who taught me, not Nepommuck."

"We are back to my original question. How did you end up living in Wimpole Street?"

"Blame us, Detective," Pickering said before she could reply. She sensed that the Colonel was not only trying to protect Higgins, but her as well. "Both Henry and I became intrigued that we could pass her off as a lady within six months' time." He smiled at her from across the table. "Of course to me she has always been a most gracious young lady."

"Hear, hear." Redstone raised his glass to her.

"They're being kind," Eliza said. "When I first laid eyes on the Professor last summer, I was a ragamuffin with dirty hair, bad teeth, and manners to match. The farthest thing from a lady one can imagine. And seeing as how you were raised in the East End, too, you don't have to imagine much."

Jack nodded.

Eliza sat back. "The night I met the Professor, it had been raining for hours, and I hadn't even made my usual half crown selling violets. I was keeping dry beneath St. Paul's, along with all the swells that had just left the opera at Covent Garden. I tried to convince the Colonel to buy a flower when someone mentioned that a man was writing down everything I said. That put the fear of God in me. I thought he was a copper's nark."

"What's a 'copper's nark'?" asked Redstone.

"A police informer," Jack replied.

"As the Colonel can tell you, I didn't take this well. I created a bit of a scene, actually. But the fellow taking these notes—Professor Higgins—got me to calm down by announcing I had been born in Lisson Grove. It seemed like magic that a person could listen to me for a minute or two and know right where I came from. Even to the very street." She took a moment to finish her blancmange. "Still impresses me, it does."

"He impressed me as well," Pickering said. "That was the night that I first met Eliza *and* Henry."

"So you all became fast friends during a summer rainstorm, did you?"

Eliza wasn't fooled by her cousin's casual tone. If phonetics ruled Higgins's actions, she'd bet her three best hats that respect for the law ruled Jack.

"The Colonel and the Professor did," Eliza said. "They have much in common, seeing as how the Colonel is a Sanskrit scholar and the Professor studies language."

"As I told you, I had come all the way from India just to meet him." Pickering reached over to pour himself another glass of Madeira from the crystal decanter. "And Henry swore he had plans to travel to the subcontinent to talk with me. I found our encounter that night most remarkable."

Jack didn't look convinced. "You still haven't answered how you ended up living here, Lizzie. The police report says you were in residence at 27A Wimpole Street from last summer until this past February. Then you apparently moved in with the Professor's mother on the Chelsea Embankment."

"This is sounding far too much like a police interrogation," Redstone said. "And you have assured Miss Doolittle that she is innocent of any crime." While he wore an impassive expression, Eliza heard a note of warning in his voice.

"It's simple, Jack," she said. "The night after I met the Colonel and the Professor, I came here to ask for lessons. Professor Higgins said he could teach me how to speak like a lady. I'd been selling violets in the rain and the fog for seven years, and all it had gotten me was a shabby room I could barely afford in Angel Court next to Meiklejohn's oil shop. Couldn't see myself doing that for the next thirty years. I thought if I could speak properly, I might be able to find work in a real flower shop."

"The Professor taught you for free?" Jack asked.

"Eliza offered to pay for her lessons, but I wouldn't hear of it," the Colonel said. "I paid for them instead, which was only right considering that we didn't have the most charitable reasons for taking her on. For that, I duly apologize."

"Oh, hang the apologies," Eliza said. "This all started as an honest wager between the Professor and the Colonel. They placed a bet that I could speak like a lady at a proper garden party, and later that I could be passed off as a duchess at the Embassy Ball. By the way,

Nepommuck helped win that wager. He had no idea of my background at the time and after meeting me, pronounced that I was indisputably of Hungarian royal blood, just as he was."

"Who knew that Nepommuck was putting on an even greater charade than we were?" Pickering muttered.

"Anyway, there was nothing dishonorable about my relationship with the Colonel or the Professor, Jack. I learned how to behave and speak properly, and Professor Higgins won his bet. Mrs. Pearce acted as a chaperone the entire time. When the Professor and the Colonel went off to Spain to do research, I began working for Nepommuck as his teaching assistant. I am far better off than I was a year ago. I even have a young gentleman who has taken a fancy to me."

"Hardly a fancy," Pickering said. "Mr. Eynsford Hill is besotted with Eliza."

Jack pushed his half-eaten dessert away. "You've both painted a most harmonious picture. Except that Professor Higgins provided the newspapers with damning accusations against Nepommuck. And the day these were published, the Hungarian winds up with a knife in his back." He frowned. "Even more suspicious, Professor Higgins is nowhere to be found."

"But the Professor did not kill the Maestro."

"Just so, Eliza," Pickering said. "Henry is incapable of such a thing."

"I know he's exasperating, sarcastic, and a bit of a bully," she said, "but he's all bluster and noise, like our drunkard of an uncle, Otis Pepper. He could no more stick a knife in a person than I could sound like one of those opera singers at the Garden."

Jack looked at her for a long moment. "I seem to recall that you had quite a nice singing voice as a child, Lizzie."

"I don't know how long you've been a copper, but think back to the toughs and dodgers we grew up with. Don't you think I'd know if the Professor had it in him to go off his chump and kill a man? You're not that many years from being on the streets yourself, Jackie. Believe me. I know if a man can be trusted."

Jack threw his napkin onto the table with obvious disgust. "I joined the Metropolitan Police when I was twenty-two, just a couple years older than you are now, Lizzie. And when I joined, I was fool enough to trust people. I took them at their word and believed in the innocence of too many friends and strangers. That wound up costing a few lives, and nearly my own."

"But you don't know the Professor. He isn't the type to be violent. Despite his bad manners, beneath it all, he's a true gentleman."

Her cousin shook his head. "Did you think I woke up one day and found myself a Detective Inspector at Scotland Yard? I had to learn to speak proper just like you did, only I didn't have two toffs paying for my lessons and taking me to garden parties. I learned by watching and listening to the swells and gents on the streets. And let me tell you, what some of those gentlemen said and did could chill the heart of Jack the Ripper."

"But why are you convinced the Professor is the murderer?" Eliza crossed her arms, still angry. "It could be any of Nepommuck's pupils, or a person from his shady past."

"I'm not saying he is the murderer, but at this moment, he is the most suspicious. Or am I the only one curious about where he's been all day, and now all evening?"

Redstone cleared his throat as an awkward silence followed. "The Detective Inspector has a point. Where is the Professor?"

Eliza and the Colonel looked at each other, both at a loss for words. Her cousin was right. Where was Henry Higgins? He had never been gone this long without sending a message or making at least one phone call.

A terrible thought occurred to Eliza. "What if whoever killed Nepommuck has also done the Professor in?"

"Dear lord, I hadn't thought of that," Pickering said in obvious alarm.

Eliza jumped up when she heard the front door close. "He's home! And it's about blooming time."

But the dining room door swung open to show Mrs. Pearce standing there with a worried expression. "Mr. Eynsford Hill for you, Miss Eliza."

Freddy entered the dining room as if blown in by a windstorm. His curly hair was mussed, his tie askew, and he looked as upset as when she had last seen him at Scotland Yard.

"Freddy, is something wrong?"

He rushed to her side. Freddy knelt down and took her hand. "Eliza, I have come to ask you to marry me."

"Are you joking?"

"This is no joke, Eliza. You must marry me, and you must marry me tonight!"

Eliza had to restrain herself from throwing one of the Professor's bellows at Freddy's head. The last thing she needed after such a trying day was a silly proposal of marriage by a man who seemed as hysterical as his sister. As soon as he blurted out his proposal, Eliza dragged Freddy off to the Professor's laboratory. She hoped to either calm him down or convince him to leave. Preferably the latter.

"Freddy, what in the world were you thinking bursting in on us like that?" Eliza flung herself down in Higgins's favorite wingback chair. Her head pounded, and now she was genuinely worried about Higgins's whereabouts. Good grief, what if he had been murdered?

Freddy once more knelt at her feet and looked up at her with adoration. "My darling girl, I am sorry if I've embarrassed you in front of the others. However, this is too important to our future happiness for me to stand on ceremony. I implore you, my love. I beseech you to marry me tonight. If not, I will perish here and now. I swear I will!"

Eliza rubbed her throbbing temples. "Please stop, Freddy."

"But you don't understand. My mother wants me to break it off with you. Immediately!"

That got her attention. "Whatever for? I thought she liked me."

"She did, until that Maestro character got murdered."

"And she thinks I did it?"

"No, my sweet. But Mother is scandalized that you worked for a man who had the bad taste to be murdered. She has been nearly as frantic as Clara all day."

"That's ridiculous. She's just upset that Clara and you were with me when we discovered the body."

"Oh no, she doesn't care about that. In fact, she was most interested in the details of how we found him. But she declared that for me to continue to associate myself with an employee of a murdered man is completely unacceptable." Freddy once more grabbed her hands, pulling her toward him. "She'll find a way to keep us apart unless we move quickly. That's why we must get married tonight. She'd never allow a divorce to disgrace the family. Once we're married, she will have to accept you as her daughter-in-law."

"Blimey, you're a grown man, not a schoolboy. She can't stop us tonight or in two weeks or a year from now. Not if you don't let her."

Freddy looked positively tearful. "I'm weak, Eliza. It shames me to admit it, but it's true. I've always done what Mother asked, even when it made no sense. You're strong, stronger than my mother. Once we marry, I'll do whatever you say, not her. And we'll be safe."

Eliza sighed. "That's not a flattering reason to marry someone."

"But I love you. I need to be with you even if Mother cuts me out of the trust fund, although I do hope she changes her mind about that. Anyway, that shouldn't matter. Colonel Pickering has promised that he would set you up in your own flower shop. Think how perfect that would be. You and I would work together at the shop all day, and then be together all night. It would be heaven. Please say yes, my darling girl. Please!"

"Freddy, I do care for you. Right now, though, I'm fighting the urge to box you about the ears."

The phone rang out in the hallway and Freddy jumped to his feet. "Damnation, I'm sure that's Mother calling. I told her I was coming to see you. Tell Mrs. Pearce to say I'm not here."

Eliza pushed herself out of the chair. "Remember that not only did I find my employer murdered today, but I was virtually kept prisoner at Scotland Yard for hours. Now I learn that Professor Higgins has gone missing. Freddy, do you realize that he may have been murdered, too?"

Freddy looked stricken. "That cannot be!"

"Do you understand why this is not a good time to be proposing marriage?"

She walked to the door but Freddy threw himself in front of her. "Eliza, if the Professor is dead, my mother will be even more adamant that we cannot marry. She'll think you far too careless for knowing two men murdered in the space of one day!"

"If you say one more thing like that, there will be a third murder today, I swear it."

The door to the laboratory swung open. Jack peeked his head in. "Is everything fine in here, Lizzie?"

"It will be as soon as Freddy leaves."

"And who are you, sir?" Freddy turned to face the older man.

"Detective Inspector Shaw of Scotland Yard," Jack said, fighting back a grin. "We met earlier at the Yard when I released you and your sister."

"Oh, yes, I remember now. Being questioned at Scotland Yard was quite an alarming experience."

"You don't know the half of it," Eliza murmured.

"I just received a call from one of my detectives," Jack said to Eliza. "I thought you'd like to know that Professor Higgins was seen this evening at the Victoria Embankment. A witness spoke with him and clearly identified him."

"Thank heaven he's alive." Eliza felt dizzy with relief.

"Mother will be so pleased," Freddy added.

"Go home, Freddy."

He grabbed her by the shoulders. "But my love, I have no home but with you. Please run away with me tonight before——"

From the hallway, a familiar voice cried out, "By Jupiter, who left their umbrella right in front of the door?"

"The Professor!" Eliza pushed Freddy aside and raced into the hallway. Jack followed close behind.

Henry Higgins stood in the foyer, shrugging off his overcoat. He looked as exasperated and arrogant as ever. Eliza didn't know whether she wanted to smack him on the nose or embrace him. Instead she crossed her arms and glared at him.

"Where in bloody hell have you been?" she asked.

Higgins gave a hoot of laughter. "So much for the celebrated duchess of the Embassy Ball. You sound just like the rude little turnip I found at Covent Garden."

"You won't get around me with insults tonight. Where were you, Henry?"

He seemed taken aback by her calling him by his Christian name. She'd done so only once before. Higgins straightened his suit jacket before answering. "I was walking about in the city."

"All day and most of the evening?" she asked. "What in the world were you doing?"

"Yes, what were you doing, Professor Higgins?" Jack came to stand beside her.

Higgins narrowed his eyes at the Inspector. "At the risk of appearing as ill-mannered as you and Miss Doolittle, I must decline to answer. I would also like both of you to leave my house. But before you depart, sir, tell me who in the hell you are?"

Freddy piped up from the doorway of the laboratory. "He's a detective inspector from Scotland Yard."

Eliza could see Higgins did not expect that. "And why is an inspector from the Yard skulking about my house?" he asked. "Without invitation, I might add."

"I invited him."

"You invited him into my house? You insolent baggage."

"Oh, shut up. Don't you have any idea what has happened today?"

Before she could continue, Freddy came up beside her and put his arm about her waist. "Professor, I am afraid that I have bad news," Freddy said solemnly. "Eliza's employer was found murdered."

"Yes, I heard." Higgins grew serious. "The newsboys have been shouting it from every street corner."

"What did you think when you heard the news, Professor?" Jack asked.

He narrowed his eyes. "I thought the world was well rid of one more scoundrel."

Eliza shook her head, trying to warn him to keep quiet.

"It appears there was no love lost between you and Emil Nepommuck," Jack said.

"If you are even moderately capable in your job as detective, then you already know that I was the one who provided the information exposing Nepommuck to the newspapers. Or did you expect me to pretend I had the slightest regard for that worthless blighter?" Higgins brushed past all three of them.

"Professor, I must ask you a few questions," Jack said.

Higgins ignored him. "Mrs. Pearce! Where the devil is that woman? I swear, a caravan of gypsies could be traipsing through the front door and she'd be none the wiser. And seeing as how she has allowed the three of you into my house, I must say the gypsies would be preferable."

"We should let him eat something before you question him about the murder," she said to her cousin in a stage whisper. "He's rather upset."

Higgins spun around. "Of course I am upset, you treacherous guttersnipe! First you run away without a 'by your leave' after all Pick and I have done for you. Then you take up with this fool here." He gestured at Freddy. "And you top it off by going to work for a charlatan who ended up stabbing me in the back!"

Eliza winced. Even Henry looked as if he wished he could take back that last sentence.

"Interesting choice of words, Professor." Jack scribbled in his notebook.

"Damn you all to hell, you know what I meant."

"Sir, you're home." Mrs. Pearce hurried into the hallway, slightly out of breath.

"Yes, and I would like to have my dinner if you don't mind. But first see that this sorry trio is sent on their way."

"Henry, my old chap. We thought we heard your voice." Pickering emerged from the dining room, followed by Redstone. "Extremely glad to have you home again."

Higgins turned around to face Eliza. "Is my mother here as well? Perhaps your father is upstairs in the bath and will be joining us, too. It will seem a fitting end to this circus of a day."

"Believe me, I haven't enjoyed it any more than you have," she said with a sigh.

"I rather think you have eaten dinner," he shot back, "which is more than I can say."

"I am not concerned about whether or not you have your dinner," Jack said. "A man has been murdered, and it is my job to track down whoever did it. That means I must ask you a number of questions. You must answer them." He paused. "If you refuse, your next meal will be served in prison."

Both Pickering and Mrs. Pearce gasped, while Higgins grew a shade paler.

"You've no reason to haul him off to prison," Eliza protested. "We all know he didn't like Nepommuck, but he wasn't the only one. I didn't even like the Maestro myself."

Jack sighed. "When I received that phone call from one of my detectives a short while ago, he didn't simply inform me that Henry Higgins had been spotted at the Victoria Embankment. The person who identified him was Corporal Theodore Trent, a veteran of the Boer War. And he swears he prevented the Professor from throwing himself into the river."

"What?" Eliza and Pickering said together.

Higgins did not respond as Eliza expected. Instead he threw back his head and laughed. "Bloody idiots. You're all bloody idiots." He laughed so hard, tears began to roll down his face.

"Idiots, are we?" Jack said sternly. "This wounded veteran claims that when he stopped you from throwing yourself into the Thames, you went on and on about how guilty you were feeling today."

Still laughing, Higgins waved Jack toward the door. "If you leave while I am in such a good mood, Inspector, I won't be forced to embarrass you in front of everyone."

"Have a care, sir," Jack said in a voice that any East Ender would know meant trouble. "My patience has limits."

Eliza put her hand on Jack's shoulder. "Why don't we go back into the dining room and let the Professor have dinner? It will give all of us a chance to calm down. And you can ask your questions while he's eating. I am sure everything can be straightened out. Please, Jack. Do this one thing for me. For your little Lizzie."

"What the devil is this?" Higgins wiped the tears of laughter from his cheeks. "When did you have the time to take up with a Scotland Yard detective?"

"Inspector Shaw is my cousin," Eliza said.

Her reply set off another wave of laughter. "What next?" Henry said. "Are you going to tell us that you're the sister of the Russian Czarina?"

Eliza turned to Jack. "Couldn't your questions wait until everyone's had a good night's sleep?"

He shook his head. "Murder has a way of upsetting people's dinner plans and their sleep." Jack turned to Higgins with a grim expression. "You leave me no choice, Professor Higgins. I am afraid that I must place you under arrest for the murder of Emil Nepommuck."

Eliza fell back a step, stunned. Higgins stopped laughing. For once in his life, the Professor was speechless.

She wished the same were true for Freddy. "One language teacher dead, the other arrested," he blurted out in dismay. "Damnation, Eliza. Mother will never let us marry now!"

SEVEN

After a lifetime spent avoiding the coppers' attention, Eliza was not happy to find herself once again at Scotland Yard. She could scarcely believe both she and the Professor had been viewed as murder suspects in the past twenty-four hours. Life was brutish in the East End, but it seemed far simpler.

"If you don't stop pacing, Eliza, you will rub the wax off the floorboards of this office." Henry's mother sat on a chair facing the room's only desk. "Inspector Shaw already appears to have a grievance against us. We don't need to add to it by marring his lovely floor."

Eliza collapsed in a heap onto the chair beside her. The older woman sat as calm and motionless as a statue. Eliza's insides boiled, however. Bad enough that Jack dragged Henry off to Scotland Yard last night, but the Professor's cavalier attitude only worsened the situation. Did the man take nothing seriously aside from the study of phonetics?

She wanted to hit him over the head for not explaining what he was doing at the Victoria Embankment. Or why that Boer War veteran thought Higgins was about to throw himself into the river. She could hardly blame Jack for arresting him. For while she knew the

Professor could never have killed Nepommuck, to an outside ob-
server Higgins had a strong motive and a flimsy alibi.

"I don't understand how you can remain so calm," Eliza said in a
hushed voice, although there was no one to overhear. The two
women sat alone in the room. Higgins had been taken for questioning elsewhere in the Yard, and Jack had let them stay in his office all
morning.

Mrs. Higgins sighed. "My dear, you have only known my son for
a matter of months. Let me assure you that Henry can be as exasperating as the Mad Hatter. I suspect that the police will be eager to
release him, if only to put a halt to his incessant talking."

The office door swung open. Colonel Pickering and Major Redstone stalked in, both looking as agitated as Eliza felt. "Have you
heard anything?" she asked.

Pickering shook his head. "Only what the sergeant out front has
been saying since we arrived. After being kept in a holding cell last
night, Henry was brought to the interrogation room about five hours
ago. He has been there ever since."

"I hope Jack hasn't let Grint and Hollaway question him." Eliza
shuddered at the memory of how viciously both detectives treated
her yesterday during her interrogation.

"It appears that Inspector Shaw is handling the situation himself."
Pickering leaned against the cherry wood desk, its surface covered
with bulging stacks of files, all securely bound. "And I have been doing what I can. I contacted the finest barrister in London, in case
this absurd mess is actually brought to trial."

"Why can't the Professor explain exactly where he was yesterday during the time of the murder?" Eliza asked. "Someone must
have seen him during the morning. This is London, after all, not the
moors."

"If Henry does not explain it adequately to the police, he had best explain it to me," Mrs. Higgins said in a threatening tone.

What a shame the police didn't allow Henry's mother into that interrogation room, Eliza thought. She'd wring answers out of him.

Eliza hoped to persuade Jack that he ought to investigate the people with real motives for wanting the Hungarian dead. She had already told Jack that the Maestro boasted at the Embassy Ball about how he made his clients pay—and for more than lessons. Higgins had passed her off as a duchess just by changing her speech. Nepommuck could also have trained his students to take on another identity. Why weren't the police questioning them, rather than Professor Higgins? Especially if their newfound positions in society depended on Nepommuck keeping their secrets.

She got to her feet and paced once more, only now she had to weave in and around Major Redstone and Colonel Pickering.

Redstone touched her elbow. "Are you all right, Miss Doolittle? You seem a thousand miles away."

She glanced up at him. "I wish I knew exactly where the Professor was yesterday."

"Oh, I know what he was doing," Pickering said. "He was walking the streets with not a care in his head. One day, he'll wander all the way to Dover. When he's listening to dialects, Henry is oblivious to everything else. He once found himself at a sheep shearing in Chesham. Had no idea how he'd gotten there."

Their exchange was interrupted when Jack Shaw hurried into the office. Her cousin's dark hair looked more unkempt than last night, and his eyes seemed bleary from lack of sleep. Eliza also noticed that he wore the same suit and tie, so he hadn't been home.

Proof to her that Jack had been working on the case all night, even while Higgins was allowed to sleep in his cell. Her spirits lifted when he shot her a quick smile.

"What can you tell us about the Professor?" she asked.

He sat behind his desk with a sigh, clearly exhausted. "Still trying to get clear answers from him."

"You do have a witness, though."

"Corporal Ted Trent? That's not good enough and you know it. In fact, it makes his innocence harder to prove."

"Why is that?" Pickering asked.

"Higgins could not have been looking out over the Thames for the better part of a day. If that was true, why can't we find anyone to corroborate that? Trent was only there a matter of five minutes or so himself. And the Professor's comment about feeling guilty is especially damning." Jack looked at Mrs. Higgins. "I am sorry, ma'am. I'm doing all I can."

She nodded. "I appreciate that, Inspector."

"Let me talk to him," Eliza said. "Maybe I can pinpoint where he walked."

"I saw how well he reacted to your questions last night, Lizzie." Her cousin rubbed his eyes. "I'm giving him a little time to stew about things. Plus he's insisting on his late morning tea and biscuit. After he's done, I'll try again to get some helpful answers."

Eliza caught a flash of movement out of the corner of her eye. She turned toward the open door. Blimey, Mary Finch was here, with her husband trailing behind her.

A moment later Mary entered the room in a fury. She looked the very picture of an avenging widow, completely garbed in black silk save for kid gloves the color of butter. Eliza shook her head. Leave it to Mary to be unable to resist a spot of bright yellow even when in mourning.

Mrs. ~~Higgins~~ Finch raised one of those gloved hands accusingly at Jack, knocking her feathered hat askew. She straightened it without a word.

"Where are you keeping that cold-blooded killer? I want to see him so I can spit in his face."

Jack got to his feet, his expression beyond weary. "May I ask who you are?"

"Mrs. Cornelius Finch."

"Mary was one of the Maestro's students," Eliza said. She flashed him a meaningful look. "And a very close friend."

Cornelius Finch stood behind Mary. "My wife and I were students of Emil Nepommuck and Miss Doolittle."

"Yes, and we've come here to make certain that monster is not set free. I knew Professor Higgins was a brute, but to think he actually stabbed the poor Maestro!" Mary began to weep. "That noble, goodhearted soul who never harmed anyone."

Cornelius handed her his handkerchief. "You're the Detective Inspector assigned to investigate Maestro Nepommuck's murder, am I right?"

"That's correct."

"We heard you arrested the killer, sir."

"And who might that be?" Jack asked.

"Professor Higgins, of course," Cornelius said. "My wife was so upset when she heard of Nepommuck's death that she insisted on confronting Higgins herself. But when we arrived at his home this morning, no one was there save the servants. They told us he'd been arrested for the murder."

"Mary, I can assure you the Professor did not kill anyone,"

Eliza said. "The two men only had a disagreement the day of your lesson."

"Disagreement? More like a battle royal, Miss Doolittle." Mary blew her nose and then flung the handkerchief at her husband. "You insufferable brat. You're the cause of this whole thing."

"What?" Pickering, Redstone, and Eliza all said at the same time.

"The trouble began when Miss Doolittle left that monster Higgins and went to work for the Maestro. The Professor was so enraged about what she'd done that he interrupted our lesson and scared the life out of me. Thank heavens the Maestro came to my rescue, only to have Higgins vilify the poor man. You were there, Miss Doolittle. Tell the Inspector what he said."

"Everyone knows the Professor has a temper, but he had good reason to be upset."

"He had no reason to act like a barbarian! I assure you, Inspector, that Professor Higgins sorely abused poor Emil. Do you know that after he accused the Maestro of stealing Miss Doolittle away, he threatened to throttle him? And he actually wondered why someone hadn't plunged a dagger in his back." Mary fought back further tears. "Then the Professor claimed that he might stab him. How much proof do you need, Inspector?"

Eliza bit her lip. She had hoped no one would remember those damning words said by Higgins during the argument with Nepommuck.

Jack nodded. "I am aware of what the Professor said that day, Mrs. Finch. I've been questioning him for hours. You haven't told me anything new."

She seemed taken aback. "Then you know he had the best reason to murder the Maestro. He's guilty."

"But was he the *only* one who had a reason to want the man dead?

I suspect not, Mrs. Finch. And until that question is answered to the law's satisfaction—and mine—I would be very cautious about proclaiming anyone's guilt."

Colonel Pickering nodded in agreement. "Well said, Inspector."

"But you did arrest him." Cornelius Finch appeared confused.

"I'm sorry to disappoint you, but at present we're only holding Professor Higgins for questioning. We do not have enough evidence to bring charges. He will be released later today."

Eliza let out a huge sigh of relief while Mrs. Higgins whispered, "Thank heaven."

Mary Finch stamped her foot. "He killed the Maestro!"

"Young woman, you really must desist," Pickering said.

Jack put up his hand to stop anyone else from joining in. "Did you witness the actual crime, Mrs. Finch?"

"Of course not."

Eliza wanted to slap the woman silly. "Then you have no reason to claim he's a murderer. He didn't murder the Maestro's reputation, either, if what was printed in the newspaper is true."

"We're still investigating that as well." Jack straightened his suit coat. "If even half of that *Daily Mail* article is accurate, then Emil Nepommuck had more than enough enemies."

"I've been saying that all along," Eliza said. The look Mary Finch shot her was so filled with hate, she took a step back.

"Perhaps you should look for another motive in all this, Inspector," Mary said. "I would not be surprised to learn that Professor Higgins was in love with Miss Doolittle and killed the Maestro in a fit of jealous rage."

Pickering gave a rude snort, while Mrs. Higgins rolled her eyes in disbelief. Even Jack fought back a grin.

Eliza took a deep breath. "You know, Mary, I'd think twice about throwing out that bit about killing in a jealous rage. The only man who had reason for such a thing is your own husband."

"How dare you!" Mary cried, but before she could go on, Cornelius laid a warning hand on her shoulder.

"I think we should go." He looked even unhappier than his wife.

Mary glared at them. "I see how it is. There will be no justice done, not with the police so cozy with Higgins's family and friends. I intend to stop at the *Daily Mail* office. Perhaps the newspapers will have a different view of his guilt or innocence. Henry Higgins deserves to be strung up without even the luxury of a trial."

Mrs. Higgins turned to face the younger woman. "Have a care, Mrs. Finch. If you utter one more word impugning my son's innocence, I will see to it that my solicitors serve you and your husband with papers accusing you of libel."

"Don't threaten me—"

"Hold your tongue, Mary." Cornelius squeezed her shoulder once more. This time, Eliza saw her wince from pain.

Mrs. Higgins stared the Finches down for a fearsome moment, before turning her attention to Jack. "Is it possible for me to see my son now, Inspector?"

"No reason why you shouldn't, ma'am." He scribbled something on his notepad. "Give this to the sergeant sitting at the hall desk. He'll take you to him."

Mrs. Higgins nodded her thanks and left the office without a glance at either of the Finches.

Mary gave an angry tug to her yellow kid gloves. "Take me out of here, Cornelius."

As the pair turned to go, Jack cleared his throat. "I am afraid you will both have to delay your departure."

The Finches turned back in obvious consternation.

Jack walked over to the open door. He gestured toward a police constable near the front desk. "Thomas, please escort the Finches to Interrogation Room 17."

"What's this all about, Inspector?" Cornelius Finch asked in alarm.

"I am detaining you and your wife for questioning in the murder of Emil Nepommuck."

"You cannot be serious!" Mary clutched at her husband.

"Mrs. Finch, I am serious about finding the murderer. I can't do that without questioning everyone who had a professional or personal relationship with the murder victim. That includes you and your husband." He nodded toward Thomas, who entered the room.

"Come with me, please." The policeman led a shocked Mary Finch and her unhappy husband away.

"I didn't expect you to do that." Eliza walked over to give her cousin a kiss on the cheek. "But I'm glad you did."

"Lizzie, I acted as a detective inspector, not your cousin. The murder happened only yesterday and I have far too many people on my list of suspects." He yawned. "And far too little sleep. Just now I also have an appointment." Jack stopped when he caught sight of someone in the corridor. "Excuse me, but I believe the lady has arrived."

"Lady?" Eliza peeked out into the bustling hall.

Jack hurried to greet a fashionably dressed older woman with a regal profile and snow-white hair. Her face was partially hidden by a feathered gray hat, but Eliza would have recognized Lady Gresham anywhere. Even in a police station, the woman seemed the height of fashion in a pale gray walking suit. A silver lavaliere necklace boasting a gemstone as large as a strawberry hung from her neck.

"The Dowager Marchioness is here," she announced to the others. "Along with her butler, Harrison. Crikey, is he the chauffeur as well?"

Pickering walked over to the door. "Don't know how many jobs that fellow does for Verena. But she always did have an eye for a handsome face. I must say, I quite forgot she was engaged to that blighter Nepommuck. I fear things are about to get even more difficult."

Eliza and Redstone followed Pickering as he went to greet Lady Gresham. They quickly offered brief—and rather unconvincing—condolences to her.

Her butler stood silent behind Lady Gresham, but this time he was dressed in a fancy chauffeur's jacket with epaulettes. Eliza thought this made him look even more debonair.

She was distracted from the man's good looks, however, when Mary Finch scurried away from her police escort. Before she had a chance to warn the others of Mary's approach, the frantic woman threw herself in their midst.

"Your Ladyship, you ought to know the Detective Inspector will be releasing Professor Higgins any minute."

The older woman gave Mary a long, cool stare. "Of course he is. The man should never have been brought here in the first place."

"You can't mean that. Henry Higgins wanted the Maestro dead. I was present when he threatened to strangle him."

"My fiancé was stabbed, was he not? I doubt a man of Professor Higgins's background would stoop to such a common method of murder. It seems the modus operandi of a dockworker, not a professor of elocution." Lady Gresham turned her attention to Jack. "Of course, many of Emil's pupils came from common backgrounds. No doubt one of them was ill bred enough to kill him."

"How can you say that? Professor Higgins is clearly the murderer!"

"Stop being tiresome, Mrs. Finch. If it wasn't a pupil, then it likely was a jealous husband."

Mary Finch went pale.

"Emil confessed that he feared being called out by many husbands over his dalliances with their foolish wives," Lady Gresham continued. "Of course, he begged my forgiveness for his mistakes. But I cared not a whit about his past indiscretions. And he cared about them even less than I did."

Mary flinched. "Then you didn't know him as I did."

"Stop talking to them, Mary!" Cornelius Finch shouted from the other end of the corridor, where Thomas the policeman had a firm grip on his arm. The poor fellow was flushed to the point of apoplexy.

"It is possible I didn't know my fiancé at all, especially if he was guilty of the things that were claimed in the newspaper."

"Lies, all of it!" Spittle formed at the corners of Mary's mouth. "I will never believe such lies. The Maestro isn't even cold in his grave, and he's being treated like a criminal. Meanwhile the real criminal will be set free. And you don't seem at all upset. You're not even in mourning dress!" Sobs racked her body. "Oh Emil, my poor darling!"

Jack snapped his fingers, and two policemen came to take Mary away.

"Please accept my apologies, Your Ladyship." Jack ushered them all into his office.

Lady Gresham stood near the doorway, refusing Jack's offer of a seat. "That woman is delusional. She has badgered Emil since she came to him for instruction. Her attentions became such a nuisance, he turned her over to Miss Doolittle for lessons."

Eliza nodded. "I've been teaching her for weeks, although Mr. Finch continued his own lessons with the Maestro."

"She threw herself at my Emil like a common strumpet. Calling at all hours, even though he refused to see her. Her behavior was positively frightful at the garden party. Miss Doolittle can attest to that."

Jack turned to Eliza. "Mrs. Finch became quite upset when Her Ladyship and the Maestro announced their engagement," she said. "Hysterical, in fact."

Lady Gresham gestured to her manservant. "Harrison had to literally carry her off the grounds. If you seek a murderer and a motive, look no further than Mr. Finch."

Eliza restrained herself from adding, Hear, hear.

"It seems I have my work cut out for me," Jack said. "Along with questioning his students, I'll have to track down all those ladies Nepommuck dallied with, as well as their husbands. That could be a lengthy list."

Lady Gresham gripped her parasol as if she wanted to batter someone about the head. "Inspector, while I want the murderer apprehended, I would prefer that my name not be associated with this case. The matter has become most embarrassing. In fact, I have already spoken to the Commissioner and he has agreed to expedite the investigation. You shan't need more than a week at most."

Jack frowned. "Talking to all these suspects will take far longer than a week, Your Ladyship, even if I put every detective in the department on it. If only we had at least one solid clue to follow."

Eliza snapped her fingers. "We do have a clue, Jack. I told you about it yesterday."

"What are you talking about, Miss Doolittle?" Lady Gresham turned the full force of her hawklike gaze on her. "What clue?"

"On the day the Professor came to Belgrave Square to confront Nepommuck, I arrived early that morning for class. I found all the lights turned off in the hallway, and someone lurking just outside the Maestro's door. Whoever it was knocked me down trying to leave."

"Good lord, Eliza." Pickering sounded as alarmed as if it had happened that morning. "You should have told us this immediately."

"Miss Doolittle believes that was how the killer got one of her tuning forks, which later turned up on the dead body." Jack shrugged. "The tuning fork is evidence, not a clue."

"That's not what I'm referring to. When I picked up the rest of my tuning forks, I found an engraved gold button on the carpeting. I believe it may belong to the murderer."

"But my dear, it most likely belonged to one of the other students who came to the apartment for their lessons," Pickering said.

"The housekeeping staff arrive just after dawn every morning. You could eat off the carpet after they finish their cleaning. If a button had been left on the floor, they would have swept it up."

"You may be right, Lizzie," Jack said. "Do you still have the button?"

"It's in my bedroom. I'll bring it back here later today."

He rapped his knuckles on his desk. "Right then, we have a possible physical clue, and a veritable throng of elocution pupils and mistresses to hunt down. Best get started."

Lady Gresham gave Jack an imperious look. "Whatever you must do, Inspector, it had best be done quickly. I will not tolerate any delay longer than a week in bringing this unpleasant matter to a close. And if Professor Higgins is still the most likely suspect, I regret the Commissioner will have little choice but to arrest him."

Jack crossed his arms. "I have always tried to solve a case as quickly as possible. But I shall not let a desire for haste overtake the pursuit of justice. Not even for the Commissioner." He gave her a hard look. "Or his friends."

She bristled at that. "Good day, Inspector. I can find my own way out. Colonel Pickering." After giving a brief nod at Eliza and Redstone, the Marchioness swept out of the room. The butler followed in her wake.

"I daresay she will not be pleased if this investigation drags on longer than a week," Redstone said.

"Quite right," Pickering said. "Verena wants things done quickly. If she had her way, the Almighty would have finished creating the world on the fifth day."

Jack shook his head. "She has already spoken with Commissioner Dunningsworth. That means he'll be running scared. Not only does Lady Gresham have powerful friends in the government, but Dunningsworth owes his appointment to her late husband. If she wants the murder of her fiancé solved in a week, there will be the devil to pay if it isn't done by then."

"So that's it? You have no say?" Eliza was alarmed by Jack's unhappy expression.

"I'm afraid so. We have one week to come up with a better suspect than the Professor."

"And if we can't?" Pickering asked.

"The Commissioner will insist we arrest the Professor on a formal charge of murder." He looked at Eliza. "I'm sorry."

"Jack, can you please spring the Professor?" Eliza gently touched his arm. "If we only have a week, I should start working with him as soon as possible to verify his alibi."

"Agreed, Lizzie. I'll get him released now. Don't see the point in another round of questioning with him anyway. I honestly think he enjoys the interrogation."

"Henry does love a challenge," Pickering said with a sigh.

"He should enjoy the next week then," Jack said as he left the office.

Her cousin was right. It would be a challenge. As soon as the Professor joined her, Eliza would drag him off immediately to trace his footsteps. Some grocer, newsboy, or street sweeper must have seen him wandering about the city yesterday.

All they needed was a little bit of luck.

EIGHT

Black as the eyes of a dead witch's cat.'" Higgins whipped out his notebook. "Never heard anyone use that phrase. Where do you suppose the fellow hails from? North Devon? Barnstable perhaps?"

"I have no idea," Eliza said with an exasperated sigh. The afternoon had been an exercise in frustration. She was amazed at how indifferent Higgins seemed at being the prime suspect in a murder case. Not even a night in jail had unnerved him.

"We should engage him in conversation." Higgins glanced back at the delivery wagon. "Eight words aren't enough to ascertain his exact birthplace. Although if I chase after every deliveryman, people will think me mad."

"And so you are." She took a firm grip on his sleeve and pulled him away from the men loading crates of beer in front of Cullen's Brewery. "We don't have time for any more of your eavesdropping. Now put that notebook away."

"Infernal female," he grumbled. "I don't know how you presume to teach phonetics when you have such little regard for its proper study."

"Professor, keep in mind why we've been wandering the streets for hours. We must find someone—anyone!—who remembers seeing you yesterday during the time of Nepommuck's death. Writing down a new turn of phrase won't help us solve anything. And it won't clear your name."

They turned the corner and almost bumped into a newsboy shouting, "Killer of royal 'Ungarian on the loose! Scotland Yard searching for who done 'im in!"

Higgins and Eliza hurried past.

"We're the detectives, are we?" Higgins finally tucked his notebook back into his suit pocket. "I know that Detective Inspector chap is your cousin, but you must admit that England has come to a sorry state when an innocent man has to play policeman. If I do end up going to trial, I'll probably have to serve as my own barrister as well."

"Then let's make certain you do not go to trial."

"We've been remarkably ineffective so far." He shook his head. "There must be a better way."

He was right. As soon as they left the Yard, Eliza forced Higgins to write down each street and neighborhood he could recall walking through yesterday. And for the better part of the day, they had walked or taken the tube to what felt like every nook and cranny of central London: St. John's Wood, Lambeth, Shoreditch, Maida Vale, St. George's Fields, and much more. Yet for all that, they had not come across a single soul who remembered seeing Higgins.

Even worse, Eliza couldn't shake the feeling they were being followed. She hadn't mentioned this to Higgins; he'd only say she was turning into a damnable policeman, suspecting every tradesman and milliner's assistant of some criminal deed. But she'd been raised on the streets of the dodgiest neighborhood in the city. Her instincts warned her that at least one person had been on their trail all day. She just couldn't figure out who it might be. Whenever she turned around, she saw only a mass of people with indifferent faces bustling along the pavement. Then again, maybe Jack had sent one of his detectives to keep an eye on her. If so, it was a sweet but irritating gesture.

A double-decker bus rumbled past them. When the exhaust cleared, Eliza spied the cupola of Covent Garden's redbrick market building. Dozens of barrows and stalls crowded the open-air square in front if it. She hadn't been back here since that fateful night when she first met Higgins and the Colonel. An odd feeling washed over her, as if she were returning home after an exciting but uncertain adventure.

Eliza tugged at her silk gloves, fighting back a sudden attack of nerves. Although the theater crowd wouldn't arrive for hours, she saw several flower girls setting off for their accustomed places at nearby St. Paul's Church and the playhouses of the West End. To think that only last summer, she had done the same thing. It seemed a lifetime ago.

Higgins followed her gaze. "So we are returning to the scene of our mutual crime."

"That's one way to describe it."

She told herself she was being a ninny. A stroll among the stalls of Covent Garden Market would not transform her back into a poor Cockney flower seller. But the voices she heard around her did bring back memories, both good and bad. Last year, she had fantasized about returning to Covent Garden dressed in her fanciest clothes. Many of the flower sellers had made fun of her when she worked here, she being one of the youngest of the group. What better way to get back at them than parading about in her linen gown and French heels while a hired taxi waited for her at the curb. But Eliza could never quite work up the nerve to come back here.

"Why did you bring us to Covent Garden? I was nowhere near the place yesterday," Higgins said.

"I have my reasons."

"None of which you seem willing to tell me. Eliza, we've already wasted enough time. Stopping at my mother's apartment for the button you squirreled away took the better part of an hour."

Eliza marched forward. "Funny how you didn't complain while eating that plate of bangers and mash Daisy served you."

"I was being polite."

"That would have been a first."

"I beg your pardon?"

"Just follow me, Professor."

The familiar aroma of oranges and onions assaulted her senses the moment they entered the market. Eliza threaded her way expertly through browsing shoppers and crates filled with fruit and vegetables. Despite the late afternoon hour—a typically slow time—most stalls still had produce on display. With the market half empty, few vendors shouted out their wares, but Eliza grinned to hear a distant fishmonger sing out, "Eels! Eels fresh from the river! All large and alive-o!"

One coster looked up from his barrow. "Parsley, miss? Penny a bunch. None greener in London."

She shook her head. The picked-over specimens weren't the best that arrived at dawn each morning from the countryside and coast, but they were still decent enough to attract buyers. Those vendors without any customers clustered in small groups near their stalls, chatting and smoking. Eliza recognized many of them. But each time she spoke a greeting to a woman in her market apron or a fellow unloading a crate of potatoes, they responded with a puzzled stare.

Why should they recognize her? Gone were her muddy boots, faded skirt, and moth-eaten coat. Now she wore a pink gown made of a soft material the dressmaker called batiste; its nautical style was said to be all the latest rage. And instead of a soot-covered straw hat she'd fished out of a dustbin, Eliza wore a new boater on her perfectly coiffed hair. The pink silk ribbon decorating her hat cost more than a week's wage of any flower seller here.

Small wonder no one realized that she was Eliza Doolittle. She was glad now that she had never come here last year to swan about. It didn't seem right. Or kind.

A wave of new scents washed over her: roses, sweet freesia, primrose, lavender, phlox, and dozens more. Eliza didn't have to look up to know they'd reached the arcade of the flower market. Baskets and pails filled with exotic lilies and orchids from as far away as Africa and Turkey sat on lavish display beneath the overhead skylight. She stopped a moment to take it all in. The Covent Garden flower market was as glorious as ever, and Eliza's heart soared to see its fragrant beauty once more spilling about her.

"Here's where I came every day to buy my flowers." Eliza bent down to sniff a basket heaped with sweet-smelling primroses. "If I had a bit more stock money than usual, I could sometimes buy two dozen bunches. Of course, I also had to buy paper and twine to tie them up with. By then, there was no money left at all until the ladies and gents in the West End bought the flowers from me." She sighed. "And heaven help a flower girl on the nights that it rained."

Higgins was silent, which so startled Eliza that she turned to him. He was looking at her with a thoughtful expression. "Eliza, we don't have to be here," he said at last. "I told you that I didn't visit Covent Garden yesterday, and this place probably brings up memories that are far from pleasant for you."

"On the contrary, I couldn't wait to come here when I was a flower girl. Take a deep breath. It smells more delightful than a hundred French perfumes. A far cry indeed from what my lodging house smelled like." She smiled. "And the flowers are so beautiful. I used to pretend it was my own private garden."

As she moved among the tulip bouquets and pails of jonquils, she smiled each time her skirt brushed a flower and sent up a wave of delicious scent. Taking another deep breath, she suddenly smelled tea roses from Spain. A moment later, she spotted the apricot yellow blooms arranged in metal buckets at Old Lucy's stall.

Eliza hurried over to the woman, who looked up from the biscuit she gnawed. "Lucy, I see you're still selling Valencia tea roses. Isn't it a few weeks past their best bloom time?"

The old woman squinted. "And who might you be, miss?"

"Lizzie Doolittle."

"Garn, you ain't Lizzie." She spat off to the side. "Don't know what you're about, miss. Did someone tell you to play a joke on Old Lucy? 'Cause I ain't never 'eard of a fancy lady trying to pass 'erself off as a poor girl what just up and disappeared."

"I didn't disappear," Eliza said, smiling. "I moved to another part of London is all. Got some new clothes and learned to speak proper, but I'm still Lizzie. I sold violets next to Carrie Vetch, the woman who makes bracelets of dried lavender."

"Now don't you be talking about Carrie. That ain't no subject for tricks or jokes. The poor woman's not cold in her grave yet."

"Oh no. Carrie's dead?"

"This past spring, of croup." Lucy now regarded her with not only suspicion but anger. "So don't be coming 'ere pretending you is one of us. Either buy one of me flowers or take yerself off. 'Cause I don't need no cheeky young miss in pretty little shoes and Mayfair clothes making fun of us 'ardworking folk."

Higgins took her arm. "Let's go, Eliza."

"I didn't mean to upset you, Lucy. Truly I didn't." Eliza fished a wad of bills from her purse. Before the old woman could reply, she pressed the money into her gnarled hand. "And I'm sorry to hear about Carrie."

Eliza hurried off. Even with his long stride, Higgins had to walk briskly to catch up with her.

"Have we come here to give out alms," he said, "or are you looking for old drinking companions to reminisce with?"

"I came here to help you," Eliza said. "Not that you deserve it, you insensitive brute."

She stopped in her tracks. Her friend Nan Barton sat wrapping bunches of violets at the exact spot that Eliza had used each day before taking up her nightly post at St. Paul's. In fact, the three baskets brimming with violets and daffodils that lay at her feet were Eliza's own. She'd given all three to Nan when she made her decision to move to Wimpole Street and begin her lessons.

"Nan," she said softly.

The young woman looked up, puzzled. "Yes, miss?"

When Nan didn't recognize her, Eliza stamped her foot. "It's me, you silly nanny goat! Lizzie Doolittle. All cleaned up and looking like a toff's fancy woman."

Nan's brown eyes widened and she dropped the bunch of violets she was tying together with twine. "Lizzie, is that really you? I 'eard you learned to talk proper and all, but kick my arse if you ain't the spitting image of a well-off snob. Blimey, you even look pretty, you skinny old natters."

Eliza knelt down beside her. The two women embraced for much longer than either intended. Behind them, Eliza heard Higgins clear his throat. She finally pushed herself away.

"How are you, old girl?"

"Not doing as blooming good as you." Nan grinned, displaying a mouth missing some teeth. Even though she was but five and twenty, poverty—and a drunken common-law husband—had taken a toll on Nan's looks and teeth.

"Is Silas treating you right?" Eliza asked. She hoped Nan would admit the lout had either died or been hauled off to jail.

She gingerly touched Eliza's sleeve, as if amazed by its color and silkiness. "Silas is a bleeding bastard, same as ever. But if he ain't in his cups, he's no worse than any other man. 'Course, he ain't giving me lovely pink dresses like your gent 'ere." Nan nodded toward Higgins, who towered over them both.

Eliza laughed. "Professor Higgins is not my gent. But he is the man who taught me to speak proper."

"Properly," he corrected.

"Properly," Eliza repeated, but only after sticking her tongue out at him. "See here, Nan. The Professor is in a spot of trouble. I wonder if you may be able to help us out."

Her expression turned wary. "Don't see 'ow the likes of me can help a gent like 'im."

"Neither do I," Higgins said.

Ignoring them both, Eliza once more opened her purse. This time she pulled out the button she'd found on the carpet that day outside Nepommuck's apartment. She was thankful she'd kept it, suspecting even then it was a clue as to the intruder's identity. Luckily it had been easy to find back in her room at Mrs. Higgins's apartment; aside from the extensive wardrobe that the Colonel had bought her, Eliza had few personal possessions.

The late afternoon sun shone through the skylight overhead as Eliza held out the button for Nan to examine. The sunlight set the golden button aglow.

"Cor, ain't that a pretty piece." Nan squinted. "I take it you want my opinion?"

Higgins gave a snort, but Eliza hushed him. "Don't be rude, Professor. Nan knows a sight more than you do about fancy buttons and jewels."

"It's true, sir," she said, displaying those missing front teeth. "Me dad fenced most of the gold and jewels boosted in south London. And 'alf of what was stolen in England. At least till the coppers run 'im into jail. 'E taught me 'ow to recognize what's quality and what ain't."

"Is this quality?"

Nan held it up to the light and then bit on the button's edge. "Ain't copper or brass. 'Tis real gold, and engraved."

"I could have told you that," Higgins muttered.

"Is the design on it a family crest?" Eliza asked.

Nan shook her head. "Don't have the look or feel of an antique button from a noble family. A fine piece, though. No more than five, ten years old. Lots of gold in this button, too. A dozen of these on a coat or jacket would cost two hundred quid at least. Maybe more."

"So a person of quality owned it?"

"A person of means anyway." Nan laughed. "The two ain't always the same."

"How about the design carved on it?" Eliza asked. "The head of a lion surrounded by stars. Have you seen that before?"

Nan examined it for a long moment. "I seen lions on a button, stars, too. Just ain't seen 'em on the same button. Seems like a fancy crest dreamed up by someone looking to move up in the world. Lots of folks what come into money feel bad they ain't got no proper family crest, so they make up one of their own. Real quality wouldn't wear something like this. A bit gaudy, y'see. But it cost plenty just the same." She handed the button back to Eliza, who returned it to her drawstring bag.

Higgins pulled out his wallet, but Nan waved him off. "No need to pay me. I'm just glad to see little Lizzie 'ere again. Besides, I ain't never paid 'er for these baskets."

Eliza gave her a great hug, making certain to slip the rest of the money from her own purse into the pocket of Nan's skirt. "Take care of yourself, please."

"Ta, luv," Nan said when Eliza stood. "And don't be afraid to come to the market for a chat now and then."

"I will." However, Eliza wasn't certain she wanted to come back to a place that held so many memories of her former life.

Nan sighed. "Sorry I wasn't more 'elpful."

"But you *have* been helpful, Nan. Now we don't have to waste time looking up old family crests. And I'll keep an eye out for a lady or gentleman wearing clothes with buttons that have a lion surrounded by stars stamped on them."

Nan resumed tying up her bunches of violets. "Don't waste time looking at the ladies. That button belongs on a gent's jacket. A lady fancies flowers or a fleur-de-lis on their buttons, not a blooming lion's 'ead." She looked up at Eliza and Higgins. "Trust me. It was a man what lost that button, not a lady."

By the time they reached Waterloo Bridge, Eliza's energy had noticeably flagged. Higgins couldn't resist a chuckle when she once again slipped her feet out of those fancy shoes Pick had bought her. She leaned against the bridge's half wall and massaged first one foot, then the other. If she wanted to be a lady, then she'd have to be as uncomfortable as one of them, too.

As for him, it had been a most productive afternoon. His notebook was filled with snatches of dialect and rough speech he'd had the good fortune to overhear. After that blasted night spent in custody at Scotland Yard, it was heaven to be out and about on a warm spring day in London. He looked at Eliza, who struggled to put her French-heeled shoes back on.

"Are we done sleuthing?" Higgins asked. "I wouldn't mind a nice cup of tea, with supper to go along with it. I say we get to the other end of this bridge and hail a cab."

"Why wait to get off the bridge? Let's hire one of the cabs driving by." She nodded toward the traffic barreling past them while they stood on the pedestrian walkway.

Higgins watched the steady stream of motorcars, omnibuses, and a few horse-drawn wagons. "Any cab on Waterloo Bridge is already hired. I am afraid you'll have to limp your way to the other side. That, or I'll sling you over my shoulder and carry you across like a side of Guernsey beef."

"I can walk on my own, thank you very much."

Wincing, Eliza jammed her left foot into a dainty rose-colored shoe. "Nan saved us a trip to the tailors on Threadneedle Street, but I'm disappointed we couldn't find anyone who saw you on the day of the murder. Still, I'm flat-out tired and ready for a cup of tea myself."

"Let's get on with it then. The sooner we find a cab, the quicker we'll be back home at Wimpole Street."

Eliza shook her head. "We have to go to Scotland Yard first. I promised Jack we'd bring the button to him before the end of the day. And it's nearly dark."

Stubborn as always, he thought; however, he admired her resoluteness, especially since this was all done on his behalf. Although it was damned ludicrous that he and Eliza were playing Holmes and Watson simply because some lying foreigner got himself killed.

Behind her, Higgins caught sight of Westminster now illuminated by the last rays of the sun. He leaned over the bridge railing and took a deep breath, enjoying the pungent smell of the river's mudbanks and the view.

"Professor, I think we should hurry. No need to stand on the bridge looking over the edge."

Amused by the concern in her voice, he grinned. "Are you worried I'll fling myself into the Thames, Eliza? You ought to know me better than that. Out of all the men in the King's empire, I am the last one to end it all in such a romantic and deluded manner. Unless you actually believe the tale Corporal Teddy spun for the police."

"Even the strongest man has a weak moment. No shame in it," she said. "You should be pleased that Boer veteran was worried about you."

"He cares because I come around now and again to write down how that Welshman slaughters his native tongue. For which he is paid rather handsomely. Hence his concern that I was going to end it all in the river."

"But he did tell the police that you confessed feeling guilty about something, and seeing as how it was the day that Nepommuck was murdered . . ." Her voice trailed off.

Higgins turned to face her, but he could barely see her features in the growing dusk. "And what do you imagine I was feeling guilty about? Do you honestly think I stuck a knife in that blighter's back?"

"No, I'd never believe that of you. Oh, you're careless of everyone's feelings, but you're not the type to put someone in the grave." She frowned. "I think you're feeling guilty all the same."

He sighed and turned back to the river. "Bloody Hungarian. Who would have thought one of his many enemies would actually do him in? All I wanted was to expose him as a liar and a mountebank. Something I did most effectively by the information I gave to the newspapers. I looked forward to watching his fraudulent house of cards come tumbling down around his ears. That was the fun I expected, Eliza."

"Would it have been fun?"

"To watch my enemy suffer a well-deserved punishment, knowing all the while I was responsible for his pain? Yes, I would have found sport in it. Why in the world would I put Nepommuck out of his misery by killing him? I'd barely begun to savor my revenge."

"But you do feel some guilt all the same."

A long moment passed. "Yes. I wanted him disgraced, not murdered. And I don't know how or why, but the information revealed in the press somehow got him killed. For that, I do share responsibility and I am sorry. However, I didn't murder the charlatan. Nor did I wish the oily bastard dead by anyone's hand."

"I know you didn't kill him, Professor. So does the Colonel and your mother and anyone who really knows you. But that doesn't include Scotland Yard."

"They're idiots. By George, it's amazing any criminal is ever apprehended in this city."

"Those idiots are the ones who will arrest someone for Nepommuck's murder. Right now, the most likely person is you. That's why we've been out here all day trying to find someone who will back up your alibi."

"A fool's errand. I've spent years eavesdropping on vendors, thieves, and ladies on the streets of London. Damn few take any notice unless I want their attention."

She drummed her fingers on the railing. "Then we have to find a more likely suspect. Starting tomorrow, we'll pay a call on Nepommuck's students. I suspect many of them are not unhappy he's dead. Nepommuck has a list in his apartment with the names and addresses of everyone who took lessons from us both. It has to be one of them."

Higgins agreed with her. Gossip had long held that Nepommuck was a blackmailer, and he was confident that some of his students had been victims of the Hungarian. "I'd certainly like a few words with that phony Greek diplomat."

"Yes, Dmitri Kollas," she said. "He was furious at Nepommuck the day of the murder. And don't forget the Finches. Cornelius may have killed him out of jealousy. He certainly had a good reason, especially after that scene Mary caused at the garden party. And who's to say that Mary didn't do him in herself? After all, the man she loved had just announced he was going to marry another woman."

"They sound a lovely pair," Higgins murmured. "And people wonder why I never married."

"I also met a young man at the garden party who didn't seem fond of the Maestro, either. We should pay a call on his students this week. Even if none of them did it, we may uncover information leading to the person who did. In fact, tomorrow morning we'll go to Nepommuck's apartment and——" Eliza tugged his sleeve. "Professor, are you listening to me?"

Higgins leaned as far as he dared over the gray granite wall of Waterloo Bridge. "Blast this traffic. It's drowning out that man on a coal barge beneath the bridge. If I'm not mistaken, he's singing a sea shanty in Old English."

In an instant, he had his notebook out once more.

"You're off your trolley! You've no more sense than one of the ravens on Tower Hill. I've crippled myself walking about London on your behalf, and all you can think about is listening to passing boatmen."

"Shhh." Higgins scribbled in his notebook. "I must remember the verse he sang."

"You can find me on the other side of the Thames when you're done. And I intend to hail the first cab I see. If you're not there when I do, you can find your own way home."

Higgins chuckled as Eliza stomped off. Silly girl. Did she forget that she had given all her money to those flower sellers in Covent Garden? And by the time she limped to the other side, he would be ten steps ahead of her. But first he had to listen to the boatman. Dodging traffic, he ran to the bridge's other side to catch further snatches of the song. It was worth a dozen cabs just to listen to this fellow warble in the night like a figure out of Chaucer.

Suddenly he heard Eliza cry out. "Ah-ah-oh-ow-ow-oh-ow!"

Cramming his notebook back in his pocket, Higgins sprinted between traffic to the other side once more. "Eliza, are you all right?"

"Help, Professor! He's getting away!"

Racing down the walkway, he pushed past a delivery boy hauling an empty wagon. "Where are you? Eliza!"

How foolish he'd been to leave her alone on Waterloo Bridge at twilight. Although most of the thieves skulked along the river's edge below, a young girl dressed as expensively as Eliza was certain to attract unwanted attention.

"Give that back, you bloody thief!"

At the sound of Eliza's voice, he ran so fast he almost tripped over her fallen figure. Higgins knelt beside her. "Are you hurt? What happened?"

With a grunt, she pulled herself up. "The blooming dodger's gotten away!"

She pointed to a figure darting off into the shadows. Even in the dark, he could see pursuit was futile. In a few more steps, the thief would come to the end of the bridge and then fling himself into the Victoria Embankment traffic.

Higgins turned to Eliza, who was brushing herself off. "Are you injured?"

"Just my pride. I haven't had something nicked off me since I was five years old when Billy Rathbone stole my cornhusk doll. It's bloody embarrassing to have my purse snatched. I should have seen that lowlife from fifty yards away."

"He attacked you?"

"I was walking along the bridge. Even said a 'how d'ye do' to that delivery boy what passed. Then someone pushed me to the pavement from behind and yanked my purse." She held up her hand. "I had the drawstring wrapped around my wrist. I gave him a bit of a struggle, but he got it off fast enough. Heard him rip that lovely pink silk, I did. If I could find him, I'd box his ears with these heels I'm wearing."

"At least you're not hurt." Higgins brushed the dirt off the back of her skirt. "Let's get you into a cab. The sooner you're home, the safer you'll be."

"But we have to go to Scotland Yard to give Jack the button." Eliza stopped. "Oh blimey! The button was in my purse."

"That's one thief who won't be happy when he realizes all he's made off with is a torn bag and a button."

"Thank goodness I gave all the money in my purse to Nan and Old Lucy. I'd rather they have it than some pox-faced pickpocket. But I've lost the button! It was a clue, too. Now we have nothing to show the police."

"Eliza, we don't know if it was a clue or not. Dozens of students went to see Nepommuck every week. That button might have belonged to any of them."

"No, it was a clue. And I'll wager that it belonged to whoever was hiding in the dark that day." She straightened her straw hat. "I know it."

"All right, Sherlock. I will concede that we lost a clue today."

She stepped closer to him and lowered her voice. "I'll tell you something else. Whoever stole my purse has been following us all day."

"Come now, Eliza. I doubt that very much."

"I've had a funny feeling ever since we left the Yard. First I thought Jack sent a detective to keep me safe. But he'd have caught the thief, you see. That dodger who stole my purse had to be tracking us all along."

Higgins moved to touch her cheek and then stopped himself. "Are you certain you didn't hit your head?"

"Oh bugger that." She spun on her heel and began to limp away. "What a wasted day. Bad enough I lost the button. But we spent hours walking around the city, and couldn't find one person who saw you yesterday. Not one!"

Nor would they be likely to, Higgins thought as he followed close behind her. He didn't expect anyone to remember seeing him the day of the murder. And he had no intention of telling Eliza his alibi was a sham. In truth, he had an airtight alibi. However, he could never reveal where he had been. Not to Eliza, and not to Scotland Yard.

No one would ever know. It was a secret he would take to the grave. Or prison.

NINE

Stifling a yawn, Eliza slowly descended the stairs. Her feet throbbed from yesterday's search, and she winced with each step. But the delicious aroma of bacon, scones, pan-fried eggs, and freshly brewed coffee drew her downstairs.

How she loved to greet Mrs. Pearce in the morning, along with the other maids at the Professor's house. Not that his mother's residence wasn't as lovely or the staff as nice. But Mrs. Higgins's palatial apartment on the Chelsea Embankment was a tad too serene and quiet. Even more important, 27A Wimpole Street felt like home.

After the attack on Waterloo Bridge last night, Higgins brought her straight back here. While it was unlikely that the attacker had targeted her personally, Higgins and Pickering were uneasy about the situation. If someone had followed Eliza, leaving her alone with Higgins's mother would only serve to place both ladies in jeopardy. They decided Eliza should move her belongings back to Wimpole Street, where she would stay until this whole murder business was resolved.

Eliza didn't protest. She looked forward to sleeping once again in her old room with its blue canopy bed and cushioned window seat.

How loverly to draw aside the blue silk curtains each morning and gaze out on the flower boxes, wrought-iron railings, and stone entrances that lined the street below. The neighborhood was elegant without being stuffy. Nannies wheeled prams to and from Regent's Park all day, while motorcars discharged well-dressed men and women calling on the many medical practices that dotted the street all the way to Cavendish Square. Eliza had even heard that a famous poetess once lived nearby. And the air of activity always present within the Professor's home—the staff setting out breakfast, the rooms being readied for the day—matched the congenial hustle and bustle outside the front door.

As she walked down the stairs, Eliza heard the maids hard at work cleaning Higgins's makeshift laboratory. She had spent so many hours in there practicing her vowels, consonants, and diphthongs, she nearly went mad. Eliza shook her head at the memory of trying to speak with a mouth full of marbles. Not to mention listening again and again to his bloody wax recordings.

It felt good to be back.

Eliza entered the dining room and smiled when both Colonel Pickering and Major Redstone jumped to their feet. Both in suits and ties, freshly shaved and their hair pomaded, they looked quite formal compared with the Professor. Like most mornings, Higgins was clad in a stained dressing gown with his hair uncombed. He lowered his newspaper to eye level and then raised it again without saying a word.

"How are you feeling, my dear?" Pickering asked.

"I hope you slept well." Redstone pulled out the cushioned chair beside him.

"I am well, thank you. Just a bit sore," she said, and sat down in relief.

"Good to see you back, Miss Eliza." Mrs. Pearce poured coffee into a china cup and placed it before her. "The cream is fresh. I'll bring you some deviled kidneys on toast if you like. There's bacon on the sideboard along with currant scones and chilled strawberries. And a platter of scrambled eggs."

"No deviled kidneys this morning, thank you."

Eliza rose again and walked to the sideboard laid out with platters of fruit, eggs, bacon, and pastry. Still ravenous from yesterday's nonstop activity, she heaped food onto her plate. Perhaps she ought to ask Mrs. Pearce to bring her a few of those deviled kidneys after all. Eliza returned to the table not only with a full plate, but carrying the tiered dish of scones.

After the first few delicious mouthfuls, Eliza shot a look at Higgins still hidden behind his paper. "In case you're curious, Professor, I had quite a restful sleep despite the incident on the bridge."

He lowered the paper a few inches. "Am I supposed to inquire about your welfare on an hourly basis? You must be mistaking me for Freddy."

"As if I could ever mistake that sweet fellow for you." She sprinkled sugar on her strawberries. "Anyway, you'd best hurry with your own breakfast and see about getting dressed. We have work to do."

"Work? I don't know of any work."

"Proving your innocence."

"Isn't that Scotland Yard's job? Murder is their business, not ours."

"Unpleasant business, too." Redstone poured himself another cup of coffee from the silver pot that sat before him. "You might have been seriously injured last night. I'm surprised a policeman wasn't on Waterloo Bridge when you were attacked. Busy thoroughfare, that."

Pickering set down his cup hard on the saucer. "Dash it all, Henry! You ought to have kept a better eye on our Eliza. Especially in that neighborhood, and with a killer running around London."

Higgins grunted. "There are always a few killers running about London. I doubt they're all after Eliza."

"I'm fine, Colonel," Eliza said, sipping coffee. "I'm upset that my purse was stolen because I wanted to give my cousin the button. Besides, I'm not certain the attack was related to the Maestro's murder. It may have been a common thief."

"Exactly. It could have happened anywhere in the city, which we explored quite thoroughly yesterday. I believe we looked everywhere but the King's bedchamber at Buckingham Palace." Higgins turned the page of his paper and continued reading.

"Well, you're safe here with us, Eliza," Pickering said. "We'll keep an eye on you. Won't we, Reddy?"

"Absolutely," the Major chimed in. "No one remotely suspicious will have a chance to get anywhere near you, Miss Doolittle. You have our word."

Eliza was touched by their concern. "Thank you so much."

Pickering turned to Redstone. "What say we head to the club then, my good man?"

She hid her smile by biting into a scone. No doubt they hadn't given much thought as to how safe she would be once they had gone off to the club. Men were an odd lot, indeed.

"Although we'll need to reserve a private room to discuss our translations." Redstone leaned closer to Eliza. "Whispers bother the older members. They're asleep most of the time, you know. I suspect a few of them have passed on and no one has noticed yet."

She returned his sly smile with one of her own.

Mrs. Pearce entered the room with another pot of coffee. "Your things will be packed and sent over shortly from Mrs. Higgins's home," the housekeeper said.

Higgins raised an eyebrow at the loud banging on the front door. "Damn tradesmen. Why can't they use the back door? Next thing you know, they'll be sitting down at table with us."

Still hungry after finishing her eggs, Eliza snitched a currant scone from the cake dish.

"I say, Reddy, what did you make of that passage we tried last night?" Pickering asked. "I wish this translation was a bit clearer."

"I believe it refers to—"

Redstone stopped as Freddy burst into the dining room. "Eliza! Mrs. Higgins told me what happened last night. Are you hurt?"

"No, not in the least," she said, intent on enjoying her currant scone.

"Why were you alone on Waterloo Bridge, my darling?"

"I wasn't alone. The Professor was with me." With his cheeks flushed redder than usual, Eliza thought Freddy looked adorable.

"I called this morning at the flat, thinking you were still there. I was dreadfully worried. Ever since Clara and I were questioned in Scotland Yard by that brute of an inspector—"

"Remember that brute is my cousin." Eliza threw him a warning look.

"Oh, I don't care about him. Mrs. Higgins told me you'd been attacked, and your purse cut from your wrist." He grabbed her hand and examined it, ignoring her wince of pain. "Look, there! A thin pink mark."

"From my purse's silk drawstring. It's nothing. Have a seat." She pushed him into the empty chair on her other side. "I'm fine, Freddy. I wasn't hurt."

"But darling, you might have been killed."

"I'm sitting here beside you, alive and well." Eliza rubbed her chafed wrist. "Have some breakfast. You'll feel better."

Mrs. Pearce topped off Higgins's cup and poured coffee for their new guest. Still upset about Eliza's attack, Freddy's hand noticeably shook as he added cream to his cup. He glanced at the others around the table. Higgins remained hidden behind his paper.

Pickering nodded at Freddy. "So good to see you survived Scotland Yard, young man."

"Yes, sir. But poor Eliza was kept there for hours." He grabbed her hand again. "I thought this whole matter was behind us, and then last night you were attacked. It's all too much, darling. I fear for your safety."

Embarrassed, she took another scone from the tray and put it on Freddy's plate. "He wanted my purse, that's all. Besides, the thief didn't make off with any money."

"Right, then," Pickering said. "Now, Reddy, about that verse we were looking at last night. I don't believe it has anything to do with romantic love. A Buddhist scholar wrote it seven hundred years ago."

"A Buddhist scholar is a man like any other. Desire is timeless."

Redstone caught Eliza's eye and nodded toward Freddy with a smile. She realized he had forgotten his concern over her as he wolfed down the scone, then reached for another.

Pickering waved his knife. "I'll prove it once we get to the club. Some of the text is so indecipherable, I can barely read it at all."

"How marvelous to imagine the two of you translating a poem that is seven hundred years old." Eliza moved the bowl of clotted cream closer to Freddy.

"And in a Sanskrit dialect long forgotten." Pickering sighed. "Unfortunately my book is useless as a reference."

"Not completely useless. We did decipher a few puzzling words with your *Spoken Sanskrit*."

"I'd love to read the poems when the translations are complete," Eliza said.

Redstone looked at her with even more interest than usual. "Do you like poetry, Miss Doolittle?"

She nodded. "Very much. Before I came to Wimpole Street, I only knew a few rhymes, usually ones the street sellers sang in the market. But the Professor and Colonel Pickering used a number of texts to teach me how to speak properly. Several were books of poetry."

Pickering smiled. "Keats, if I remember right."

"And Emily Brontë, Kipling, Tennyson. Although I didn't care much for Tennyson." Eliza eyed the plate of scones, wondering if she dared have another. "Poems are perfect for teaching someone the rhythms of speech. Even Nepommuck told me to use books of poetry for my lessons."

The Professor muttered behind his newspaper again.

Pickering raised an eyebrow in distaste. "I can only imagine the sort of poetry that fellow had a taste for."

"Limericks," Higgins said.

"Not at all." Eliza dabbed her mouth with a napkin. "He recommended Kipling. He also gave me poetry by writers he said were now forgotten: Temperance Burns, Hiram Daniels, Jasper Willoughby. My favorite was this little book of love poems called *The White Rose*."

Redstone seemed puzzled. "I've never heard of any of these poets. Who wrote *The White Rose*?"

She shrugged. "Anonymous, which seems a funny sort of name. Anyway, the poems were written for a young woman. The book is dedicated inside to the White Rose of Rossendale, wherever that is."

"Lancashire," Higgins said from behind the newspaper.

"Well, whoever this Anonymous fellow was, he wrote some lovely poems. I imagine him as a handsome young soldier in the cavalry, pining away for his lady."

Higgins peeked around the side of his paper. "He probably was a fat old man from the suburbs of Manchester, with a nagging wife and an even worse mother-in-law."

"Henry, really," Pickering said. "If ever there was a man resistant to poetry, it would be you."

"Not at all, old chap. I have committed every line of Milton to memory. Now there's a poet, all thunder and gloom the way it ought to be."

Redstone winked at Eliza. "Pay him no mind. A great love poem is like a song from God."

She smiled at him. "You don't have to convince me. I quite enjoyed using the poetry books in my lessons. And Nepommuck was generous enough to make a gift of them to me."

"Where are they now?"

"Back in my classroom at Belgrave Square. I should return and pack up what remains of my things. I certainly have no intention of resuming lessons just a few feet away from where he was murdered."

"I'd like to see these poetry books when you retrieve them, especially the love poems in *The White Rose*. Interesting to see how they compare with the ancient Sanskrit poets that Pick and I are working on."

"Of course," she said. Sitting beside Redstone, Eliza realized for the first time that he was a handsome man. How had she not noticed that before? In fact, Freddy seemed quite boyish next to the tall strapping Major. And despite Freddy's love-struck chattering, she doubted he knew—or would even understand—a single poem.

A thought occurred to her. "The Professor and I have plans to visit Nepommuck's apartment today."

"We do?" Higgins lowered his paper.

"How many times must I tell you? We need to get the list of Nepommuck's students and their addresses."

"I've turned into a blasted police constable."

"While we're there, I'll pop across the hall and retrieve the poetry books from my classroom," Eliza said to Redstone.

"Excellent." He looked across the table at Pickering. "I say, why don't we accompany them on the way to the club? We can take the books with us."

"Fine idea, Reddy."

"Good," she said. "As soon as we're done with breakfast—and the Professor gets out of his pajamas—we can take a cab to Belgrave Square."

Redstone cleared his throat. "Speaking of poetry books, Miss Doolittle, this seems an opportune time to give you a little something I found at the booksellers this week." He reached inside his jacket and pulled out a slim leather-bound volume.

Higgins put down his paper.

Eliza's eyes widened. "What is it?"

Redstone placed the thin book in her hands. *"Hamlet,"* he said quietly.

Eliza was touched that he remembered her chagrin at the garden party about never having read the play. "What a thoughtful gift," she said when she could finally trust her voice. "Thank you so much."

Redstone smiled. "I hoped you'd like it."

"I say, this seems most improper, Eliza. The gentleman scarcely knows you," Freddy protested. "I insist you return the book to him at once."

"Do be quiet, Freddy." Eliza fluttered the pages of the book.

She stopped at the title page where Redstone had inscribed: "To the poetry lover of Wimpole Street." He was such a considerate gentleman. No wonder he and Colonel Pickering were good friends. Elisa impulsively leaned over to give Redstone a quick hug. Freddy almost dropped his coffee cup.

"Since you care so much for poetry," Redstone said, "you may like to hear a stanza from the poem we're translating."

"Please."

Redstone's blue eyes fastened on her intently. " 'Flushed with love, the moon puts forth his hand upon the cloud breasts of the night whose dark robe he has opened, revealing the silver honey within—' "

"How dare you!" Freddy sputtered so hard, crumbs landed on the tablecloth and his suit. He stood. "First you have the bad manners to give Eliza a volume of Shakespeare, and now you dare quote lewd poetry to her! I can't believe the liberties you take with the woman I love."

Eliza tugged at his coat. "Sit down, Freddy."

The Major shrugged. "I merely gave the lady an example of what we're translating, Mr. Eynsford Hall."

"Hill. Frederick Eynsford Hill the Third."

Redstone inclined his head with a worldly smile. "I beg your pardon. Mr. Eynsford Hill." He paused. "The Third."

The younger man's stammering indignation was no match for Redstone's confident tone and manner. "Eliza, you're coming home to live with me."

"What?" Eliza choked on her coffee.

"I meant, you must come live with Mother and me," Freddy corrected. "And Clara, of course. Mrs. Pearce, please fetch her things. I'm sorry, but I'm putting my foot down."

"No. Now finish your breakfast."

"But that poem was revolting. I couldn't possibly let you spend another hour, let alone another night, under the same roof as this man. You must leave with me at once."

"Freddy, don't be absurd."

"I'm not being absurd." He pulled Eliza to her feet. "Come with me immediately."

Higgins folded his newspaper and slapped it down onto the table. "What the devil, young man! What are you implying? That my home isn't fit for decent company? That I ought not tolerate ancient poetry, however bad it is?"

"Of course not—"

"Eliza is perfectly safe under my roof. And stop manhandling her. She will remain here until either she or I decide otherwise." Higgins wagged his finger at the younger fellow. "And if you ever upset my breakfast again, I shall put my foot on your arse and send you flying out into the street!"

Freddy stammered, "B-but my darling is in danger and I cannot let her remain here."

"Cor, I've had enough," Eliza said. "Excuse us, gentlemen."

Ignoring his protests, she dragged Freddy into the foyer. Grabbing his hat from the wall hook with one hand, Eliza opened the front door with the other. She pushed him out on the steps. "Now stop making a scene and go home."

He opened his mouth to speak, but Eliza stopped him with a lingering kiss. When she finally broke away, Freddy was speechless and euphoric.

"You're sweet to worry about me, Freddy, but I shall be fine. And I'll be in touch after we make more progress on the case."

"But Eliza, my darling, please let me—"

She shut the door on his pleas. *If* they made progress, she thought with a sigh.

Freddy had no reason to worry about the Major. Although Redstone could quote the most delicious poetry, Freddy was far more suited to her. He was such a dear boy, so handsome with his golden mane of hair and endless declarations of love. Even his hysterical concern for her was flattering. And he was easy to manage. Besides, Aubrey Redstone was a man of thirty-seven, just three years younger than Professor Higgins. Both of them were much too old for the likes of her. She had to keep reminding herself of that, especially now the Major had been kind enough to give her that lovely copy of *Hamlet*.

Higgins and Redstone were merely her friends, while Colonel Pickering was like a father, far more generous and loving than Alfred Doolittle had ever been. And she owed the Colonel and Higgins her loyalty for all their help. Without them, she'd be sitting next to Nan at Covent Garden tying bunches of violets. No matter what, she'd find a way to keep both Higgins and the Colonel safe from harm. That meant Freddy and his romantic plans would have to wait until she finished solving a murder.

"Here we are," Eliza announced to the trio of men clustered about her.

Higgins looked up at the whitewashed building with its Ionic pillared porticos, ironwork balconies, and first-floor railings. "It cost that scoundrel a pretty penny to rent one apartment here, let alone two."

"Do you know where Nepommuck kept his list of students?" Redstone asked.

"The writing desk in his sitting room." Eliza entered the imposing building. She threw a quick glance at the heavy doors that led to the solicitors' office before walking toward the stairwell.

"Perhaps we should also take a look around his apartment for threatening letters or cryptic notes," Pickering said as they climbed the stairs. "Anything to suggest blackmail."

"Absolutely," Higgins said. "Blackmail is the likeliest motive."

"I wouldn't be surprised if the police missed something important when they searched his rooms," Eliza added.

Higgins gave a bitter laugh. "Nothing the police do would surprise me."

Upon reaching the second floor, Eliza faltered. The last time she was here, Nepommuck's corpse was lying in the hallway. Perhaps this wasn't such a good idea after all. It took every ounce of her will to continue walking toward the Maestro's apartment. But Eliza stopped cold when she saw the large dark stain on the carpeting in front of his door.

"Are you all right, Eliza?" The Colonel put his hand on her shoulder. "No need to go any farther. We can turn around and leave. Or we can simply send Higgins into the apartment to get the list you need."

Higgins nodded. "Pick, why don't you take Eliza downstairs while I rummage about his desk. I just need the key."

She took a deep breath. "No, I can do this. Besides, I promised to get the poetry books from my classroom for the Major afterwards."

"Please don't worry about that now, Miss Doolittle." The Major gave her a concerned look. "We should have known better than to allow you to return here so soon after your employer's death."

"I'm fine." None of them looked convinced. "I'm fine," she repeated in a stronger voice.

She rummaged in her pocketbook for the brass key to the apartment. Eliza carefully stepped over the bloodstain. A second later, she stood before Nepommuck's door. She inserted the key into the lock, turned it, then tried the knob. It didn't budge.

"Why won't it open?"

"Maybe it was already unlocked, and you locked it again." Higgins reached over and twisted the key. "Try it now."

Click.

"You're right. But why would it be unlocked in the first place? Maybe the police are inside." Eliza pushed the door open.

Her gaze swept over the ornate furnishings of Nepommuck's apartment. It was hard to believe he was dead. She could still smell his Turkish cigarettes in the air, along with his favorite eau de cologne, Kölnisch Wasser. At any moment, she expected to hear him call her into the sitting room and give her the name of yet another new pupil. Nepommuck may have been an insufferable man—and possibly a criminal back in his native Hungary—but no one deserved to die such a terrible death.

"Eliza, are we going inside or not?" Higgins said from the hallway.

She stepped inside the apartment and froze. Cornelius Finch sat on the sofa in the middle of the room. He seemed not to notice Eliza and the others. Instead he stared down at the floor. Eliza craned her neck to see what he was looking at. She clapped a hand over her mouth.

Higgins and the other two men crowded in behind her. "By Jove, what is this?" Pickering said in horror.

A woman in a black dress lay faceup on the Persian rug. Eliza instantly recognized the blond hair. "It's Mary Finch," she whispered.

Higgins pushed her backward into Pickering, who stepped on

Redstone's foot. When the Major let out a howl, it stirred Cornelius Finch into movement. He finally glanced over at them.

"My wife." He spoke as if in a trance.

"Is she ill? Help me get her onto the sofa." Eliza hurried to kneel by Mary. She let out a cry when she saw the woman's bruised neck and lifeless eyes.

"It's too late." His calm voice stunned them.

Higgins knelt beside Eliza. "Damnation, man. What happened?"

"She's dead." Cornelius sighed. "I killed her."

TEN

Eliza tried to avert her gaze from the large map of London that hung on the wall of Jack's office. But her eyes kept coming back to it. The detailed street map of the city was covered with a profusion of colored pins. Jack told her yesterday the map showed where various crimes had been committed this year; each color represented a different offense. Red pins denoted a murder. She shivered to think another red pin had been placed at the Belgrave Square building where Nepommuck had lived.

"I can't believe we're back at Scotland Yard again," Eliza said.

"If we come one more time, we may as well rent our own office." Higgins stood by the window, staring down at Whitehall Place. "I doubt your cousin is thrilled we seem to have moved into his."

"What a beastly day." Colonel Pickering tamped tobacco into his pipe.

"If we'd been a few minutes earlier, we might have been able to stop Mr. Finch from strangling Mary."

Higgins let out an exasperated sigh. "Eliza, you must stop saying that. Jack told you Mary had been dead for at least an hour before we got there."

"I know, but maybe he's wrong. Maybe we could have saved her."

"There was nothing we could have done, my dear." Pickering reached over and patted her hand.

"I feel guilty." Eliza couldn't get the image of poor Mary out of her head. It didn't seem possible that in only forty-eight hours, she had discovered the dead bodies of two people she had known well.

Redstone looked up from the periodical he was reading in a corner chair. "None of us has reason to feel guilty, Miss Doolittle, least of all you. We simply had the misfortune of stumbling upon a murder. At least this crime will be easy to solve."

"Thank heaven," she said. Although horrified at Mary's death, Eliza was immensely relieved they had the killer in custody. It seemed clear that Cornelius Finch had murdered both his wife and her lover. Higgins would now be seen as an innocent man.

"You'd think at least one blasted policeman would come in and tell us something." Higgins rattled the loose change in his pocket, which Eliza knew he did only when he was agitated. "We've been here for three hours without even a cup of tea, let alone any useful information."

"One good thing has come out of this tragedy, Professor," Eliza said. "The Maestro's murderer has been caught and he isn't you."

Redstone cleared his throat. "We may want to hold off on celebrating. After all, the Inspector has told us nothing aside from Mrs. Finch's approximate time of death. Who knows what sort of story Mr. Finch is telling the police?"

"What can he say?" Eliza said. "We caught Cornelius standing over Mary's body, and he even announced he killed her. It seems obvious to me."

"But did he kill Nepommuck as well?" Pickering puffed on his pipe. The older gentleman invariably brought out his pipe when he felt uneasy. Higgins wasn't the only one in the office on edge.

"Of course he did. You remember the scene Mary created at the garden party when Lady Gresham announced their engagement. Mary was obviously in love with Nepommuck. And her jealous husband knew it."

Pickering drew on his pipe. "I say, I feel awfully bad about it all. Especially when you consider that Mrs. Finch said something about a baby when Lady Verena's butler took her away. If she was carrying Nepommuck's child, this is a doubly tragic situation."

Eliza had forgotten what Mary cried out during the party. How dreadful if the woman had been with child. She shuddered at the brutal consequences of an illicit tryst. The clock on the opposite wall chimed half past two. How much longer were they going to be kept here? She was weary of Scotland Yard, police detectives, and the uncertainty over the Professor's fate.

"Surely now, life can go back to normal," Eliza said, not realizing that she had spoken aloud. The others looked at her.

"And what will that life be for you?" Redstone asked. "Will you continue giving lessons?"

"I don't know."

"My dear, I have told you many times I will set you up in a flower shop." Pickering squeezed her hand once more. "Or perhaps you'd care to be the proprietress of a millinery store. You've become the most fashionable young lady I know."

"Due to you, Colonel," she said with fondness. "I quite enjoy teaching, but Freddy would prefer having a shop."

"I didn't realize this was Freddy's decision," Pickering said as he tapped a finger on his meerschaum pipe.

"I'll make the final decision, of course, but you know he wishes to marry me. It makes sense that he's already thinking about our future."

"He might think about finding a job," Higgins muttered by the window. "He's twenty-one. High time he had a profession."

"I wouldn't ask him to get a job." Eliza was appalled at the very idea. "He was raised to be a gentleman, not a common laborer."

"Gentlemen usually have private incomes," Redstone said quietly. "That's how they came to be gentlemen."

"But his family has fallen on hard times. It must be far worse to have known a life of wealth and lost it than to never have known it at all."

Higgins only sneered. "I doubt the inhabitants of the poorhouse would agree."

"I'm not saying that being without money is easy for anyone, but Freddy and Clara were brought up to expect a much different life than I was. I feel sorry for them."

"You are much too kind," Redstone said. "If you had remained a Cockney flower seller, Mr. Eynsford Hill would never have paid you a moment's notice."

"No more than you would have," Eliza said.

"Touché," Redstone murmured.

"Let's not get carried away about Freddy's lamentable station in life," Higgins said. "The Eynsford Hills boast no knights, dukes, or even baronets in their family tree. They are solidly middle-class, with the pretentious manners to prove it."

Eliza didn't fancy the criticism about her Freddy. "I don't know why we're discussing his family or their manners. All I care about is that he loves me and I love him."

The room fell silent.

"*Do* you love him, Eliza?" Pickering finally asked.

For a moment, she regretted her words. Did she love Freddy? Or was she just in love with the idea that a proper young gentleman was smitten with her?

"Of . . . of course I do. Why else would I defend him so?"

Higgins laughed. "Sheer pigheadedness."

"As if you're in a position to talk about men and women in love. Unless a woman comes to you with a stammer or a Scots brogue that needs correcting, you don't give her a second's attention."

"I take that as a compliment."

"You would, you brute." Eliza slumped down in her chair, arms crossed. Sometimes the Professor could make her forget all the pretty manners she spent so much effort to acquire.

"Henry, if our Eliza wishes to make an honest man of Mr. Eynsford Hill, then we should support her," Pickering said.

"No doubt financially as well."

"I'll make my own way, Professor, as I always have. I wouldn't take a shilling from you, even if I have to go back to Tottenham Court Road with me blooming flowers."

"I believe you owe me more than a shilling. Your father demanded five pounds from me last year, otherwise he threatened to remove you from Wimpole Street."

Eliza glared at him. "Don't drag my father into this. I've known him to try to sell everything from a barrow of old clothes to an actual building off Bishopsgate. None of which he actually owned. I'm not surprised he tried to shake you down. More fool you for giving him so much as a halfpenny."

Higgins shrugged. "You came cheap. I offered to give him ten."

"I'll pay you back your blasted five pounds as soon as we get out of here."

"I'd prefer you work it off as my assistant," he said with a grin.

"It's the least you can do after running off to teach for that dishonest Hungarian."

Eliza didn't know if Higgins was serious about taking her on as his assistant. The prospect of working with him did tempt her. But if he was teasing, she'd box him about the ears, she would. "I have to talk about this with Freddy first. He has his heart set on having a shop."

"Oh, hang such girlish nonsense. I thought you learned to think for yourself. You are *my* handiwork, Eliza, and I don't fancy my efforts being wasted on a fellow with the brains of a bilious pigeon."

"Henry, really," Pickering protested.

Furious, Eliza snatched off one of her shoes and flung it at Higgins's head. He ducked at the last second and it bounced off the window. "You're nothing but a bullying monster. And I'll throw my other shoe at you if you say one more insulting thing about Freddy!"

"I believe you owe Miss Doolittle an apology, Professor," Redstone said.

"For what? Speaking the truth about that boy with the floppy hair and insipid prattle? By the way, I engineered their first meeting at my mother's when we were training Eliza to enter society. Of course, I get little thanks for that."

Eliza stood to face him. "You weren't the one to introduce Freddy and me. I met him the same time I first laid eyes on you, at Covent Garden that rainy night."

Higgins beamed, obviously pleased. "Just so. You did meet Freddy that night, while trying to harangue him into buying your violets. But he had no recollection of it because you were just a squashed cabbage leaf of a girl who called every man 'Freddy.' He left that night without a backward glance at you. While I left you with the correct impression that I could better your life. Else why did you turn up on my doorstep the next day, asking for lessons?"

Eliza sat back down. "I hate it when you're right."

"You must hate me a great deal of the time then." Higgins tossed her shoe back and Eliza caught it.

"Don't know why I'm trying so hard to prove your innocence. I should let Scotland Yard drag you off to prison."

"If they did, Eliza, you'd miss me."

That she would. Drat the man, but sometimes she felt he knew her better than anyone else. And there was no one she trusted more than Higgins. Not even the Colonel. It was true that she'd met Freddy at Covent Garden the same night Higgins scared her by writing down her Cockney speech. But Freddy didn't recognize her weeks later when he and his family were invited for tea at Mrs. Higgins's. All he saw then was a young woman, cleaned up and dressed like she had been born with an "Honorable" before her name. Of course, Freddy knew all about her past now, but he thought her transformation from poor Cockney girl to Belgrave Square lady was an amusing lark. He didn't understand how difficult her life had been, or how damnably hard she had worked to better it.

Maybe that was why she found Freddy endearing. He was such an innocent, and he loved her so much. Eliza couldn't imagine marrying anyone else. And if she wanted to support him while he enjoyed a life of leisure, it was no one's concern but her own. But no matter how she decided to make her living, it would be best to wait until Cornelius Finch's double-murder trial was over.

Jack must be dancing on air right now. Surely he'd be given a commendation for solving the case so soon. Pride swelled in her bosom for her cousin. As if in answer to her thoughts, Jack hurried into the office. Lines of worry creased his forehead. Her high spirits tumbled at his troubled gaze.

"What is it, Jack? What's wrong?" Eliza asked.

"Trouble, that's what. You won't like the news, either."

"But you've solved the Maestro's murder."

"Not exactly, Lizzie."

Higgins moved closer to the center of the room, while Redstone and Pickering both got to their feet.

"Is he refusing to talk to the police?" Pickering asked.

"Oh, Finch refused to cooperate at first, but we managed to change his mind. He's still in the interrogation room in fact. He did confess to his wife's murder."

"What about Nepommuck's murder?"

Jack shook his head. "I'm sorry, Professor, but Finch claims he did not kill Emil Nepommuck. And he has an alibi."

"What?" Eliza exchanged shocked looks with Higgins. "Finch admitted killing her and he had the best motive to kill the Maestro as well."

"Maybe so, but his alibi is airtight."

"Alibi? By George, if that man has an airtight alibi, then I'm the King of Bohemia," Higgins said.

"There's your crown then, Professor." Jack pointed at a set of handcuffs on his desk. "We've spent the day checking his story. It appears he is telling the truth."

"That can't be," Eliza said, dismayed beyond belief. "Finch had the perfect reason to want him dead. And he showed that he's capable of murder. Jack, he must have killed the Maestro. He must."

Her cousin shook his head. "According to Finch, he took the train from London to Leeds the day before the murder. We could gather hundreds of people as witnesses. We've already talked to some of them. At his woolen factories, at King's Cross station—half a dozen reliable people verified seeing him at his factory office on the morning of the murder. He spent the rest of the day in Leeds before returning."

"Then what about Mary Finch?" she asked. "Perhaps she stayed here while Cornelius went to Leeds. She was very upset that the Maestro was marrying another woman. I wouldn't be surprised if she killed him."

"Finch claims his wife was with him in Leeds." Jack shrugged. "And even if she wasn't, I don't see how she could have killed Nepommuck given the force of the wound. Most women wouldn't have the strength to deliver such a blow."

"Unless she had good reason," Eliza said. "Jack, it had to be one of the Finches who killed him."

Jack sighed. "I'll have the detectives question the witnesses we have on record about whether they saw Mrs. Finch at King's Cross and on the train. But don't get your hopes up. Chances are the Finches went back to Leeds together. Especially if she was that upset."

"Damnation," Higgins said. "I regret the day I ever agreed to teach that infuriating Hungarian."

"What should we do now, Inspector?" Pickering asked. "Can we go home?"

"Not quite yet. It seems that Mr. Finch has something he would like to say." Jack paused. "To Professor Higgins."

Higgins followed Jack out into the hall. Eliza kept step with them, her chin jutting out defiantly. Even though Jack insisted that Finch wanted to speak only with Higgins, she wouldn't hear of them leaving her behind. And Higgins was glad of her company. He needed to be reminded that someone believed in his innocence.

The busy hallways were filled with uniformed police and a dizzying variety of Londoners, some victims of a crime, others the likely perpetrators. Just walking along the corridors, Higgins heard at least a dozen fascinating dialects amid the cacophony. If only circumstances were different, how instructive this setting would be. He frowned. No doubt he'd be privy to an even wider variety of speakers if and when he ever found himself in prison.

They followed the inspector down a narrow hall until they reached a door, one all too familiar. Higgins had spent hours being interrogated in that room. Jack poked his head inside, spoke a few hushed words, and then stepped back. Detective Hollaway emerged, letting the door shut behind him. He avoided glancing in Eliza's direction.

"Finch clammed up again, sir. Not about his wife, but about Nepommuck," Hollaway said. "Can't get him to confess no matter how much I tried to convince him."

"I won't have any of that, Detective," Jack said in a sharp voice. "He has witnesses who verify his innocence in the Nepommuck murder."

Hollaway flushed. "But sir, he did kill the lady. Don't see why we're treating him so gentle."

"Mr. Finch has not been brought to trial yet. When he does, he may very well get off. Or have you forgotten that he's a rich man? I can assure you, whenever you cross a man of means, you are likely to regret it. Stop playing the bully boy and get to work."

"Yes, sir." Hollaway was so eager to get away, he nearly broke into a run.

Jack shook his head. "Bloody idiot. He's fool enough to cuff a duke about the head if he had the chance."

"I'd like to think the police treated everyone fairly, duke or dustman," Eliza said. "Unfortunately I know that isn't the case."

Jack gently touched the bruise behind Eliza's ear. "I'm sorry about that, Lizzie."

Higgins cleared his throat. "May I see Finch now? I'd like to get this over with."

After he opened the door, Jack allowed Eliza to enter the room first. The businessman was slumped in a chair at the table.

"Here's the Professor." Jack stood against the far wall. "But whatever you want to say to him, you'll have to say in front of me as well."

Surprise registered on Cornelius Finch's face at the sight of Eliza. "Miss Doolittle. I didn't expect you to be the one to discover my wife's body. My apologies if I upset you."

"I've been upset since finding the first body." Eliza sat across from him.

He nodded. "Ah yes, the Hungarian. I forgot you'd found that body, too."

Higgins sat down beside her. "I hope there are no more bodies after this."

"I can only be blamed for one of them," Finch said. "I was in Leeds with Mary the day Nepommuck was killed."

This close to Finch, he could see a bruise had formed on his cheek. Higgins frowned. No one dared touch him when he was brought in for questioning. And he didn't see the need for any roughhousing now, especially if the man had confessed to one of the murders. Pickering told him one of the detectives by the name of Grint had struck Eliza. If Higgins saw that man outside of the Yard, he'd give him a bruised face and maybe a broken bone or two to go along with it.

"Why did you do it, Mr. Finch?" Eliza said in a soft voice, as if they were in danger of being overheard. "Why did you kill Mary?"

"I had good reason." He looked as exhausted as he sounded. "As well you know."

"I know the Maestro had a talent for seducing ladies. He even tried on occasion with me."

Higgins stiffened. This was the first he had heard of it.

"I watched him play the romantic swain with a dozen or more of his pupils," she continued. "Sometimes, they couldn't resist. His being an aristocrat and all."

"You resisted, Miss Doolittle. Mary should have done likewise."

Jack leaned against the wall, arms folded over his chest. Higgins wondered how many times the Inspector had listened to a murderer's words.

"I'm sure Mary meant no real harm. You two were quite happy when I first met you. And she seemed to love you so."

"I loved her, too," Finch said. "How could a man not love Mary? She was the prettiest girl in west Yorkshire. Ask anyone. She was a bit of a flirt, though. That always was a worry for me, seeing as how men liked to flirt with her as well. How could they not, looking as she did. Like a little golden bird, that's how I thought of her. How fitting she took on the name of Finch. And when the money started coming in, I could finally afford to buy her the fancy things she'd always wanted. It made her even more beautiful."

Higgins hadn't thought Mary Finch a particularly attractive woman, but then he had no patience for empty-headed ladies who cared about nothing except fashion and flattery.

"Beautiful enough that Nepommuck had to have her." Finch's voice grew hard. "Oh, I knew he was a poncy fellow, with no regard for decent hardworking people like us. But he was a good teacher.

I'll give the blighter that much. He had Mary and me sounding like gentry."

"How long did you take lessons from him?" Higgins asked.

"Three months. We were almost done. That's the joke in all this. He said we only needed a few more weeks of instruction. I thought it would remain a harmless flirtation until then. I was glad when you began working for him, Miss Doolittle. I insisted that Mary finish her lessons with you. I hoped things wouldn't get out of hand. But I was wrong."

"Perhaps it did remain a flirtation."

Finch let out a harsh laugh. "I can't believe you were as blind and stupid as I was. Oh, I suspected Mary had taken a strong fancy to the bloke, but I didn't know how bad it was. I didn't know the whole truth until that garden party she dragged me to. I didn't want to go. I'd already learned how to speak proper. I didn't like being forced to show off what that bloody Hungarian taught me. Mary insisted, though."

"Yes," Eliza murmured. "She was keen to attend."

"Keen? She was desperate to see Nepommuck and tell him she was carrying his child." Finch pounded the table with his fist. "Bloody whore! That's what she was. Can't deny it now."

"How do you know it wasn't your child?" Eliza asked.

"We've been married ten years, Miss Doolittle. How many children do you think we have? None. We went to doctors, too many doctors. Seems the problem lies with me, and I won't go further than that, seeing how you're a lady."

"So you didn't know the whole truth until the garden party?" Higgins asked.

Finch ran his fingers through his hair, as if he wanted to tear it out in frustration. "She took bad at that party. You saw her, Miss Doolittle. Running through the crowd, yelling at the top of her lungs, begging for a second's notice from a man who had just announced his engagement to another woman. Bloody nightmare, what with all the swells watching us. And then the butler had to carry her off the lawn. She was so hysterical, I called a doctor."

"Is that when you learned about the child?" Eliza asked.

He nodded. "She'd been muttering about a child all the way home, but it was the doctor who confirmed it. Hell, he even congratulated me!" Finch pounded the table again. "And how do you think that felt? I'd wanted a son since I married the girl. And now I learn some nasty foreigner fathered the child I wanted for ten years." He turned to Higgins. "Do you blame me? Would any man blame me?"

Higgins only stared back at him. It would be futile to explain wounded pride was no justification for murder.

"I wonder that you waited so many days to kill her," Eliza said quietly. "Seeing how upset you were."

"I didn't know what to do. I loved the woman. Don't you understand that? God help me, I love her still. I felt gutted, destroyed. It took days just to process the truth, and the whole time she was weeping and wailing with grief, like a bleeding widow."

"Seeing how upset Mary was about Nepommuck's engagement, perhaps she was the one who . . ." Eliza's voice trailed off.

"What? You think Mary killed him?" His laughter had a horrible sound. "She would never have harmed a hair on that devil's head. Oh, she might have stuck a knife in the Marchioness, but never the Hungarian. She was talking so crazy, in fact, that I worried about her hurting Lady Gresham. When I had to go to Leeds on business, I forced her to come with me. She fought me tooth and nail. But I couldn't let her stay in London after making a spectacle of herself at the party."

"Then you were both in Leeds the day of the murder?" Higgins asked.

"We heard the news in the papers about him being stabbed, and Mary had another knockdown fit. She created such a ruckus while we were in Leeds that I gave in to her demand that we return to London. We have family and friends in Leeds, and there's only so much humiliation a fellow can tolerate."

"Indeed." If Higgins ever had a moment's doubt about the perils of matrimony, these last few minutes dispelled it.

Jack finally spoke up. "Did Nepommuck threaten either you or your wife with blackmail?"

Finch shook his head. "He'd have no cause to blackmail me. Mary perhaps, but she never admitted to it. Sure, she played fast and loose with her pin money. I never kept track of what she spent. Mary did love to shop. She squawked on and on about your wardrobe, Miss Doolittle, enough to make me sick."

Eliza knew that was true, given Mary's obsession with every fashionable article she wore from Whiteleys and Harrods. "She may have given her lover blackmail money."

"I can't say for sure. She seems to have given him everything else."

"I don't understand, Mr. Finch. You were enraged to learn your wife had been unfaithful and was carrying another man's child. But you left her unharmed for over a week. Why did you decide to kill her when you did?"

"The shock finally wore off, Miss Doolittle. I was beginning to feel something besides pain and humiliation. And she never stopped carrying on for the man, never stopped weeping and sobbing, falling to the floor, talking to his ghost in the middle of the night."

"She sounds a bit mad," Higgins said.

"I think we both went a little mad." Finch sat silent a moment.

"This morning was worse than ever. It appears today was that devil's birthday. And she was grieving as if she hadn't already cried an ocean's worth of tears. I didn't know what to do. I was near the end of my patience, and maybe my sanity. When I went to get dressed, I'd left Mary weeping on the couch. But when I came out, she was gone." His face hardened. "I knew exactly where she went."

"To Nepommuck's apartment?"

"Yes, Miss Doolittle. She'd gone to weep and worship at the altar of her lost love. I went after her, I did. And when I got there, she was on her knees, kissing his photograph like he was a bloody saint, and not some lying fat foreigner."

"How did she get into the apartment?" Eliza asked. "It must have been locked."

"He'd given her a key for their trysts. Only he never got a chance to ask for it back."

"That must have been a terrible scene between you two this morning." Eliza shuddered.

"No, no scene at all." Finch stared down at his clasped hands. "I looked at her there on the floor, crying out his name, telling him how much she loved him, would always love him, how their child would know how wonderful he was. So I walked over to her and put my hands around her neck." He paused, eyes still downcast. "And it was over."

Higgins and Eliza looked at each other. Neither of them wanted to be in this room any longer.

"She deserved to die," Finch added. "Both of them did."

Higgins waited for him to admit anything else about the Maestro's murder.

"But you didn't kill Nepommuck." Jack came to stand by the table.

"No. I wish I had, though."

"You're a rich man," Eliza said. "You could have paid any number of lowlifes to do the job for you."

Finch shook his head. "I might have, but someone else got to him first. That's why I wanted to see you, Professor Higgins."

Higgins sat back in disappointment. "Why?"

"To thank you, of course."

"Whatever for, man?"

"You've done a great thing, Professor." He grabbed Higgins's hand and shook it. "You killed Emil Nepommuck."

ELEVEN

Higgins regarded himself as an ordinary man who only wished to lead a quiet bachelor life. So why was he skulking about the city chasing after murder suspects? Women, that's why. As he feared, females brought only disorder into a scholar's peaceful existence. And Eliza Doolittle had so far brought more trouble than a police wagon filled with suffragettes. She wasn't the only woman currently complicating his life, of course, but she was at the top of his list.

If not for her traipsing off to work for Nepommuck in the first place, he would never have been dragged into this bloody circus. Now instead of researching the dialects of a Devonshire farmer, he was stumbling over corpses, being hauled off by the police, and waiting like a messenger boy outside the home of that fraudulent Greek diplomat, Dmitri Kollas.

He looked up from the newspaper he pretended to read. Directly across from where he sat was Kollas's lodgings. When Higgins read the addresses of Nepommuck's clients, he had been surprised to see that Kollas lived in such a prestigious neighborhood. What sort of income did this fellow have access to that he could afford an elegant mansion in Kensington? This was just a step or two down from the heady environs of the aristocracy in Mayfair.

Of course, if the man posed as a retired diplomat, Higgins didn't expect him to be living above a brewery in Lambeth. But it looked as though Kollas enjoyed a lifestyle that could only be termed posh. A steep ascent indeed for one secretly rumored to be a watchmaker's son from Clerkenwell.

"I'm back, guv'nor."

Higgins nodded at the boy who suddenly appeared next to the wrought iron bench he was seated on. "Where did the gentleman go, boy?"

"I followed him to Holborn. St. Giles-in-the-Fields."

"He went to a church? Whatever for?"

"Seeing how it's Sunday, sir." The twelve-year-old raised an eyebrow, and even Higgins felt the rebuke.

"Yes, of course. He went to Sunday service. Anywhere he stopped along the way?"

"Bought a griddle cake from the muffin man at Tottenham Court Road. He sells griddle cakes special on Sundays."

Higgins fished a pound note from his wallet and handed it over. The information he had just received was more helpful than anticipated. And how lovely to learn it was Sunday.

"Would you like me to wait outside the church and follow him some more?"

"No need for that." Higgins rose to his feet. "He's sure to be busy singing hymns for the better part of an hour, which is more than sufficient for my purposes."

The boy tucked the money into the lining of his cap. "If you ever need me to follow anyone else, guv, you'll find me in the same place:

making pretty pictures on the pavement in Piccadilly. Leastways on a sunny day. Otherwise, ask around for Toby Greene."

As the boy vanished into traffic, Higgins made his way to Kollas's mansion. No better time to discover the sort of man one was dealing with than taking a look about his home, especially if he was absent. Higgins had met Kollas only once at the infamous Embassy Ball. Even during their short conversation, he had been struck by the man's atrocious Greek accent. And he seemed a florid and overbearing poseur. But Higgins swore he heard a Cockney flavor in the few words Kollas spoke in his presence. For certain, he was no Greek. Then what was he?

Higgins rang the mansion doorbell. The brass doorknob and address plate looked well polished, and the porch was swept as clean as the front stoop of a Dutch housewife. The door opened and a young maidservant peeked out at him.

"Sir?"

As he suspected, only a skeleton staff remained at the house on Sunday; most of the servants would be given permission to attend church. This was easier than he hoped, with no head housekeeper or butler to persuade. Higgins gazed upon a girl no older than sixteen.

"Mr. Kollas, please."

"I'm afraid Mr. Kollas is at church, sir."

"I see. I have an appointment with him at eleven. I realize I'm a bit early, but I was hoping to find him in."

"He'll be back in time for luncheon. Cook has a roast in the oven."

Higgins handed his calling card to the girl, whom he guessed to be the under-house parlor maid. "No doubt you are aware that Mr. Kollas had engaged a gentleman to help him with his English. Sadly that individual is recently deceased. As you can see from my card, I am a language specialist as well. Mr. Kollas wished to speak with me about continuing his instruction."

The girl seemed impressed by his embossed card. "Since you have an appointment, Professor Higgins, you may wait inside." She opened the door wider.

He needed no further invitation. Within minutes Higgins was comfortably ensconced in Dmitri Kollas's front parlor.

"Can I bring you tea, Professor? Or coffee? Ambassador Kollas prefers Greek coffee."

Higgins settled back in a dark purple divan. "I will wait for Mr. Kollas to join me. Besides, I am sure you must have a great deal to do getting luncheon ready."

"Indeed yes, sir. There's only me and the scullery maid here right now and a dozen things on the stove. If you need anything, just ring, sir." She bobbed a small curtsey.

As soon as the oak door swung shut behind her, Higgins sprang to his feet. It was a small room with overlarge furniture. He had to skirt carefully around the ottomans and polished tables. There were no family photos in evidence, although a portrait of King George I of Greece hung in a prominent spot above the fireplace.

He examined the many paintings in the room. Each portrayed a scene in Greece: three were of the Acropolis alone. A pedestal near the window held a first-rate marble reproduction of a bust of Pericles. On a side table sat a brass tray with demitasse cups and several bottles of Greek wine. Nothing surprising about that. Only a fool would pretend to be a foreign diplomat and not have several objects related to their so-called mother country.

There wasn't a book to be seen, but the Sunday *Times* lay neatly folded on a cabinet by the door. Higgins sighed. He would have no further luck in here. Opening the door, he peeked out into the hallway. The aroma of roasting meat already wafted through the house. Higgins's stomach gave an involuntary growl. He remembered he had not eaten breakfast.

Stepping out farther, he heard two female voices below along with the sound of clattering pans. Through the open door across the hall, he spied what must be the library. Crossing the hallway as quietly as a house burglar, he ducked into the room and slid the pocket doors shut behind him. Due to the cloudy morning, Higgins swept the curtains open wide before turning to inspect the room. The oak writing desk was free from any clutter save an inkwell, blotter, and a neatly stacked pile of vellum stationery.

He pulled open each desk drawer, but they held little of interest. Next he turned to the bookshelves filled with leather volumes; most appeared remarkably new. Several bore Greek titles on the spines. When Higgins pulled these out, they opened as if they had never been touched. Some had pages still uncut. Just so, Higgins thought. The books were as much a false front as the portrait of the Greek king and the bust of Pericles in the parlor.

The bottom shelf held several medical journals and two thick volumes on tropical medicine. He flipped these open. All the spines were cracked, with pages repeatedly marked in the margins. Unfortunately, there were no bookplates or names scribbled on the flyleaf to identify the owner.

Kollas would be home soon and he had discovered nothing except that the fellow wasn't actually Greek. Yet who really believed that he was?

Discouraged, Higgins returned to the hallway to think over his next move. He paused by the stairs. The library and parlor might hold no clues as to Kollas's real identity, but the bedroom was where a man might feel safe enough to be careless.

Without giving himself time to change his mind, Higgins ran up the carpeted stairs two at a time. He stood for a moment in the upper hallway. Only two bedrooms on this floor, and a quick glance at the narrow dark stairway to the third floor suggested it probably led to the servants' quarters. Peeking into the nearest room, Higgins dismissed it as a rarely used guest bedroom, devoid of decoration or decor. They may as well have covered up the few pieces of furniture with a sheet.

Higgins entered the remaining bedroom filled with well-polished mahogany furniture. It was an imposing masculine room with not a hint of the frivolous about it. If Higgins liked Kollas, he may have allowed himself a moment of appreciation for the fellow's taste. But he had no time to admire the Oriental rug or the maroon bed coverings.

He headed for the largest wardrobe and flung it open. Over a dozen neatly pressed suits hung inside. He glanced at the labels. All carried the mark of Savile Row tailors, except for three suits hidden in the back. After examining them, Higgins raised an eyebrow. The labels on the three jackets claimed they had been made by "HSM, Chicago, Illinois."

Next Higgins yanked open bureau drawers, not caring if he left the contents noticeably askew. In one drawer, he pulled out a silver cigarette case buried beneath expensive ascot ties. The case was empty, and its tarnished state indicated it had not been used for some time. However, the initials inscribed on the front of the case were "TR." Inside was another inscription: "Congratulations, Dr. Richards. From your proud father."

Now he began to look in earnest, under the bed, beneath the plump pillows, even behind the potted ferns along the bay window. In a smaller bureau of drawers, Higgins discovered a book tucked away among a careless jumble of leather gloves and cashmere mufflers. The well-thumbed volume contained essays by Ralph Waldo Emerson.

Higgins fluttered the pages and came upon one whose corner had been turned down. Someone had underlined the quote: "It was a high counsel that I once heard given to a young person, 'Always do what you are afraid to do.'"

Curious, Higgins fanned the other pages and stopped when he saw a folded piece of paper. Taking it from where it had been tucked away—or hidden—he quickly read what turned out to be a newspaper article. After reading it twice, he stepped over to the window to make out the date.

"October 10, 1912," he said aloud. "And a Chicago paper, too."

"What in hell do you think you're doing?" Kollas stood glowering in the doorway.

Damnation, how could he not have kept track of the time? Sensing the man's fury, Higgins was grateful he had insisted that Eliza question the young Mr. Nottingham while he tackled the more intimidating Kollas. And although Higgins was a good four inches taller, Kollas had the physique of a boxer, and a temper he suspected easily turned violent. He'd have to proceed with care if he wanted to exit this room unbloodied.

"I asked you a question, you barmy excuse for a man!"

Higgins shuddered at the labored imitation of a Cockney accent. "Drop the dialect, sir. You obviously needed a few more lessons with Nepommuck to school you in how the people of Clerkenwell speak."

"Bollocks! I find you in the bedroom, handling me property, and you 'ave the piss to challenge me!" His expression grew more menacing when he saw the book and newspaper article in Higgins's hands. "Give me that, or you'll be wishing you were skagged on a rocky cliff."

Higgins folded the article and replaced it in the book. He tossed it at Kollas, who caught the volume.

"I apologize for the intrusion, but I may be thrown into prison for a crime I did not commit. I need to discover if anyone else had a reason to murder the Hungarian."

"You're a meddler, you are. And the sooner I call the police and tell them how you broke into my home—"

"But I've done no such thing." Higgins sat down on the bay window's cushioned seat. "Your maid let me in. You may ask her if you like."

"I already have. She told me a Professor Higgins was waiting to have a word with me. Thought you'd done a runner when you weren't downstairs." Kollas shook his head. "Instead I catch you going through my things like the Artful Dodger 'imself. Yes, the police would like to get an earful about this."

Higgins gave a careless shrug. "Don't know what they'd find so interesting about it. I needed to use the water closet. Not wanting to disturb the servants, I came upstairs in search of it. I've always been a bit too curious for my own good, so I couldn't resist a little poke about your bedroom. Rude? Certainly. But hardly criminal."

"Liar."

"That's a strange thing to hear from a man pretending to be both a Greek and an Englishman. By the way, if you insist on posing as a Greek diplomat, you should keep up to date on what is actually occurring in Greece. For example, the Greek king died in March. At some point, even the insular English will notice that you have never donned a black armband in mourning."

"You'll regret this, you arrogant blighter."

"Like Nepommuck did?"

Kollas narrowed his eyes. "Last I heard, the Yard was looking at you as the bloke who done him in."

"That may change when the police hear about your activities in America. You are American, aren't you? I should have discerned the occasional flat vowels in your speech. And I am certain Inspector Shaw will be fascinated to learn about your colorful past. Or were the Chicago papers mistaken when they claimed that you killed your father?"

After a long tense moment, Kollas closed the bedroom door. Higgins noticed with misgiving that he also locked it.

"You *are* the man mentioned in the article," Higgins went on. "Dr. Thaddeus Richards, renowned surgeon of Chicago. The journals and medical books downstairs were the first clue."

"Are you playing detective now? If so, it's a poor imitation. Although in some respects, you are like all detectives in that you lack imagination." He paused. "And compassion."

Struck by the abrupt change in Kollas's speech, Higgins raised an eyebrow. Now that the man had dropped all pretense, it was clear that Kollas was a highly educated man from the American Midwest.

"You expect compassion for doing in your own father?"

"What do you know of it?"

"I only know what I just read in that newspaper article. It stated that railroad magnate Ambrose Joseph Richards was found dead at his home of an overdose of morphine in October 1912. A dose administered by his only son, a doctor."

"That is true."

Higgins didn't know what to say to this. Had the fellow just confessed to murder? "So the papers were right, Dr. Richards?"

He flinched. "Do not call me Dr. Richards. My old name and the life that went with it are as dead to me as my father. I am Dmitri Kollas, at least for now."

"You didn't answer my question."

Kollas leaned back against the bedroom door. "Did I murder my father? No, I did not. I did, however, end his life."

"I don't understand."

"My father was a good man who deserved a more fitting end than the cancer that ravaged him for two years. He wanted only me to treat his illness, and why should he not? His son was a celebrated surgeon, a superb diagnostician, the recipient of numerous fellowships and honors. And through my work I had saved so many lives. Except I couldn't save his." Kollas grew silent for a moment. "I couldn't."

Higgins felt uncomfortable and a little ashamed. He had trespassed on something private and deeply painful.

"I had been giving my father morphine in increasingly stronger doses," Kollas said in a voice so soft, Higgins strained to hear him. "But the pain was unrelenting, I could barely stave off even an hour of it. At the end, he begged me to set him free of the agony. Jesus only suffered for three hours upon the cross, Professor. My father and so many like him suffer for months, sometimes years. As a physician—as a son!—I did what my conscience dictated. I gave my father peace. I gave him eternal rest. Some may call it murder. I call it mercy."

Neither man spoke for a time. "How did you become involved with Nepommuck?" Higgins finally asked.

"When my father died, his sister suspected I had given him a fatal dose of morphine. Aunt Hortense was his last surviving sibling, and I his only living child. A great fortune would be divided between us, but Hortense is as greedy as she is heartless. She wanted it all. So she went to the police with her suspicions. I was arrested within a week of his death."

"Was there a trial?"

"I was in the middle of the trial when I made my escape. It seemed obvious I would lose, and the sentence would have been thirty years in prison. But I needed a new identity, and time to fashion a new life." He shrugged. "Ironically, I had made enough money on my own that my father's fortune was negligible to me. And with enough money, Professor Higgins, one can buy many things. Not least of which is information."

"Someone told you about Nepommuck?"

He nodded. "I needed to lose my American accent and become someone else as fast as possible. I was put into contact with Nepommuck, who suggested that I pretend to be a retired Greek diplomat. He schooled me first in how to speak like a Greek who had a poor command of English. But the more important aspect of the charade was to teach me the speech patterns of a fellow from Clerkenwell. This way people who were dubious about my Greek identity would hear traces of Cockney dialect and think I was hiding a lower-class English past."

Higgins admired Nepommuck's capacity for deviousness. "It was a double blind. Quite brilliant. Two false identities hid the truth."

"Exactly. It gave me time to separate myself from who I was."

"And who you will become next."

Kollas hesitated before replying. "Yes."

Higgins thought a moment. "But on the morning Nepommuck was found dead, you had an encounter with Miss Doolittle. She claims you were furious about the newspaper article exposing Nepommuck, and that you had gone to confront him. Why were you angry to learn the truth?"

"That blackmailing creature was living as secret a life as I was. I can only guess how many of his other students were like me, desperate to hide their past and living under constant fear that Nepommuck would reveal our dirty secrets. He made us pay quite handsomely. All the while, he made us feel like scum. It wasn't enough to take our money, he took what was left of our pride as well."

"It must have been galling to learn of his own dark past."

"Of course it was. I only put my father out of his pain and misery. But Nepommuck was a repulsive fellow from birth. The papers claim he raped a young cousin when he was seventeen. Three years later he and his blue-blooded friends beat a fellow university student insensible. The poor man is still confined to a wheelchair. Then there was the fire he drunkenly started at a party in which at least five guests were severely burned. But no matter how vicious his actions, his father the Count always saw to it that he was never punished." Kollas paused. "Until he cheated a Hungarian prince at baccarat."

No need to explain further. They both knew that Nepommuck's downfall came when he crossed the son of a man even more powerful than his father.

"A pity he was only kept in prison two years," Higgins said.

"When I read that article about his unsavory past, I wanted to kill him. He acted as sanctimonious as Queen Victoria, claiming he dirtied his hands by giving me instruction. How I hated the hypocritical bastard."

"You said that you wanted to kill him. Did you?"

Kollas surprised him by laughing. "If I was bent on that, do you think I would go banging on his door the day he was killed, yelling his name at the top of my lungs? Indiscreet behavior for a murderer, wouldn't you say?"

"Men do reckless things when they're in a rage."

"I am not reckless, Professor. I never have been. Besides, I don't have a strong enough motive."

"Blackmail? One of the stronger motives, I'd say."

"I am not the only one the Hungarian was blackmailing."

"No doubt Scotland Yard will be interested in all the students who were being blackmailed." Higgins paused. "Even the ones who are not reckless."

A thoughtful look crossed Kollas's face. "Yes, I imagine they will be. Lucky for me I have an alibi."

"But you were at Nepommuck's apartment the morning of the murder, noticeably upset."

"Yes, I was. And while I shouted outside his apartment door, one of the law clerks on the first floor came up to tell me to stop. The solicitors sent him to discover what the racket was about. He escorted me out of the building. Since there was no corpse lying in the hallway when he came upstairs, obviously I had not just plunged a dagger into Nepommuck's back."

"Damn," Higgins said under his breath.

"Exactly." Kollas smiled. "Are we done with the interrogation?"

Embarrassed, Higgins felt fortunate that Kollas hadn't called the police. He got to his feet. "Forgive me for intruding on your privacy."

This time Kollas looked surprised. "I know what it is like to be under threat of the law. I am not unsympathetic to your plight. I hope that you are as sympathetic to mine."

"You have nothing to fear from me. I may be arrogant, but I am not malicious. Whatever happened in America had nothing to do with Nepommuck's murder. I have no reason to say a word about your past to the police." Higgins gestured toward the locked door. "However, if we remain in here any longer, the servants will begin to wonder. There are enough rumors circulating about me at the moment. I don't need another."

Kollas unlocked the door. As Higgins moved past, he said,

"You weren't wrong to want to question Nepommuck's students, Professor."

"I suspect there are many of us who have a motive for wanting him dead. The trick is finding the person without an alibi for the morning of the murder."

"Why is Scotland Yard especially interested in you?" the American asked. "As you say, there are many who wanted him dead."

"That is true."

"Do *you* have an alibi, Professor?"

A wave of fear swept over him. "No."

Higgins now understood why Kollas fled his country and took on another identity. He hoped he would not have to do the same.

TWELVE

Pickering was in a rare bad temper. "I won't hear of it, Eliza. You are not going off to interview a murder suspect unchaperoned. What can Henry be thinking to let you put yourself in such jeopardy?"

"Calm down, Colonel. It's not dangerous." Eliza stared at her image in the foyer mirror. Her hat needed another pin to keep it in place.

"Did you tell Detective Inspector Shaw that you and Henry intend to question Nepommuck's students?"

"Of course not. He has no idea I took the list with everyone's addresses on it when we were at the apartment yesterday. Jack thought we were in the building to retrieve the books from my classroom." She frowned. "Of course, I forgot all about that once we found poor Mary."

"By heaven, when you took the list from Nepommuck's desk, I assumed you had done so with your cousin's permission and knowledge."

"Hardly." She took a last poke to the hat's silk ribbons. "Jack would have my head if he knew. He thinks we're still asking people on the street if they remember seeing the Professor the day of the murder."

Pickering flushed even redder. "Yes, the first murder. And now there's been a second. Eliza, if you keep throwing yourself in the middle of all this, you may be the next dead body that is found. I thought I taught you better behavior than this."

She fought back a grin. "I didn't know there were rules of etiquette for chasing down murder suspects."

"If not, there bloody well should be. See now, you have me so upset I have quite forgotten my own manners. Eliza, please don't put yourself in danger by asking questions of someone who may be a murderer."

Eliza kissed him on his cheek. "If we do not discover who the murderer is very soon, Professor Higgins is certain to be arrested. And the Yard detectives are moving much too slow. It's up to me and the Professor to track this killer down." She pulled on her white silk gloves. "And I have nothing to fear from the young Mr. Nottingham."

"Then let me question this fellow. Along with the rest of the students on that list."

"They would never open up to you, Colonel. No more than they will to Scotland Yard. But they know me. I worked with the Maestro, and that gives me a legitimate reason to speak with them. No, the Professor and I are the best ones to handle this."

"Better than the police?" Major Redstone leaned against the open doorway to Higgins's laboratory, his arms folded.

Eliza nodded. "Police frighten people, whether they're guilty or innocent. They'll feel more relaxed talking to me. And if Professor Higgins keeps his temper in check, they might reveal themselves to him as well. Anyway, we're running out of time. Which is why the

Professor is off right now speaking with Kollas while I plan to arrange an 'accidental' meeting with Mr. Nottingham."

Redstone shot her an approving glance. "Looking even prettier than usual, which I didn't think possible."

Eliza didn't know whether to be flattered or unsettled by the older man's obvious interest. She was surprised to find that she was both. "Since Mr. Nottingham acted quite flirtatious at the garden party, I thought it wouldn't hurt to appear as appetizing as I could."

"I believe you look a bit too appetizing," Pickering said in exasperation.

She glanced at her reflection once more. The last time she appeared this elegant and alluring was at the Embassy Ball, and that was only because she'd been decked out in glittering borrowed gems and the finest Worth gown. But the results were just as gratifying today. She brushed her hair for an hour before the maidservant pinned it up in the latest fashion. A wide-brimmed hat decorated with a large apricot silk ribbon perched atop her coiffure. The ribbon matched the color of her sleek walking skirt, which clung to her figure. However, she suspected her white blouse had caught the attention of both Pickering and Redstone. While it boasted a high collar, bands of French lace running down the front were transparent enough to reveal a glimpse of her white camisole beneath.

Shocking no doubt to an older gentleman like Pickering, but according to the fashion magazines, the style was all the rage in Paris. And after all, she *was* wearing a bolero jacket over it. Although she was certain Pickering considered it a tad too snug. Yes, she believed Nottingham might be diverted enough by her appearance that he wouldn't mind her questions.

"Exactly how do you plan to arrange this so-called accidental meeting with Mr. Nottingham?" Redstone asked.

"When we spoke at Lady Gresham's garden party, he mentioned spending his Sunday mornings at Kensington Gardens. He said watching the other swells and listening to their conversation was as helpful as a lesson with the Maestro." Eliza tightened one of her pearl earrings. "Time to be off."

Pickering guarded the front door. "You must allow the Major and me to accompany you."

"He will never be candid with me if the pair of you are within earshot." She gave his arm a squeeze. "I am going to be in the middle of London surrounded by dozens of people enjoying a Sunday stroll. I shall be quite safe."

"We should trust Eliza's judgment," Redstone said.

"Very well." His face a mask of disapproval, Pickering opened the front doors.

Eliza turned to smile at Redstone. "Thank you," she mouthed silently.

He nodded. Before Pickering could lodge another protest, Eliza picked up her parasol and darted out the door.

If she circled the pond one more time, Eliza planned to start feeding the ducks. Pickering ought to see her now. Far from being in danger, she was actually bored. She had already spent over an hour wandering about the vast expanse of gardens, hoping to catch sight of Nottingham. But she hadn't spotted him near the Albert Memorial or outside Queen Caroline's Temple. And she'd marched up and down the Lancaster Walk like a drilling soldier.

Given the daunting size of Kensington Gardens, Eliza wasn't surprised she had not been successful. Prepared to call it quits and leave, she finally caught sight of Nottingham sitting near a row of trees along Budge's Walk. He was close enough to the large pond that she could watch him safely from there. But Nottingham was not alone. Two young men sat on the bench with him, engrossed in conversation.

The dapper young Nottingham looked quite the swell this morning in his cream-colored pants, beige striped jacket, and jaunty straw boater. His companions were not dressed anywhere near as fancy, although they seemed roughly the same age as Nottingham.

She kept her distance during their conversation. It wouldn't do to have Nottingham recognize her while he was otherwise engaged. He might exchange a pleasant greeting, only to return his attention to his companions. Eliza opened her silk parasol. On such an overcast day, it might cast enough shade upon her face so she could watch the trio without attracting notice. If only she could overhear a few words of their conversation.

All three men were animated. Although they didn't appear angry, their conversation seemed intense. She doubted they were discussing the latest cricket scores.

Eliza stiffened. Cor, but she once more had the feeling of being watched. She looked over her shoulder with feigned nonchalance. Whenever her instincts told her to put up her guard, she did. And right now, the sensation of being observed was strong. But who watched her? At least four dozen people were in the immediate vicinity: couples, nannies with prams, men in their Sunday best, children and their mothers crowding around a cart selling fresh strawberries. No one, however, seemed interested in her. Perhaps it was time for another stroll around the pond.

Before she had time to move, Nottingham got to his feet.

He tipped his hat to the two fellows, who remained seated. Nottingham walked down the pathway toward the large pond. Eyes down, he didn't notice her standing there. Should she perhaps bump into him? Or call a greeting from several yards away, although that seemed brash.

While she mulled over her next move, Nottingham looked up. His broad grin was reassuring.

When he reached her side, he swept off his boater and bowed. "Miss Doolittle, what a delightful surprise. Or did you perhaps remember that I enjoyed a Sunday walk in the gardens? I'd be flattered to think that."

"Actually, Mr. Nottingham, I hoped to see you today."

His eyes narrowed with a bit too much interest. For a moment, he once again looked the image of a fox; all that was missing was the long luxurious tail. His gaze traveled over her figure with blatant approval. "This seems most promising. Perhaps we can find a quiet corner and enjoy a little privacy."

"Lord, but you move faster than a horse at Epsom Downs. And I made a proper fool of myself there last year." Eliza took his arm. "There's no need to go hunting for a lover's corner. A little turn about the park will suffice, Mr. Nottingham."

"That still sounds promising, if a little mysterious. Should I worry?"

She gave a dramatic sigh while they strolled up Budge's Walk. "I don't know. It seems that everyone who knew the Maestro should be worried. After all, the police haven't caught his murderer. It must be someone we know."

"Certainly someone Nepommuck knew. Don't know about the rest of us." He cocked an eyebrow in her direction. "And if anyone should worry, it's Professor Higgins. I heard he leaked the truth about Nepommuck to the papers. The man must have had a strong reason to destroy someone else's reputation like that. I believe the police call it a motive."

"Professor Higgins did not kill the Maestro."

"How do you know?"

"I know him. He isn't the type of fellow to do such a thing."

"Anyone is capable of murder, although I admire your loyalty." Nottingham leaned too close to her, and Eliza immediately put a few inches between them.

The young man seemed amused by her sudden skittishness. "You must admit Higgins had a serious grudge against Nepommuck." He lowered his voice. "Maybe deadly serious."

"He was not the only one who disliked the Maestro."

"True enough. Cornelius Finch, for one. I told you his golden-haired wife had been indiscreet. And now the silly woman is dead. Although I never thought Cornelius had it in him for a crime of passion. He struck me as a milksop, but sometimes it's the quiet ones you have to keep your eye on. I could hardly believe it when I read about him being charged with her murder. I wonder if they have the right man."

"I discovered the dead body," Eliza said with a shudder. "Along with Cornelius Finch standing over it, announcing to us that he had done her in."

That surprised Nottingham. "For an elocution teacher, Miss Doolittle, you lead quite an eventful life. Didn't you also discover Nepommuck's body?"

She nodded. So far the conversation had only dampened her spirits.

"Why are you concerned about the fate of Professor Higgins? If Finch killed his wife for being unfaithful, it seems likely he also killed her lover."

"He was at his factory in Leeds on the morning of the murder, as well as the night before." She sighed. "Finch has witnesses to vouch for his presence. Many of them."

"I see. Now I wonder why you came to the park today to find me," he said. "Do you believe I have information that will lead to the killer? Or do you think I have my own reasons for wanting the Hungarian dead?"

"I don't know. Do you?"

Nottingham laughed. "You may dress like a Mayfair miss, but you still have the brashness of a Cockney flower seller."

"You didn't answer my question."

"I have no more information than you do. Blimey, girl, it could be any of three dozen people. From what I could see, the bounder had seduced most of his lady students under fifty. Some of their husbands might be upset."

"But aside from his womanizing, who else would want him dead? Professor Higgins said Nepommuck boasted at the Embassy Ball that he made his students pay, and for more than elocution lessons."

"You believe he was a blackmailer?"

"Yes, I do."

He shrugged. "Makes sense to me. All of us are trying to become something we're not. I suppose Nepommuck was the keeper of an alarming number of secrets."

"What secret of yours was he hiding?" Eliza asked.

"I told you at the garden party why I took lessons," Nottingham said. "Don't let me fancy dress and pretty vowels fool you, girl. I'm a rough lad from Liverpool. If I'd stayed there, I'd be a drunk by the time I was thirty. No money in me pockets and a face punched in from dockside brawls. But I'm not so ashamed of my Liverpool past to pay a blackmailer."

"You did want to distance yourself from it, though. Enough that you came to London and paid the Maestro for lessons on speaking proper English."

"Isn't that why everyone takes elocution lessons? I went to Nepommuck to learn how to sound like a gent, instead of a Scouser. What's suspicious about that? After all, you did the same thing last year. Did you have a sinister reason for wanting to speak like a lady? I doubt it."

Eliza thought he was a clever fellow indeed. "I remember you said you wanted to work in a bank."

"And so I do. In fact, I got hired as a bank clerk in the City. Starting tomorrow, I'll be off in my clean-pressed clothes and fancy cane and hat to help oversee the wealth of the Empire."

"Congratulations," Eliza said, and meant it. "Although you don't seem the bank clerk type."

"Oh, I don't plan to remain a little clerk scribbling away. I aim to attract the notice of the influential gents who bring their money to the bank. After that, I shall very likely catch the eye—and the heart— of a wealthy man's daughter. It's a short step from there to becoming his son-in-law. Sometimes a good accent, fine clothes, and a handsome face are worth more than an Oxford degree, Miss Doolittle."

"Until today I thought Professor Higgins was the most arrogant man in London. It seems I was wrong."

Before he could reply, she realized they were approaching the same two men Nottingham spoke with earlier. They had remained on the park bench and now gave a friendly nod to Nottingham. He didn't respond. They didn't notice, since their brazen attention was focused on Eliza. She felt as if she was strolling through the park in nothing more than her corset.

Matching their boldness with her own, she stared back at them. The ruddier bloke had the cheek to wink at her.

"Morning to you, miss," he said. "But I think you could do a sight better than him."

Startled, she noticed his broken nose and glass left eye.

Both fellows laughed. Nottingham shot them a dark look and hurried her away. Eliza heard one of the men say to the other under his breath, "I don't Adam and Eve our Jimmy sometimes. He's got too much flash for a tea leaf."

As their laughter faded behind them, Eliza did her best to keep up with Nottingham. They were nearly halfway to the Speke Monument before she convinced him to slow down.

"Enough, Mr. Nottingham. We're not competing in a race through the park. You'll have us jumping steeples next." She stood still and panted for breath.

"Sorry, but I didn't want to subject you to those rude men any longer."

"I didn't find your friends so offensive that we had to run away."

Nottingham looked surprised. "Those men are not my friends. In fact, I've never seen those blokes before."

"Please, Mr. Nottingham. Or should I call you Jimmy as they just did?"

He paled. "What are you talking about?"

"When I arrived at the park, you were already deep in conversation with them."

"All right, all right. They're a couple of mates from Liverpool. Came to the city they did, and wanted advice on where to find some honest work."

"Try again. The man who spoke to me did not have a Scouser accent. He's a Cockney from Wapping."

Nottingham swore under his breath. "I keep forgetting you're a teacher of dialects."

"I didn't have to be a teacher to peg him for an East Ender. Being an East Ender myself, I knew exactly what he said."

The young man looked uneasy. "What do you mean?"

She snapped her parasol shut. "Your friend said, 'I don't Adam and Eve our Jimmy sometimes. He's got too much flash for a tea leaf.'"

He looked about, as if worried someone might be eavesdropping. "So?"

"Translated into proper English, he said, 'I don't believe our Jimmy sometimes. He's acting much too flashy for a thief.'"

"That bloody eejit. He never knows when to keep his head down and his mouth shut." He took a deep breath. "Look, back in Liverpool, I was a bit light-fingered. But I never pulled off a job that landed me in jail. And I was a boy. Don't think what I did at fifteen should be held against me now. I haven't pinched anything for years."

"Really? Then why are you meeting with Hyde and Rathbone, two of the most clever and accomplished thieves in London?"

His expression grew even more alarmed. Nottingham led her to a park bench partially hidden by rhododendron bushes in full flower. Neither spoke until they were seated.

"Okay, Miss Doolittle, I know two men who are thieves. Can't arrest me for that. But maybe I should be suspicious of you, seeing as how you happen to know who they are."

"Don't turn this around on me. I told you I was raised in the East End. Not only do I know Cockney-speak, I know most everyone who lives within the sound of St. Mary's Bells. And that includes the fellow with the broken nose and glass eye. His name is Bill Rathbone and he grew up around the corner from me." Eliza shook her head in disgust. "He's been a 'tea leaf' since he was eight years old and nicked my corn husk doll. He hasn't stopped stealing since—except for a stay in Walton Prison in Liverpool, where no doubt you first met him. So you may want to change your story about never being arrested."

"Bloody hell." Nottingham sat back, clearly shocked. "Then why didn't he say anything to you, seeing as how you grew up in the same neighborhood?"

"Billy boy looks as he always has, in need of a wash, a shave, and a few pints of stout. Last time he saw me, I looked as scruffy and unkempt as he does now. I don't wonder he didn't recognize me." She paused before adding proudly, "I've changed. He hasn't."

Leaning forward, Nottingham clasped his hands over his knees. "You want the truth, Miss Doolittle? I'll give it to you. I am a thief, one of the best in the south of England. I grew up on the Liverpool docks and had a hand in nabbing something off every ship that came in." The young man's voice grew hard. "Should have stayed on the docks, but I fell in with some mates who wanted to break into houses. Regular burglars we were, sneaking about like shadows. Right fun, too, unless someone woke up and discovered us. One of those times was enough to send me to Walton for a few years."

"Where you met Bill Rathbone?"

He nodded. "We became mates. Bill got out first and told me to look him up if I ever came to London. Stealing from Liverpool judges and ship owners was too dicey. Since Bill had all sorts of connections in London, I decided to come to the city and work on one big score."

"But why were you taking lessons from Nepommuck if you planned to remain a thief?" Eliza gasped when she realized the truth. "You wanted to get a job at a bank so you could steal from it."

"Yes."

"That's why Nepommuck was blackmailing you."

"He wasn't blackmailing me." Nottingham looked smug.

"I don't understand. You would be a perfect person to blackmail."

"Not really. Nepommuck wasn't stupid. It's one thing to blackmail cheating wives, quite another to threaten men like Bill or me. We know too many dangerous people."

Eliza grew uneasy. Pickering was right. It was reckless to confront murder suspects on her own. She knew how unsavory the criminal element could be. And yet here she was sitting beside a man who realized she knew his secret plan to rob the Bank of England. Cor, would she ever learn?

As if reading her thoughts, Nottingham gave her a sly grin. "Don't worry, Miss Doolittle. I'm a thief, not a murderer. I'm a good thief, too. Problem is I have a hard time keeping the money I steal. I like to buy things—for myself, for my mates, for my lady friends. I'm like a modern Robin Hood. That's why I gave myself the name 'Nottingham.' But I never had to kill anyone to get what I want. And I certainly wouldn't start with you or even a fellow like Emil Nepommuck."

"Did he know about your past?"

"Oh, the devil take my past. All he cared about was my future. I needed him to teach me how to speak like an educated man, one who could toady his way up to a bank manager's desk. I only sought a position at the bank to have access to their vaults. Once I learn how the bank is run, I can go in there one night and make off with a fortune to last even me for a few years." He paused. "With a little help from Bill and his friends."

"And Nepommuck knew this?"

"Of course he did. I didn't even pay for my lessons. But I had to agree to hand over a portion of the bank haul once I'd pulled off the robbery." Nottingham shrugged. "It seemed a fair deal for both of us. I've spent my life splitting the spoils with fellow thieves, fences, or crooked police. Don't know why you think I would suddenly go off my head now, and take to killing a man for his fair share."

Nottingham could be lying to her, yet the whole story seemed strangely plausible. He was cocky and young enough to think he could pull off such a robbery. Who knows? Perhaps he could. Whatever the truth, her instincts told her she wasn't sitting next to a murderer. Which was good news for her and Nottingham, but bad news for Higgins.

"Who do you think murdered Nepommuck?" she finally asked.

"I don't know. Probably the most unlikely suspect." He turned to her. "And what will you do with this information, Miss Doolittle? Run off to the police?"

"If I was that foolish, I would never have survived twenty years in London's East End."

He frowned. "I believe you, but I don't know about Bill. Despite how fancy you look now, it may occur to him later on that you are actually Lizzie Doolittle, the girl who knows far too much about him. About both of us, in fact."

A nervous shiver ran through her. "Is this a threat?"

"A warning."

Again, she had that feeling of being watched. Eliza rose to her feet and scanned the area about her.

"What's wrong?" Nottingham jumped up to stand beside her.

"Someone is watching us."

"Bollocks," he muttered. "It better not be the bloody police."

"I don't know who it is."

"Let's get out of here then." Nottingham grasped her elbow so tight, she winced. "Together. Right now, I don't trust you out of my sight."

Before Eliza could react, a familiar voice rang out. "Miss Doolittle, how charming to come upon you like this."

Eliza and Nottingham turned to see Major Redstone emerge from around the corner. Pulling free from the young man's tight grip, she hurried to meet Redstone.

"Major, I am so glad to see you."

He reached out for her hand and held it. "Are you all right, Eliza?" he said in a voice so low only she could hear.

She nodded. "I am now."

"Perhaps you would like to join me for a cup of tea?" He drew her closer. Eliza felt like she had taken shelter under a strong tree.

"I would join you for a bowl of cold porridge," she whispered back, "as long as it doesn't include Mr. Nottingham."

Redstone looked over to confront the younger man, but Nottingham had vanished.

THIRTEEN

The day went from bad to worse. Hadn't it been frustrating enough that Higgins was forced to strike Kollas off the list of murder suspects? Yesterday he and Eliza had spoken with five of Nepommuck's students; all of them either had alibis for the time of the murder, or were physically incapable of committing such a crime. Now he had to place Kollas among them.

There were only a few of Nepommuck's current pupils left to question. And all of them were ladies. Who among them had the motive and the ability to kill a man in such a manner?

The minute he learned Kollas's story, the first person Higgins wanted to tell was Eliza. The two of them arranged to meet at one o'clock at the Princess Louise pub. They planned to compare notes on their respective encounters with Kollas and Nottingham. But the last thing he expected was to see Eliza arrive at the pub clinging to the arm of Major Redstone.

How had that poetry-spouting chap become so involved in this investigation? Wasn't he supposed to be translating Sanskrit folderol with Pickering? Honestly, the man traveled halfway across the world for a chance to elevate his status as a Sanskrit expert, and instead wasted time following a flower seller about.

Of course, Eliza didn't look like a Cockney flower girl today. Higgins had never seen her so elegant and refined, not even at the Embassy Ball where they tricked her out like a prize pony in feathers, diamonds, and silks. Sitting across from him at the table, in her pale apricot skirt and jacket, she appeared as much a lady as his own mother. And there was no higher compliment he could extend to any woman but that she compared favorably to Lady Grace Honoria Winslow Higgins. What a metamorphosis for the little guttersnipe he'd found screeching outside St. Paul's last summer.

Eliza raised a dainty hand in the barmaid's direction and pointed at her empty glass.

Higgins smiled. He was happy to see traces of the Cockney cabbage leaf remained. Apparently she worked up quite an appetite parading about Kensington Gardens. She spent the better part of the past hour tucking into her shepherd's pie and sipping Guinness. His own appetite vanished when he was forced to sit through lunch with Redstone as well.

"You should inform the police that Kollas is wanted for murder in America," Redstone said for the third time.

"What happened in Chicago has nothing to do with Nepommuck."

"How do you know? My word, a fellow gives his father a fatal dose of morphine and you think Scotland Yard should remain ignorant." Redstone seemed more puzzled than exasperated. "At least let the police decide for themselves if this information is pertinent."

Eliza swallowed another piece of pie. "The Professor gave Kollas his word he wouldn't tell. And I agree with him. It has nothing to do with the Maestro's murder."

"Except the Hungarian knew a damaging secret about a wealthy and desperate man." Redstone shook his head. "Kollas—or Dr. Richards, as he more rightly should be called—had an excellent reason to want Nepommuck dead. He also confessed to killing his own father. I don't understand what either of you think qualifies as a likely suspect."

Higgins regretted telling both of them the details of his conversation with Kollas. He should have waited until he could speak with Eliza alone. "As I explained, the man has an alibi for Nepommuck's murder. I wish he didn't, but the fact is he does. Running off to the police like an informer will not change his innocence. Nor will it prove mine."

"True." Eliza sipped her Irish beer.

Redstone sighed. "But dear Eliza, the man is leading a fraudulent life. How do you know if Kollas is being honest about anything, including his alibi?"

" 'To be honest, as this world goes, is to be one man picked out of ten thousand.' "

He smiled at her with obvious pride. *"Hamlet?"*

"Act 2, scene 2. It's a marvelous play. I read it all in one night. Thank you so much for giving it to me, Aubrey."

Higgins rolled his eyes. Bloody hell, what a cozy pair they seemed. And when did she start calling him "Aubrey"? The man was old enough to be her father. As for Redstone, he hung on her every word. The glances he cast her way showed the man found her attractive. More than that: desirable. As if Freddy wasn't bad enough, now he would have to deal with a middle-aged Lothario in his midst. And with Eliza living at Wimpole Street, Higgins wondered if he should toss the Major out of his house. Maybe Pick could convince him to move his lodgings elsewhere, preferably back to India.

Redstone returned to his plate of kedgeree. "I shall say nothing of Kollas's past history, if that's what you both wish."

"I should hope not," Higgins said. "Especially since none of this concerns you."

"Professor." Eliza shot him a warning look.

"But it does concern me. First, you are a close colleague of Colonel Pickering and he would be crushed to see you unjustly convicted of murder. Second, you are a renowned language scholar whom I have long admired, and I would regret the loss of your future work. Last, but perhaps most important, Eliza regards you as a friend and mentor. She would be heartbroken to see you in prison."

Her mouth full, Eliza could only nod.

Higgins tapped his spoon against his dish of half-eaten cod cakes. "We've been so busy speaking about Kollas and Eliza's conversation with Nottingham that I never learned how you came to be in Kensington Gardens today. Was this something the two of you planned?"

"Oh no, it was a complete surprise when he turned the corner. And glad I was to see him. Nottingham was getting too nervous and wanted to hightail it out of the gardens—and me with him. He got scared at seeing Aubrey and slipped out of the park like the dodger he once was." Eliza frowned. "Still is, I suppose."

"Then we can keep James Nottingham on our list of suspects?"

Higgins bristled at Redstone's use of the word "our." "Of course he is still a suspect. Even if the young upstart manages to come up with an alibi, no doubt it would include one of his criminal cronies. And the police would dismiss them out of hand."

"We must think carefully about what we tell my cousin." Eliza's expression turned somber. "He will bring Nottingham in for questioning. Knowing Jack, he'll discover his criminal record. But I don't think we should reveal his plan to rob the bank."

"Why not?" Higgins said. "Better now, rather than after they've done it."

"No. I saw Bill Rathbone and Charlie Hyde with him at the park. They're all in on the plan. And such a big job would take more than three men to have any success, so there must be others we don't know about. If we blow the whistle, the police will arrest the three of them. But you and I will be targeted by the rest of their gang. No one will be able to protect us, Professor, least of all the police."

"She's right," Redstone said.

This was all getting too murky. Higgins could scarcely believe that only last month, he had been enjoying the sun and sonorous dialects of Spain. Now he was being hauled in and out of Scotland Yard, learning unhappy secrets about men he barely knew, and worrying that he had dragged Eliza into what had become a deadly situation.

"I should never have allowed you to become involved in this, Eliza," Higgins said. "It's far too dangerous."

"Now you sound like the Colonel. I'm not some nervous little girl in pantaloons. When I was nine years old, I saw two men beat each other bloody on Cordelia Street. It ended when one of them bashed the other's head in with a brick."

"He killed him?" Redstone sounded shocked.

"Don't know how else you could bash someone's head in without sending him to the undertaker. And I've been witness to much worse, believe me." Eliza sighed. "Sometimes I think the folks in Whitechapel have seen more bloodshed than the soldiers who fought the Boers."

Higgins turned back to Redstone. "You never answered my question. How did you happen to be at Kensington Gardens today? It seems a remarkable coincidence."

"As I told Eliza on the way here, it wasn't only Pickering who was concerned about her meeting Nottingham alone. Even if she were with him in a public place, lots of treacherous things are done in public places. I decided to follow her, discreetly of course, and make certain she remained safe."

"Rather sweet, don't you think?" Eliza smiled at Redstone. "Although I would have been angry at him if I'd known of his plan this morning."

Higgins smirked. "And now you couldn't be more grateful for your Galahad."

"I don't know who Galahad is, but I'm sure you're being sarcastic." Eliza drank down the last of her beer. "And I don't see why. Aubrey didn't upset my conversation with Nottingham, and he got me out of there when I needed an excuse to get away." She stood, and both men rose to their feet. "If you gentlemen will excuse me for a moment."

As Eliza left the glass-paneled room, Higgins noticed that more than one man at the surrounding tables stared at her departing figure. He'd have to speak with Pickering about buying the girl less alluring dresses. Her lace blouse verged on scandalous. In another year, she'd be flouncing about London looking like a dancer from the Moulin Rouge. When did this little cabbage become so damnably pretty?

"I'm glad that you and Pickering are as concerned for her welfare as I am," Redstone said as they sat down once more. "Between the three of us and her detective cousin, we should be able to keep her safe from harm."

"She's too young for you."

"I beg your pardon?"

"You heard me," Higgins said. "Your interest in her is neither scholarly nor avuncular. So I am telling you once and for all that you are far too old to harbor fancies about Miss Doolittle."

Redstone sat back. "I do not harbor fancies about the young lady. I find her charming, of course. Who wouldn't? And I admire that she has worked so hard and so successfully to better her station in life. If you ask me, Professor, you take far too much credit for her transformation, while giving her scarcely any credit at all."

"I didn't ask you. And I know better than anyone how hard Eliza has worked."

"I wonder. You seem at times like Pygmalion with his Galatea." Redstone picked up his glass of port. "If I recall the myth correctly, Pygmalion fell in love with his creation. I suspect that you have as well."

"What a cheeky fellow. The more I know you, the less like a scholar you seem."

"There are all sorts of scholars, not all of them confirmed bachelors who only view women as a nuisance." Redstone gave him a pitying look. "Even the Colonel has had a romance or two in his life, not that I imagine he has ever confided such things to you."

Higgins snorted. "True enough. Pick and I don't sit around mooning about romantic love like girls who have just danced their first quadrille at a ball. You must spend an inordinate amount of time mooning about it, what with all that poetry you're forever reading and translating."

"I make no apologies for devoting my life to translating poetry. Some of the greatest minds have written poems, many of them paeans to love. A shame you don't understand any of it, aside from meter."

"It probably impresses the ladies. How many young women have you declaimed verses to, I wonder. Of course since you are a bachelor as I am, it appears that either you are not serious about your romantic sentiments, or the ladies found you lacking."

"I have had my moments." Redstone threw back what was left of his port, then set his glass down hard on the table.

"I don't care what you have had," Higgins said quickly when he caught sight of Eliza's return. "As long as you do not plan on having any moments with Miss Doolittle."

Eliza rejoined them. "It seems the skies have opened up, so we'll have to hire a cab to return home." She hiccupped. "Excuse me."

"Are you and the Professor questioning any more of Nepommuck's pupils today?" Redstone asked.

"Not until tomorrow. We're going to the theater to talk with Miss Page. She's in dress rehearsal for *Hamlet*." Eliza adjusted her hat. "I can't wait to see what her dressing room looks like, and how many costumes she'll be wearing. I hope some of them have feathers."

"And she may have information about who else Nepommuck was blackmailing," Higgins added. "A minor concern compared to the costumes."

"Allow me to pay for lunch." Redstone placed several pound notes on the table.

Eliza clasped her hands. "Oh, thank you, Aubrey."

Higgins fought hard not to laugh. It seemed the Cockney temptress was tipsy.

"You were sweet to watch over me at the park," she went on. "Now I want to do something nice for you. Let's say we stop by my classroom in Belgrave Square and I'll get those poetry books."

"You can't be serious, Eliza." Higgins grabbed her elbow as she swayed on her feet. "You went white as a ghost walking down the hallway to his apartment yesterday. Not that I blame you. But it's much too soon for you to go back. I'm afraid you'll faint."

She gave him a shove. "Garn, I never fainted in my life. And unless there's another dead body lying up there right now, I'm going to march into my classroom and take what belongs to me." Eliza grinned. "Besides, I drank three glasses of Guinness to give me courage. Now let's get going. I want me books!"

Higgins feared the girl might indeed faint away, but from drunkenness.

"Inspector Shaw told us yesterday that both apartments were now off-limits," Redstone said.

She waved a dismissive hand. "I'll tell the policemen on guard that Jack gave us permission to retrieve my belongings. He won't mind."

"Yes, he will," Higgins warned.

Eliza shoved him again. "I don't care if he minds or not. Those ain't his books. And if the coppers try and stop me, I'll brain them with my parasol, like I did that nasty red-haired detective. What's so funny?"

"You," Higgins said, laughing. Eliza rarely drank more than a small glass of claret. Downing three pints of Irish stout in one hour had been foolish. Had she drunk a fourth, she'd be dancing on the table right now.

Redstone turned to Higgins with an equally amused expression. "If we don't accompany her, she'll end up going there alone, and when we least expect it, too."

Eliza hiccupped again. "Right then, gents. We're off."

The two men started after her, but not before Higgins muttered to Redstone, "Remember, you're too old for her."

Redstone raised his eyebrow. "So are you."

———

By the time they reached the door to her classroom, Eliza was having a hard time putting one foot in front of the other. Drinking three pints of Guinness was a mistake. Two would have given her courage; the third seemed likely to make her lose her shepherd's pie. Outside the weather had turned stormy. An occasional roll of thunder rumbled overhead—just like the morning she found a stranger lurking in the dark hallway. The whole building now seemed cursed. She hoped to retrieve all her personal belongings because she never wanted to visit this place again.

"I thought there would be a policeman standing guard," Redstone said.

Although signs warning off trespassers were posted on both Nepommuck's door and the room where Eliza gave lessons, the hallway was empty and silent. Eliza pressed an ear to her classroom door, but heard nothing.

She hiccupped. "I don't think anyone's inside."

"Knowing Scotland Yard, they're probably having a pint at a corner pub," Higgins said. "And no, Eliza, you are not joining them."

Trying to stand upright, she gave him her haughtiest look. "Are you implying that I drank too much Guinness?"

"Yes," Higgins and Redstone said at the same time.

"I wish you'd let us take you back to Wimpole Street, Eliza," Redstone added. "You should lie down for a bit. Maybe have a strong cup of tea. We can come back here when the police have finished their business."

She patted him on the shoulder. "Nonsense, I'm fit as a fiddler. And I've come to get those books for you."

Still, Eliza hesitated to unlock the door. When she did this yesterday across the hall, she'd found a dead woman lying on the floor. Taking a deep breath, she opened the door and stepped inside. The curtains were pulled open, but due to the cloud-tossed skies, the room remained dark. She switched on the electric lights.

"Bloody hell!"

The entire room was in complete disarray. Drawers yanked out of cupboards, papers strewn over the floor, her teaching tools scattered about like debris left after a violent windstorm. The three of them stepped carefully to avoid further damage to her overturned books, tuning forks, and broken phonograph records. She whirled about, taking in the havoc.

"I wouldn't be surprised if those blooming detectives Grint and Hollaway did this. They don't like me a bit, especially after learning that Jack was me cousin."

"Eliza," Higgins said softly.

"I mean, *my* cousin." She stopped as a wave of dizziness swept over her.

"I doubt that Grint and Hollaway would risk angering your cousin further, especially where you're concerned," Redstone said.

"He's right. This is probably normal search procedure for the police." Higgins couldn't help being sardonic.

"I'm going to talk to Jack about this right away." Eliza hiccupped yet again. "How dare the police turn my classroom into a barmy wreck!"

She knelt down to examine pieces of her teacups scattered about the floor. The small table the tea set sat on had also been knocked over. Muttering under her breath, she took note of what was broken and what had been flung about without care. It would take hours to tidy up, and it had best be the police who straightened up her room.

"Where are your books, Eliza?" Redstone helped her to stand. "We can collect the whole lot of them and take them back to Wimpole Street."

Higgins picked up the stray tuning forks. "I shall collect all your teaching implements and pack them. I have no intention of leaving behind perfectly good phonetics tools for the police to commit further mayhem with."

Eliza stepped over to the bookshelves along the far wall. All the books had been thrown to the floor, and she had no choice but to start piling them on the nearby sofa, which—mercifully—remained upright and clear of debris.

"If this is how they search for evidence, I'm not surprised they haven't caught the Maestro's killer yet." Eliza frowned when she reached the last book. "Those blasted Scousers."

Higgins looked over at her. "What now?"

"*The White Rose* isn't here."

Redstone knelt beside Eliza. He scanned the titles of the books stacked on the sofa. "Are you certain? Let's look through all of them again."

But none of them proved to be the volume by the anonymous poet that she'd planned to give him.

"How dare the police steal that book," Eliza said. "It had nothing to do with either of the murders."

Redstone didn't look happy. "This doesn't make sense. Why would the police care about a book by an unknown poet? Unless it was a rare book. Did it look antique?"

Standing with arms akimbo, she scanned the mess in her classroom. The sight of the wrecked room had sobered her up. "How would I know what an antique book looked like?"

"Maybe the police are poetry lovers like the Major," Higgins said from across the room. "They came upon the poems while searching for evidence and ran off to swoon."

Redstone looked at him with irritation.

"I'll have the coppers swooning the minute I find out who did this," Eliza said. "And if they have taken anything else of mine, I swear I will——"

"What do you people think you're doing in here?" Two uniformed policemen stood in the doorway dripping rainwater on the carpet.

"No one's supposed to be in here by order of the police," the taller one said. "Didn't you read the sign? You better have a good explanation as to why you ignored it."

"I'd like an explanation, too. I am Miss Doolittle and this is my classroom. The wreckage behind me is what is left of my teaching tools."

"I advise you to adopt a more respectful tone when speaking to us, miss."

"And I advise you to answer my question, or else my cousin Detective Inspector Shaw will be the next person to listen to my complaints."

The shorter policeman gestured at the chaotic state of the room. "I'm sure the Inspector will have a complaint of his own when he learns about this. Why the devil have you and your friends ripped this room apart?"

"What!" Higgins said.

"We found it this way," Eliza said. "Blame the police for this sorry mess."

Both men looked at each other. "The police haven't been in here since the day of Mr. Nepommuck's murder."

"You can't be serious," Redstone said.

"I am Detective Newell and this is Detective MacDonald. I assure you that we take our work seriously. Let me inform you again that no one from the Yard has been here since Thursday last. The room was left in order with every item in place. I can vouch for it since I was here."

"But Jack told me the rooms would be searched yet again by the police."

"He was correct, Miss Doolittle. We are the police assigned to search the room." He paused. "And we have only just arrived."

Eliza grew cold with fear. "That means another person has been here since then. And looking for something important."

Redstone touched her arm. "Are you all right, Eliza?"

"No. Not really."

She once again felt unsteady on her feet. If the police hadn't ransacked her classroom, it could be only one other person.

The killer.

FOURTEEN

Eliza vowed never to touch a drop of Irish ale again. When she'd discovered her ransacked classroom yesterday, she had to undergo yet another round of questioning at Scotland Yard—made worse by a queasy stomach and only the dimmest recollection of what she actually told Jack. Today her stomach had mercifully settled, but she woke with a terrible headache. Blimey, she had a hangover. Wouldn't her dad crow to see her now? Gin was mother's milk to Alfred Doolittle, and he'd always teased her for being a teetotaler. Eliza rubbed her throbbing temples. Lord, how did half the population of the East End throw back pints all blooming day without collapsing in the street?

Sipping her tea, Eliza was grateful the Colonel and Redstone had left early for the club. With them gone and Higgins buried behind his newspaper, she was spared having to make conversation. The only thing less desirable at this moment was breakfast. She stared down at the platters of poached eggs, kippers, and raspberry buckle that Mrs. Pearce had laid out for her. But she couldn't even bring herself to nibble the toast.

When the busy housekeeper called her out to the telephone in the front hallway, Eliza welcomed the chance to leave the table.

"Alfred Doolittle wishes to speak with you." Mrs. Pearce handed her the candlestick base and receiver.

"My dad?" Eliza hadn't heard from him since his wedding day in February.

Mrs. Pearce seemed as surprised as Eliza.

"Hello?" Eliza said.

"Liza? Izzat you?"

Wincing at his bellowing voice, she moved the receiver several inches away from her ear. "Yes, Dad. What—"

"I need to see you straightaway, girl. No excuses."

"Why? Is something wrong?"

"Since when does a loving father need a reason to see his daughter? I'm your dad and I want you to come see the family."

"The family?"

"Me and your stepmother, who else?"

Eliza bit back a groan. There weren't many women she disliked more than her stepmother. Rose Cleary was the sixth in a long line of "stepmothers" and by far the worst. This one was likely to be around for a while, too; she was the only "stepmother" that Alfred Doolittle actually married.

"I can't visit today. Professor Higgins and I have an appointment later this afternoon."

"I don't give a blooming fig if you're expected at Buck'nhem Palace. Besides, it's only nine o'clock. You got time to come see your family. Or are you thinking you're too good for the likes of us?" His voice grew louder with each word, and her head threatened to explode.

"Dad, you don't understand. The Professor and I are helping the police with the investigation into my employer's murder."

"That's one of the reasons I wants to see you. I been reading about this murder business in the paper and I need to talk to you. Now get your skinny arse over here. And don't be bringing that Professor fellow, either."

Eliza sighed. "All right, I'll come round this morning. But it may take me some time to get to Wapping."

"Nah, we've moved up in the world. We ain't in Wapping no more."

She memorized the directions he gave and the address. Wasn't that in Pimlico? What were they doing there? After her father nattered on for a good five minutes about how easy this newfangled telephone was to use, compared with the old days of finding a boy to send a message and pay him a halfpenny, Eliza finally rung off in relief.

As soon as she hung up, Eliza had second thoughts about the visit. She didn't relish seeing Rose Cleary. Her father claimed respectability had transformed Rose from a bullying harridan to a meek housewife. Unicorns trotting down Oxford Street would be easier to believe.

An hour later, Eliza emerged from the tube station in Pimlico. The day threatened rain again, and she set off along Belgrave Road through a fine mist. She glanced around at the white stucco terraces lining the road. Her father had moved up in the world, all thanks to Professor Higgins. On the day Eliza visited 27A Wimpole Street to ask for speech lessons, Alfred Doolittle came banging on the door soon after to shake Higgins down for a few quid. Not only did he get his five-pound note, the Professor had been so amused by the dustman's gift of gab that he mentioned him to an American millionaire.

Although Higgins did this as a joke, the wealthy Ezra D. Wannafeller thought an articulate Cockney dustman sounded like the perfect person to work for the Wannafeller Reform Moral Societies. And when Mr. Wannafeller died, he left Alfred Doolittle an annuity of three thousand pounds if he would lecture for his Moral Reform League six times a year. Now her father was a respectable gentleman with the money—if not the manners—to prove it.

Finally spotting the correct address, she crossed the street. "Would you look at that?" she said aloud. "Flowers in the window and polished railings on the stoop."

Eliza couldn't help admiring the pristine house with its narrow portico and colorful mass of pansies planted in window boxes. This house had cost her father a pretty penny. She lifted the heavy brass knocker shaped like a horse's head and rapped three times.

A parlor maid in black with a crisp white apron and cap opened the door. "Yes, miss?"

"I'm here to see Mr. Doolittle. I'm his daughter."

The maid led her through a hallway covered in gold-and-white striped wallpaper and into the large parlor. The familiar smell of boiled cabbage and corned beef wafted through the house. Even with a windfall of three thousand a year, her father had apparently not developed a taste for mint jelly and capon.

The parlor also reassured her that newfound wealth hadn't resulted in either her father or her stepmother acquiring good taste. The crowded room was crammed full of tapestries, paintings of horses, potted ferns, and plush velvet furniture. Whatnot shelves stood in every corner filled with ceramic vases and souvenirs. And framed family photographs were scattered on every possible surface. While Eliza didn't recognize any of the people in the photos, she did notice a distinct resemblance to Rose Cleary. She frowned when she caught sight of the framed marriage certificate propped against a carved statue of an Indian elephant.

From upstairs came the sound of a slammed door and shrill voices. More noises and footsteps rippled above the parlor. She swore she heard a baby's muffled wail. Had the entire Cleary family emigrated from Ireland and taken up residence here in Pimlico?

Eliza leaned out of the doorway and peeked up the carpeted stairs. Two small heads stared back at her between the topmost banister's spindles and then vanished. A moment later her father appeared at the top of the stairs. Despite his age, he had more energy than an Eton boy and nearly galloped down the steps. Of course, he hadn't bothered to get dressed. Instead he sported a tattered plaid robe over his trousers. He hadn't shaved yet, either, and his eyes looked bleary. Even three thousand a year couldn't change some things.

"Well, well, my girl, high time you got here." He charged past her into the parlor.

"You never mentioned moving out of Wapping the last time I saw you," Eliza said as he sat back in a large velvet wingback chair.

"Ah, your stepmother rooked me into buying this place. Ain't it a beaut, though? We're movin' up in the world, that we are."

She didn't have the heart to tell him this area of Pimlico was on its way downward in terms of the fashionable neighborhoods. Still, it was a damn sight better than the rundown streets of Wapping.

"Why is there a photograph on the mantel of a horse and jockey?"

"Noticed that, did you? That's the sire of the horse I bought," he said, puffed with pride. "All his offspring have been winners, and so will the Donegal Dancer. Thought the name was a bit of luck, too, since your mum was from Donegal. That little colt is sure to beat the rest of the field at Ascot. Wait and see if I'm right."

Eliza rolled her eyes. First a house and now a racehorse! Oh well, it wasn't any skin off her nose. Let him waste his money at the races while Rose filled these rooms with lavish knickknacks. Before too long they'd have to make do on a budget—or head back to Wapping. Her father spotted a decanter on a side table and rose to pour a glass of water. She suspected the water might be gin.

"Money can be a terrible burden, Eliza. Here I am tied hand and foot, and the ropes tightening every day." He took a hefty swig and sighed. "Me wife's family moved in lock, stock, and barrel. Her nephew and his family are stuffed in the attic, and her brother and sister-in-law in the spare bedroom. Blimey, there ain't no room left for the rats, although some of those Clearys could pass for 'em."

"I haven't heard from you in months, Dad. I near fainted from shock when you called me today."

He returned to the armchair. "You're my daughter. Why shouldn't I call you? Wonder what your mum would think of you now, all gussied up like a lady. She'd be proud as a peacock, I wager."

"I wish that were true." Eliza sighed. "I also wish I could remember her."

"You were barely three when she passed. No reason you should remember."

Eliza sat down on a settee. "What did Mum die from again? You once told me it was a fever that took her, but Aunt Maud said it was the croup."

"I didn't call you here to talk about your mother. It's about the Governor what put me in this muddle. That Professor of yours." He tossed back another swig, and then wiped his mouth. "Wish now I'd never shown up on his doorstep, I do. That was the end of my free and easy life, the day I asked him for five quid."

"You can't blame Professor Higgins for giving you what you asked for."

"Well, I never asked him to send my name to that rich American bloke, did I? Now I'm one of the blasted middle class, and it's a sorry state to be in." He pulled out a handkerchief from his robe pocket and blew his nose. "Then I hears about you and all the messy business you're in, so what's a father to do, I asks ya!"

"What are you talking about?" Eliza resented his sudden interest in her welfare. He had never worried about her before. "I'm not involved in any messy business."

"You telling me you ain't involved in that murder business with the Hungarian?"

"It's hardly my fault that my employer was killed. I had nothing to do with it."

"Nothing, is it? Are you knackers? Come on, girl. I read the papers. You know as well as I do that the Governor ain't above taking a rival down. Who's to say he didn't stab that foreign bloke in the back?"

"Me, for one. It's ridiculous to think Professor Higgins could kill anyone."

"Oh, you just can't see straight 'cause he taught you to speak proper and took you to balls and such. But the Governor is a danger to you, and you'd best not forget it, Lizzie girl."

"How is he a danger?" Eliza asked. "And when have you ever cared a brass farthing about me?"

He drained his glass. "I'm your father, ain't I? It was me what brung you into this sorry world. Your mum, too, only she ain't here. She'd be worried sick, though. She'd want me to warn you about the Governor and take you back."

"Take me back?" She looked around the parlor in disbelief. "You mean move in here?"

"We've a big house. There's plenty of room yet. Didn't Mrs. Higgins say I should take you back and provide for you? It's my duty as a father." He pointed his finger at her. "Murder's a bad business, and you're in the thick of things. We want you back home where you belong."

The visit had gone on long enough. "I am exactly where I belong at this moment, residing with Professor Higgins and the Colonel at Wimpole Street. Now if you'll excuse me, I have other errands to see to."

"Sit down. I got more to tell you, if you gimme half a minute."

"You won't convince me the Professor had anything to do with the murder."

Rose Cleary Doolittle suddenly swept into the room carrying a maroon silk robe. Without sparing a glance for Eliza, she pulled her father up by the neck ruff. "Oh, Alfie! Wasn't I telling you to take off that tartan rag? Come on, old thing."

Her husband grumbled loudly, but exchanged his old bathrobe for the silk one. Rose smoothed his lapels while the parlor maid brought in a tray with tea and tiny cakes. Rose handed a cup to Eliza, who not only refused to accept it, but got to her feet.

Rose shot her a forced smile. "So good to see you again, luv. And ain't you the height of fashion. Although I have two new hats in that same style as yours."

Her gaze fixed on Eliza's beribboned hat before traveling over her smartly tailored navy suit and high-topped shoes. Rose's own ensemble was nearly as expensive: a bright pink daytime silk gown over a cream lace underskirt, with a large lace collar overlay. She was also decked out in too many jewels for this hour of the morning, with a ring for nearly every finger as well as large pearl earrings.

Rose turned to Alfred. "Spread your napkin, Alfie. Over your lap, for heaven's sake. Like this."

Done fussing over him, Rose plopped herself on the divan with a grunt. Too much powder layered her freckled face. And her thick hair seemed streaked with some odd dye, making her copper-colored curls appear orange. Rose always did remind Eliza of an Irish witch, but now she looked like a clown as well.

She turned her demanding gaze on Eliza. "Your da and I are worried sick over you."

"It will be the first time then." Still refusing to sit, Eliza returned Rose's hard stare with one of her own. "Neither of you gave a thought as to what would happen to me when you tossed me out of my home with not even a shilling in my pocket."

"Not that again," Alfred said as he slurped his tea.

"You were seventeen, high time you were on your own." Rose reached for a tea cake. "My own parents kicked me out when I was just fourteen so you were lucky, girl, and don't you forget it. Anyway, you were selling oranges and violets long before I moved in. Your da and I knew you could make a honest living at Covent Garden."

"At least I got to keep my earnings once I left, instead of you taking every last penny I made."

"And why shouldn't you be paying rent, I ask you?" Rose shook her head. "Even then, you thought you were a bleeding duchess."

Eliza looked at her father. "No doubt this is why you asked me to visit. Now that I'm making good money giving lessons, you want me to pay rent again."

"Why would I be wanting your rent money when I'm getting three thousand a year?" Alfred said, peering at her above his teacup. "In fact, we'll let you stay here rent-free as long as you give us lessons on how to speak proper."

Finished with her tea cake, Rose brushed crumbs from her skirt. "Now ain't that a grand idea? And you could steer clear of that Higgins fellow. I been reading how your Professor accused that dead foreigner of stealing his pupils. The coppers seem to think he's the one what done him in."

"Not that it's any of your business, but the Professor and I have been working hard to see that the killer is caught. And we're getting assistance from Detective Inspector Shaw at Scotland Yard. You remember Jack Shaw, Dad. He's Mum's sister Polly's oldest boy."

"Little Jack Shaw? From Kennet Street, back in Wapping?" Alfred sat back with a shocked expression. "That little blighter is working for the Yard! Jack was always nicking an onion or tater for Polly to add to the soup. Quick fingers, little Jackie had. A real nice touch."

"Jack's a proper detective now, he is."

"Garn!" Alfred slapped his knee. "That's even harder to choke down than you swanning about London like the Queen Mother."

Eliza heard the clock chime the half hour. She had already wasted too much time here. "As charming as this visit has been, I have no interest in hearing the two of you sling insults at Jack and me. I also have no intention of moving into your household. Let's say our goodbyes since I must get back to helping the police solve the murder."

"And how are you doing that? By working alongside that bloke what killed the foreigner?" Rose asked.

"Professor Higgins did not kill the Maestro. In fact, he was wandering about London on the day of the murder conducting phonetics research."

Rose and Alfred exchanged meaningful glances. "Was he now?" Alfred asked. "According to the papers, no one remembers seeing him that day."

Eliza's frustration had reached its limits where Higgins's alibi was concerned. It troubled her that no one could verify his whereabouts. But it rankled deep to see her father and Rose pointing out that unhappy fact. "We just need more time. London's a big city, you know. I'm sure to find someone who saw him in London that day."

"Maybe it's not London you should be asking around in." Rose tipped back her teacup for a sip, taking care to lift her pinkie finger.

Eliza's headache returned full force, along with a sense of uneasiness. "What are you talking about?"

Rose took her time sipping tea, then leisurely placed the cup back on the tray. "I seen your shifty Professor Higgins that day, and he weren't in London. I happen to know he left London right after he killed the Hungarian bloke."

"That's a lie, you blooming witch!"

"Witch, am I?" With a great push, Rose got to her feet. "At least I ain't no murderer."

"Neither is the Professor."

"Then he's a bloody liar, 'cause I seen him in Surrey the day the Hungarian was stabbed."

Eliza could scarcely take this information in. She knew Rose resented her. Indeed, she probably hated Eliza, and the feeling was mutual. But to think she would concoct such a terrible lie to get back at her. Rose knew Eliza would be heartbroken if the Professor was thrown into prison. And it seemed the blasted woman was willing to help convict an innocent man just to wound her.

"First, you've never even met the Professor," Eliza said, trying to keep her temper in check. "You wouldn't know if you'd seen him or not."

"Is that so? Your da pointed him out to me just three days after the wedding," Rose said. "We was taking a hansom ride through

Hyde Park—we do that regular now—and Alfie pointed out Professor Higgins. He was listening to the speakers on the corner. And when your da yelled at him, the Professor tipped his hat to us as we drove by. Ain't that right, Alfie?"

"Right as rain, luv," Alfred said. "It was the Governor for sure."

"So I know what that tall fellow looks like," she went on. "And I saw him in Tilford village in Surrey when I went to visit me Aunt Sarah. He was sitting in a motorcar waiting for a herd of sheep to cross the road. I walked past with Sarah, and I saw him close up, I did."

"Let me guess. You were returning from the pub at the time." Eliza glared at her.

"How d'ye know that?" Rose seemed taken aback by Eliza's correct guess. "Anyways, that don't matter. Aunt Sarah and me always enjoy a pint or two during my visits. I weren't drunk if that's what you're implying, Miss La-dee-dah. And I seen the Professor in that motorcar. I also know it was the day the Hungarian got killed. When I got back to London that night, the newsies were screaming it out from every corner."

Despite her morning vow never to drink ale again, Eliza wished she had a glass of Guinness at that moment. "I don't believe you."

"But you believe that lying Professor, don't you? And lying he is if he swears he was in London all day." Rose stalked to the parlor door. "I told Alfie it was no use trying to help you. Run back to that fancy house in Wimpole Street for all I care. Only don't turn your back on the Professor, else you might find a knife sticking out of it!"

Eliza waited until Rose stamped her way upstairs before turning to her father. "Is this true? Did Rose tell you she saw Professor Higgins in Surrey?"

"That she did, my girl." With his wife out of the room, Alfred reached for the gin bottle.

"Why hasn't she gone to the police with the information?"

"What? Are you bleeding daft? Did you forget everything you ever learned in the East End, Lizzie? You was taught to run the other way any time you saw a bluebottle on the streets. Coppers don't help people like us, no matter how much money we come into or how fancy we start talking. And don't tell me about your cousin Jack. Now that I learn he's working for the Yard, I trust him even less than when he was nicking potatoes." He gave her a world-weary look. "Me or Rose go to the police with a tale like this, they ain't gonna believe us. They may even start to think we're involved in this murder. Before you know it, I'll be forking over solicitor fees, and then I'm back to being a poor dustman."

Eliza stood silent for a time. Rose was mistaken in what she saw that day in Surrey. And probably drunk into the bargain as well. After all, she had seen the Professor only once before, and just for a few seconds. No doubt the man in the motorcar merely resembled the Professor.

"Professor Higgins doesn't even own a motorcar," Eliza said finally.

Alfie shook his head. "If I can rent a hansom carriage every week, Higgins can rent a motorcar to drive to Surrey."

"I simply don't believe it." Indeed, the longer she thought about it, the less likely it seemed. Goodness knows, she had a far higher opinion of Professor Higgins's character than she did of either her father or Rose.

"I knew you wouldn't listen to reason. Stubborn as your mum, and that's the sad truth. Leastways I did what I could to save you from being knocked off by that fellow."

Eliza allowed herself a smile. "I'll be all right. We'll solve this murder. Jack's sure of it."

"The offer's still open if you be wanting a room upstairs," he said, wiping his nose on his handkerchief. "And you don't even have to give us lessons. Fact is, I'll kick out her worthless brother-in-law for you, I will."

"Thanks, Dad. Take care of yourself." She pecked his cheek, more out of sympathy than affection.

Once outside, she almost broke into a run. Cor, it felt good to be out of that house. It was nearly noon, and her stomach growled. Not surprising since she hadn't felt well enough to eat breakfast. Eliza couldn't wait to sit down to Mrs. Pearce's lunch, while exchanging pleasantries with the Colonel and Redstone. And she was eager to set off for the Drury Lane Theatre with Higgins later today. Hang Rose Cleary Doolittle and her silly accusations.

Humming a favorite music hall song, Eliza headed back to Wimpole Street, where she belonged.

FIFTEEN

Higgins shook the raindrops from his lapels with a muttered curse. "I grew too accustomed to the sun and heat in Spain. Every rainy day since I returned sets my teeth on edge."

"I don't mind the rain so much as the fog." Eliza ducked under the portico. "Never liked trying to find my way in that pea soup. And if you can't see where you're going in Whitechapel, you might end up with a cut purse or a cut throat."

"Yes, I can see how that could be bothersome." Higgins walked behind stacks of newspapers while a boy yelled out the headlines in a singsong patter.

A moment later Higgins strode into the theater, but Eliza didn't follow. Instead she gazed in awe at the fancy colonnade and imposing front of the Theatre Royal, also called Drury Lane, on Catherine Street. On performance nights, she'd seen gorgeously gowned ladies swathed in velvet, satin, and fur walk right up these steps escorted by gentlemen in black tie and tails. Eliza tried to be on her best behavior when approaching them to make a sale. The violets they bought paid her weekly rent at Angel Court.

Eliza looked over her shoulder. Her shabby "piggery" was but a few blocks away. It now seemed as distant from her present life as the moon. After all her bowing and scraping on these very steps, she would attend the theater on Thursday evening with the rest of the swells. What a blooming miracle.

She was almost as excited about today. What a thrill to see Drury Lane from the inside instead of standing out in the street. Eliza hoped for a tour of the backstage area, too, especially since they had come here to speak with Miss Page.

Higgins stood waiting in the theater lobby, and Eliza hurried to catch up to him. She let out a cry of delight at the gilt trim, marble columns, and red carpet. Higgins explained that the columns were called "Doric." Next he drew her attention to the grand staircase leading to the boxes and the vast rotunda with its three statues of Shakespeare, Edmund Kean, and David Garrick. A peek into the Grand Saloon revealed more marble columns and statues, along with a magnificent glittering chandelier.

"It's near as beautiful as Westminster Abbey," she finally said.

"To an actor, the Drury Lane is more holy," Higgins replied with mock seriousness.

As they headed into the actual theater, Eliza cast one last look behind her. "I had no idea it was like this inside."

He shrugged. "I'm not a devoted theatergoer, but the Drury Lane is impressive. And it's the oldest theater in London. Not a bad place for you to see your first *Hamlet*."

"I'm glad Aubrey gave me the play. I've read it five times. I bet I know the lines better than most of the actors. But I don't care much for that Hamlet fellow. He seems like he can't make up his mind."

"I believe his Uncle Claudius is none too fond of him, either."

"Do you know they kill each other in the end?" Eliza bit her lip.

"I shouldn't have said anything. Maybe you haven't seen the play yet, and now I've ruined it for you."

Higgins smiled. "I heard the play doesn't end well. But for future reference, please remember any play calling itself a tragedy means that the main characters die in the last act. Macbeth dies in *Macbeth* and Romeo and Juliet die in *Romeo and Juliet* and Othello dies in *Othello*—"

"Stop!" Eliza covered her ears. "You're spoiling it for me. Now I'll know how they end when I finally see these plays."

"Tragedy may not be your cup of tea. It might be better if we attend an Oscar Wilde production next. I think we'd both prefer it."

After speaking with the box office manager, Higgins led the way into the theater hall. The theater was bigger than Eliza expected. Its horseshoe shape was ringed with ornate balconies and dizzying tiers of private boxes trimmed with red velvet drapery and gilt. Her attention fastened on the actors rehearsing on the large open stage. Unfortunately, the sound of hammers drowned out what they were saying. Not until they walked down the aisle could Eliza finally hear them speak.

" 'Peace, break thee off; look, where it comes again,' " an older man said in a monotone. He squinted at a dog-eared book he held and then flipped a page.

Another man answered from the stage's far side. " 'In the same figure, like the king that's dead.' "

" 'Thou art a scholar; speak to it, Horatio.' "

" 'Most like: it harrows me with fear—' "

"No, no, no! You skipped Bernardo's line again," a deep voice roared from afar. "You ought to know that line, it's your cue."

The actor who missed his line stalked in a circle onstage. He was dressed in a velvet doublet and tights. His deep bass voice sounded like thunder.

"'Looks it not like the kind? Mark it, Horatio. Most like: it harrows me with fear.'" He flashed a black scowl at Eliza when she knocked over a small ladder in the aisle.

"Sorry," she said, looking around for Higgins. She caught sight of him walking up the side stairs by the stage. An instant later, he disappeared behind the red curtain.

Eliza ran after him. She dared not look at the actors as she clambered onstage. Why couldn't the Professor wait up for her? He had such blooming long legs.

Once backstage, she stepped with caution. Props, wiring, and half-finished sets covered the entire area. The hammering got louder, as did the shouts of the workers. An older woman rushed past, holding a jeweled purple cloak. An actor in costume went in the other direction, muttering lines to himself; Eliza was pleased that she recognized the lines as coming from Act 3. She saw Higgins with a wizened old man in overalls.

"Easy, easy, steady on," someone called out overhead. She looked up to see two men balancing a heavy lamp along the catwalk.

"Watch out, Eliza!" Higgins pulled her aside as two more workmen headed straight for them. "They're coming this way with what looks to be a castle rampart."

Curious, she touched the wall when they walked by and was amazed that the stone brickwork they carried was only painted plaster.

"So, would ye like a tour of the backstage then?" the wizened fellow asked.

"Yes, please," Eliza said. "It's my first visit."

The man pointed out many oddities of the backstage area that Eliza would have passed by, such as the fireproof curtain and alcoves crammed with set furnishings stacked in haphazard fashion. Rickety shelves and hidden dark rooms held belts, shoes, boots, a painted crown, swords, a bouquet of silk flowers, and even a gruesome skull. The shelves bore odd markings, such as "II/2" and "IV/3."

A worker's armful of rolled muslin knocked her into the brick wall. "Sorry, miss! You all right?"

He didn't wait for an answer. As Eliza righted her wide hat, he hefted the bolts over his shoulder and staggered toward the direction of the stage.

"Which way are the dressing rooms?" Higgins asked the elderly man at last. "We've come to see Miss Rosalind Page, if she has any time to spare."

"Mayhap a few minutes, guv, but that be all. Follow me then, watch your step."

The old man threaded his way through the maze of posts, up a slanting ramp, down a slope, and along a narrow corridor between closed doors on either side.

Eliza peeked around an open doorway. The strong scent of linseed oil and paint fumes tickled her nose, as did tiny bits of sawdust speckling the air. Inside the huge room, workers stood on a rickety scaffold facing a canvas backdrop that hung from the ceiling. Brushes protruded behind their ears or from the pockets of their spattered overalls as they painted details of castle turrets and trees.

"Eliza, we don't have time for all the gaping."

"But there's so much left to see."

Higgins took her arm. "The tour is finished. We're here to speak with Miss Page."

"What can she tell us that we don't already know?" Eliza frowned. "I doubt Miss Page broke into my classroom and nicked *The White Rose*. And I bet whoever did that was the killer. Tell me what Miss Page has to do with my book."

"Please stop going on about that insufferable book. We've come to learn if Nepommuck blackmailed Miss Page, or any other student we don't know about." He led her along another hall. "Your cousin is no doubt right, however. Only a man would have the strength to stab the Hungarian in such a fashion. Therefore Miss Page seems an unlikely suspect."

"Which is why you're still a suspect." She paused. "Unless you tell Jack where you really were the morning of the murder."

Eliza saw that her comment startled him.

"I told both of you where I was. Walking about London and listening to whatever interesting dialects I could hear."

She shook her head. "You never showed me your notebook from that morning. And I know your methods. You always log the date and place you find your subjects."

"I have about three hundred notebooks back at the house." Higgins helped her walk around coils of wiring on the floor. "You may look through each of them if you like."

Eliza hesitated before continuing. "I also visited my dad and step-mother this morning."

He laughed. "Good grief, if ever there was a time for you to get drunk, that was it."

"My stepmother swears on the day the Maestro was killed, she saw you sitting in a motorcar in the village of Tilford."

Higgins stopped in his tracks. "One of us must be drunk right now because I don't believe what I've just heard."

His disbelief seemed genuine, and akin to what she felt when Rose told her. "I don't believe her, of course. And she had been drinking that day, too. Only I thought you should know. Dad and Rose aren't the type to go to the police, but my stepmother hates me. Which means she also hates my friends. If she wanted to be malicious, there would be no better way than to spread rumors about you."

"Just when I thought this charade couldn't get any worse," he said under his breath.

"Professor, I know you're innocent. But the police—and the public—require proof."

"Eliza, I spent the entire day on the streets of London, listening to strangers talk to one another. The key word here is 'strangers.' They didn't know me, and I didn't know them. Makes it hard to find them now. Or do you actually believe that I am the killer? Perhaps we should leave the theater right now so I can surrender to Scotland Yard. You'd like that, no doubt. There may be a reward."

"Don't be blooming dramatic. I know you didn't kill anybody. But it doesn't make sense that not a single soul remembers you from that day."

He sighed when they finally reached Rosalind Page's dressing room. "Few things have made sense since the day I met you."

"Very funny," Eliza said.

"I'm quite serious." Higgins knocked on the door.

A handsome young man yanked it open. He was dressed in a white loose-flowing shirt tucked into rumpled trousers. His dark eyes swept over Eliza with interest.

"We're here to see Miss Page, " Eliza said.

The actor looked over his shoulder. "You have two more visitors, Roz. That makes five in the last hour alone. I swear I can't get a moment's worth of attention."

"Aren't you John Barrymore?" Higgins asked. "I saw you in Wilde's *The Importance of Being Earnest*. Marvelous performance, but I'm surprised that you're in *Hamlet*. I thought comedy was your forte."

The actor grinned. "Time to try my hand at a bit of Shakespearean drama. My brother, Lionel, claims it will season me as an actor. He's also putting me in a few films this summer."

"You'll be acting in the cinema?" Eliza asked. "How wonderful."

"Aye, my lady," Barrymore said with a bow. "Just a few small parts for now. Still learning the trade. As my character the good Guilden-stern says, 'There is much brains thrown about.'"

"Don't you mean 'there has been much throwing about of brains'?" Rosalind appeared in the doorway. Her dazzling smile lit up the hall. "You'd better get your lines right, John. Miss Terry will have your head if you do anything to spoil the performance."

John Barrymore bent over the actress's hand for a lingering kiss. "Until later, my sweet." After bowing once again to Eliza, he headed toward the stage.

Rosalind waved them inside the small dressing room. "Please come in."

She sat down before her mirrored dressing table and picked up an ivory-handled brush. "Excuse me while I finish getting ready. I'll be called back onstage soon."

What a looker, thought Eliza as she watched Rosalind brush one of the auburn curls cascading over her shoulder. And her lashes were so long. Blimey, how could a person even see through them? As it had at the garden party, a velvet ribbon circled her neck. It made her throat even more swanlike. How futile to be jealous of someone so beautiful. One might as well be envious of a rainbow or a field of spring flowers.

Rosalind smiled at her in the mirror. "How nice to see you again, Miss Doolittle, even if the setting isn't as grand as the gardens of the Marchioness. And who is this gentleman?"

"Professor Henry Higgins. He's the fellow who taught me to speak like a lady."

"I am most happy to make your acquaintance, Professor. You did an excellent job with Miss Doolittle. She sounds as if she were born and raised in Mayfair."

"Thank you," he murmured.

Eliza realized the Professor was dumbstruck by Miss Page's beauty. She fought back a grin.

"Will you both be at the opening night performance?" Rosalind asked.

Eliza nodded. "I can't wait."

They looked over at Higgins, who roused himself to say, "I'll be there, too."

The two women exchanged amused looks. "Are you a fan of Shakespeare, Professor?"

"I prefer Wilde," he said after another long pause. "But I am looking forward to your performance as Ophelia. And I didn't realize Miss Ellen Terry was taking on Queen Gertrude's role in the production."

"Yes. We're lucky to have her."

"I saw her golden jubilee benefit, seven years ago this June. She was extraordinary, I must say."

Rosalind straightened her silk Chinese dressing gown embellished with teal, pink, and canary yellow flowers. "I'm afraid I'll never live up to Miss Terry's past performances as Ophelia."

"I'm sure you will," Higgins said.

"Is this one of your costumes?" Eliza eyed the embroidered blue velvet gown draped over a mannequin. "It's beautiful. In fact, everything is beautiful here at Drury Lane."

"It is a glorious theater, isn't it?" Rosalind stroked the costume's rich fabric. "Then again, the theater world itself is glorious. I cannot imagine a more satisfying profession. Acting means more to me than life itself. Being able to become another person onstage is a sort of magic, you know. And how thrilling to fool the audience by changing one's identity, voice, and appearance."

"But is the audience really fooled?" Higgins asked.

"They are if the actors do their job correctly. I daresay most people would like to transform themselves like we do. As I quoted at the garden party, 'All the world's a stage, and all the men and women merely players.' "

" 'They have their exits and their entrances; And one man in his time plays many parts,' " Higgins said with a slight bow.

"I thought you weren't a fan of Shakespeare."

He smiled. "I've a fondness for the comedies, especially *As You Like It*. And you would make as impressive a Rosalind onstage as you do off. I'd be first in line to buy a ticket."

Eliza cleared her throat. At this rate, the Professor would be openly flirting with the actress soon. "You were right about Nepommuck, Miss Page. At the garden party you wondered if he was playing at something. We've learned since then he had far too many secrets."

"The papers have speculated that you killed him, Professor." Rosalind frowned. "Surely you had nothing to do with his death?"

His expression turned grim. "Of course not."

"I didn't think so."

"The Maestro must have been pleased when you became his student, Miss Page," Eliza said. "I know he had an eye for pretty women, and you're more beautiful than most. You've probably received plenty of attention all your life because of it."

"Too much attention sometimes, but I'm not as beautiful as you imagine. It's the makeup, you see." She picked up a smaller brush and swept powder across her high cheekbones. "Without it, you wouldn't recognize me at all."

Eliza didn't believe that for a minute. "I recognized my favorite film actor on the Strand one day. But I was too afraid to ask for an autograph. That reminds me. I brought my copy of *Hamlet*. Would you sign my book, Miss Page?"

"With pleasure."

After admiring the leather binding, Rosalind turned to the first blank page. She plucked a fountain pen from a tin cup, checked the ink, and then signed the photo with a charming flourish. While she did that, Eliza's attention was drawn to the wondrous contents heaped about her dressing room table: jars and pots of cold cream, rouge, fine powder, pencils and brushes of every size. She even spied cigarettes and a razor buried behind the array. The actress undoubtedly had a lover. Perhaps the handsome John Barrymore.

Eliza knew many actors and actresses led scandalous lives. Even the regal Miss Terry had borne children to a lover while married to another man. And anyone who looked like Rosalind Page must be pursued by hordes of admirers. A beautiful young actress could not be expected to behave like a maiden aunt.

Rosalind handed the book back to Eliza, who waved the open pages, hoping for the ink to dry faster.

Higgins cleared his throat. "Forgive us for interrupting your rehearsal, but Miss Doolittle and I have a serious purpose for our visit."

The actress looked up at him with those wide innocent eyes.

"As you said, the papers have been insinuating that I had something to do with Nepommuck's murder," he continued. "I am afraid Scotland Yard is taking these rumors seriously. We are trying to discover who else had a reason to want the Maestro dead."

She sighed. "No doubt there are many, both here and in his native Hungary."

"Can you explain why you took lessons from the Maestro?"

"I needed help to mask my flat Canadian speech. Ophelia at the Drury Lane does require a proper English accent and Nepommuck came highly recommended. But not as recommended as you, Professor." She gave him a scolding look. "I did make inquiries into becoming your pupil, but was told you were in Spain."

"My sincere apologies for not being at your service. I would have been happy to instruct you. I hope Nepommuck was of some assistance."

"He was an irritating braggart, but I can't fault his teaching abilities. Now we will have to see if the critics agree."

"We know the Maestro blackmailed some of his students," Eliza said. "Were you aware of any of this?

She shook her head. "We spent four weeks doing little else but reciting lines from Shakespeare. I never spoke more than two words to his other pupils until the garden party. I wish I could help you, but the police have already visited me and asked questions about Maestro Nepommuck. I could not help them, either."

"Did you by chance overhear any threatening exchanges with other students?" Higgins asked.

Her long, lithe fingers curled into tight fists. "I'm afraid not. Whenever I arrived for lessons, the Maestro was alone in his apartment."

"And he never threatened you?"

"Why in the world would he threaten me?" Miss Page turned back to the mirror, and began to rearrange her makeup jars and pots. "If you two will excuse me, I must return to the rehearsal. And I haven't checked to make certain my costume is properly fitted. I'm sorry I cannot help you."

"If you'll allow me one more question, Miss Page," Higgins said, but she shook her head.

"Please, Professor. I cannot be late for my cue. Our interview is at an end."

"Of course, and thank you, Miss Page. You've been so kind to speak with us." Eliza dragged Higgins out to the hall and down the stairs. She didn't see any reason for bothering the poor woman any longer. Also, if Higgins became frustrated, his usual arrogance would make an appearance.

They dodged several actors hurrying to and from the dressing rooms. At the stage door, Higgins finally shook off her grip.

"Why the devil did you rush us out like that?" he said. "I didn't even have a chance to pinpoint where she grew up in Canada. Canadian dialects are tricky, almost as puzzling as regional American accents. For certain, she's not from Toronto. Somewhere in the western provinces, perhaps."

"Miss Page was frightened by your question about being threatened," Eliza said. "A blind man could see it. Badgering her right now would only make her clam up. I think she does have information. But we should wait until after the performance on Thursday to ask her more questions. After all, she's in the middle of rehearsal."

"Perhaps we should tell that cousin of yours to do his job better so we don't have to keep questioning everyone."

Eliza sighed. "You have a point." She opened the stage door, only to slam it shut again. "Blimey. I forgot my copy of *Hamlet* that she was nice enough to autograph. I can't leave it behind. Stay here. I'll be right back."

She went only a few steps before turning around. "While I'm gone, why don't you have a little conversation with that Barrymore fellow? The two of them looked a bit fond of each other when we found them in her dressing room. He may know if Miss Page was frightened of Nepommuck."

Higgins grumbled aloud. She ignored him and headed upstairs. Miss Page had to be onstage by now since she had been in such a hurry for them to leave. Eliza marched toward the dressing room and twisted the handle without knocking.

She stopped dead in her tracks.

"Oh!"

Eliza and Rosalind gasped at the same time. She stared at the actress, who was indeed a wonder to behold stark naked. The cause of the real wonder, however, was the sight of her flat chest and the sprinkling of red hair that led down to shocking proof that Rosalind was not a woman at all. She was a man.

———

"Do you need another sip of water?"

Rosalind knelt before Eliza, who had collapsed on the dressing room table chair. Those violet eyes showed only kindness and sympathy. She held the glass to Eliza's lips.

Eliza gulped down the rest of the water. "Did I faint?"

"No, but your knees buckled." With a rueful smile, Rosalind stood.

Eliza was grateful that she—or was it he?—had gotten dressed. The actress now wore Ophelia's blue velvet costume, her long red hair spilling down her back. She looked nothing like a man. Eliza could scarcely believe what she had just seen. However, the wide ribbon about Rosalind's neck caught her eye, and Eliza realized it must hide a slight Adam's apple.

Someone knocked on the door. "Five minutes, Miss Page."

"Thank you," she called back.

Eliza sat back, stunned.

"I suppose you have questions, Miss Doolittle."

"About a hundred, actually."

Rosalind took a deep breath. "As you saw, I was born male. That is my tragedy. I should have been my parents' first-born daughter, not their son."

"I don't understand."

"How can I explain?" Rosalind paused. "It was as if I had been dressed in the costume of another actor's character and pushed on-stage without knowing my lines. Being a boy was the one role I could never play well. For one, I was much too pretty, and far too feminine. That made growing up in a small town difficult. I was the oddity." She frowned. "And the recipient of much unkindness. My family was ashamed to call me their son."

"How terrible," Eliza murmured.

"Yes, it was. I was only thirteen when I left Alberta. It's farmland, for the most part, with nothing to offer someone like me. Since being a boy brought only misery, I decided to become the girl I was meant to be. I took the train to Vancouver and got a job in a dress shop. They thought I was pretty enough to model the clothes for customers. A year later, a traveling variety show came to town, and I caught the attention of several performers who visited the shop. And when the variety show left, I went with them." Her voice became filled with wonder. "The first time I walked onstage, I knew I was home. In the theater my only purpose is to pretend to be something I am not. And few people are as good at it as I am."

Eliza's confusion cleared, and she remembered what Rosalind had told Higgins and her earlier: "How thrilling to fool the audience by changing one's identity, voice, and appearance."

"No one ever guessed the truth?"

"Why should they? People see only what they expect to see. And I was Rosalind Page, the actress. After years of misery and shame, I felt truly myself: authentic, honest, the woman I was destined to be." She shrugged. "Of course, it helped to be attractive."

"It can't all be based on how beautiful you are. Everyone says you are a wonderful actress."

"Thank you," Rosalind said quietly. "But my looks won me my first role in musical theater, and bigger roles after that. By the time I became a theater star in Toronto, I was as celebrated for my beauty as my thespian skills. I am proud of both."

"But you must be afraid someone will discover your secret."

"Always. It is why I take such great care. For example, I never employ a dresser. Everyone assumes I change my own costumes because I am shy about undressing in front of others. And I have spent years training my voice to speak in a higher register. Although if I want to, I can sound as masculine as Mr. Barrymore."

Eliza wasn't sure she wanted a demonstration of that. It was unsettling enough dealing with the fact Rosalind was male. She didn't need further proof. "You said no one guessed the truth for a long time. Did someone learn your secret?"

"A businessman in Toronto almost did." Rosalind's voice grew hard. "Porter Collings was as disagreeable as he was wealthy. He sent endless flowers and gifts, but I refused all his advances." She shuddered. "How I dread the gentlemen callers. I live a life more celibate than a nun's, but it's a price I am willing to pay. This particular suitor refused to give up, and his attempts at seduction grew aggressive. Nothing I said would dissuade him."

"What did you do?"

"I left Toronto. I had no choice. It was only a matter of time before he'd take me by force. When that happened, I knew he would expose me to the world. Fortunately my manager arranged this engagement at the Drury Lane. When I arrived here, I hired

Nepommuck for help with my accent." Her expression grew even more unhappy. "How I wish I had waited for your Professor Higgins to return from Spain."

Eliza thought a moment. "Nepommuck had a talent for sniffing out other people's secrets. I suspect he discovered yours as well."

"Yes. During our third lesson, that filthy Hungarian groped me most shamefully." She wrapped her arms about herself. "After his shock at finding me not quite the woman he fancied, his greed replaced his desire. He wanted money, a lot of money. I paid him two hundred pounds, enough to buy a racehorse at Epsom."

"I suppose he asked for more money after that."

"Of course. I became desperate."

"So you killed him," Eliza said softly.

Rosalind looked at her in horror. "No! Certainly not."

Eliza had trouble believing that, however. Being a man, Rosalind Page had enough brute strength to kill Nepommuck, along with a bloody good motive. If Rosalind's secret were exposed, it would spell the end of her life in the theater. And Eliza thought that might spell the end of her actual life as well.

"Where were you on the morning of the murder?"

"Sleeping until noon. I usually stay up late after performances and rehearsals."

"Excuse me for asking, but was anyone with you?"

"No, I was alone. I'm always alone." Rosalind met her gaze without flinching. "You must believe me, Miss Doolittle. I am not a violent person. When things become too difficult, I run away. I would never harm someone simply to protect myself. It is not in my nature."

Eliza was moved by the emotion in her voice, and the unshed tears welling in Rosalind's eyes. Poor woman. And yes, Eliza still thought of her as a woman, not a man. Except for what lay hidden beneath her gown, everything about Rosalind Page was womanly in the extreme. It didn't seem possible this beautiful, sad lady could murder anyone. But a great actress could make an audience believe anything. Was Rosalind acting now?

Rosalind seemed to sense her doubt. "My life is ruined if anyone learns my secret now. I would be arrested as a suspect in Nepommuck's murder, and jailed. You must realize I'd never last a day in the men's prison."

Eliza bit her lip, uncertain of what to do. "I have to tell Inspector Shaw and Higgins," she said at last.

Rosalind gave a cry of dismay.

"I swear on my life, Higgins will tell no one. He's an honorable man. And Inspector Shaw is my cousin. I shall make certain that Jack—and only Jack—questions you."

With a sinking heart, Eliza retrieved her autographed book and left the dressing room. Poor Miss Page, or whatever her real name was. A pity Nepommuck wasn't still alive. Eliza would love to beat that blighter silly.

She hurried downstairs to find Higgins, who paced outside the stage door in the fog.

"Good heavens, Eliza. Where have you been? Barrymore had nothing of interest to tell me, except for a few salacious tales of actresses he's known. And none of them was about Rosalind Page."

"I didn't think so."

In a low voice, she related the entire story as they walked up Catherine Street. Higgins said nothing the whole time, only shaking his head.

"You realize what this means, don't you?" Eliza said finally.

"We must pass on Miss Page's sad story to your cousin."

"Yes, and I pray Jack doesn't clap her in irons right away without better proof of her guilt. From where I sit, she's about as likely a murder suspect as you are."

"I beg your pardon," Higgins said. "You aren't comparing motives, are you? If so, her motive is a bit stronger than mine."

"It's not motives I'm comparing," Eliza retorted. "It's alibis. And I'm afraid I don't know which of you has the weaker one."

She also feared that both Rosalind Page and Professor Higgins were lying.

SIXTEEN

Henry Higgins tipped his hat to a fellow Etonian on his way to the playing fields. The late May sunshine bathed his face. Ah, spring. He'd best enjoy it before the jail cell slammed shut behind him. It was an odd time of year to be heading for Eton's cricket ground. But thanks to a whim of the Prince of Wales, the players and fans of both Eton and Harrow were gathering weeks early for an unprecedented exhibition match.

He walked at a brisk pace past the copse surrounding Fellow's Pond. At the sight of the pond, he broke into a grin. Years ago, he'd pushed a rival batsman into the water for being a sore loser. Higgins's team had beaten Harrow, and the boy dared to call them cheats. As if Eton needed to do that to defeat Harrow. He continued on along oak-lined Pococks Lane, and then toward Agar's emerald green fields.

Given recent events, Higgins wanted only to enjoy the afternoon. Who knew if he would still be a free man once cricket season officially began? The restful train ride to Windsor had been much needed. He hadn't even bothered to note down a single odd turn of speech. And Higgins didn't care one whit if Detective Inspector

Shaw forbade him to leave London. He had to get away from Scotland Yard, Wimpole Street, and Belgrave Square.

The weeks since returning from Spain had been frustrating beyond belief. Scotland Yard's investigation into Nepommuck's murder let Higgins see firsthand how wrong the police could be. And yesterday's encounter at the theater with Miss Page made the hunt for the killer only sadder and more puzzling. He couldn't imagine how Jack would handle the startling revelations about Rosalind Page. Higgins hoped he would not be unkind to the actress. Actually she was an actor. Or was he an actress? Blast, he felt as if he had fallen down the rabbit hole.

Higgins walked faster. He disliked being late for an Eton match, but Mrs. Pearce had trouble finding the correct silver-topped cane. She'd pressed his morning coat last night, and set out his top hat and gloves. While he preferred wearing his daily outfit of tweeds and fedora, attire at these matches was far more formal. Especially since the students' own uniforms included black morning coats and top hats.

A bit winded, Higgins at last joined the back of the crowd watching the under-sixteen cricket match. An Eton-Harrow match always elicited high spirits, but as Higgins moved through the crowd, he sensed a growing excitement. He looked about and spotted the source of the fevered attention.

Several yards away stood the Prince of Wales. The Earl and Countess of Craven flanked the young royal, who was not yet nineteen years of age. Rather dull company for the boy, Higgins thought. However, from every corner of the playing field, blue-blooded girls cast flirtatious looks his way. As if any of them had a chance. When the time came, Prince Edward would be married off to whatever dull young woman his parents deemed sufficiently royal and suitable. Higgins couldn't think of anything grimmer.

Today the Prince of Wales was here for only one reason: cricket. As a student at Oxford's Magdalen College, Edward's interest in cricket and racing was well known. It was he who requested today's special demonstration between the two celebrated teams. The usual Eton-Harrow exhibition match took place in July at Lord's in London. Higgins had also heard Prince Edward favored Harrow. And while the lad seemed charming enough—especially in his naval hat and uniform—Higgins hoped his future king would be disappointed with the outcome of today's match.

Bored by the royal watching, Higgins moved on. He scanned the crowd for a lovely woman wearing what would surely be an unusual hat. After a moment he caught sight of two sweeping white swan wings mounted on an upturned rose-hued straw brim. This absurd creation sat perched at an angle atop the Duchess of Waterbury's honey-blond head. Only Lady Helen could appear graceful and charming in such a ridiculous chapeau.

When he recognized the two elderly ladies who accompanied the Duchess, Higgins sighed in relief. Then again, the Duke was not a fan of cricket. It was no surprise his wife had attended without him.

With the match now under way, Higgins moved to a different vantage spot where he watched the Harrow batsmen score more than a half-dozen runs. Damnation. They were probably playing all out because the Prince of Wales was here. Eton's home crowd applauded with restrained politeness.

A new bowler from Eton stepped up, cheeks reddened from the sun, and delivered a spectacular ball. The ball bounced once and knocked down a wicket before the batsman could make any contact. Loud cheers rose above the crowd. Higgins let out a cheer of his own. The boy accepted his teammates' congratulatory cuffs on the shoulder with a wide grin. As he watched the strapping young Etonian,

Higgins swelled with pride. Good man, good play. His mother would be proud.

"They're all growing up so fast," he murmured.

Higgins continued to watch the match for at least fifteen minutes, aware that Lady Helen had noted his arrival. She slowly made her way along the sidelines, heading toward the trees that divided the playing fields. He followed ten minutes later. Careful to remain discreet, he ducked under the low-hanging branches. Higgins circled the area to allow her to catch up with him. When they met up, they didn't exchange a word but only walked together in silence.

Several Eton boys passed by, complaining about their various beaks and chiding each for having to sign the Tardy Book this past month.

"I say, let's go watch the wet bobs on Sunday," the shortest one said. "We've nothing else to do."

"They can row to kingdom come for all I care."

"Beg pardon, sir. Didn't see you walkin' there," the tallest student said as he dodged Lady Helen.

"Have a care where you step, young man," Higgins said. "And it's walk*ing*, not walk*inn*. Practice correct diction and the world will be at your beck and call."

"Yes, sir."

As the boys hurried off, Lady Helen smiled at him. She looked radiant in a rose dress set off by a wide lace collar and pearls. "Must you always play professor, Henry?"

"I'm hardly playing at it. I am a professor."

She laughed, which made her hat's ridiculous swan wings bob. "I think you're still irritated Oxford didn't create a chair for you."

"By George, the last thing I want to waste my time on is reading dryasdust papers written by students who have trouble diagramming a compound sentence."

"I suppose you're even less interested in acting as Master of Literature here. Would it really be so bad to join the college faculty? You've always said your finest memories took place at Eton."

"Only in the cricket fields, not the classroom." Higgins shook his head. "I would never fit in as a professor at Eton. The students would hang me from Lupton's Tower in the space of a week. I'm too demanding when it comes to teaching phonetics. Only paying pupils are willing to tolerate such draconian treatment from a martinet like me."

"Martinet? You've a heart of gold."

"I believe you've forgotten all the tears you shed over our own elocution lessons."

Actually, he doubted either of them would forget that they met soon after she arrived in England as the fiancée of the Duke of Waterbury. Helen was yet another lively American millionairess about to marry an English lord. But unlike the Astor and Vanderbilt heiresses, this pretty American had an appalling Bostonian accent.

The Duke hired Higgins to eradicate Helen's dreadful flatness of vowels and the lack of the 'r' consonant. The entire ducal family—along with Higgins—cringed whenever she opened her mouth. Although the Marsh family boasted an impressive fortune, their ancestry paled beside those of the Boston Brahmins. The one thing lacking was an English title, which Helen's mother insisted on securing for her oldest daughter. Only that troubling accent stood in the way of perfection.

Helen initially agreed with the plan to lose her Boston speech, at least until she met the arrogant young Professor Higgins. They battled for weeks over his teaching methods, but at last he succeeded. In fact, he'd been quite proud of the result—and her. He was also reluctant to see her married.

She winced. "Don't remind me about those lessons. But you ought to give yourself more credit, Henry. My husband was so pleased at the result, he paid double your fee."

Higgins stiffened at the mention of her husband. "And how is Lord Edward?"

"Very well, thank you. He's meeting with the Chancellor of the Exchequer this afternoon. Otherwise he would have been here to watch William play."

"Really?" Higgins couldn't disguise his skepticism. "I don't believe I have ever seen the Duke at one of these matches."

Lady Helen's smile faded. "I feared that you would not be here, either. With everything going on, I don't know how you managed to find the time to attend."

"I wanted to be here. You know that."

She turned to face him. Even in the bright sunlight, Helen looked almost as young and fresh as the girl of twenty-one he'd taught when she first arrived in England. Only a few fine lines around her hazel green eyes hinted that she was now close to forty. "I'm worried about Scotland Yard's handling of the Hungarian's murder."

"Let's not talk about that. I came here for cricket, not crime. I haven't given a single lesson since that scoundrel was found dead. It's a messy, unpleasant matter. You ought not concern yourself with it."

"Of course I must concern myself about it. I've been alarmed since I first heard about the murder. I told you it was madness to expose that man in the press. You've drawn attention to yourself, Henry."

"I don't want to discuss it."

Helen slammed the tip of her silk parasol into the gravel walk. "Well, I do."

He'd forgotten how stubborn and unconventional she could be.

At this moment, she reminded him of Eliza. Higgins chalked it up to her being a brash American. It was ironic that he had trained two young women to be duchesses, even if Helen was the only one to marry an actual duke. It was even stranger that both ladies had become far too important to him. How had a reasonable man such as himself become so infernally concerned with the welfare of two exasperating females? Sometimes he feared he was a bigger romantic fool than the poetic Major Redstone. But at least he took care to conceal this absurd side to his otherwise sterling character.

"Right then. What is it you want to discuss?"

"Don't take that tone with me. I am hearing ominous things about this police investigation. In my own circle of friends, it's been a constant topic of conversation, especially because the murdered man was engaged to Lady Gresham."

That caught his interest. "What are your friends saying?"

"Everyone believes Verena was a fool to accept the marriage proposal of that preening bore. His premature death was seen as a blessing, except for the garish fact that it was a murder. But I don't know if Verena's reputation can recover from the revelations in the newspapers. The consensus is that she'd best take herself off to the Continent for a year or two until this scandal is forgotten." She sighed. "As for Verena, she's complaining to anyone who will listen that she was shamefully deceived by this Nepommuck. Was she?"

"Helen, she's a woman of seventy. Verena ought to have hired a detective to investigate him, rather than agreeing to marry the cad so soon after they met. I'm not sorry for exposing Nepommuck. He was a fraud."

"But why do most of Verena's circle believe you were the one who stabbed him?"

If Lady Helen had heard such gossip from her aristocratic friends, it didn't bode well. "Because the dreary lords and ladies in her set have as little imagination as the police. I had nothing to do with the murder."

"Good grief, have you forgotten I am the one person who knows for a fact that you did not murder him? Why do you think I'm so worried?"

"There's no need." His feigned cheerfulness didn't seem to reassure Lady Helen. Higgins held out his arm. With a resigned sigh she tucked her hand into the crook of his elbow.

Just that slight touch was enough to set his blood afire. If only . . . But it was too late to dwell on the past. Helen Louise Marsh was the fifteenth Duchess of Waterbury now, and he was Henry Higgins, London's most celebrated professor of phonetics—and a confirmed bachelor. But only Higgins and Lady Helen knew why he was so averse to marriage. The only woman he had ever wished to marry was another man's wife. Even in their impulsive youth, both knew that divorce was out of the question for the Duchess. And once her son was born, any foolish dreams of one day being together were dashed.

Higgins believed duty and responsibility trumped passion. Without it, life would be chaos. At least the Duke of Waterbury was not a malicious fellow. Higgins didn't think he could tolerate the idea of Helen being tied to a drunken lout or a mean-spirited tyrant. However, the Duke was a cold man, far more interested in politics and gardening than his lovely American wife. Had he been at all attentive to Helen, Higgins doubted they would ever have begun their romance.

To their credit, they behaved honorably during the months of elocution lessons as Helen prepared for her aristocratic wedding. And while their affection for each other was obvious from the beginning, they never acted upon it. But Higgins never forgot the charming American heiress. How could he? During the first two years of her marriage, she was a society darling. Photographs of the pretty young Duchess of Waterbury appeared almost daily in the papers during the Season. All that was needed for a happy ending was the birth of an heir and a spare. Yet she was still childless when Higgins bumped into her at the Cambridge wedding of a mutual friend.

It didn't take long to learn that Helen was trapped in a loveless marriage. The Duke came to her bed but twice a year, and only in the hope of producing a son. Despite the vivacious face she presented to the world, Lady Helen was lonely and unhappy. Indeed, she was almost as lonely and unhappy as he was. Soon after, Higgins and she became lovers and the most reckless—and unexpected—chapter of his life began.

Two older men turned onto the path. Lady Helen took her hand from Higgins's arm. She opened her parasol as they approached.

"Your Grace," one of them said with a bow of his head.

She gave a playful twirl to the parasol resting on her shoulder and nodded in return. "Good morning, Sir Charles. I hear you have a horse running at Ascot. Should I tell my husband to place a wager?"

"Not unless he wishes to lose his money, Your Grace," he said, laughing. "Prince Palatine is sure to win again this year."

After the men moved out of earshot, she turned to Higgins once more. "Don't worry about those two. Sir Charles has such poor eyesight, I doubt he even knew I had a walking companion. If I weren't wearing this hat, he would have passed by without a word."

"And the other fellow?"

She shrugged. "Some obscure German count who couldn't identify King George, let alone the author of the *Universal Alphabet*."

"Speaking of Ascot, will you and the Duke be there this year?"

She gave him a stern look. "We were speaking of the murder investigation of Emil Nepommuck, not Ascot. Were you questioned by Scotland Yard?"

"Yes. Several times." He avoided her penetrating gaze by focusing on what he could glimpse of the distant cricket match.

"No doubt your customary arrogance was on display during the questioning, which did you even greater harm."

Higgins couldn't help smiling. She knew him only too well. "I told them I'd been walking through London the day of Nepommuck's murder. I always do, you know, writing in my notebook. I often find someone with a new dialect in the oddest parts of the city."

"Speak plainly. Did the detectives believe your story or not?"

"I'm afraid it's not much of an alibi. Or so they tell me."

Lady Helen twirled her parasol for moment, clearly trying to control her agitation. "I have heard that your arrest is imminent. Verena is calling in every favor she has, especially from the Commissioner. And everyone knows Wilfred Dunningsworth has the backbone of a jellyfish. Henry, I see no way around it. They are going to arrest you."

He turned away from her obvious concern. "I'm afraid that is all too possible. Unless I find the real killer."

"Nonsense. It is not your purview to hunt down murderers. What sort of buffoon passes as a police detective in London? A sheriff in the Wild West did a better job of tracking down killers. Anyone who believes England is a civilized country has never spent more than three months here."

Higgins chuckled. "Seventeen years as an English duchess, and you're still as American as Thanksgiving dinner."

"I merely added a title to my name, I didn't give up my birthright." She halted. "And I will not let you give up your freedom. As soon as this match ends, I shall go to London and speak with Scotland Yard."

"Out of the question."

Her expression grew more stubborn. At moments like this, Higgins thought she could be Eliza's older sister. In truth, given the span of years between them, she could be Eliza's mother. That gave him even greater pause.

"You are not going on trial for a murder you did not commit, Henry. They could send you to the gallows."

"You have no say in the matter, I'm afraid."

"Do not presume to tell me what I have a say in. I am involved in this matter." She paused before adding in a lower voice, "Intimately involved."

"If you go to the police, you risk everything: your reputation, the Duke's good will, your family's honor—"

"I would not be the first duchess to take such a risk, as well you know."

"Yes, and some of them came to bad ends."

Helen frowned. "For pity's sake, I'm not Madame Bovary. Why are you being so obstinate? Louisa, Duchess of Manchester, had a thirty-year affair with the Duke of Devonshire."

"And they were noted for their discretion. Their relationship did not become public fodder during a murder investigation." Higgins held up his hand. "I don't require a list of titled names who had illicit unions. I refuse to allow you to sacrifice yourself."

"Stubborn man." She glared at him. "I will not see you arrested when I can end this matter with one conversation with the police. After all, I am your alibi for that day. And we have at least one other witness who could prove it."

Higgins shook his head. On the day of Nepommuck's murder, he paid an early morning call on his mother. But directly afterward, he left for a quaint village in Surrey where he spent the rest of the morning and afternoon with Helen. Since the beginning of their romance, he and Helen always met at a remote cottage owned by his cousin, who also loaned him the motorcar. Leonard was discreet and dependable; the man also worked in the offices of a Cabinet minister. If anyone learned Leonard provided the secret love nest of Henry Higgins and the Duke of Waterbury's wife, it could spell the end of his career.

"Do you really wish to drag my cousin into a police investigation? He's been a decent fellow to us for many years."

Tears filled her eyes as she shook her head. Higgins decided not to tell her that Eliza's stepmother caught a glimpse of him in Surrey. It would make her only more upset.

They walked in silence for a few minutes. It was not a pleasant scenario either way. If Higgins stuck to his original alibi, the police would likely arrest him soon. But if Lady Helen explained that she and the Professor had been secretly meeting for fifteen years, her marriage would be in jeopardy—along with something much more important.

Higgins knew she meant well. But he wouldn't risk everything. Not even for her. "Remember the Cardinal Rule," he said finally.

"Hang the rules."

"It's one rule, not many. And crucial."

She waved a hand. "Rubbish."

"You wouldn't say that if you'd experienced what I've gone through the past week. Scandal is a heavy weight to carry."

"Then let me help you."

"No."

Her sweet mouth thinned. "I don't care if anyone finds out. Not anymore. And why should they guess at the rest? There's no real resemblance."

"I forbid you to interfere, Helen. No one must learn the truth."

As far as he was concerned, their conversation was at an end. With a firm hand at her elbow, Higgins led Helen back toward the playing field before she could defy him again. He feared they had been gone too long. People may have taken notice of them speaking together for longer than a five-minute period in public. That would be unwise.

Lady Helen's shoulders drooped as she stumbled on the gravel path.

"Don't sulk," he said, several yards before they neared the crowd's edge. "You know I'm right."

"I'm trying to save your life."

"And I'm trying to save your marriage."

"If we divorced, I doubt the Duke would even realize I was gone. What would I really lose if I left him?"

"It's not what you or I would lose."

They looked at each other. "I know," she murmured.

He stepped away from her. They couldn't afford any hint of impropriety. Not after all these years of taking the utmost care to avoid it.

Higgins followed Lady Helen's gaze out over the brilliant green swath where the schoolboys continued the cricket match. The batsman hit the ball far over the fielder's head and ran back and forth, exchanging places with his partner.

Both he and Helen gave a jubilant yell, proud as always of fourteen-year-old Lord William Fairfield, Marquess of Woburn, Baron of Tarlington—and the only son of Lady Helen and Henry Higgins.

As the boy scored another run, Higgins felt his heart swell with paternal love. When William was born, Henry bitterly regretted not being able to claim him as his own. But he realized that as the only heir of the Duke of Waterbury, Will enjoyed a life of privilege and opportunity that would be denied him otherwise. And the boy loved the Duke, who was the only father he had ever known. Higgins and Helen had taken enormous pains these past fifteen years to hide their relationship and protect William as best they could. That must continue, no matter what.

Higgins would be damned before he let this sordid mess with Nepommuck interfere with his son's life. Nothing could be allowed to call into question the legitimacy of the next Duke of Waterbury. Even if it meant Higgins must sacrifice his own freedom.

SEVENTEEN

The oldest woman in the world stared down at Higgins. He thought her face remarkably unlined for someone who had seen more than one hundred winters. Then again, the caption appearing on the screen announced that she hailed from Brussels. After the French and Italians, there were few foreigners he trusted less than the Belgians.

"Blimey, she says she remembers the Battle of Waterloo." Eliza sat beside him, gazing up at the cinema screen with a look of wonder. "Maybe she even saw Napoleon."

Higgins gave a rude snort. "I'd like to know what a six-year-old girl was doing on the battlefield."

"It has to be true." Eliza never took her eyes from the screen. "Otherwise they couldn't put it up there as news, now could they?"

For someone reared in the back alleys of London's East End, Eliza had managed to remain far too gullible. What use to tell her that the newsreel was put together by blokes trying to mix a bit of current affairs with a lot of claptrap.

So far the Pathé News had reported on the birth of a monkey at the London Zoo, the opening of the Chelsea Flower Show, and the world's record set by aviator Frangeois, who kept his airplane aloft for an amazing seventy-five minutes.

The audience seemed especially entranced by the story of 104-year-old Jeannet Schell, the oldest woman in the world. And yes, one of the captions claimed she had indeed laid eyes on Napoleon. Such nonsense. Higgins watched in relief as the next news story appeared on the flickering screen. With luck, it would concern the recently failed women's suffrage bill in the House of Commons, or President Wilson's recognition of the new Republic of China.

Instead, film of a man scaling the outside of the U.S. Capitol building appeared onscreen. The crowded theater buzzed with excitement. He heard at least a dozen colorful turns of speech and local dialects murmuring around him, but the blasted theater was too dark for him to write legibly in his notebook.

"Lord, look at him," Eliza said. "Climbing all the way up there just to put his hat on the Dome. No wonder they call him 'the Human Fly.' Why doesn't an Englishman do something that daring, like climb Big Ben?"

"Because the idiot would be arrested, just like they're doing to the Human Fly up there."

Higgins tried to find a comfortable position yet again in his odorous chair. Why had he let Eliza convince him to accompany her to the cinema? They had a four o'clock appointment at Hepburn House. Lady Gresham had requested the meeting, and he hoped to persuade her to allow the authorities more time to investigate Nepommuck's murder.

As things stood now, an arrest would be made the day after next, neatly meeting the deadline worked out between Lady Gresham and the Commissioner. And since he was still the prime suspect, he had few illusions about who would be hauled off by Scotland Yard.

Murder was a sorry affair. Not just for the victim, but for every-one under suspicion, each with a sordid tale. He could scarcely be-lieve the lovely Miss Page was, in fact, a Mister. After Eliza told her cousin about their discovery, the lady—or gentleman—was brought in for questioning by Jack himself. Neither Eliza nor he had heard a word since. Surely if Rosalind Page had appeared guilty to Jack, she would have been arrested by now. But today's penny dailies still trum-peted her West End debut in *Hamlet* tomorrow night. And for all he knew, tomorrow might be his last day of freedom.

A new offensive odor assaulted him. Twisting about in his seat, Higgins spied one of the theater attendants walking down the aisle. Holding an enormous glass bottle aloft, she sprayed the air with some sort of liquid.

"What the devil is she doing?"

Eliza spared a quick glance before turning back to the screen. "Oh, she's spraying Jeyes Fluid. It helps to cut down on the stench. Otherwise the smell would be so awful in here, you'd faint dead away."

"By George, what sort of pig attends the cinema?"

Eliza sat up straighter. "The pianist is here. That means the main feature is about to start. Be quiet now."

"Why must I be quiet for a silent film?"

This finally caught Eliza's attention. "Have you really never been to the cinema before?"

"No, and I've never attended a rat fight, either. But I wouldn't be surprised if you had."

"Look, it's starting."

The title, *Nan of Northumberland,* appeared on the screen as an out-of-tune piano played what sounded like an Irish jig.

"I am not sitting through this."

"But Bransley Ames is in it. You must see him. He's my favorite actor." Eliza leaned forward. "Look, there he is. Isn't he the most handsome fellow you've ever laid eyes on?"

A dark-haired man costumed in a Victorian cloak and hat suddenly filled the screen. "He certainly is wearing more makeup than any fellow I've run across," Higgins said with a smirk.

"I think Her Ladyship's butler looks very like him."

"And I think the Jeyes Fluid is giving you hallucinations."

"There's the actress who's playing Nan." Eliza's eyes opened wide with excitement. "Her name is Jemima Castle and I read that she's only sixteen years old. Imagine, sixteen and already a leading lady in the cinema. You can see why, though. Looks like an angel, she does."

With all the pipe and tobacco smoke wafting about the theater, Higgins could barely make out the simpering blond girl on the screen. However, he could discern the caption cards that flashed before them. The film portrayed a romance between an English lord and a vicar's daughter. He desperately wished for the return of the newsreel and more footage of the Human Fly. Higgins sat back with a groan nearly as loud as the pounding piano music.

"Oh, don't take on so," Eliza said. "The main feature never lasts more than twenty minutes. That leaves us plenty of time to get to Hepburn House."

"Seems like we've already been here for days." He crossed his arms, resigned to suffering through the romance of two absurdly costumed fools as best he could.

After a few minutes, Eliza whispered, "I wish I'd thought to bring the Major."

"Don't you mean 'Aubrey'?" Higgins said sarcastically.

"I think he might have enjoyed *Nan of Northumberland,* seeing as how he's from there himself."

"Are you mad? Redstone's not from Northumberland."

"Of course he is."

"Shhhhh," a voice hissed from the row behind them.

He sighed. "Eliza, you may be able to mimic any accent in England, but you still can't place a person's speech outside White-chapel."

She turned to face him. "But he said that he was from Northumberland. Corbridge, in fact, east of Hexham. You must be mistaken."

Higgins raised an imperious eyebrow at her. "Don't insult me. I am never mistaken about a person's speech. The man's from Lancashire. The southeast part of the county."

"Please keep your voices down," someone whispered.

"Why would he lie about something like that?" Eliza asked.

"Maybe he thought it more poetic to hail from Northumberland rather than the mill towns of Rossendale."

"Rossendale? But that's the dedication in the book."

"What book?"

"Be quiet," the voice hissed again.

"Don't you remember? The book of poems titled *The White Rose* by that anonymous chap I wanted to give the Major. The book someone nicked from my classroom. It's dedicated inside to the White Rose of Rossendale. This doesn't make any sense at all."

Higgins pointed at the screen. "Neither does this film."

"You're not listening to me. If the Major is from Rossendale, how could he not mention it when——"

"Will the two of you stop talking!" A matron in the row behind them grabbed onto the back of Eliza's seat and thrust her forward. "One more word and I'll have the attendant throw both of you out of the theater."

"Oh, don't get your knickers in a twist. We're leaving." Eliza stood. "Come on, Professor."

He scrambled to his feet. "But the vicar's daughter hasn't even gotten her hand kissed yet. We ought to see that at least."

"You must be quiet," the woman said, her hat feathers trembling with anger.

"Crikey, why do we have to be quiet?" Eliza shot back. "It's a blooming silent film, or ain't you noticed!"

"I believe this creature is called a cockatoo." Higgins stared at the large crested bird grooming its feathers on the other side of the cage bars. "Pick would know. The Colonel spent two years in the Malay Peninsula. I can see why Lady Gresham bought the bird, too. It looks rather like her: white, haughty, and living in a most expensive cage."

"Most people would be happy as a Bolton brewer to be living in a cage such as this." Eliza paced about the drawing room.

This was the same room Eliza had accidentally walked into the day of the garden party at Hepburn House. She'd thought it grand then, but now that she and Higgins had been kept waiting for over thirty minutes, she realized the parlor was as intimidating as Westminster Abbey.

"I wonder if I could teach this bird to talk?" Higgins laughed. "Can you say anything, Lord Cockatoo? Has anyone taught you to say you'd like a biscuit? You know, it might be amusing to teach you to speak like a person from Bristol. That's where your Lady Gresham was born, though she pretends to hail from Hampshire. Imagine if she heard you talking in an accent she'd spent decades trying to forget."

"How can you bother about that parrot when we've just discovered Major Redstone is a liar?" Eliza said.

Higgins shrugged. "In my experience, everyone is lying about one thing or another. It's far more amazing to learn a person has been honest."

"But why should the Major lie about where he was born? What difference does it make if he came from Lancashire?"

"Apparently it matters to him." Higgins sat down in a nearby chair. "A pity he made that claim about being from Northumberland when I wasn't there. I would have enjoyed pointing out his east Lancashire vowels and flat consonants."

"I think it's right dodgy behavior. Here I am, going on about this lovely little book of poems from a fellow what lived in his own hometown, and he doesn't say a word about it." She paused. "What if he wrote the poems?"

"That I can believe. I'm sure the poems were all treacle and tripe, something I can see the rhyme-loving Major wallowing in."

"Let's say Redstone wrote these poems, and he wanted to keep it secret for some reason. When he learned I had the book in my classroom, he broke in and stole it."

"Seems a tad melodramatic, even for him."

Eliza ignored that. "Now why would he keep it a secret? It must have something to do with Nepommuck."

"Why?"

"Because Nepommuck gave me the book to use for my lessons. Maybe Nepommuck knew the Major had written the poems."

"Writing poems, even bad ones, is not a crime."

She thought a moment. "What if Nepommuck knew something about the poet, something that person wanted to keep secret?"

"I thought you introduced Major Redstone to Nepommuck at the

Marchioness's garden party. Did either of them have an odd reaction to seeing each other there?"

"No, but they could have been *pretending* they were strangers. As Shakespeare wrote, 'Though this be madness, yet there is method in it.'"

Higgins sighed. "I want to find the murderer as much as you do, Eliza, but linking Redstone and Nepommuck is a bit of a stretch. The Major has been living in India for the past fifteen years. When would his path have crossed with the Hungarian?"

Eliza had no answer to that.

"Although I am amused you are so ready to view Redstone as a murderer," Higgins went on. "You seemed to find him a most congenial fellow."

"'That one may smile, and smile, and be a villain,'" she said.

"If you quote *Hamlet* one more time, I'm going to resume my conversation with the cockatoo."

A sonorous bell chimed through the house. A moment later, Harrison the butler strode past the parlor entrance.

"I hope that's Lady Gresham," Higgins said. "She clearly doesn't seem to be at home."

Instead the butler entered the parlor with Jack Shaw. Eliza ran to her cousin and gave him a quick hug. He hugged her back with affection.

"Jack, what are you doing here?"

"I was about to ask you the same, Lizzie. Lady Gresham sent for me."

"She sent for us as well," Higgins said from his chair. "With luck, someone will send for her. We've been waiting without even a pot of tea to keep up our strength."

Harrison sniffed. "Her Ladyship shall be down shortly. The tea will follow."

Once the butler left, Eliza led Jack to a divan and pulled him down beside her. "It appears Major Redstone is a liar. And there may be a connection between him and Nepommuck."

Jack placed his derby on the divan beside him. "And what has Redstone lied about?"

"On the day of the murder, you came back with me to Wimpole Street after my interrogation at Scotland Yard. At dinner, you asked the Major if he had any reason to be blackmailed by Nepommuck."

"I remember. He said that a Northumberland accent was nothing to be ashamed of."

"Exactly. A pity the Professor wasn't there, because he would have told everyone Redstone comes from Lancashire, not Northumberland."

"Rossendale, to be exact," Higgins added. "His use of flat vowels is characteristic of the region."

"And there's more than that to raise our suspicion." Eliza explained about the book of poems, and how it was stolen from her classroom.

Jack seemed more impressed by this information than Higgins had been. "You may be on to something, Lizzie. I shall have Major Redstone brought to the Yard today for questioning."

"You'll have to wait until tomorrow, Inspector," Higgins said. "Redstone and Pickering are presently at a linguistics symposium in Cardiff. They're scheduled to take the train back tomorrow. Both men are quite keen on being here for Miss Page's debut."

Jack cocked an eyebrow. "Since I have a ticket as well, it should be no problem to have the Major accompany me to the Yard as soon as the curtain falls."

"While I'm not a champion of Major Redstone, I have no wish to see yet another man unjustly targeted by Scotland Yard," Higgins said. "Yes, he lied about where he was born, but I hardly think that automatically makes him a murderer. I hope Redstone can expect better treatment from the police, even if I have not been the recipient of it."

Jack stood. "See here, you've been treated far better than your flimsy alibi deserves."

Higgins rose to his feet as well. "Oh, so I seem more guilty than *Mister* Rosalind Page?"

"Don't push me, Higgins. I questioned Miss Page yesterday, as well you know. And yes, Page has an alibi even worse than yours, along with a far more compelling motive. Then again, so does Nottingham. Or did you think I wouldn't discover his criminal past, or what his plans were for working at the bank?" He turned a disapproving eye on Eliza. "You could have trusted me with that information, Lizzie. Instead you protected a known thief."

Eliza squirmed with embarrassment.

He shook his head. "I sent the pair of you off to try to discover if anyone could verify the Professor's alibi. Instead you both went chasing off after Nepommuck's pupils. Not only do you interrogate them as if you were police constables, you didn't relay any pertinent information back to me. You chose not to tell me about Nottingham. Then Higgins here went to question Kollas. I never learned what became of that interview. And now that Kollas has done a runner, it seems no one will know why he hated Nepommuck so much."

"Kollas is gone?" Eliza asked.

"Kollas packed his things and left London two days ago. Don't know where he went, but I suspect he's fled the country."

With a heavy sigh, Higgins quickly told Jack about Kollas's past. He related everything from the morphine he'd given his dying father back in America to the charade he'd concocted with Nepommuck about pretending to be both a Greek diplomat and the son of a watchmaker from Clerkenwell.

"I regret withholding the information," Higgins said when he was through. "But I didn't see any need to expose the fellow when he had a perfectly good alibi for the time of the murder."

"What are you talking about?" Jack asked, even more exasperated.

"Kollas told the Professor that on the morning of the murder, one of the law clerks downstairs came up to the second floor to get him to stop pounding on Nepommuck's door," Eliza said. "Then he escorted Kollas out of the building. Since there was no dead body lying in the hallway when the clerk went up there, how could Kollas have killed Nepommuck?"

"Are the two of you completely mad? Do you think police work consists of questioning a murder suspect and then believing anything he tells you? You have to check out the blooming alibi to see if there's any truth to it!"

"Was there any truth to it?" she asked in a small voice.

"Of course not. Yes, the law clerk heard Kollas pounding and yelling up there. He was about to climb the stairs to get Kollas when he met the fellow on his way down. The law clerk never got to the second floor. It is quite possible Kollas stabbed Nepommuck just two minutes earlier."

Eliza and Higgins looked at each other. "Bloody hell!" they said in unison.

"Yes, bloody hell." Her cousin flung himself back down on the divan. "This is what I get for letting amateurs meddle in a murder case. I wouldn't be surprised if I lose my job when the Commissioner gets a full report."

"I feel like a complete idiot," Higgins muttered.

"Imagine how I feel," Jack said.

Eliza took to pacing again. Agitated, she tugged at her string of pearls. "It might be a good thing for the Professor, though. I mean, now we have at least three solid suspects. Four, if we include Redstone. And since the Professor is not the only suspect, there's no reason for him to be arrested in two days."

"Don't be too sure of that, Lizzie. The Commissioner wants this case wrapped up by the end of the week. Lady Gresham and her friends are putting enormous pressure on him. And they've settled on Higgins as the culprit. It was that blasted newspaper article you're responsible for, Professor. They believe it's a simple motive, one the public is already familiar with." He frowned. "Her Ladyship wants this matter brought to a close. Now."

"Damned toffs," Eliza muttered. "Who do they think they are?"

Suddenly the ornate parlor seemed like a mausoleum. She needed some fresh air. When Eliza stepped into the corridor, she saw Harrison and Lady Gresham by the grand staircase. They took no notice of her, however; the pair were kissing with an alarming display of passion.

Eliza rushed back into the parlor. "You won't believe what I just seen. Her Ladyship and the butler are all over each other like two cats in heat."

"What?" Higgins said.

"Impossible." Even Jack looked shocked.

"Come out here right now if you don't believe me. I'm telling you, they're a sight. I can't hardly believe it meself."

She tugged at her pearls again, which sent the beads flying. With a cry, Eliza fell to her knees to retrieve them. Jack and Higgins tried to scoop up the rest.

"What is so interesting on my floor?"

Everyone looked up. Lady Gresham stood in the doorway, as serene and majestic as Queen Mary.

"I broke my necklace." Eliza held up a fistful of pearls.

"Pity. You'll have to have them restrung." The older woman swept past her.

Eliza handed her pearls to Higgins, who slipped them into his pocket.

The Marchioness settled into the chair recently vacated by Higgins. "I'm glad all of you could come this afternoon. We have something important to discuss."

Jack nodded. "Indeed we do, ma'am."

"We hope you will ask the Commissioner to extend the investigation," Eliza said.

Lady Gresham shook her head. "Out of the question."

"Why?" Jack asked. "We have at least three excellent suspects: Kollas, Nottingham, and Page. We simply need more time to pursue our inquiries."

Harrison entered the room carrying a silver tea tray. He set it down on the table nearest the Marchioness.

"You can't mean Miss Rosalind Page?" Lady Gresham raised a haughty eyebrow. "Really, Inspector, Scotland Yard has no business bothering such a lovely young woman."

"Lovely young women murder people all the time," Jack said.

"Lovely young men, too," Higgins muttered.

Harrison poured tea into a delicate china cup and handed it to the Marchioness. Eliza caught the two exchanging quick but affectionate glances.

"Did you hear that, Harrison?" Lady Gresham took a sip of tea. "The Inspector thinks an actress may have killed the Maestro. Isn't that the most absurd thing you have ever heard?"

"Begging your pardon, madam, but an actor did kill President Lincoln." Harrison poured another cup, this one for Eliza, who took a seat on the divan.

"I should warn all of you that Harrison is rather biased against people in the acting profession," Lady Gresham said.

"Actors, Your Ladyship, not actresses. I bear no prejudice against women treading the boards. But it is no fit profession for a man."

Eliza thought him quite cheeky for a servant. And now that he stood so close, she was struck once more by his startling resemblance to Bransley Ames. "A pity you don't care for actors. I was telling the Professor only today that you seem very like one of my favorite actors of the cinema: Bransley Ames."

The teacup in Harrison's hand rattled, and some of the tea spilled onto the saucer.

"That will be all, Harrison," Lady Gresham said. "Miss Doolittle can finish pouring."

With a curt bow, the butler left the parlor.

"Did I say something upsetting?" Eliza poured two cups of tea for Jack and Higgins and handed them out.

"Only to Harrison," Lady Gresham said. "Bransley Ames is his younger brother."

She almost spilled her own tea. "What?"

"True. Bransley Ames's real name is Billy Harrison."

"I told you Harrison looked just like him," Eliza said to Higgins.

"I disagree, Miss Doolittle. I've seen photographs of the young man, and Harrison is far more attractive than his brother. Fortunately for me, he finds acting a disreputable profession, at least for a man. He is most excited at the prospect of seeing Miss Page perform tomorrow night, however." She shrugged. "Then again, aren't we all?"

"Harrison is attending the performance as your chauffeur?" Jack asked.

"No, I have kindly given him the night off. The fellow wants to dress in his best clothes rather than a uniform. It is the Drury Lane, after all. For a servant he has amassed quite a wardrobe, thanks to my generosity. I was reluctant to grant such a frivolous request from a mere butler, but Harrison can be most persuasive."

Eliza gulped the rest of her tea.

"Back to why we were summoned here," Jack said. "I assume it concerns the investigation into Nepommuck's murder."

"Of course it does." Lady Gresham set down her cup. "I discussed this at length with Commissioner Dunningsworth and we are in complete agreement. The investigation ends Friday."

"That is not your decision to make," Jack protested.

"But it is my decision, as well as the decision of the Commissioner. Sir Wilfred and I both concur. This sorry affair has gone on long enough."

"It's not even been a week," Eliza said. "The police need more time to find the killer. You're not being fair."

"Fair? Do you think it's fair that I am made to suffer because my fiancé was murdered? Bad enough Emil was killed in such a lurid manner, but that dreadful newspaper article trumpeted the most sordid accusations about his past. I have been the unwitting subject of innuendo and foul gossip every day since. Another week of this, and I shall become a complete laughingstock in my circle."

"Surely your friends do not blame you for anything the Maestro did," Eliza said.

"You are ignorant of how society works, Miss Doolittle. One has friends only as long as one does not become a figure of fun. Oh, the horror of this past week. My late husband, the Marquess, was vigilant about *not* having our name bandied about in the press, and here I am being mentioned in the penny dailies with the frequency of a music hall singer. No, someone must be arrested by the end of the week, with a speedy trial to follow."

"And it doesn't matter if the person arrested is actually guilty." Higgins put down his teacup with so much force it nearly broke.

Her expression grew even stonier. "I had hoped the police would have found a likelier suspect than you by now. But it appears you have run out of luck while I have run out of patience. Unless a better suspect turns up by Friday, you shall indeed be arrested."

"You're a fine piece of work, Verena." Higgins rose to his full towering height. "First you were stupid enough to get engaged to that charlatan. And when he's murdered, you care more about getting your name out of the papers than seeing justice done. You quite shame all those Bristol dockworkers you're descended from. At least they were honest folk."

The Marchioness pushed herself out of her chair. "I should have Detective Shaw arrest you right now."

"I am not arresting an innocent man," Jack said. "Not for you, not for a Scotland Yard Commissioner, not even for Prime Minister Asquith."

"I'll have your job then, Inspector. I intend to ring Sir Wilfred immediately."

"Ring away. I am a Detective Inspector, not your bleeding footman."

Lady Gresham gasped.

"And he's not your bleeding butler, either," Eliza said. "So don't expect him to be pawing you behind the stairs like Harrison does."

Lady Gresham turned as white as her hair. "I don't know what you are talking about."

"Don't act all innocent like Nan of Northumberland," Eliza said. "I saw you out there kissing the butler. And his hand was on your blooming arse, too."

"Emil told me you were common as Cockney dirt, and he was right." Lady Gresham's expression turned murderous. "You should be sent back to the squalor of the East End where you belong."

"At least in the East End we put on a bit of black when someone dies, even if it's only an armband. We don't go flouncing about like we're off to a spring wedding." Eliza pointed at the Marchioness's ivory silk gown. "If you had a veil and an orchid bouquet, you'd look just like a blooming bride. Although you're a bit long in the tooth to be wearing a white dress, you are."

"Let's go, Eliza," Higgins said. "In another moment, you'll be dropping your aitches."

"I'll drop what I like. She ain't even in half mourning. Then she's all cozy with the butler, and the Maestro only six days cold in the ground. Looks to me like she might have done her fiancé in 'erself."

"One more word, and I will ask the Commissioner to arrest *you* as Professor Higgins's accomplice." Lady Gresham trembled with anger. "You both deserve to be behind bars."

"I got an alibi, and probably a better one than you 'ave!"

"And you're a worthless girl that Emil saved from the streets, where no doubt you will soon return. By next month, you'll be back to selling flowers, along with yourself!"

"Not bloody likely. I'm a good girl, I am. Not like you. I'm not the one who went straight from burying a sweetheart to diddling with the butler. So don't try to harm the Professor because if you do, we'll have a right dustup. And Jack 'ere will tell you I knows how to play dirty!"

"Lizzie, stop." Jack tried hard not to laugh.

"Let her babble on, Eliza." Higgins grabbed her arm. "She can't simply snap her fingers and have people arrested like an Oriental potentate. This is England, not Siam."

"If they arrest you, Professor, I'll go to the papers and raise such a stink about her and the butler, they'll both have to run off to Siam—wherever that is—to escape the gossip!"

"Harrison!" Lady Gresham tugged frantically at the cord to summon him.

"I ain't afraid of that pretty boy of yours, neither." Eliza grabbed the teapot as Harrison rushed into the room. "Don't you be laying a finger on me, boyo, or I'll crown you with this."

"Get that filthy girl out of here," the Marchioness cried.

Harrison stood before Lady Gresham. "If all of you do not leave immediately, I shall ring for the authorities."

Eliza pointed at Jack. "He is the authority, you steamin' Friar Tuck!"

Harrison took a step toward her—and slipped on one of her missing pearls. He landed flat on his back with a grunt.

"We're done here, Eliza." Higgins took the teapot from her hands. "But I believe this has been more entertaining than anything we will see tomorrow night."

EIGHTEEN

Higgins found it difficult to eavesdrop over the din of the packed theater lobby. He leaned so close to two conversing women, the feathers from their headpieces tickled his nose.

"I had quite a gelder when I learned Francis bought tickets for tonight," one lady whispered to her companion. "They say Miss Page is lovelier than a spring morning of sea mist and flowers."

Higgins scribbled the phrase down. "Blast," he said when his pencil broke.

"Don't tell me you're working, Professor." Inspector Shaw pushed through the crowd of richly dressed theatergoers to join him.

With a sigh, Higgins tucked his notebook and pencil into the inner pocket of his formal suit jacket. "The linguistic pickings are slim. Most everyone here is from the greater London area. However, that lady behind me in the purple-feathered monstrosity had an interesting turn of phrase. It is obvious she spent a forlorn decade or two in the Orkney Islands."

Jack shook his head. "Don't know how you do that, Professor. It would be a handy skill to have when questioning suspects."

"Speaking of suspects, any sign of Major Redstone yet?"

"No, but I have men posted at several train stations in the area, as well as detectives watching your residence."

"I hope they're not going to make a scene. The Colonel is with him, and he has no idea the police want Redstone for questioning. Pick will be most alarmed."

"When he arrives at Wimpole Street, my men will take him directly to the Yard. If he comes here first, we shall let him enjoy the play. No need to disrupt everyone's evening, especially since the Major has no idea he's under suspicion." Jack lowered his voice. "But as soon as the curtain falls, we'll bring him in."

"That's assuming they make it in time for the performance. Pick called from Cardiff to complain about a delay with the trains. He said they would come straight here from the station. And I won't be able to miss them since they're sitting with my mother and me in our box."

Jack frowned. "Please try to keep Eliza calm. I don't want her accusing Redstone of anything until we've got him safely at Scotland Yard."

Both men exchanged rueful glances. They remembered too well the scene Eliza threw yesterday at Hepburn House. Granted, she had been a marvel to watch, and Higgins was touched more than he would admit by her staunch defense. However, it would be a disaster if she did the same thing tonight. The theater was packed with peers, Cabinet ministers, and the titled women who controlled society. This was not the time or place for an angry Cockney flower girl to confront a possible murderer.

"Eliza won't be in the gallery box with us," Higgins said. "The besotted Mr. Eynsford Hill insists that she sit with him and his family. Good thing, too. They're in the orchestra seats, stage right. I can keep an eye on her from our box."

Jack looked around the lobby, which was a sea of top hats, feathers, and jewels. "Where is Lizzie, by the way?"

"She and my mother went to remove their cloaks." Higgins was taller than most, and saw both ladies approaching. "Here they are."

Jack whistled. "My little cousin can clean herself up proper, now can't she?"

Indeed she could, Higgins thought with approval. The crowd made way for the two women, both of whom were as finely dressed as any lady boasting a coronet. Higgins was accustomed to his mother's unerring elegance, so he was not surprised when people nodded in deference to her regal figure. Just as many appreciative glances were cast Eliza's way as she walked arm and arm with Mrs. Higgins.

"Who is buying Lizzie's wardrobe? You?"

"Don't be mad. Pick is the fellow with the bottomless wallet and the paternal desire to dress her like a princess."

"It's money put to good use." Jack grinned. "Don't know I've ever seen her look more like a grand lady—and with a pearl tiara, too."

But even Higgins marveled at the sum of money Pick must have paid for Eliza's pale gold gown of tulle and brocade. Her fashionable slim skirt drew stares, as did the glittering metal beading and pearls dangling in profusion from a low-cut bodice layered with lace flowers and jewels. Her arms were seductively bare, but almost as eye-catching was a robin's egg blue sash wrapped about her waist, then draped lushly along the back of her skirt.

Higgins was glad Redstone was not sitting with Eliza tonight. He suspected that romantic fellow would find Eliza's charms a bit too difficult to resist. She threw him a smile when she caught sight of him. He reminded himself again that she was his former student and his friend. Nothing more.

"This is so exciting," Eliza said when she and Mrs. Higgins joined them. "And everyone is here. We even caught a glimpse of Churchill and his wife."

Higgins raised an eyebrow. "Didn't know our Lord of the Admiralty was such a fan of Shakespeare. I'd heard he preferred paintings to plays."

"I believe the titian-haired Ophelia is the real draw," Mrs. Higgins said. "Is this Canadian actress as ravishing as the press claims?"

"She's unlike any woman I have ever met," Higgins said.

Eliza bit back an obvious smile. "Such a pity that the murder investigation has to spoil tonight's fun."

"I don't expect anything to happen to ruin the performance tonight, Lizzie." Jack gave her a warning look. "Let the police handle things from this point on."

"That includes you, Henry." Mrs. Higgins tapped her son on the shoulder with a Battenberg lace fan matching her tea-colored gown. "You are a linguistics professor, not Sherlock Holmes. I'm surprised the pair of you haven't been arrested for interfering."

"But we must keep Lady Gresham from having the Professor arrested tomorrow." Eliza stood on her toes to see over the crowd. "There's the Marchioness now."

They watched her enter the lobby on the arm of a corpulent, red-faced gentleman. As she glided past, Lady Gresham shot them a venomous look.

Higgins laughed. "It appears she took your advice, Eliza. She finally put on mourning."

"With a vengeance, too," Eliza added.

Although Lady Gresham wore black, the low-cut gown seemed more suited to a ball or royal gala than a performance at Drury Lane Theatre. The black velvet bodice was partially hidden by scallops of embroidered rhinestones, and the sweeping skirt boasted an overlay decorated with countless silver jewels. She literally glittered with every step. And with her upswept snow-white hair, the Dowager Marchioness of Gresham proved once again to be the most striking woman in the room.

Mrs. Higgins sniffed. "Verena should know better. Her gown is more suited to Anna Karenina than an English matron of seventy."

"She knows enough to show up on the arm of the Commissioner," Jack said with obvious bitterness.

"What!" Eliza and Higgins said at the same time.

Jack nodded. "That's Sir Wilfred Dunningsworth. I knew they were friends, but they look a bit cozier than that."

"What a quaint way of phrasing it, Inspector." Mrs. Higgins threw a scornful look at the couple over her shoulder. "Verena and Sir Wilfred had a liaison over forty years ago, back when they were part of those now moribund layabouts known as the Marlborough House Set. I'd forgotten about their romance until this moment. It's difficult to keep count of the men Verena has cut a swath through. During Cowes Week in 1890, Alice Keppel found her in a compromising position with the Prince of Wales. Any fool ought to know it is bad form to cross the mistress of the future monarch. When Alice went to the Marquess with the tale, it nearly cost Verena her marriage."

"You never told me any of this," Higgins said.

"As if I would speak of such things to my son." She shuddered. "I only bring them up now because I may be forced to wreak a bit of havoc on Verena's reputation."

"You'd expose the Marchioness publicly to save your son?" Eliza hugged the older woman. "You're what I call a real lady."

"Thank you, dear, but I see no need to expose her publicly. In our circles, a private word in the right ear causes far more damage. And I know exactly which ears will be the most receptive." She adjusted the gold and emerald brooch on her gown. "Distasteful business, but if Verena goads Wilfred into arresting Henry, I shall go to battle for him like Athena Nike."

Now it was Henry's turn to embrace his mother. "And you wonder why I never married. How could I find any woman to match you?"

Mrs. Higgins gave him a playful push. "They don't need to match me, dear boy. I only care that whatever woman you choose doesn't irritate me too much." She sighed. "Lord and Lady Isling are trying to get my attention. No doubt they wish to bore me with another tale of their suffragette daughter. Luckily the play is due to begin, so I shan't be trapped long."

"I rather like your mother," Jack said as Mrs. Higgins went to greet the couple.

Higgins nodded. "How could you not?"

Eliza looked relieved. "I feel better now that I know she has a plan. And once the Major shows up and you question him, we'll have another good suspect to consider."

"Speaking of which, there's young Nottingham," Jack said.

The dapper fellow was flirting shamelessly with several young women on the mezzanine stairs. "I'm not surprised to see him," Eliza said. "All the Maestro's students were thrilled about Rosalind Page. I bet most of his pupils are here tonight." She paused. "Except for Kollas and Finch, of course. But since you figured out about the bank robbery Nottingham planned, why haven't you arrested him?"

"I can't arrest him for a crime he has neither committed nor admitted to planning. For now, I am giving the brash boy enough rope to hang himself."

"Oh, there's Freddy. I'm sure he's looking for me."

Eliza turned to go, but Jack grabbed her arm. "Wait."

Higgins leaned close. "Your cousin has something quite interesting to show you."

She looked at them both with a curious expression.

Jack cleared his throat. "As you're aware, my men and I have done several exhaustive searches of Major Redstone's bedroom at Wimpole Street, but turned up nothing."

"I know," Eliza said. "I went through his things about a dozen times last night myself."

"Lizzie, you didn't! I told you yesterday to stay out of the investigation."

"I am sure she will," Higgins said. "Eventually."

With a weary shake of his head, Jack pulled a small book from his jacket and handed it to Eliza.

"Crikey!" She turned to the dedication page where the inscription 'To the White Rose of Rossendale' stared up at her. "Where did you find it, Jack?"

"At Colonel Pickering's club. Redstone had originally booked rooms there, and he still uses it as a study. We went through them this afternoon and found the book."

Jack told Higgins earlier about the book. While he was relieved the mystery of the theft was solved, the discovery had shaken him. So much for his detecting skills. Now he felt a combination of anger and fear. Perhaps they had been living under the same roof as a murderer all week. A chill ran up his spine. Redstone had had ample opportunity to be alone with Eliza. They should be grateful the poor girl hadn't been harmed.

Eliza grew pale, and Higgins knew she had realized her own danger at last. "So the Major killed Nepommuck," she said in a sad voice.

"We don't know that. All we know is that he broke into your classroom and stole this." He took the book back from Eliza. "Whatever else he may be guilty of, the police will handle it. When Redstone shows up tonight, act as if nothing has happened. I have a half dozen men at the theater right now. As soon as the curtain falls, we will take him to the Yard, hopefully without incident or notice."

Eliza bit her lip. "Maybe he was only another person Nepommuck was blackmailing, and the poems are connected to that. He could just be a liar and a thief, like Nottingham."

"I don't care if he's a blooming street sweeper, Lizzie. Steer clear of him until we get him to the Yard."

"Listen to him, Eliza." Higgins gave her his sternest look.

Freddy burst in upon them, breathless as always. "My darling girl, I've been looking all over for you." He kissed her cheek, and Eliza leaned against him. "Don't know why it took me so long since you are the most exquisite lady here."

The lights in the lobby flickered once, and a uniformed usher stood on a small podium announcing, "Curtain," in a booming voice.

"The show is about to begin," Higgins said.

"Did you know Eliza has memorized every line of *Hamlet*?" Freddy kissed her again. "Isn't she amazing?"

She smiled up at him. "I want to see if any of the actors miss their lines. They won't get anything past me."

Freddy stared at her in adoration. "I don't think there is any young woman as marvelous as my Eliza. I hear everyone in the theater going on about how pretty this Rosalind Page is, but she cannot hold a candle to the beauty and magic of Eliza Doolittle."

"Garn," she murmured.

Higgins rolled his eyes. "We are all fond of Eliza, but if you persist with this drivel, you will make us quite sick."

"I agree," Jack said.

Eliza stuck out her tongue. "Come on, Freddy. Some gents don't appreciate a cultured young lady like you do."

"Remember what I said, Lizzie," Jack called after her. "You're only here tonight to watch the play."

She took Freddy's arm. "Of course. Like Hamlet says, 'The play's the thing to help me catch the conscience of the king.'"

"I don't like the sound of that," Jack said while they watched Eliza and Freddy disappear into the crowd.

Higgins sighed. "And she misquoted, too."

———

As long as Rosalind Page was onstage, Eliza followed the play with rapt attention. In full makeup and costume—with the stage lights making her almost luminous—Rosalind seemed like an angel come down from the heavens. The audience actually gasped when she made her entrance in Act 1. Every time she walked onstage, a murmur ran through the crowd. The unlucky fellow who played Hamlet didn't have a chance. Eliza couldn't even remember his name, although she had read the program twice. A pity they couldn't retitle the play *Ophelia*.

But it wasn't fair to say all this attention was due solely to Rosalind's beauty. Eliza bawled like a baby in Act 4 when poor Ophelia went mad. And she wasn't the only one choking back a sob in the audience. Rosalind was a fine actress indeed if she could wring tears while looking like a goddess with all those flowers in her long red curls.

Of course, with such a stunning Ophelia, it made no sense when Hamlet rejected her. Blimey, as if any bloke would turn down a looker like that. It made Hamlet seem even more balmy on the crumpet than

Shakespeare had written him. Eliza already thought Hamlet a weak-kneed fool when she read the play. Cor, some dodgy uncle marries Hamlet's mum after doing in his father, then the uncle gets to be king into the bargain. If this happened in Whitechapel, the uncle would be lying outside the Ten Bells with his head bashed in by the end of the first act.

Eliza was also glad she had memorized the play, thanks to Major Redstone's gift. She bet most folks sitting in the theater didn't know those cheeky actors were cutting lines in every act. Either they forgot the words, or the actors wanted to ring down the curtain and get to the pub early. Thinking about the Major reminded her that he had stolen the book of poems, and lied to her about where he was from. Whenever Rosalind or that exciting ghost wasn't onstage, Eliza's thoughts wandered back to the murder investigation.

Maybe Rosalind knew something important about Major Redstone. After all, when she and Higgins visited the actress the other day, they asked only about Nepommuck's students. They didn't bother to discuss anyone else. Rosalind may have heard the Maestro mention Redstone at some point, or heard a reference to that blooming book dedicated to the White Rose. A snore sounded beside her. She jabbed Freddy with her elbow. The sweet man was clearly not a fan of Shakespeare; he'd been asleep since Act 3. And Freddy didn't wake up at her latest nudge, either.

She peeked over at his mother and sister, who both sat on the other side of Freddy. Mrs. Eynsford Hill was deep in conversation with the lady next to her, while Clara played with the beads on her fan. Onstage, Hamlet held up the skull of Yorick, which meant that soon Ophelia's dead body would be brought to her grave. Since Rosalind's character didn't appear in the play's final scene, it seemed a perfect opportunity to dart backstage and ask her about Redstone.

Before she could talk herself out of it, Eliza gathered up her skirt and stepped past the other people in her row as quickly as possible. Trying not to attract the attention of an usher, she made straight for a side door near the orchestra pit. On Monday, she and Higgins were given an extensive tour of the Drury Lane. She felt confident that she could find Rosalind's dressing room without any problem.

Once backstage, it was darker than she expected. Walking with caution over cables, coiled ropes, and sandbags, Eliza was surprised at the number of props and equipment scattered on all sides. She heard the actors' muffled voices while they fought over Ophelia's body onstage, and hoped she wouldn't knock anything over to disturb their performance. The helmet belonging to the ghost of Hamlet's father blocked her way. Eliza hitched up her skirts and took a giant step over it. Once she found the stairs, she'd be standing right outside the dressing room door before the actress even arrived.

A moment later, she barged into a storage room. She was lost. Retracing her steps, Eliza caught sight of the actor who played Polonius. He wore a robe over his costume and held a mug of tea. Deciding to follow him, she grinned in relief when he led the way up the steps to the dressing rooms. As he disappeared through a door on the left, Eliza continued down the dimly lit corridor. She stopped short.

Lady Gresham's butler stood knocking on Rosalind's dressing room door. It appeared Eliza wasn't the only one waiting to see Miss Page.

Blimey. Why couldn't Harrison dislike actresses as much as he disliked his actor brother? She remembered the Marchioness said he was eager to see Miss Page perform as Ophelia. And that he'd been given the night off so he could wear his best clothes. Eliza sighed as she watched him from around the corner. Dressed in black tie and tails, he looked anything but a servant. No doubt Lady Gresham had sent him to the best tailor in London. Even when doing his duties as a butler, Harrison was twice as handsome as most men. Tonight he appeared more princely than Hamlet.

She spied a large bouquet of flowers in his hand. Obviously Harrison thought he'd be a fine match with Rosalind. Ain't he in for a surprise, Eliza thought. Time was running out. Rosalind would exit the stage any moment. If she waited here, Harrison would see the actress at the same time as Eliza, and she'd lose her chance to speak with Rosalind in private.

Better beat him to the punch. If she took a shortcut through the costume area, then descended the stairs, Eliza would be right off-stage as soon as the curtain came down between acts.

A burst of distant applause signaled the burial scene had ended. She quickened her steps through the clothes racks standing along the corridor. Confronted with the armor of the ghost, Eliza snuck around it but her skirt got caught. She tugged to release it. Instead she felt herself pulled forward. Reaching through the racks to find what had snagged her gown, Eliza let out a strangled cry when someone grabbed her arm. A second tug pulled her through the rack itself and into the next row of hanging costumes.

In horror, she stared at Major Redstone.

———

Higgins hadn't been this bored since his mother forced him to sit through a performance by the Ballets Russes with that Nijinsky fellow decked out as a blasted rose. At least Rosalind Page was prettier to look at, and her Ophelia was impressive. Even he found her mad scene moving. But he couldn't forget that her best performance was not as the Shakespearean heroine, but playing Rosalind Page herself.

If the audience knew how great an actress she was, they'd bring the house down at curtain call. Then there was that abysmal man starring as Hamlet. Couldn't they find a better actor in London to play the melancholy Dane? This fellow's performance was weak as mother's milk. He did enjoy Mr. Barrymore's Guildenstern. Such a shame the young man preferred light comic roles. Higgins suspected he'd make a passable Hamlet.

The time passed even slower when Pickering and Redstone never arrived. Just how delayed were those Welsh trains anyway? If only Eliza was in the box with him. She'd keep him entertained, especially if he asked her to mimic all the actors. And since she'd memorized the play, he was sure she would be far more interesting than what was actually happening onstage. But the poor girl was stuck with the Eynsford Hills tonight. Every time he looked down to where she sat, Freddy was fast asleep beside her. It almost made him like the silly boy.

Higgins gave a great sigh, and his mother threw him a forbidding look. He hadn't seen Jack Shaw since the play began. Numerous times Higgins borrowed his mother's opera glasses to scan the theater, but he caught no sign of the inspector. He whiled away a good hour trying to figure out which of the men in the audience were Scotland Yard detectives. Another hour was spent guessing where each of the actors hailed from. Polonius was Aberdeen born and bred, while Queen Gertrude was a native of Coventry. Higgins found it amusing that an actress as talented as Miss Ellen Terry had not managed to erase traces of her West Midlands dialect.

He didn't dare converse with his mother; she abhorred anyone who spoke during a theatrical performance. Just now, she seemed riveted by Hamlet and Laertes struggling with each other in Ophelia's grave. A pity Laertes couldn't kill Hamlet a scene early and save the audience from another thirty minutes of bad acting. At least the swordfight in the final scene ought to liven things up.

Playing about with the opera glasses again, Higgins heard the door to their box swing open. He swiveled around. "It's about time, Jack. I wondered where you were all this time."

"It's me, old fellow," a voice whispered back.

Colonel Pickering tiptoed into the box and sat in the chair behind him. "Sorry to be so infernally late," he said in Higgins's ear. "The train was delayed for hours in Cardiff."

Higgins looked at the door to the box, but no one else came in. "Where's Redstone?"

Pickering nodded a greeting to Mrs. Higgins, who cleared her throat in irritation. The Colonel leaned forward again. "Reddy needed to stop at the club first. His shoes got mud spattered in Cardiff. He has an extra pair in the trunk he keeps at his rooms there."

"Have you seen Inspector Shaw?" Higgins asked, growing alarmed.

Pickering shook his head. "I assume he's in the theater."

"Gentlemen, please," Mrs. Higgins said, a note of warning in her voice.

Higgins stood. "What are you doing, Henry?" his mother whispered.

He leaned over the box, scanning the seats, aisles, and other galleries with the opera glasses. On his third sweep, he spotted a familiar profile. Jack sat on the aisle near the rear of the theater. "Inspector," Higgins said in a loud voice.

Several people glanced over at him. "Shhh."

Fortunately Jack looked up. Higgins waved and said, "Get your men and meet me in the lobby."

Jack sprang out of his seat.

"Henry, I am never coming to the theater with you again," Mrs. Higgins said.

He next turned the opera glasses on the orchestra seats up front. Higgins was reassured to see Mrs. Eynsford Hill and Clara as restless and distracted as ever. And Freddy was still asleep. But the seat beside Freddy was empty.

"Bloody hell!"

"Henry, whatever is the matter?" Pickering stood beside him.

Higgins pointed below. "Eliza's gone."

NINETEEN

"What are you doing here, Major Redstone?" Eliza fought to keep her voice calm.

"I might ask you the same." Redstone's smile seemed as kind as ever. But his gaze was too intense. "And why so formal? I thought we were friends, Eliza."

She hesitated. "Why are you backstage, Aubrey?"

"When I saw you leave your seat, I assumed you were heading for the lobby salon. But you slipped through a side door instead. I thought it rather curious."

Eliza didn't like the fact that he had been watching her rather than the play. Freddy would have a proper fit when he heard, assuming she lived to tell him. "I came backstage to have a word with Miss Page. I find it strange you're hiding in the wardrobe racks."

"Hiding? Hardly that. I followed you because we need to speak."

His grip on her arm relaxed, and Eliza let out a sigh of relief. "Calling out my name would have frightened me less than pulling me into these costumes."

"I never meant to frighten you, my dear. But I didn't want to spoil the performance. If we make too loud a racket, the actors on-stage might hear us."

Thank heaven for that, Eliza thought. If he didn't let her go in another minute, she planned to yell as loud as a Covent Garden fish-monger. "I can't breathe among all this fabric. Why don't we talk in the hallway? No one will hear us there."

He gave her a knowing look. "But we wouldn't be alone, not with that butler hanging about Miss Page's door."

"What do you want to say to me?" she asked.

Redstone stared at her for a long moment. "The book of poems missing from my luggage at the club. Did you think I wouldn't find out you had stolen back *The White Rose*, Eliza?"

Hang the performance. With a murderer clinging to her arm, Eliza didn't give a fig about *Hamlet*. She started to yell, but Redstone clapped his hand over her mouth. He pulled her tight against his chest. Eliza was certain he could hear her heart pounding with fear. How stupid not to scream as soon as she saw him. That was the prob-lem with trying to be a well-mannered young lady. Being polite was a bloody nuisance.

She should have kicked the blighter in his orchestra stalls the mo-ment he pulled her in among the cloaks and armor. It was not too late. Squirming to get free, Eliza landed several hard kicks to his shins. That made him only tighten his grip.

"Stop, Eliza. I won't hurt you."

"Not bloody likely," she tried to say, but his hand still covered her mouth.

"Are you mad? I never harmed a lady in my life. And I certainly would not lay a hand on you."

At that obvious lie, Eliza stared hard at him.

A sheepish expression crossed his face. "My apologies for the manhandling, but you leave me little choice. You have only yourself to blame for taking the book."

She jerked her face free long enough to yell, "It's my book!"

He clapped his hand once again over her mouth. "You have no right to that book, nor did Nepommuck. I've only taken back what rightfully belongs to me. Or did you never wonder who that anonymous poet might be?"

Eliza stopped struggling.

"Yes, that's right. I was the poet. I wrote those poems fifteen years ago for the only woman I have ever loved. And I had just two copies printed and bound: one for me, one for her. The fact that it came into the possession of that vile Hungarian is intolerable."

As Eliza twisted about, Horatio's doublet from Act 2 fell over their heads. They both jumped. "Damn, this won't do," Redstone muttered.

Holding her close, he peeked out from the hanging costumes, then dragged her around the corner to the prop room. Once he shut the door behind them, it was dark as night. Eliza panicked. The cramped room, fear, and the lack of air made her dizzy. When Redstone turned on the electric light overhead, her knees buckled. She must have blacked out for a second. There was no other explanation for how she found herself perched on the velvet stool Ophelia used in Act 1.

Redstone crouched before her. Perspiration beaded his high forehead, and he looked as unhappy and frightened as she did.

"Please don't yell or scream, Eliza. And don't make me gag you. I don't enjoy holding you prisoner."

"Then let me go."

He shook his head. "I never meant for you to be involved in this. But you are."

Eliza wiped her damp brow. "Nepommuck simply gave me the book to use for my lessons. I never asked for it. And I was going to give you the blooming book. Don't know why you up and stole it."

"The longer it remained in your possession, the more likely the police would discover it. Even a cursory investigation would reveal where the book was written and by whom."

"Were you afraid they'd find out you came from Lancashire and not Northumberland?"

Redstone looked startled. "How do you know that?"

"Professor Higgins told me. You were lucky he wasn't there that night when you lied about being from Northumberland."

"No doubt he also figured out exactly where in Lancashire."

She nodded. "Rossendale. Just like the White Rose."

He frowned. "My ill luck to share the hospitality of a man renowned for his knowledge of English dialects."

"What does it matter if you came from Rossendale? Unless you committed some horrible crime there." She grew more nervous. "Did you?"

"My only crime was being born into a family that boasted an ancestry as ancient as the Earl of Thornton; but not as wealthy. If I had been richer, Arabelle Brandt's parents would have allowed us to wed. But the Redstone properties weren't enough. The Brandts were distantly related to the House of Saxony, although they'd grown impoverished in their native Germany. They sold their angelic girl to that English pig of an earl."

His face contorted with rage. Eliza shrank back. She didn't understand what he was talking about. Who were the Brandts?

"My poor Arabelle was barely seventeen and innocent," he continued. "Far too innocent to be handed over to a man who had already brutalized three wives. How do you think I felt to see her married off to that monster? That's why I left England when I was twenty-two and never returned until now. I couldn't bear being on the same continent as the Earl of Thornton, let alone the same country."

Eliza glanced at the closed door. Didn't they need any of these props for the final act? At some point, she hoped even Freddy woke up from his nap and came looking for her. She'd also like to know what in blazes Jack and his detectives were doing out front. Wasn't the plan to keep an eye on Redstone as soon as he arrived? She didn't blame Higgins. Sometimes Scotland Yard seemed as useless as a suffragette in a sporting house.

Best stall for time. Eventually the play must end, and someone out there might notice she was missing. "You wrote the poems for this Arabelle lady?"

He nodded. "I called her my white rose because her golden hair turned white in the sunlight. We fell in love soon after we met. I wrote *The White Rose* when I thought her family would agree to our marriage. The book of love poems was meant to be a wedding gift to my bride. Then the Brandts refused my suit. I begged her to run away with me, but she lived in terror of the Earl. She feared what he would do to her family—and her—if she was caught trying to leave him. So she became the fourth wife of the Earl of Thornton. And I joined the army and went to India."

"But I don't see why the police would care that you wrote love poems."

Redstone gave her a sardonic look. "Because the book links me to Nepommuck."

"How did Nepommuck get his hands on it?"

"Although I left England, I never forgot about Arabelle. We corresponded secretly for years with the help of a trustworthy maid. That was how I learned of Thornton's increasing hatred of her German accent. He brought in one private tutor after the other to make her speak like an Englishwoman. But none were successful until last year when he hired a Hungarian aristocrat to journey to Lancashire and rid his wife of her coarse German speech."

"Nepommuck." Eliza was beginning to understand. "Knowing him, he probably used poetry to teach her, especially local poets."

"Exactly. Arabelle wrote that he found her reading *The White Rose* one day and insisted they use it during her lessons. That was no hardship for her; she treasured my poems and welcomed the chance to read them aloud."

Eliza cast a furtive look around her. The nearest shelf held goblets, a garland of artificial flowers, and a silver cross on a pedestal she recognized from the scene where Hamlet came upon Claudius praying. Her hopes rose when she also spied wooden lances used by the guards manning the ramparts in the first scene.

"Is all this fuss because Nepommuck nicked the book from your sweetheart?" If this was why Redstone was upset, he was more of a sentimental ninny than Freddy.

"Of course not. Or did you forget where the man's real talents lie?"

Eliza turned her attention from the lances back on Redstone, who was still crouched before her. "He blackmailed her? But how?"

"He surprised Arabelle when she was writing to me and snatched the letter away. We wisely never used our Christian names, but the letter's contents were incriminating. He threatened to take the letter to the Earl if she didn't give in to his demands, which included sexual favors along with money." Redstone's face grew cold and hard. "He didn't know my Arabelle. Of course she refused and the bastard made good on his threat."

Eliza inched to the left to get closer to the nearest lance.

"Get away from those lances, Eliza," Redstone said.

Anger overwhelmed her fear. "What do you want me to do? Sit here like a rag doll while you decide when you're going to kill me?"

"I am not going to kill you!"

Eliza bit back a nervous grin. If she got him riled up, he might start yelling his fool head off. That would call attention to the noises in the prop room. But how far did she dare push him?

"Don't know why you wouldn't. Or are you going to tell me that you didn't want Nepommuck dead?"

"Of course I wanted him dead." Realizing his mistake, Redstone lowered his voice, which made his words seem more sinister. "Because Arabelle thwarted him, Nepommuck exposed her to the Earl. And Thornton was notoriously jealous. He almost beat her to death."

Fearful of the answer, Eliza paused before asking her next question. "Did you kill the Earl as well?"

Redstone laughed, a hollow sound. "I didn't have to. Thornton was certain that once Arabelle healed from the beating, she would run off to join her lover. He decided to take her to America. The pig booked passage for both of them." He paused. "On the *Titanic*."

Eliza didn't say a word. His malevolent expression scared the life out of her.

"I only learned about their deaths when Arabelle's maidservant wrote me the news. Yes, I wanted Nepommuck dead. Arabelle would still be alive if he hadn't gone to Thornton with the letter. I spent months plotting my revenge. When Pickering wrote to say he was remaining in England, I saw my chance."

"Then you came here to kill Nepommuck, not work on the translations." The walls of the prop room seemed to close in on her. There was nowhere to run and hide, and Redstone blocked the only escape.

He nodded. "Imagine my surprise when I learned the Colonel's young friend actually worked for Nepommuck."

"I introduced you to him at the garden party," she said in a whisper.

"Yes. Through you, I gained access to him. But I had no idea Nepommuck had taken Arabelle's book. It was an even greater shock when I realized you now owned *The White Rose*. Don't you see I had to get the book back before the police got their hands on it?"

"But I was going to give it to you."

He shook his head. "The police would have gotten to it first. I had to retrieve it as soon as I could. But you went off to Pickering's club to play detective. You must give it back to me."

"I don't have it." Her heart began to race once more.

His eyes narrowed in suspicion. "Who does?"

She swallowed hard. "The police."

Redstone stood. "The police! Why would you give it to the police? Do you know what you've done, you foolish girl? They'll clap me in prison before the week is out."

Eliza leaped for the nearest lance. Startled, Redstone took several steps back, giving her enough room to point the lance at him. "Back up, mate, or I'll run you through."

"Eliza, put that down. You don't want to hurt me."

"Yes I do. Now let me by."

Aiming the lance at his chest, Eliza inched her way along the wall until she was at the door. She took one hand off the weapon to turn the knob. When she did, Redstone grabbed the lance. For a moment they both struggled. A loud crack sounded. Eliza looked in dismay as the lance broke in two.

"Blooming prop!" She flung herself out the door and into the hallway.

Dashing through the wardrobe racks, Eliza wasn't certain which way to turn. Then she remembered Harrison. She hurried along the corridor. Behind her she heard a clatter. Redstone had probably collided with the suit of armor belonging to the ghost of Hamlet's father. When she reached the dressing room area, she almost burst into tears. Harrison was gone. The bouquet of flowers lay like a floral tribute before Rosalind's door.

Should she hide in Rosalind's dressing room? But if Redstone found her there, she'd be trapped all over again. When she turned to leave, she saw Harrison turning the corner.

Eliza couldn't have been happier if Bransley Ames had just strolled in. With a cry of relief, she rushed over to Harrison and threw herself in his arms.

"Miss Doolittle, what do you think you're doing?" He smelled of men's cologne and cigarettes. The butler must have stepped out for a quick smoke.

"Thank heavens you're here." Her voice was muffled against his jacket. "We must call the police! Major Redstone is after me."

She felt him nervously pat her on the back. "Why is he after you?"

"He killed Maestro Nepommuck, and I'm the only one who can prove it."

Eliza felt better now that the strapping Harrison was there to protect her. She had to stop acting like a silly goose. Besides, her face was pressed far too tight against the buttons on his jacket. One nearly poked her in the eye.

She lifted her head, only to stare in disbelief. Harrison's buttons were made of gleaming gold—and embellished with the head of a lion surrounded by stars.

TWENTY

I see you recognize the buttons, Miss Doolittle." Harrison tightened his arms around her.

Eliza stared in shock at the gold-engraved lions' heads and stars, which gleamed in the light above the door. Impossible. Every button on his dress coat matched the one she'd found outside Nepommuck's apartment. The same button that was stolen from her on Waterloo Bridge.

"I knew someone was following me that day," she said in a hoarse voice. "It was you."

Harrison shook his head. "Not me, you little fool. I'm a handsome fellow, and that attracts attention. I had an old friend follow you about. You led him a merry chase, too: Covent Garden, Bloomsbury, Southwark. When you wandered onto the bridge after dark, you finally made it easy for him to snatch back the button. A pity he also didn't throw you in the river."

"How did you know I had the button?" As soon as she said this, Eliza remembered that he had accompanied the Marchioness to Scotland Yard the day they released Higgins. Good grief. He stood right beside her as she told Jack about finding the button on the hallway carpet.

She tried to push him away, but his grip was like iron. What she wouldn't give right now to have only Redstone to deal with. "Let go of me! Let go!"

Harrison dragged her into Rosalind Page's empty dressing room and slammed the door shut. Eliza kicked his shins. When he let out a howl, she sprang for the door. But he blocked her. He raised his arm to hit her, and she threw herself backward. Eliza banged her head so hard on the wall she literally saw stars—and not just the ones on his buttons.

He put up his fists as if she were a boxer he faced in the ring. Cor, what a night. First Redstone chases her, and now this ape of a butler. Had the whole of London gone mad?

"Keep quiet, girl. You've caused enough problems. Poking your nose into what doesn't concern you, running around asking questions. Why in bleeding hell do you care who killed that damn Hungarian anyway?"

"Because everyone thinks the Professor killed him. And I know he didn't." Eliza rubbed the back of her head. "I also know who the killer is now. You."

"Brilliant deduction. What was the first clue? Oh, let me guess. It's these buttons." He looked down at them with pride. "They're worth over twenty quid each. For blooming buttons, can you believe it? A gift from Verena. I was angry as hell when I realized one of them came off my coat that day in the hallway." Harrison glared at her. "The day you interfered again. You and those stupid tuning forks."

Eliza wished she had the tuning forks now. She'd throw them at his head. "Oh, did I stop you from killing the Maestro that day? My apologies. But if the likes of me scared you off, maybe you weren't ready to stick a knife in him."

Harrison pinned her against the wall, and she let out a strangled cry. When would she learn to keep her mouth shut when crazy men held her prisoner?

"You're the one I should have killed that morning. Funny thing is, I went there only to scare Nepommuck. I didn't have a reason to kill him until the garden party."

With his angry face only inches from her own, Eliza marveled she had ever thought him handsome. He was a devil, he was.

"You're hurting me," she gasped.

"Good."

Voices sounded out in the hallway. He released her, but only to clap his hand over her mouth. She prayed it was Rosalind Page or one of her many admirers. Eliza wanted to weep when the voices died away.

He waited another excruciating moment before releasing her. "You open your mouth again, and I'll snap your neck. Not that I wouldn't love to do it, but this isn't the most convenient place for a murder."

"We're in the middle of a crowded theater," Eliza said. "The actors will be coming back to the dressing rooms soon. If you kill me, they'll find you."

"Idiot. Why would they even think to look for me? It never occurred to anyone to suspect me as Nepommuck's killer. Scotland Yard spent all its time questioning those students of his, and your Professor." He smiled. "That's why I left the tuning fork on the body. The one I stole from you that day in the hallway. I only grabbed it because it felt like a weapon. Didn't even know what it was until I got outside. I figured it was something you language teachers used. Came in handy, though. Sticking the tuning fork in that scoundrel's mouth made it seem like an angry student finished him off."

Eliza rubbed her sore shoulders. "Quite the theatrical touch."

"Yes, it was. My actor brother isn't the only one with a flair for the dramatic."

She groaned. How could she ever watch her favorite actor Bransley Ames again? The two brothers looked as similar as twins. It occurred to her that she might never go to the cinema again. Crikey, she'd probably never leave the dressing room—at least not alive.

After running from Redstone, she now wished he would burst through the door. Not that she trusted the Major, but the two madmen might be distracted by each other long enough to let her get away.

She pointed at the buttons on his coat. "You've no right to be calling me an idiot, mate. You're the one parading around Drury Lane wearing a jacket with gold buttons I'd be sure to recognize."

He smirked. "I didn't plan on seeing you tonight. I don't even have a ticket for the play. My only purpose was to come backstage and introduce myself to Miss Page. Last time she saw me I was wearing a butler's uniform. To romance a famous beauty like her, I need to look like a proper gentleman."

Gentleman my arse, Eliza thought. "I don't know if Lady Gresham would like the idea of you romancing Miss Page. The two of you seemed quite lovey the other day."

"I work hard for Her Ladyship, in more ways than one. I deserve a night off now and then." He laughed. "Besides, who's going to tell her that I'm with another woman? You?"

"I guess not," Eliza muttered. The actors had to be in the middle of the play's final scene. Eventually the performers would take their bows and return to the dressing rooms. If only she could stay alive until then.

"Not that she would believe you anyway," he continued. "The old woman is in love with me. She has been for the five years I've worked at Hepburn House. She adores me so much, I'm in the will as her primary heir."

Eliza was stunned.

"Yes, that's right. Me—Frank Harrison from Putney—heir to the estate of the Dowager Marchioness of Gresham. I told you she was smitten with me. And why shouldn't she be? There aren't many men as good-looking as I am. And how many young men would even glance at a woman her age, let alone make love to them?"

"Nepommuck, for one," Eliza said. She was determined to keep the conversation going for as long as possible.

His face reddened with anger. "That fraud. He spotted Verena two months ago at some reception for the Princess Royal, and saw how the bigwigs danced attendance on her. Being an ambitious clown, Nepommuck began dancing around her as well. He came to Hepburn House so often, he should have brought his steamer trunks and moved in. And when he was there, I had to play the servant. I even had to bow to that hairy fool."

"That must have been hard to take."

"You don't know the half of it," Harrison said. "He put on more airs than a dozen dukes. And him just some silly Hungarian with a worthless title. I'd had enough. He spent too much time with *my* marchioness. I couldn't let this preening foreigner push me out of her bed. Not that he realized I kept her warm on the nights he wasn't there. I finally decided to pay him a visit at his apartment. Rough him up a little, shake some sense into him." Then his voice hardened. "Scare him so much, he'd take his phony medals and run back to the Continent. But you got in my way."

"Sorry," she murmured.

"No, you're not. I was, though. Especially when Verena announced their engagement at the garden party. I almost stabbed him right there on the lawn. There was no way I could let Nepommuck become her husband. Where would that leave me? Out of her will, for one. And I didn't spend five bleeding years devoting myself to that white-haired witch just to watch some puffed-up foreigner take it all away."

Eliza eyed the narrow space between them. She wondered if she could throw something at him. The dress dummy, maybe? A heavy costume?

"The Maestro knew he had enemies, but I bet he never figured you for one of them."

"No, he didn't." Harrison nodded with obvious satisfaction. "Not until I stuck the knife in his back."

He reached for a silk scarf on the dressing room table, and started to wrap it around his hands. She had to do something. Harrison blocked her escape out the door. But there was another door to her left that led to the water closet. If she could get in there, she might be able to lock it behind her, assuming the water closet had a lock.

What she really needed was a weapon. Her gaze swept over the small dressing room. She looked at the jumble of jars and brushes on Rosalind's mirrored table and mentally checked off the items: makeup, cigarettes, greasepaint, combs, razor. Razor! When she visited Rosalind the other day, she remembered seeing the razor buried beneath the jars. At the time she thought it belonged to one of her male lovers.

Now she realized that Miss Page used it to shave her own morning whiskers.

"They'll trace the knife back to you," Eliza said, trying to distract him.

"Impossible. It's a common kitchen knife. Nothing special to point to—"

Eliza threw herself onto the dressing room table. A dozen jars crashed to the ground. As she frantically searched for the razor, Harrison slipped the scarf around her neck. It wrapped about her like a noose. Eliza fought against it even as she choked. Just when she thought her breath would stop, her fingers felt the sharp blade. In one swift motion, she slashed at Harrison's hand. He cried out in pain, and the noose loosened. Eliza reached one hand under the scarf, and cut herself free.

She slashed at him again, but he grabbed her arm. He banged her hand against the mirror until she dropped the razor. Together they fell backward onto the dressing table, scattering its remaining items to the floor.

A deep male voice suddenly boomed. "Who said either of you could come into my dressing room?"

Harrison and Eliza froze. Standing in the doorway of the water closet was Rosalind Page—naked. Eliza wanted to kiss her. The butler fell back in shock at the sight of a totally nude Rosalind in full makeup and with her long hair flowing down her back.

He pointed. "You're . . . you're . . . you're a man!"

"More of a man than you are for sure!" Rosalind replied again in that low voice. "Best run for it, Eliza. I'll take care of him."

In a flash, Eliza was out the dressing room door. She raced toward the costume racks. Maybe she could hide among the thick velvet or brocade cloaks. But clattering footsteps followed close behind. Harrison had recovered from his shock sooner than expected. Eliza almost dodged into the same prop room where Redstone had dragged her, but changed her mind. That would be a dead end. She'd never escape Harrison. She kept running, weaving through the narrow spaces, always on the move. Eliza rushed downstairs.

Lucky she had that tour of the backstage and knew her way around the theater. She needed to get to the front of the house where she could wave down Jack or Higgins. Her heart pounded in her ears and she panted for breath. Suddenly she spotted Major Redstone coming toward her from the opposite direction. His eyes widened when he caught sight of her.

"Eliza, wait!"

She plunged sideways. Blimey. How the devil was she to avoid both of them? Eliza shoved her way into a crowd of actors in the wings. They must be waiting for the final curtain call. She heard the sound of clanging swords from onstage.

"Who the blazes are you?" One of the actors did a double take at her formal gown and jewels. He pulled her away from the stage area. "Audience members aren't allowed in the wings."

"Get your mitts off me!" she cried.

Eliza ducked as Harrison lunged for her. He overshot and crashed into the armor-suited actor who played the ghost of Hamlet's father. Both men tumbled to the floor, making an awful din. Every actor and stagehand hissed at them to keep quiet.

Redstone pushed aside a sandbag a few feet away, and she jumped back. "Eliza, stop running. We have to talk!"

"Ah-ah-oh-ow-ow-oh-ow!" She shoved one of the grave-digging actors at him.

"Are you mad, lass?" The actor waved his shovel.

She snatched it out of his hand. "Get the police up here now!"

Harrison scrambled to his feet. Redstone fought past the actors trying to keep him back.

"Bloody hell!" Eliza dodged around the fire curtain and ran behind the stage. The actors in front of the scenery flat continued with the performance, unaware of the uproar in the wings.

"Eliza, stop!" Redstone called from behind her.

She threw the shovel at Redstone with all her strength. It missed and hit the scenery flat instead. The stage wall wobbled several times, then fell backward. Redstone jumped aside as it crashed to the floor, but Harrison was knocked off his feet. Were the two of them in cahoots? How else to explain why they were both after her?

The lights from the stage spilled through the space where the wrecked wall once stood. "Where's Collins?" an actor cried from the wings. "Someone get the manager over here!"

After a moment of stunned silence, she heard the actors onstage resume sword fighting. Sounds from the audience grew louder as well. They were no doubt amazed that part of the set had fallen down. At least she had gotten everyone's attention. If only Jack would get his blooming arse backstage.

Harrison began to crawl out from beneath the scenery. Meanwhile Redstone circled around her and stood in the wings to her right. She couldn't afford to wait any longer for Scotland Yard.

Without thinking, Eliza ran right through the space where a moment before a castle wall had stood. The audience let out a collective gasp when Eliza burst onto the stage.

She stopped short. The hot lights along the stage's edge half blinded her. Beyond the glare, she discerned a sea of faces staring at her out front. It took another moment of adjustment before she became aware of the two dozen actors in robes and tights clustered about. Everyone wore a stunned expression. Hamlet and Laertes gaped at her from center stage, their swords upraised but motion-less.

Claudius leaned toward Eliza from his throne and said in a loud whisper, "Get off the stage."

Near Eliza's feet, Queen Gertrude lay on the floor beside a ta-ble where the poisoned goblet sat. Looking still as death in her regal robes, Miss Terry suddenly opened her eyes. "Are you mad?" she hissed.

Eliza jumped back and fell onto Gertrude's empty throne. With Redstone lurking in the wings, she figured the stage was the safest place to be just now. "I am Lady Eliza Doolittle come to Elsinore," she announced.

The theater went dead silent. If only one of the actors would say their lines.

Growing nervous, Eliza said, " 'I am but mad north-north-west. When the wind is southerly, I know a hawk from a handsaw.' "

Titters of laughter rippled through the audience. When no one moved onstage, she clapped her hands at the actors. "C'mon, mates. Let's get on with the show!"

If they'd start saying their lines, she would sit here quiet as a mouse until the play ended. Jack was sure to have seen her run onto the stage. With luck, he'd get to her before either Redstone or Harrison.

Suddenly thirsty, Eliza caught sight of wine goblets on a nearby table. She signaled to one of the court attendants. "Stay, give me drink." No one could say she didn't know her Shakespeare.

The audience's laughter grew louder. The attendant looked at his fellow players for help, then shrugged. "Here you are, miss," he said, handing her a goblet.

She tipped it back, only to spit the wine all over Queen Gertrude.

The poor woman sputtered in protest. Some of the actors began laughing along with the audience. Blimey, that stuff wasn't wine at all. Whatever it was tasted right sour.

Eliza gestured for Hamlet to continue. "Go on, say your line."

His face red with anger, he pointed his weapon at her.

"Get that sword away from me." She shrank back on the throne.

"It's a rapier," he hissed. "Now get off the stage."

"Actually it's a foil." This came from the fellow Eliza remembered as the Osric character. He sat on the steps to the king's throne, his face creased in a silly grin.

"In your cups again, are you?" Hamlet's ire now focused on Osric.

The actor playing Laertes cleared his throat. "The girl's right. Say your line."

With a scowl, Hamlet stuck his poison-tipped rapier at King Claudius. " 'Drink off this potion. Is thy union here? Follow my mother.' "

The dying Claudius slumped to one side on his throne, but not without a last bewildered look at Eliza.

A loud bang erupted from behind them. Eliza peeked around the throne and saw Harrison pushing the last of the fake castle wall off him.

Eliza shot to her feet. "It isn't Hamlet who's to blame for the king's death!" Every actor onstage stared at her in shock. "I know who did the poor queen in, too. It was the same fellow who killed Maestro Nepommuck. The murderer's backstage right now! And his name is—ah-ah-oh-ow-ow-oh-ow!"

An enraged Harrison burst onstage, his dark hair covered in plaster. The blood that ran down his hand made him appear even more dangerous. If only she'd managed to cut his whole hand off with that razor.

"Gimme that sword!" Eliza grabbed it from Hamlet.

"It's a rapier!" he cried, ignoring the loud buzz from the audience.

Harrison reached for her, but she skittered away at the last moment. Eliza waved her sword—or whatever it was—at his face.

The butler yanked Laertes by the collar. "Give me yours!" After snatching his weapon, Harrison shoved the actor away.

In response, Laertes scooped up a handful of goblets from a velvet-covered table. He flung them, one after another, at Harrison. All of them missed, although the last one hit the dead Claudius right in his face.

Claudius sat bolt upright. "What in hell are you doing?"

Another goblet landed in the wings, eliciting a yelp of pain. While crossing swords with Harrison, Eliza saw one of the gravediggers dart onstage. With a muttered curse, he hurled the goblet back at Laertes. But his throw fell short, and smacked poor dead Queen Gertrude in the head. Miss Terry sat up with a shriek.

Harrison and Eliza squared off. Neither of them knew what to do with the weapons. They dodged and weaved, smacking each other with the sides of the swords. But they quickly learned the blunt-tipped weapons were as fake as the castle wall that fell on Harrison.

Eliza spied an actor in the wings, waving wildly. "Get the manager! He's the only one who can ring down the curtain!"

Someone grabbed Eliza from behind. She thought it was Redstone and kicked him hard. Didn't seem fair for both men to gang up on her. But she recognized the answering curse as belonging to Hamlet. Cor, if only his character had died earlier in the play. He was giving her far too much trouble.

A new figure ran onstage. He pulled Harrison backward, and both men went down hard on the wooden floor. Surprised, Eliza realized Major Redstone had just attacked Harrison.

Someone yanked her backward by the hair. "Ow, what are you doing, mate?"

Once Eliza fought free, she whirled around on Hamlet. Blimey, he looked angrier than Harrison. "You've ruined everything, you miserable chit," he spat. "Get off the stage."

"I got a killer—maybe two—to take care of!" She smacked him with her sword. "I ain't got time to worry about you!"

"I'd like to kill you myself!"

"Here now, we can't have you harming this nice young lady," one of the gravediggers said. Hamlet turned and knocked the smaller fellow to the ground.

"We can't have you harming the gravediggers, either." Eliza stuck the tip of her fake rapier into the back of Hamlet's tights and gave it a yank. His tights ripped all the way up.

Covering his now bare buttocks as best he could, Hamlet ran offstage. Waves of laughter filled the theater. Eliza grinned and gave a small bow. The audience was certainly enjoying the performance.

She needed to get to the front of the stage and wave down Jack or Higgins. But on the way there, she tripped over Claudius and Laertes wrestling with each other on the floor.

"This is insufferable!" announced Miss Terry, who was now as completely out of character as the rest of the performers.

The recently deceased Queen Gertrude got to her feet with a flourish. Swirling her cloak about her, she tried to make a grand exit. But Harrison punched Redstone, which sent him flying right into the actress. She and Redstone fell back against the set, and yet another castle wall came tumbling down. Eliza ducked as broken plaster showered the stage.

" 'A hit, a very palpable hit.' " The actor who played Osric clapped his hands.

Eliza looked in wonder at the young actor. He sprawled over Queen Gertrude's throne, a brandy flask tucked into his tights. She shrugged. At least the fellow was still quoting lines from the play.

Laughter roared out again from the audience. Eliza could only make out those people sitting by the far edge of the stage. And they were bobbing up and down, holding their stomachs and wiping their eyes. The play's a success, she thought.

Now was the time to yell for Jack and his detectives. Redstone was all tangled up in Gertrude's cloak, the other actors were distracted—or fighting with each other. And somewhere out front was Jack and Higgins. But so was Harrison. And he was a lot closer.

Shaking off the plaster dust, Eliza looked around the rubble. "Where is that sneaky bastard?" she asked aloud.

"Right here, you miserable tart."

She spun around to see Harrison looming over her.

He gripped her throat. "You've ruined everything. Everything!"

Eliza clawed at his hands, but this time he wouldn't let go. The bright lights dimmed. The sounds of shouting and objects crashing all around her began to ebb. Would he strangle her here, in front of all these people? If she had any breath left, her last words would be, "Where in blooming hell is Scotland Yard?"

Right before she blacked out, she saw a skull float in the air above her. I must be already dead, she thought. A second later, the skull came crashing down on Harrison's head.

He collapsed in a heap onto the stage without a sound. Eliza staggered back. The spry actor who played one of the gravediggers stood over the unconscious butler. The remains of Yorick's skull were still clenched in his hands. With a satisfied grin, the gravedigger handed what was left of the skull to Eliza.

Ignoring her pained throat, Eliza held it aloft. "Alas, poor bastard!" she shouted. "Yorick has done you in!"

The audience roared with approval. Applause and laughter thundered from every corner of the theater. Clasping the gravedigger's hand, Eliza and he bowed for the cheering crowd. Cor, but this was exciting. No wonder Miss Page loved the theater so much.

Spread-eagled on the floor, Miss Terry raised her head and looked in horror at the standing ovation out front. A broken crown sat askew on her head. An infuriated Hamlet threw his bent rapier at Eliza. In the wings, she glimpsed John Barrymore doubled over with laughter. A red-faced man in a formal suit stood beside him, his mouth hanging open.

A piercing whistle broke through the din. Everyone stood still, except for Claudius and Laertes, who continued to wrestle each other at the back of the stage. Eliza felt dizzy with relief as Jack marched onstage, followed by six of his plainclothes detectives.

She grinned wider when Higgins bounded up the stairs from the front of the stage. He looked happier than she had ever seen him.

"Professor, come here, I want you to meet the gravedigger." Eliza gave the fellow a kiss on his cheek. "He saved my life, he did."

But Higgins pointed behind her. "Eliza, watch out!"

She turned to see Redstone only a few feet away. Jack was on him in a heartbeat, and detectives immediately surrounded them.

"Are you hurt, Lizzie?" Jack asked as he gave Redstone an angry shake.

"I'm fine now." Picking up one of the rapiers, she pointed it at

Redstone. "And don't worry. If he makes a move, I'll run him through. Along with Harrison."

The red-faced fellow from the wings staggered onstage. He looked aghast at the wreckage. The actor who played Osric hiccupped. "The manager's here. Everyone look sharp!"

Jack seemed concerned over the man's stricken expression. "Are you all right, Mr. Collins? You look ill."

He opened and closed his mouth at least three times but no words came out.

"I think he's in shock," Higgins said.

Jack stepped closer. "Sir, do you want to say anything?"

The manager took a deep breath. "Curtain down!"

TWENTY-ONE

Higgins kicked aside what was left of Yorick's skull. He settled back on the throne with a satisfied grin. Without a doubt, this was the greatest performance of *Hamlet* he had ever seen. His only regret was that he had missed part of the wild theatrics onstage. After Pickering informed him that Redstone was headed for his rooms at the Club, he knew the Major would discover the missing poetry book. And that made him even more dangerous. How was Higgins to guess that while he met with Jack, his detectives, and the manager in the lobby, Eliza was wreaking delightful havoc in the final scene? Luckily he caught the last few moments of it.

To his delight, the performance continued. Although the audience out front had gone home, the actors remained onstage, as did Eliza, Major Redstone, and Harrison. And like Roman soldiers guarding the lion pit at the Coliseum, Jack Shaw's detectives ringed the stage. None of the actors who participated in the final scene were allowed to leave, not even the nervous fellow who played Fortinbras. Higgins suspected the young man was close to tears.

"I am bringing suit against everyone in the last act!" Theater manager Arthur Collins stood in their midst. "Do you realize that the critics from four London papers were out front tonight? Critics! How dare all of you turn the hallowed boards of the Drury Lane into a boxing exhibition! What in blazes came over you?"

The actor who played Hamlet pointed an accusing finger at Eliza. "She's the one who started it. I'm dueling with Jimmy as nice as you please, and suddenly this lunatic girl knocks down the castle wall and takes a seat on the queen's throne! Why didn't someone come out and drag her away? Instead she's drinking from the flagons and quoting *my* lines. Then she takes off with my rapier. We rehearsed our fencing duel for weeks. What do I get for all that hard work? A bloody nose and tights ripped up my arse!"

Higgins chuckled. Sitting in the throne that belonged to King Claudius gave him a perfect view of the results of tonight's mayhem. That included a startling look at the bare buttocks of Hamlet. Shakespeare himself might have enjoyed the new ending to his play. Certainly both Higgins and the audience laughed more tonight than at any production of *Twelfth Night* or *The Taming of the Shrew*.

"What did you want me to do, mate?" Eliza piped up from where she sat cross-legged on the stage. "I had two gents chasing after me, one of them a murderer. The way I see it, I needed a sword a lot more than you did."

"It's a rapier!" Hamlet shouted.

She stuck out her tongue.

"I don't care if Jack the Ripper was after you, young woman." The manager's face flushed with rage. "You had no reason to run onstage and ruin the performance."

"That Hamlet of yours was doing a pretty rum job of ruining it before I got here," she said, picking pieces of broken plaster out of her hair.

"If I had my rapier back, I'd run you through myself," Hamlet said. Eliza tossed a chunk of plaster at him. "Damnation, stop that!"

Higgins's burst of laughter drew everyone's attention. "Come now, Collins. Tonight's play was far more enjoyable than those annual Christmas pantomimes of yours. In fact, if they were as rousing as tonight's performance, I'd buy a ticket right now."

Collins ignored him. "And I can't blame only this impertinent girl and those two ruffians over there." The manager gestured toward Redstone and Harrison. "The rest of you lost complete control of yourselves. You're all to blame. The set is destroyed, and the props into the bargain. And at some point during the melee, I saw the dead King Claudius get to his feet and tackle Laertes!"

The actor who played Claudius seemed insulted. "Not without cause. Laertes flung a goblet right at my face."

Laertes wore a contrite expression. "I was aiming for that fellow there." He nodded at Redstone, now guarded by two detectives. "Wait, maybe it was the man on the stretcher. I don't know. There was simply so much commotion, the esteemed Mr. Hopkins got in the way. My dear man, I am so sorry."

Mr. Hopkins, an actor renowned for his Shakespearean roles, looked up from examining his black eye in a hand mirror. "Apology not accepted."

"Never mind about your eye. Who threw the poisoned goblet at me?" Miss Ellen Terry rose to her full height. Higgins winced at the sight of an egg-shaped bruise forming on the famous actress's forehead.

"I think it was one of the gravediggers," Eliza said.

The chaps who played the gravediggers hurried to hide behind Fortinbras's attendants.

Collins flung his arms into the air. "Why were the gravediggers onstage anyway?"

"It was a lucky thing they were." Everyone turned to look at Higgins again. "After all, one of the gravediggers knocked out that man"—he pointed to Harrison, who lay moaning on a nearby stretcher—"with the skull of Yorick. Poetic justice, I say. Especially since Miss Doolittle claims that Harrison is the man who murdered Nepommuck."

"Who the bloody hell is Nepommuck?" one of the actors asked.

The manager shook his head. "I have never seen such a performance of *Hamlet* in all my years in the theater. It was absolute bedlam. And don't think I have forgotten that someone threw a lance right into the audience. It landed in the lap of the Liberal MP from Ipswich! I guarantee we haven't heard the last of that."

Higgins noticed that one of the king's attendants averted his eyes in shame.

"I'm stunned the audience didn't demand we refund their tickets," Miss Terry said.

"From where I sat, they got their money's worth tonight," Higgins replied.

"Hear, hear!" The actor who played Osric leaned against an overturned table, waving his torn cloak like a flag. "Well done, I say."

"Drunken sod." Hamlet kicked one of the broken crowns in the young man's direction.

Pickering cleared his throat. "Since your own actors fought like pugilists tonight—one of them inebriated—I do not see how you can criticize the actions of Miss Doolittle." The Colonel stood over Eliza in a belated attempt to protect her.

Higgins realized that even he had underestimated the Cockney cabbage. Eliza had proved that not only could she take care of herself, she could bring the house down while doing it.

"Because Miss Doolittle is the hooligan who started it all." Collins ran a finger along his white formal collar, clearly getting hotter under the stage lights. "As if it wasn't appalling enough she set off a brawl onstage, she then had the audacity to quote lines from the play!"

A look of pride crossed her face. "I memorized all of it, I did."

Higgins gave another hearty laugh, prompting the tipsy Osric to pass him a silver flask. He took a sip. The brandy went down his throat like fire. If the lad had been gulping this all night, it was a miracle he was still upright.

With a contented sigh, Higgins surveyed the stage strewn with broken props, bruised actors, and Scotland Yard detectives. Who knew a night at the theater could be this thrilling? He had prevailed on Freddy to see to it that the Eynsford Hill ladies, as well as his own mother, were safely escorted home. No one needed the excitable Mr. Eynsford Hill stirring things up even more.

"I hope they arrest you, Doolittle, along with that fellow on the stretcher," Hamlet shot back. "You ruined the performance *and* butchered the sonorous words of Will Shakespeare!"

Eliza got to her feet with the assistance of Pickering. "Look, mate, I'm sorry I spoiled the play, I really am. I didn't plan on being onstage tonight. And I didn't think I'd be ripping off your tights while crossing swords with the blooming butler there." She pointed at the semiconscious Harrison. "But don't forget I discovered this brute killed Nepommuck, and kept him from doing anybody else in. Including me! Everyone should stop carrying on about the play, and give me a bit of thanks for bringing a murderer to justice."

"Are we supposed to take your word for that?" The manager sneered.

"You can take mine." Jack strode onstage. "Along with the word of Miss Page. She overheard everything."

Now fully dressed in a fashionable gown, Rosalind Page followed behind him. Higgins noticed that she bit back a grin at the sight of the wrecked set and disheveled actors.

Jack stood in the middle of the stage. "Miss Page was privy to the conversation between Miss Doolittle and Mr. Harrison. She has corroborated Harrison's confession to the murder of Emil Nepommuck, otherwise known as the Maestro. In fact, she is coming to Scotland Yard now to give her official statement."

A loud moan sounded from the stretcher. Harrison had revived enough to catch sight of Rosalind, who was gorgeously gowned in flounces of rose tulle with a wide-brimmed hat atop her auburn curls. "She ain't no lady. She's—she's a chap." He pointed a shaky finger at her. "A right bloke with a set to match my own!"

The fellow who played Horatio rolled his eyes.

Higgins worried at what Harrison might say next, but Eliza stepped in.

"He's off his nut, he is. The gravedigger over there smacked him over the head good with that skull. I wouldn't be surprised if he's never quite himself again." Eliza threw Harrison a look filled with contempt. "Plus he's a blooming liar and a murderer. I don't think anyone will ever believe another word that comes out of his trap."

Jack cleared his throat. "I assure you the police will listen to both Miss Page and Mr. Harrison, but I am confident that only one will be given the attention and respect they deserve." He bowed to Rosalind. "My men will escort you to the Yard for your sworn statement. Thank you again for your cooperation and your honesty, Miss Page. I will not soon forget it."

"You are quite welcome, Detective Inspector. And thank you."

Rosalind gave him a gracious curtsey before gliding offstage. Higgins chuckled at the awestruck expressions on the detectives' faces. He felt relieved. No one would believe anything a cold-blooded killer like Harrison said, especially a whopper that claimed the most beautiful woman in London was, in fact, a man.

"While I am happy that your job is done, Inspector, I must still deal with the consequences of this ludicrous opening night performance," Collins said. "As manager of the Drury Lane Theatre, I demand justice of my own."

"Then you will have to seek it elsewhere, sir," Jack said. "I am certain this wasn't the first time a criminal has walked into the Drury Lane, and it's not likely to be the last. Yes, it is regrettable the play was disrupted. But apprehending a killer is worth disrupting a hundred plays." His expression softened. "And perhaps you should think of the publicity, not all of which will be unwelcome. The papers won't be talking about any other play but yours for weeks."

Jack gave instructions to the actors and manager about giving their own statements, and waited until the disgruntled performers left the stage. He next ordered the detectives to carry Harrison, now unconscious, outside to the police wagon.

Higgins stretched out his legs, trying to find a more comfortable position on the throne. It appeared that the action hadn't yet drawn to a close. All he cared about, however, was that the real killer had been caught—and by Eliza Doolittle, no less. He fought back the impulse to yell from the throne, "I told you I was bloody innocent!" Higgins felt so lightheaded with relief, he considered grabbing Osric's flask and downing the rest of his brandy.

Eliza looked at her cousin. "What are we going to do about Major Redstone?"

"Indeed, what are we going to do about him?" Jack frowned at the Major, who remained expressionless and silent.

"I'm confused over what Aubrey has to do with all this," Pickering said.

With a sigh, Eliza told everyone what had transpired backstage before she encountered Harrison. Higgins raised an eyebrow at the account. As he feared, too much romantic poetry turned a fellow into a dangerous idiot.

Jack walked over to Redstone, still flanked between two detectives. "So, Major, if Harrison hadn't killed Nepommuck first, would you have done the deed?"

Redstone stirred to life. "I don't know. But I'd like to think I would have had the courage to kill him. He deserved it."

"And how much courage did it take to drag Eliza off into a closet and frighten her?" Higgins said, unable to keep the scorn from his voice.

Redstone shook his head. "I never meant to frighten her."

"You did a pretty good job of it," Eliza said.

He seemed ashamed. "Eliza, all I wanted was for you to return the book."

"There was no need for you to steal the book in the first place, Aubrey." Pickering was still confused. "On the day of Mrs. Finch's murder, we all went to Belgrave Square so that Eliza could give you the book. It makes no sense you would steal it from her classroom, and then chase her about the way you did tonight. You are a cad, sir."

"Don't you see? If Eliza had given me the book, the police would have asked to see it." Redstone grew more animated by the minute. "Everything in her apartment and Nepommuck's was evidence in a murder investigation. And Eliza had already said Nepommuck gave her *The White Rose*. I had no choice but to steal it. Only two copies were ever printed, and it would be easy to find the man in Lancashire who produced the books for me."

"What if they had?" Pickering asked.

Higgins sighed. "It would show that our poetic Major had a motive to murder Nepommuck."

"But he didn't murder him," Eliza said.

"Lizzie, he just didn't get the chance." Jack brushed a stray piece of plaster from her shoulder.

"Don't know how you can arrest a man for *wanting* to kill somebody." Eliza had a familiar stubborn look on her face. Higgins thought Jack should give in. He wouldn't win the argument. "There were plenty of times I wouldn't have minded running one of these swords through the Professor's back when he was bullying me about my vowels."

Higgins laughed. "The feeling was mutual."

"That's not the same thing——"

"Yes, it is," Eliza interrupted Jack. "I don't know the law as well as you do. But how can you arrest someone just for being angry enough to want to do them in? Half of London would be in prison if that was true."

"You know she's right," Higgins said.

"I wish she wasn't." Jack walked over to Redstone. "You're lucky, Major. I'd arrest you for threatening Eliza and dragging her off against her will, but I'm afraid she wouldn't press charges."

"Let him go, Jack. He scared me is all——and stole back a book that belonged to him."

Jack nodded. "You can leave, Redstone, thanks to your young friend Eliza."

"He's not my friend," she said with obvious sadness. "Not anymore."

Redstone walked across the stage, but stopped before Eliza.

"Please accept my deepest apologies. I behaved like a scoundrel, but I would never have harmed you. Never. After Arabelle, I regard you as the dearest and best young woman I have had the honor to meet."

Eliza turned aside, unwilling to meet his gaze.

Higgins leaned forward. "And you're not coming back to Wimpole Street, either. So that's the end of all the free room and board."

With a last glance at Pickering, who avoided his eyes, Redstone exited stage left. His loud footsteps echoed in the empty theater.

"We'd best let the cleaning staff in here." Jack stepped over the shattered remains of Yorick's skull. "I still have work back at the Yard, but I'll wait until tomorrow to take Eliza's statement. I think she's had more than enough surprises and drama for one night."

"Indeed yes," she said. "I've only been to the music hall. This is the first respectable play I've seen. Cor, but it was exciting."

Higgins got to his feet and stretched. "Being chased by a killer probably made it more thrilling than the usual Shakespearean performance. However, I do admit this *Hamlet* is the most splendid night I have ever spent in the theater. The same cannot be said for the murder investigation itself."

Eliza, Jack, and Pickering turned puzzled faces in his direction. "What do you mean, old chap?" the Colonel asked.

"He didn't fancy being the prime suspect, I suppose," Eliza said.

"That, too," Higgins said. "But look how predictably the case ended."

They stared back at him.

"Don't you see?" Higgins grinned from ear to ear. "The blooming butler did it."

The other three let out a collective groan.

"I'm just glad this is over and the killer's been caught." Eliza scanned the littered stage with obvious satisfaction. "As Shakespeare would say, 'All's well that ends well.'"

"That's the wrong play," Higgins corrected.

"But the right sentiments," Pickering added as he kissed the top of Eliza's head. "And the right lady to express them."

"I agree, Pick," Higgins said. "Our Eliza has shown herself to be resourceful, bold, and unstoppable, but a lady all the same." He smiled over at her with affection. "A fair lady indeed."